SUBHUMAN

SUBHUMAN

A UNIT 51 NOVEL

MICHAEL McBRIDE

PINNACLE BOOKS
Kensington Publishing Corp.
www.kensingtonbooks.com

PINNACLE BOOKS are published by

Kensington Publishing Corp.
119 West 40th Street
New York, NY 10018

Copyright © 2017 Michael McBride

All rights reserved. No part of this book may be reproduced in any form or by any means without the prior written consent of the publisher, excepting brief quotes used in reviews.

If you purchased this book without a cover, you should be aware that this book is stolen property. It was reported as "unsold and destroyed" to the publisher, and neither the author nor the publisher has received any payment for this "stripped book."

All Kensington titles, imprints, and distributed lines are available at special quantity discounts for bulk purchases for sales promotions, premiums, fund-raising, educational, or institutional use. Special book excerpts or customized printings can also be created to fit specific needs. For details, write or phone the office of the Kensington special sales manager: Kensington Publishing Corp., 119 West 40th Street, New York, NY 10018, attn: Special Sales Department; phone 1-800-221-2647.

This book is a work of fiction. Names, characters, businesses, organizations, places, events, and incidents either are the product of the author's imagination or are used fictitiously. Any resemblance to actual persons, living or dead, events, or locales is entirely coincidental.

PINNACLE BOOKS and the Pinnacle logo are Reg. U.S. Pat. & TM Off.

ISBN-13: 978-0-7860-4158-9
ISBN-10: 0-7860-4158-7

First printing: November 2017

10 9 8 7 6 5 4 3 2 1

Printed in the United States of America

First electronic edition: November 2017

ISBN-13: 978-0-7860-4159-6
ISBN-10: 0-7860-4159-5

For Gary Goldstein

Special thanks to Steven Zacharius, Elizabeth May, Lou Malcangi, Arthur Maisel, and the entire team at Kensington Books; Alex Slater and Tara Carberry at Trident Media Group; Chris Fortunato; Andi Rawson and Kim Yerina; Jeff Strand; my amazing family; and all of my loyal friends and readers, without whom this book would not exist.

PROLOGUE

Man is not what he thinks he is; he is what he hides.

—ANDRÉ MALRAUX

Queen Maud Land, Antarctica
December 30, 1946

Their compasses couldn't be trusted this close to the pole. All they had were aerial photographs taken six days ago, which were useless in this storm. The wind propelled the snow with such ferocity that they could only raise their eyes from the ground for seconds at a time. They couldn't see more than five feet in any direction and had tethered themselves to each other for fear of becoming separated. Their only hope was to maintain their course and pray they didn't overshoot their target, if it was even there at all.

Sergeant Jack Barnett clawed the ice from his eyelashes and nostrils. He'd survived Guadalcanal and Saipan, two of the bloodiest battles in the Pacific campaign, with no more than a few scars to show for it, but no amount of experience could have prepared him for what he'd found down here at the bottom of the world. When his commanding officer assigned him to an elite expeditionary squad, he'd assumed he was being sent back to the South Pacific with the rest of the 2nd Marines.

It wasn't until his briefing aboard the USS *Mount Olympus* that he learned he'd been drafted for Operation Highjump, whose stated mission was to establish a research base in Antarctica.

His mission, however, was something else entirely.

Jagged black peaks materialized from the storm. He'd studied the aerial reconnaissance and committed the configuration of the Drygalski Mountains to memory. They had to be nearly right on top of the anomaly they'd been dispatched to find.

The Nazis had made no secret of their interest in the South Pole, but it wasn't until eighteen months ago, when two German U-boats unexpectedly appeared off the shores of Mar del Plata and surrendered to Argentinian authorities that the intelligence community sat up and took notice. All charts, books, and identification papers aboard had been destroyed, and the captains had refused to divulge the nature of their mission to Antarctica, the whereabouts of a jettisoned dinghy, or the reason their passengers were covered with bandages.

The Counterintelligence Corps had been tracking various networks used to smuggle SS officers out of Europe and into South America, but none of those so-called ratlines passed through the Antarctic Circle. During their investigations, however, they'd encountered rumors of a mysterious Base 211 in Queen Maud Land, a veritable fortress commissioned by Hitler in the face of inevitable defeat. They couldn't dismiss the stories out of hand and potentially allow the Nazis to regroup and lick their wounds, so nearly 5,000 men had boarded a squadron of aircraft carriers, destroyers, and icebreakers under the auspices of scientific research and embarked upon a perilous four-month journey through a gauntlet of icebergs and sheet ice. Sorties were launched in every direction in an attempt to reconnoiter the entire continent, upon which, in addition to vast stretches of snow and ice, the cameramen aboard the planes photographed surprising amounts of dry land, open water, and what appeared to be a bunker of German design nestled in the valley ahead of them, which was why Barnett's squad had parachuted into this frozen wasteland.

The wind screamed and nearly drove Barnett to his knees. The rope connecting him to the others tightened and he caught a fleeting glimpse of several of his men, silhouetted against coal-black cliffs rimed with ice. Barnett shielded his field glasses from the blizzard and strained to follow the course of the ridgeline eastward toward a peak shaped like a shark's tooth. He followed the sheer escarpment down to where it vanished behind the drifted snow. The ruins of a rectangular radar tower protruded from the accumulation.

Barnett lowered his binoculars, unclipped his line, and unslung his M3 carbine. The semiautomatic assault rifle had been equipped with an infrared spotlight and a special scope that allowed him to see in complete darkness. The Nazis had called the soldiers who wielded them *Nachtjaegers*, or night-hunters, which struck him as the perfect name as he struck off across the windswept snow, which broke like Styrofoam underfoot.

The twin barrels of a FlaK anti-aircraft turret stood up from the drifted snow, beneath which a convex slab of concrete protruded. Icicles hung from the roof of the horizontal embrasure like fangs, between which Barnett could see only darkness.

He crouched in the lee of the bunker and waited for the others, who were nearly upon him before they separated from the storm. Their white arctic suits would have made it impossible to tell them apart were it not for their armaments. Corporal Buck Jefferson, who'd served with him since the Solomon Islands, wore the triple tanks of his customary M2 flamethrower on his back. They'd rehearsed this scenario so many times that he didn't need to be told what to do. He stepped out into the open and raised the nozzle.

"Fire in the hole."

Jefferson switched the igniter, pulled the trigger, and sprayed molten flames through the embrasure. The icicles vaporized and liquid fire spread across the inner concrete floor. Gouts of black smoke churned from the opening.

Barnett nodded to the automatic riflemen, who stood, sighted their M1918 Browning automatic rifles through the gap, and laid down suppressing fire. The moment their magazines were empty they hit the ground in anticipation of blind return fire.

The thunderous report rolled through the valley. Smoke dissipated into the storm. The rifleman cautiously raised their heads.

Barnett waited several seconds longer before sending in the infantrymen, who climbed through the embrasure and vanished into the smoke. He rose and approached the gun slit. The flames had already nearly burned out. The intonation of their footsteps hinted at a space much larger than the unimpressive façade suggested.

He crawled into the fortification, cranked his battery pack, and seated his rifle against his shoulder. The infrared spotlight created a cone of what could only loosely be considered light. Everything within its range and the limitations of the scope appeared in shades of gray, while the periphery remained cloaked in darkness, through which his men moved like specters.

The bunker itself was little more than a storage corridor. Winter gear and camouflage fatigues hung from hooks fashioned from exposed rebar. A rack of Sturmgewehr 44 assault rifles stood beside smoldering wooden crates filled with everything from rations to ammunition. Residual puddles of burning gasoline blinded his optics, forcing him to direct his sightline toward walls spattered with what looked like oil.

"Sergeant," one of his men called.

A haze of smoke collected near the ceiling amid ductwork and pipes that led him into a cavernous space that reflected both natural and manmade architecture. To his left, concrete gave way to bare stone adorned with Nazi flags, golden swastikas and eagles, and all kinds of ornate paraphernalia. Banks of radio equipment crowded the wall to his right. He recognized radar screens, oscilloscopes, and the wheel that controlled the antenna.

"It's a listening station," Jefferson said.

There was no power to any of the relay boards. Chairs lay toppled behind desks littered with Morse keys, handsets, and crumpled notes, both handwritten and typed.

"Give me some light," Barnett said.

He lowered his weapon and snatched the nearest man's flashlight from him. He didn't read much German, but he recognized the headings *Nur für den Dienstgebrauch* and *Befehl für das Instellunggehen*. These were top-secret documents, and they weren't even en-crypted.

Barnett turned and shined the light deeper into the cavern. The rear wall was plastered with maps, the ma-jority of which were detailed topographical representa-tions of South America and Antarctica, all of them riddled with pins and notes. His beam cast the shadows of his men across bare rock etched with all sorts of bizarre and esoteric symbols before settling upon an orifice framed with wooden cribbing, like a mineshaft. Automatic shell casings sparkled from the ground, which was positively covered with what could only have been dried blood.

"Radioman," he said.

A baby-faced infantryman rushed to his side, the an-tenna from the SCR-300 transceiver on his back whip-ping over his shoulder.

"Open a direct line to Rear Admiral Warren. Ears-only."

A shout and the prattle of gunfire.

Discharge momentarily limned the bend in the tun-nel.

Barnett killed his light and again looked through the scope. The others followed his lead and a silent dark-ness descended.

A scream reverberated from inside the mountain ahead of them.

Barnett advanced in a shooter's stance. The tunnel wound to his right before opening into another cavern, where his infrared light reflected in shimmering silver from standing fluid. Indistinct shapes stood from it like islands. He placed each footfall gently, silently, and quieted his breathing. He recognized the spotted fur of leopard seals, the distinctive patterns of king penguins, and the ruffled feathers of petrels. All of them gutted and scavenged. The stench struck him a heartbeat before buzzing flies erupted from the carcasses.

He turned away and saw a rifle just like his on the ground. One of his men was sprawled beside it, his boots pointing to the ceiling, his winter gear shredded and covered with blood. Several hunched silhouettes were crouched over his torso and head. They turned as one toward Barnett, who caught a flash of eyeshine and a blur of motion.

His screams echoed into the frozen earth.

BOOK I

*Two possibilities exist: either we are
alone in the Universe or we are not.
Both are equally terrifying.*

—ARTHUR C. CLARKE

1
RICHARDS

Queen Maud Land, Antarctica
Modern day: January 13—8 months ago

The wind howled and assaulted the command trailer with snow that sounded more like sleet against the steel siding. What little Hollis Richards could see through the frost fractals on the window roiled with flakes that shifted direction with each violent gust. The Cessna ski plane that brought him here from McMurdo Station was somewhere out there beyond the veritable armada of red Kress transport vehicles and Delta heavy haulers, each of them the size of a Winnebago with wheels as tall as a full-grown man. The single-prop plane had barely reached the camp before being overtaken by the storm, which the pilot had tried to use as an excuse not to fly. At least until Richards made him an offer he couldn't refuse. There was no way that he was going to wait so much as a single minute longer.

It had taken four days, operating around the clock, for the hot-water drill to bore through two miles of solid ice to reach a lake roughly the size of the Puget

Sound, which had been sealed off from the outside world for an estimated quarter of a million years. They only had another twelve hours before the hole closed on them again, so they didn't have a second to waste. They needed to evaluate all of the water samples and sediment cores before they lost the ability to replenish them. It wasn't the cost that made the logistics of the operation so prohibitive. The problem was transporting tens of thousands of gallons of purified water across an entire continent during what passed for summer in Antarctica. They couldn't just fire antifreeze into the ice cap and risk contaminating the entire site, like the Russians did with Lake Vostok.

Richards pulled up a chair beside Dr. Max Friden, who worked his magic on the scanning electron microscope and made a blurry image appear on the monitor between them. The microbiologist tweaked the focus until the magnified sample of the sediment became clear. The contrast appeared in shades of gray and at first reminded Richards of the surface of the moon.

"Tell me you see something," Richards said. His voice positively trembled with excitement.

"If there's anything here, I'll find it."

The microscope crept slowly across the slide.

"Well, well, well. What do we have here?" Friden said.

Richards leaned closer to the monitor, but nothing jumped out at him.

"Right there." Friden tapped the screen with his index finger. "Give me a second. Let me see if I can . . . zoom . . . in . . ." The image momentarily blurred before resolving once more. "There."

Richards leaned onto his elbows and stared at what

looked like a gob of spit stuck to the bark of a birch tree.

"Pretty freaking amazing, right?" Friden said.

"What is it?"

"That, my friend, is the execution of the bonus clause in my contract." The microbiologist leaned back and laced his fingers behind his head. "What you're looking at is a bacterium. A living, breathing microscopic creature. Well, it really isn't, either. We killed it when we prepared the slide and it's a single-celled organism, so it can't really breathe, but you get the gist."

"What kind?"

"No one knows exactly how many species of bacteria there are, but our best estimate suggests a minimum of 36,000 . . ."

Richards smiled patiently. He might have been the spitting image of his father, from his piercing blue eyes to his thick white hair and goatee, but fortunately that was all he'd inherited from his old man. He could thank his mother—God rest her soul—for his temperament.

Friden pushed his glasses higher on his slender nose. The thick lenses magnified his brown eyes.

"I don't know," the microbiologist said. "I haven't seen anything quite like it before."

Richards beamed and clapped him on the shoulder.

"That's exactly what I wanted to hear. Now find me something I can work with."

Richards's handheld transceiver crackled. He snatched it from the edge of the desk and already had one arm in his jacket when he spoke into it.

"Talk to me."

"We have eyes," the man on the other end of the connection said.

Richards's heart leapt into his throat, rendering him momentarily speechless.

"Don't go any farther until I get there."

He popped the seal on the door and clattered down the steps into the accumulation. The raging wind battered him sideways. He pulled up his fur-fringed hood, lowered his head, and staggered blindly toward the adjacent big red trailer, which didn't appear from the blowing snow until it was within arm's reach. The door opened as he ascended the icy stairs.

"You've got to see this," Will Connor said, and practically dragged him into the cabin. The former Navy SEAL was more than his personal assistant. He was his right-hand man, his bodyguard, and, most important, the only person in the world he trusted implicitly. The truth was he was also the closest thing Richards had to a friend.

The entire trailer was filled with monitors and electronic components fed by an external gas generator, which made the floor vibrate and provided a constant background thrum. The interior smelled of stale coffee, body odor, and an earthy dampness that brought to mind memories of the root cellar at his childhood home in Kansas, even the most fleeting memories of which required swift and forceful repression.

Connor pulled back a chair at the console for Richards, who sat beside a man he'd met only briefly two years ago, when his team of geologists first identified the topographical features suggesting the presence of a large body of water beneath the polar ice cap and he'd only just opened negotiations with the government of

Norway for the land lease. Ron Dreger was the lead driller for the team from Advanced Mining Solutions, the company responsible for the feats of engineering that had brought Richards to the bottom of the Earth and the brink of realizing his lifelong dream.

The monitor above him featured a circular image of a white tube that darkened to blue at the very end.

"What you're looking at is the view from the fiber-optic camera two miles beneath our feet," Dreger said. He toggled some keys on his laptop, using only three fingers as he was missing the tips of his ring and pinkie fingers, and the camera advanced toward the bottom. The shaft was already considerably narrower than when the hot-water drill broke through, accelerated by a surprise flume of water that fired upward as a result of the sudden change in pressure, which had inhaled fluid from the surrounding network of subsurface rivers and lakes they were only now discovering.

The lead driller turned to face Richards with an enormous grin on his heavily bearded face, like a Viking preparing to pillage.

"Are you ready?"

Richards stared at the monitor and released a long, slow exhalation.

"I've been waiting for this my whole life."

The camera passed through the orifice and into a vast cavernous space, the ring of lights around the lens creating little more than a halo of illumination. The water had receded, leaving behind icicles hanging like stalactites from the vaulted ice dome. There was no way of estimating size or depth. There was only up, down, and the unfathomable darkness in between.

"Should I keep going?" Dreger asked.

Richards nodded, and the camera slowly approached the surface of the lake, which remained in a liquid state due to a combination of geothermal heat rising from beneath the mantle, insulation from the polar extremes by two vertical miles of ice, and the pressure formed by the marriage of the two. The image became fluid. When the aperture rectified, it revealed cloudy brownish water through which whitish blebs and air bubbles shivered toward the surface. A greenish shape took form from the depths, gaining focus as the camera neared. The rocky bed was covered with a layer of slimy sediment, from which tendrils of sludge wavered. It looked like the surface of some distant planet, which was exactly what Richards hoped it was.

There were countless theories regarding the origin of life on earth, but the one that truly resonated with him was called *lithopanspermia* and involved the seeding of the planet by microbes hitchhiking through space on comets and asteroids, whether having survived on debris ejected from a collapsing planet or by the deliberate usage of a meteorite to plant life on a suitable world by some higher intelligence. Fossilized bacteria of extraterrestrial origin were found on a meteorite recovered from this very continent less than twenty years ago, but it wasn't until living samples were collected from Lake Vostok that Richards realized what he needed to do.

Ever since that fateful night sixty years ago, when he'd run into the wheat fields to escape the sound of his father raining blows upon his sobbing mother, he'd known mankind wasn't alone in the universe. He remembered every detail with complete clarity, for it was that single moment in time that altered the course

of his life. He recalled staring up into the sky and beg-
ging for God to answer his prayers, to take his mother
and him from that horrible place. Only rather than a vision of the Almighty, he saw a triangle formed by three
pinpricks of light hovering overhead. He'd initially
thought they were part of a constellation he hadn't seen
before until they sped off without a sound and vanished
against the distant horizon.

He'd been looking for them ever since.

"What's that over there?" Connor asked.

"Where?" Dreger said.

Connor leaned over Richards's shoulder and tapped
the left side of the screen. The driller typed commands
into his laptop, and the camera turned in that direction.

"A little higher."

The change in angle was disorienting at first, at least
until Richards saw what had caught Connor's eye.

"What in the name of God is that?"

2
EVANS

El-'Amarna, 194 miles south of Cairo
Minya Governorate, Egypt, September 15—5 days ago

The tunnel was barely wide enough to accommodate his shoulders, forcing him to drag himself deeper into the darkness with his palms and push with his toes. Dr. Cade Evans could barely raise his head high enough to shine the light mounted to the side of his helmet beyond his outstretched arms. He hoped the HD video camera affixed to the other side was capturing the details that were lost to him. The bare sandstone was coarse underneath him where sections of the walls had been crumbled and furrowed by what looked like the claws of a burrowing animal of some kind. Structures elsewhere in the royal tomb complex were reinforced with gypsum plaster, which likely meant that this passage had been abandoned, incomplete, with the rest of the city of Akhetaten.

"How are you holding up in there, Cade?" Dr. Andrea Ferrence asked from the surface, where she and her graduate students monitored the live feed from his camera on her laptop.

"I'm still trying to figure out how you talked me into doing this."

"Undoubtedly my sexy British accent."

Her voice was too loud in his earpiece, but he drew a measure of comfort from it. They'd been friends—and sometimes more—since grad school. Like her, he'd studied Egyptology at Cambridge and had been well on his way to becoming one of the world's foremost authorities on the Old Kingdom—at least in his own mind—until he read about the discovery of human remains with strangely elongated craniums in Peru and mere hours later found himself aboard a plane bound for Lima. During his subsequent examination of the remains and the petroglyphs of normal and cone-headed people alike on the walls of the cave in which they'd been found, the seeds of a theory about spontaneous evolutionary divergence took root and launched a quest for answers that had taken him around the globe and exhausted the funds from the sale of his deceased parents' estate in Montana.

It had taken Andrea several days to track him down in the remote Swabian Alps of Germany, where he'd been studying skeletal remains with a marked divergence in their mitochondrial DNA that suggested the abrupt replacement of European hunter-gatherers by an unidentified mystery population in the years following the last ice age.

She'd discovered something intriguing in her current excavation of Tomb 29, on the other side of the main valley from where they were now. The southern necropolis had been carved from unstable strata, leading to the collapse of chambers they were only now finding, including one with remnants of hieroglyphics she believed had once told the story of the sudden abandonment of the El-'Amarna region. While the majority of the tale had crumbled with the sandstone walls, she was able to isolate a passage that warned of a curse that would befall anyone who disturbed a hidden tomb in the royal necropolis where—literally translated—"a devourer god" was entombed, the depictions of which immediately made her think of Evans.

Within half an hour of opening her email and viewing the attached picture, he was packed and on his way to Friedrichshafen Airport.

Using a combination of ground-penetrating and through-wall radar, they'd discovered a hollow space of indeterminate size behind the northeastern wall of Pharaoh Akhenaten's tomb and beneath the floor of the one built for his wife, Queen Nefertiti, although they hadn't been able to find a way to reach it. It wasn't until they expanded their search to the surrounding hillside that they found a mound of stones heaped against the base of an escarpment that somehow looked too purposefully stacked to have been caused by the erosion of the cliff. They had spent an entire day moving several tons of boulders and were on the verge of collapse when they finally revealed the tunnel through which he now slithered.

A spider crawled over the back of his hand. He reflexively jerked his arm, hit his head on the low roof, and cursed.

"We can edit that out, right?" he said.

Andrea merely laughed in response.

Evans dragged himself through the webs and tried not to think about the countless tons of earth above this ancient tunnel carved by primitive men without any formal training in structural engineering. Not that the Pyramids of Giza wouldn't still be standing long after the last skyscraper had fallen to ruin. Of course, they were built during the Fourth Dynasty of the Old Kingdom, while Akhetaten was a hastily erected cultural and architectural anomaly that served as the capital city for little more than the blink of an eye during the Eighteenth Dynasty.

Pharaoh Amenhotep IV, son of Amenhotep III and Queen Tiye, was considered a heretic. He shunned polytheism and the traditional pantheon of gods in favor of the monotheistic worship of Aten, who he claimed appeared to him in a vision as a disk descending from the sky. So powerful was this vision that he changed his name to Akhenaten, which meant "Of Great Use to Aten." Seemingly overnight the capital city of Thebes was deserted in favor of a site nearly two hundred miles away on the eastern bank of the Nile, where the city of Akhetaten—Horizon of the Aten—rose and fell in little more than a decade, leaving behind some of the most fascinating, yet least understood ruins.

Following his death, Akhenaten's son Tutankhaten—"the Living Image of Aten"—not only moved the capital back to Thebes, but had his family's remains disinterred and brought with him. The worship of Aten was abolished and Amun, their forsaken creator-god, and his pantheon were restored to supremacy. He even changed his name to further distance himself from his father's misguided devotion to this disk from the sky and became Tutankhamun, millennia later to be shortened to King Tut.

Or so the story went.

The hieroglyphics Andrea unearthed spoke of the vengeance of renounced gods and the abandonment of a city besieged by devourer gods.

The tunnel wound to the left and opened into a natural formation Evans estimated to be approximately the size of Akhenaten's tomb, roughly six feet away through solid rock. He stood and surveyed his surroundings, slowly tracing the earthen walls with his light so the camera could record them for posterity. Motes of dust sparkled in his beam as it passed over sandstone adorned with petroglyphs that were markedly different from the hieroglyphics throughout the city.

"Do you recognize any of these symbols?" he asked.

It took Andrea several seconds to reply.

"No, I don't believe so."

They were symmetrical and reminded him of stylized suns. There was something strangely familiar about the pattern in which they'd been carved into the walls and ceiling of the cavern, almost as though in an attempt to mimic the pattern of the stars in the sky.

He advanced slowly in an attempt to absorb everything around him. It smelled of an ancient time perfectly preserved inside this sealed chamber, of dust and age and the faintly biological taint of a crypt.

"Were there lions around here?" he asked.

"Their historical range covers the entire Nile Valley. Why?"

He swept his light across heaps of bones at the rear of the cavern. The long horns of gazelle and cattle protruded from skeletal remains that appeared to have been unceremoniously cast aside without regard for

species. There were humans and animals alike, their
skulls cracked open like coconuts and their long bones
broken and scored with what could only have been
teeth marks.

"Can you think of another animal capable of doing
something like . . . this?"

"You saw the hieroglyphics. They clearly depicted
something other than a lion."

Evans thought about the picture she had sent him
while he followed the trail of carnage to a recess in the
cavern wall nearly obscured by all of the bones. The
remains inside were curled into fetal position and
mummified by the dry desert air.

"Can you get any more light in there?" Andrea
asked. "I can't tell . . . is it human?"

"Give me a second."

He skirted the bones, crouched in the mouth of the
recess, and shined his light down onto the body. The
ground beneath it was carpeted with shriveled pelts
and a crust of bodily dissolution. Its desiccated legs
and feet were undeniably human, its skin like parch-
ment stretched over its skeletal infrastructure. He
raised his light from its sunken chest to its bony shoulders, and finally to its—

"Jesus," he gasped, and toppled backward onto the
pile of bones.

He suddenly understood why the ancient Egyptians
had barricaded the tunnel and abandoned the city in
such a hurry.

3
JADE

Musari, Nigeria

The smell hit her the moment she got out of the camouflaged truck. Fires still burned inside the scorched mud buildings. Smoke twirled lazily up into the sky from where the tin roofs had once been. The dirt roads were paved with charcoal and ashes. The silence was a physical entity skulking through what was left of the village. There were no dogs barking or birds singing from the trees, only the huffs and grunts of the vultures wheeling overhead and in the skeletal black treetops. What little hadn't burned was pocked with automatic gunfire. Pools of blood had clotted on the ground where bodies had fallen. Judging by the scuffmarks, not all of them had been dead when they were dragged through the center of town in a macabre parade of the dead.

Dr. Jade Liang wrapped her hijab over her raven-black hair and covered the lower half of her face until only her green eyes showed, not in deference to the religion that had spawned such horrors, but as a practical means of dampening the smell, which suggested the massacre had occurred sometime between twenty-four and forty-eight hours ago.

The Nigerian Red Cross volunteers with their white smocks and red elbow-length gloves had already begun to disperse since there was no need of their services. There were no survivors, not even the young girls often left raped and bleeding in the gutters. They made themselves scarce at the sight of the United Nations peacekeeping troops, who climbed from the trailing convoy of trucks and took up position to either side of what had once been a market. Fruits and vegetables had been flattened beneath the caravan of vehicles that had carried death across the savanna.

An officer in Nigerian Army fatigues emerged from between two burned homes with a cadre of soldiers who hardly looked out of their teens, too young to be wielding the AK-47s slung over their backs. Then again, the men in her entourage weren't a whole lot older. They wore the powder-blue helmets and Kevlar vests of the United Nations, with the flags of their home countries on their shoulders.

The man who'd greeted her on the tarmac at Maiduguri International Airport, a Canadian who'd introduced himself only as Billings, ordered his men to secure the perimeter and approached the Nigerians. Whatever they had to discuss didn't concern Jade. She was here for one purpose and one purpose only.

"Where are they?" she interrupted.

The Nigerian officer looked her up and down contemptuously, then nodded vaguely back over his shoulder in the direction from which he'd appeared.

"You don't go anywhere without your escort," Billings said. He spoke with a French accent and in a tone of command.

"Then escort me," she said, and continued toward the tree line. Soot came away on the bottoms of her shoes, leaving behind distinct tread marks in the reddish soil.

The fires had burned to within mere feet of the high weeds, which, had they caught, would have carried the blaze into the forest and consumed the evidence. Several Nigerian soldiers stood among the sumac and flowering legume trees, looking more than a little green around the gills. They were happy to step aside and let her take their place on top of a freshly exhumed mound of dirt roughly a hundred feet long. She estimated that the trench from which it had been excavated was maybe five feet deep, although it was hard to tell with all of the bodies heaped in the bottom.

She imagined these poor souls lined up and forced to kneel where she stood at that very moment, looking down upon their dead friends and neighbors, knowing that within a matter of seconds they would join them.

The inhumanity of it all sickened her. Just when she thought mankind had reached the fullest depths of depravity, it found a way to dig even deeper. Sights like this one were becoming so commonplace that they were losing their power to shock, not that the media back home even bothered to report on the tragedies that unfolded here on a daily basis. The Western world was too busy keeping up with the Kardashians to recognize that genocide was being committed beneath their very noses. Sure, people changed the overlays on their Facebook profile pictures to show solidarity with the country most recently victimized by terrorism, but they were blind to the fact that jihadists were waging a war of extinction across an entire continent, slaughtering innocents, abducting their daughters, and creating a literal hell on earth.

That was why she'd volunteered three months of her time to the U.N. International Criminal Court's investigation of Boko Haram. The militant faction considered itself the de facto Western branch of the Islamic State, but in terms of violence and bloodshed it knew no peer. Despite the formal declaration of a state of emergency and the creation of several new infantry divisions, the number of extremists continued to grow, fueled by the prospect of marauding the countryside in hordes straight out of the Middle Ages. A trail of scorched earth followed them from one village to the next as they expanded their territory. To date, they'd murdered more than 25,000 people and displaced millions in the process of securing 50,000 square miles of Nigeria, Cameroon, and Chad. They needed to be stopped and forced to stand for their crimes against humanity before their numbers swelled to the point that they no longer could be.

Jade skidded down the dirt mound and into the pit, where the remains of bloated men, women, and children lay, discarded and seething with black flies. She removed her camera and digital voice recorder from her bag and began the laborious process of documenting the nature of the wounds and the various causes of death. Those near the bottom had been butchered in the most horrific ways, while those nearer the top had been shot point-blank in the back of the head. Whether the executioners had already sated their taste for killing or had simply needed to expedite the process was a matter of speculation.

While her skills as a forensic anthropologist were overkill at this juncture, they were crucial in establishing a case for genocide. They needed the kind of incontrovertible proof that only someone intimately familiar with the subtle skeletal distinctions between not only races, but the various ethnicities and geographic variances within those races could provide. If they could prove that Boko Haram was targeting a specific ethnicity or religion, then a formal tribunal could be assembled, without which there could be no direct intervention, at least not without the majority of nations on board, and that wasn't about to happen as long as military action would be perceived as a war against Islam in this climate of political correctness.

The problem was that until the civilized world acknowledged that it was at war with extremism, the forces aligning against it would continue to rally the disenfranchised to their cause.

Sometimes it seemed to Jade as though she inhabited two different worlds. Back home she taught osteology and genetic mutation within the safe environs of the University of Colorado Medical School. It was often staggering to think that while we were all the same on the inside, it was the almost trivial variations in genetic expression that divided humanity, and man's very nature that pitted him against those he identified as different when there was otherwise such beauty in the world.

She stared down at the outstretched arm of a woman who'd died while trying to reach a baby in a bloodstained diaper. Her fingers rested inches from those of the infant.

Jade knelt and brought their hands together. It seemed like the very least she could do.

She was about to stand again when she noticed the body beneath theirs. Flies crawled all over its grayish skin and misshapen skull. She rolled the body sideways so she could see its face and features that weren't entirely human.

4
ROCHE

Wiltshire County, England

"You're certain it wasn't vandals," Martin Roche said.

"I was in that field yesterday afternoon," Abe Grafton said. The farmer spoke with a thick British accent and had the look of a man who'd spent a lifetime in the sun. "I'm telling you, it wasn't there. And there's no way any number of people could have made it in so little time. Least of all without me hearing them."

Roche plugged the Smart Geiger into his cell phone as they tramped through the waist-deep barley toward the distant row of beech trees, above which the sun, having dispelled the morning fog, commenced its ascent in earnest.

"What's that for?" Grafton asked.

"This app measures radiation exposure in microsieverts per hour."

"You're saying my fields are radioactive?"

The readings rose with every step until they reached a point where it looked like a shadow had fallen upon the wavering crops, at least from this elevation. Roche held up the screen so the farmer could see it.

"Bloody hell," Grafton said. "This is just wonderful. What will it do to my sheep?"

"Do your sheep graze in your crops?"

"Well . . . no."

"Then you probably don't need to worry about them."

They stepped from the sea of green tassels into a clearly demarcated flattened section. Roche unplugged the mini Geiger counter, took several photographs, and then crouched in the barley. None of the long stems were broken. It was as though they'd simply collapsed to the ground in a radial pattern. The nodes, which reminded him of knuckles along the stalk, were all artificially elongated, a curious anomaly he'd been able to independently reproduce using boiling water, microwaves, and electricity. Considering the nearest power lines were little more than toothpicks against the horizon and the closest cell tower was twice that far away, he could safely rule out spontaneous induction, although that wouldn't have explained the design of the crop circle or the tiny dead gall flies perfectly preserved on the grains as though flash-frozen.

"What are you looking for?"

Roche broke off one of the tassels and handed it to the farmer, who plucked off one of the dead flies and inspected it before crumbling it between his fingers.

"The devil can do something like that?"

Roche attached the 150x magnification lens to the camera on his phone, grabbed a handful of dirt, and appraised it on the view screen.

"What kind of fertilizer do you use?"

Grafton puffed out his chest.

"This is an organic farm, sir. The only fertilizer comes from my sheep."

Roche held up the screen so the farmer could see the microscopic, pearl-like spheres mixed in with the soil.

"These little balls are silicon dioxide, commonly found in industrial fertilizers and cosmetics."

"I assure you, neither are in use here. You saw the wife, didn't you?"

His laughter boomed across the plains.

Roche cast aside the dirt, brushed off his palm on his thigh, and put the magnifying lens back into his field kit. With each passing year, researchers like him discovered more and more seemingly inexplicable anomalies in these crop circles. While the prevailing theory was that most were elaborate hoaxes, there were similarities between them that simply defied logical explanation. How were the crops flattened without breaking a single stem? What caused the spike in radiation and the malformed nodes, some of which appeared as though they'd been popped from the inside? What could have killed the flies in such a manner and why was there such a high concentration of silica?

More important, what did these crop circles mean?

A growing faction believed they were created by extraterrestrial life in an attempt to communicate with us. After all, how could such precise patterns, formed from sacred geometry and higher orders of mathematics, be created in the middle of nowhere? Some even claimed to have seen plasma spheres hover over the fields and patterns form beneath them like magic.

Roche didn't believe in magic any more than he believed in aliens, but the fact remained that there was simply too much that he couldn't explain.

"Do you mind if I collect samples of grain from both inside and outside the circle?" Roche asked.

"What good can that possibly do?"

"I can compare their rates of germination against known standards and see if there are any variations in growth patterns."

"You've done this before?"

"As a general rule, seeds collected inside the pattern exhibit stunted growth."

"But not always?"

"If the crop circle is formed right before harvest, when the grain is fully matured, the seeds actually grow faster."

"Figure out what causes that and we can sell it. We'll be millionaires."

"I don't think that's the best idea."

"Why the hell not? I need to recoup the loss of this harvest somehow."

"Look around you. Don't you notice anything unusual?"

"More unusual than the radioactive pattern in my bloody barley?"

"There aren't any birds. All of this grain. All of these dead flies. And there's not a single bird in the sky."

"What are you, some kind of scientist?"

"Something like that," Roche said, although nothing could be further from the truth.

He wasn't one of these New Age freaks who traveled hundreds of miles to lay in the design and commune with the universe or experience the surge in mystical energy, or whatever it was they did. He was an educated man, a skeptical man, but one who couldn't walk away from a mystery of this magnitude without cracking the code. As a cryptanalyst first for the Marine Cryptologic Support Battalion and later the National Security Agency, he'd been trained to see patterns where there were none, to identify signals within intelligence that could mean the difference between life and death for operatives in the field.

His grandfather had emigrated from French Basque country as a child and served as a U.S. Marine in World War II. Francois de la Roche had utilized his ability to speak the obscure Basque language as a code talker, translating official communications in a way the Germans couldn't understand. While he and his team were ultimately replaced by the legendary Navajo Code Talkers, whose language was built upon complex grammar that wasn't mutually intelligible to any known language, the way he described his service and his subsequent years in intelligence had stirred Roche's imagination. Cipher machines and the bombe used to break the encryptions. Wiretaps and listening devices. Informants and double agents. His whole life he'd wanted nothing more than to be an operative in this game of cloak-and-dagger like his *pépère,* who had made himself sound like a cross between James Bond and Indiana Jones.

The reality, of course, was something else entirely.

Linguists like his grandfather were sent to the front lines. Several of the men he'd known at Fort Meade had died in Afghanistan, where it was impossible to tell the difference between innocents and suicide bombers until they pushed the detonators on their explosive vests. Roche had served from thousands of miles away in a dark room where written communications whipped past on a computer screen so fast that he barely had a

chance to glance at them in search of hidden messages
and patterns. He'd been good at it, though. Whether as
a consequence of his training or some innate gift, he'd
helped locate and eliminate terror cells all over the
globe and prevent attacks that would have made 9/11 a
historical footnote. He'd been so good, in fact, that the
NSA had snatched him from the Marines and set him
up at a fancy station making ten times as much money
and granted him a high-enough security clearance that
he probably could have figured out the identity of the
second shooter on the grassy knoll, if he'd had the
time.

His sole task had been to evaluate cell phone calls
plucked from the ether. Not just those flagged because
of certain trigger words, but communications of all
kinds. After all, terrorists were ingrained into society
like ticks on a deer's back. They lived invisible lives
and recruited nationals who weren't hindered by Arabic accents or the color of their skin. He'd believed in
the importance of his job clear up until the moment that
realization struck him like a lightning bolt from the sky.

He was spying on his own people.

Not only was he violating the constitutional rights
he had sworn to uphold, he was doing the exact same
thing as the imaginary Communist spies he'd spent his
childhood thwarting with secret codes and plastic
guns. He'd become Boris Badenov, only rather than
wearing a black trench coat and fedora and skulking
through the shadows, he sat in a dark room drinking
Starbucks and pissing on the very notion of freedom.

So it was that six months later—after jumping through
flaming hoops and signing countless documents that ensured that if he so much as *thought* about breaking his

oath of confidentiality he'd be executed for treason—
he was no longer employed by the federal government
and traveling the world in search of his place in life
when he encountered his first crop circle in a field in
Nebraska. He'd been driving west to see the Rockies
when a hand-painted sign on the side of the highway
caught his eye. The farmer had charged him twenty
dollars and told him to follow a simpleton in overalls
into the cornfield, where the design had supposedly
appeared overnight a week prior.

From the ground, it had looked like a poorly con-
ceived corn maze. The leaves of the standing stalks
were strangely withered and, after driving hundreds of
miles with starlings and crows lining every fence and
telephone wire, he became suddenly conscious of the
fact that he hadn't seen a single bird since climbing out
of his car.

From that day forward, he'd dedicated his skills to
deciphering the riddle that had plagued some of the
brightest scientific minds dating back to the seventeenth century. The problem was that if there was a
pattern to their formation, it eluded him. The only one
he could find was in geographic dispersion. There was a
stretch in southwest England where not only did the
crop circles appear more than anywhere else in the
world, but they did so in a pattern that mirrored the flow
of a large subterranean aquifer, as confirmed by over-
laying a map of known crop circles on top of a hydro-
geological map of England, which was why he'd
moved to Trowbridge and set up a makeshift laboratory in his garage.

This was now the third crop circle he'd investigated
in as many months.

Roche opened an app on his own design on his phone that used a sophisticated geolocation algorithm to create a map from his movements. He walked the perimeter, following each and every curve and contour. When he was done, he stopped in the center of the crop circle, where the matted barley formed a clockwise pattern as though swirled by a tornado, and studied the image of a pentagon with circles of equal diameter at each of its five points.

"Have you ever seen this symbol before?" Roche asked.

Grafton shook his head.

Neither had Roche, but he was certain that the key to unlocking the secret was out here somewhere, whether celestial or terrestrial in origin, and it was only a matter of time before he found it.

5
KELLY

Seaside, Oregon

The Sikorsky MH-60 Jayhawk thundered low over the spruce forests and grassy bluffs of Tillamook Head until the steep cliffs abruptly gave way to the Pacific, where they veered to the north and followed the coastline. Kelly Nolan was harnessed in the back, twirling a shock of green-dyed hair around her index finger. She looked from the open laptop on her thighs to the window, where the vast ocean vanished into the night, and then back again.

2:03 a.m.

Never in her life had she been so nervous, and not just because she'd hadn't been on a helicopter before, let alone one traveling at what had to be nearly 200 miles an hour. If it turned out she was wrong . . .

She couldn't afford to think about that now. Her greater concern was what was about to happen if she was right.

"The evacuation's proceeding on schedule," the pilot said through the noise-canceling headphones, which made the *thupp-thupp-thupp* of the rotors sound like the heartbeat of some great mechanical being. Everything had happened so quickly that she couldn't remember his name, or even if he and his copilot had introduced themselves.

"Excellent," Dr. Davis Walters said from the seat beside her, his voice somewhat garbled by the microphone touching his lower lip. "We have confirmation from all five assembly areas?"

"Yes, sir. We should be passing over Assembly Area Five any second now."

The fingers on Kelly's left hand tapped a restless rhythm on the pad of her thumb, faster and faster, as though soloing on an air guitar. It was an unconscious tic she'd developed as a small child, and one she couldn't turn off without an absurd amount of concentration. Her multicolored fingernails moved in a blur, so fast that even she couldn't figure out if there was a pattern to the tapping.

2:04 a.m.

A collection of lights materialized below them, where the plateau had become a parking lot for evacuees gathered in the hope that this was just another drill. The town sprawled across the shoreline below them, a sandy oasis among the rugged escarpments. The red and blue lights of emergency vehicles flashed through the streets while search-and-rescue choppers swept their spotlights across the vacant beach and desolate boardwalk. A seemingly endless parade of brake lights led inland toward higher ground, where the lights of the other four assembly areas stood in stark contrast to the dark forest.

"There are going to be a lot of pissed-off people if you're wrong about this," the copilot said.

"Even more if we're right," Kelly said.

She focused on her laptop, which displayed the incoming data from the oceanic hydrophone array and the search coil magnetometer she'd installed at the USGS's seismic monitoring station in Corvallis. The SCM was a fairly simplistic sensor that monitored fluctuations in the Earth's magnetic field. These subtle oscillations manifested as sounds of such low frequency that the human ear couldn't hear them, but they were often used to detect impending avalanches or the formation of tornadoes nearly half an hour before they hit. Her theory was that the same technology could be applied to predict earthquakes.

The Earth's magnetic field was formed by a combination of minerals turning around a solid iron core, which generated an electrical current, and the spin of the planet on its axis, known as the Coriolis force. Together they created an enormous electromagnetic field from one pole to the other that produced constant background noise at 7.83 Hertz, below the range of hearing, in much the same way that the flow of electricity through power lines made them buzz.

Her entire graduate thesis was built upon the premise that a localized variation in that sound suggested geological upheaval corresponding with the movement of tectonic plates against one another, which added to the strength of the magnetic field as their edges compressed like springs, storing inordinate amounts of energy just waiting to be released. She'd even been granted access to the moored, autonomous infrasonic hydrophone arrays that the students at the Hatfield Marine Science Center used to listen to the whales. The idea was that not only would the hydrophone capture the sound of the subauditory variance in the magnetic field, it would allow her to run it through an amplifier and a subwoofer to create a physical expression of that sound in a shallow liquid medium—a process called Cymatics, which she likened to the scene in *Jurassic Park* when ripples formed in the cup of water on the SUV's dashboard as the *Tyrannosaurus rex* approached—a literal waveform that could be used to predict not only an impending quake, but its severity.

2:05 a.m.

"Still no alerts from the NOAA," the pilot said. "Tell me you have access to data we don't."

"Hydrophones off the coast have picked up a substantial increase in noise in the infrasonic range over the last six days," Kelly said.

"What exactly does that mean?"

"If I'm right—"

"If?" the copilot interrupted.

"—we're looking at a seismic event that could wipe this entire coastline off the map. Are you willing to take the chance that I'm wrong?"

At first, the SCM readings had been chaotic and seemingly incoherent. She'd despaired that her entire thesis was a failure and she'd wasted years of her life and tens of thousands of dollars, at least until she realized that any tectonic activity along the Cascadia fault line—the subduction zone running from Northern California to Vancouver—would create a proportional disturbance in the surrounding ocean, which, when digitally subtracted, left her with data that could be plotted as a perfect sine wave of increasing frequency and intensity. Initially, the spikes in activity were erratic and interspersed with periods of relative calm, but since 8:53 P.M. the readings had assumed an element of steady escalation, inside of which she detected a pattern she couldn't quite explain, one that when isolated appeared to form what could loosely be considered a countdown.

2:06 a.m.

She glanced nervously at Dr. Walters. She'd never seen him so pale. He alternately tore his fingers through his hair and checked his cell phone, which was logged into the National Oceanic and Atmospheric Administration's Tsunami Warning Center. As her graduate adviser, it was his neck on the proverbial chopping block.

"Any reports of flooding anywhere along the coast?" he asked.

"Nothing that's been reported to the Coast Guard," the pilot said.

Kelly caught Dr. Walters looking at her from the corner of his eye and wondered if even he was beginning to doubt her. She'd spent two panicked hours trying to convince anyone who would listen to evacuate a stretch of the Oregon coast from Manzanita to Astoria corresponding to the increased activity in the Cascadia Subduction Zone. She'd been in tears when she finally called Walters, who for the last five years had been predicting a massive and long overdue earthquake off the shore of the Pacific Northwest. Even he had been difficult to convince, and had only been persuaded by the threat of having to live with the deaths of thousands on his conscience if he didn't act. It didn't hurt that he was obviously into her. She felt guilty about taking advantage of his feelings, but as one of the designers of the Tsunami Early Warning System, he'd been able to set the gears in motion with a single text. Evacuations had commenced within a matter of minutes, and the USCG Jayhawk had been dispatched to ferry them to the Seaside command center at the Hilltop Assembly Area.

"How long until we're on the ground?" Walters asked.

"Just a few more minutes," the pilot said.

2:07 a.m.

"We're too late," Kelly said. She closed her eyes and slowly exhaled in an effort to calm her nerves. She opened them again just in time to watch the magnetometer readings flatline. "The countdown's complete."

Kelly stared at Dr. Walters, whose expression ran the gamut from apprehension to sheer terror at the thought of having thrown away his career alongside millions of dollars of emergency funds.

She had to look away.

2:08 a.m.

The magnetometer readings spiked by a full 3 microteslas, and the background noise on the hydrophones jumped 20 hertz. The ground below them appeared to shiver.

An alarm sounded from Walters's phone. He read the warning into his microphone so they all could hear.

"Preliminary quake information . . . Location: off the coast of Oregon . . . Depth: 7 miles . . . Estimated magnitude: 7.8 . . . Christ." Another beeping sound. "The early warning buoys just alarmed."

"Sweet baby Jesus," the copilot said.

Kelly leaned against the window so she could look straight down at the row of hotels lining the boardwalk. The wheels of the chopper nearly skimmed their roofs as they banked around the town toward the command center. The beach grew longer and longer before her very eyes as the Pacific receded.

She heard a grumbling sound outside, followed by the shrill cry of what sounded like an air-raid siren. One of the hotels fell straight down to the ground beneath them. The helicopter lurched violently, as though caught in a downdraft.

The night grew suddenly silent and so still that the chopper seemed to float effortlessly.

Kelly knew exactly what that meant.

"Get us above it!" she shouted.

The Jayhawk banked sharply and streaked inland, climbing as it went.

Kelly pressed her cheek against the window and looked back. A tsunami rose from the black horizon, thrust upward by the seismic event. It seemed to pause for the briefest of moments before bearing down upon the coastline at nearly 500 miles an hour. Moonlight shimmered from the seamless crescent of water as it raced into the shallows and rose in a churning wall of destruction that swallowed the beach, hammered the line of hotels, and washed over the business district, sending cars and debris tumbling into the surrounding neighborhoods, where entire houses vanished beneath the sea. The massive tidal wave tore through the foothills and broke against the cliffs, throwing so much water into the air that it nearly submerged the airborne chopper.

She stared down upon the devastation in mute horror.

Walters placed his trembling hand on her shoulder.

"You did good. Imagine how many people could have died tonight."

Kelly looked away from where she could see little more than rooftops protruding from water roiling with the detritus of ruined lives. All she could think about were those who hadn't made it to safety because she hadn't recognized the pattern in time.

She wiped the tears from her eyes and watched the readings on her laptop continue to spike with the aftershocks, although with diminishing intensity until, finally, they returned to normal.

6
ANYA

Johann Brandt Institute for Evolutionary Anthropology
Chicago, Illinois

The main public exhibit hall was filled with shatter-proof glass cases positioned beneath recessed lights that made them appear to glow. Each contained skeletal remains and artifacts related to the various stages of human evolution. The exhibit had closed hours ago with the rest of the Johann Brandt Institute for Evolutionary Anthropology. Only a handful of researchers remained cloistered in their labs, lost in their work and oblivious to the time. Security guards prowled the dark hallways of the 220,000-square-foot complex, which was spread out over four floors, including a subterranean level primarily used for storage and curation. One of them had been nice enough to keep Anya Fleming company for as long as he could, before leaving her alone in front of a long display case in what they jokingly called "Headhunter's Hall."

She scrutinized her reflection in the glass. If she tilted her head just right, she could superimpose her green eyes and freckles over the hollow sockets and cheekbones of the two-thousand-year-old skull inside. Its cranium, however, was a different story. It was disproportionately large and elongated, which was why the guys in the genetics lab called it a conehead, after the old *Saturday Night Live* sketch with Dan Aykroyd and Jane Curtin. To Anya, though, it looked more like a Xenomorph from the *Alien* films.

She'd exhumed this specimen herself, from beneath the red clay soil in the steppes of the Southern Ural Mountains at a site called Arkaim, colloquially known as Russia's Stonehenge, which was built in the seventeenth century BCE, at the height of the Sintashta-Petrovka culture. It consisted of two concentric rings of dwellings surrounded by fortifications nearly twenty feet tall and a moat another six feet deep. A single entryway served as a bottleneck to repel invading forces, although no one knew precisely which enemies were aligned against them or why they abandoned the fortress. It wasn't until recently that anyone even knew it was there. Had surveyors not recognized its significance, it would have vanished beneath the floodwaters used to create a reservoir.

While the settlement was found burned to the ground and nearly indistinguishable from the plains around it, archeologists were still able to piece together its functionality as a celestial observatory, similar to those from the same time period in Egypt, Mesopotamia, and throughout Central and South America, contemporary sites where—whether coincidentally or not—dozens of other coneheads like the one Anya had been staring at had been unearthed.

The prevailing school of thought was that their misshapen heads were a consequence of artificial cranial deformation, a process by which the growth of an infant's pliable skull was altered by binding it between two pieces of wood or wrapping it tightly in a cloth. While many primitive cultures like the Huns and the Alans were known to employ such methods as recently as the third century BCE, the practice largely died out shortly thereafter. Their craniums were easily distinguished by an indentation that almost looked like a headband across the frontal bone and along the parietal sutures, with associated forward protrusion of the mastoid processes and a bulbous occipital bone.

The skulls in the case before her now were different, though. They were elongated more in the vertical axis than the horizontal and had been exhumed from burials near known ancient observatories. The majority were collected from a cave in Paracas, Peru, near the enigmatic Nazca Lines, yet they shared several striking physical characteristics with the others, some of which had been collected on the other side of the globe. Traditional deformation merely changed the shape of the cranium. These were a full 25 percent larger and 60 percent heavier. No amount of squishing or flattening could add mass or change the volume of the brainpan. More important, analysis of their mitochondrial DNA, which was inherited through the maternal line, demonstrated mutations distinct from all other species of primates, including modern humans, Neanderthals, and Denisovans. And this one—the one she'd personally disinterred—could potentially help them understand the nature of these mutated sequences and determine their function.

Previous remains had been discovered in caves and other regions where the climate wreaked havoc on their DNA, degrading samples to the point that sequencing had been unable to produce a complete genome. Her skull, on the other hand, had been so perfectly preserved in the dense mud that the entire skeleton remained articulated. At this very moment, a sample from this cranium was down the hall in the genetics lab, its genome being sequenced by some of the most accomplished geneticists in the world, the same team that had sequenced Denisovan DNA from a single finger bone.

The process was taking forever, though. The results should have come back a full eight hours ago, although no one had been willing to commit to a formal timetable. She was just a postdoctoral fellow, which, in this esteemed company, was the equivalent of being an undrafted rookie playing on an all-star team. Those on staff at the Brandt Institute were the very brightest minds in their respective fields, the kind of brilliant researchers who could secure tenured positions at any university in the world just by picking up the phone. They'd been lured here not because their mere presence would secure funding for the institution, but rather because the institution secured that money for them. Third-party funding ensured they could write blank checks from inexhaustible accounts in order to perform any research they wanted, anywhere in the world, without anyone looking over their shoulders.

That had really just been the icing on the cake for Anya. There weren't many institutions willing to concede the possibility that these coneheads, which were essentially the equivalent of roadside curiosities in the scientific community, could actually be a discrete lineage of extinct hominin, a terminal branch on mankind's family tree. There were simply too many similarities between individual remains discovered on completely different continents that defied coincidence.

More than 500 candidates had applied for the posting she'd secured with a single interview. Even better, she'd been given an office of her own and keys to pretty much every laboratory in the entire state-of-the-art facility. She'd immediately become the envy of every other fellow, and even a few department heads. Not bad for a four-eyed girl from Scranton, whose first archeological dig was in a sandbox that produced what the other kids convinced her was a piece of chocolate.

She probably should have just gone home to wait, but she knew someone would call from the lab the moment she walked through the door. What in the world was taking so long? The institute's new DNA analyzer could sequence the entire human genome in twenty-six hours and it had been—she glanced at her watch—nearly thirty-five hours. It was already nine o'clock, and the building was a graveyard. Maybe the lab had decided to call it a day and no one had bothered to tell her. If that were the case, she was going to storm into the department head's office first thing in the morning and scream—

"Dr. Fleming?"

Anya flinched at the sound of the voice. She hadn't heard anyone enter the cavernous room.

"Yes?"

She turned to face a man she'd never seen before.

Granted, there were nearly 400 staff and another 80 doctoral candidates at any given time, but she would have remembered this man. He wore a custom-tailored suit and a practiced smile that didn't reach his eyes, which surreptitiously surveyed the exhibit hall. His bearing was upright and regal in a way she attributed to either wealth or military service, almost like a Secret Service agent, although this man appeared more accustomed to the limelight than blending into the woodwork.

He strode toward her and proffered his hand. He was handsome in a rugged way, although he was both too old and too angular for her. Too many sharp edges: from his buzz-cut hair to the line of his jaw to the shoulders of his jacket.

"My name is Will Connor. It's my distinct pleasure to finally meet you."

"Nice to meet you, too. You'll have to pardon me, but I'm kind of preoccupied right now—"

"Waiting for the results from the genetics lab." His smile morphed into an amused smirk. "Don't look so surprised. That's the whole reason I'm here. And I do apologize for making you wait so long."

"The results are in?"

"Do try to keep up, won't you?"

"I don't understand."

"Let me start over. I represent the interests of the corporation that funds your research. In fact, you could say my employer was integral in securing your services here."

"My research is funded by the institute—"

"Which, in turn, is funded by the generous dona-tions of benefactors like my employer, who's just dying to meet you."

"What about the results?"

"Don't worry. They've already been sent to your faculty email so you can evaluate them on the plane."

"What plane?"

7
RICHARDS

"The suspense is killing me. Can't I just get a quick peek?"

Hollis Richards had been in the middle of dinner when Friden interrupted and hustled him down into the sublevel of the research station, where the laboratories had been installed inside a natural formation.

"Just give me a few more seconds."

Richards paced Friden's lab while the microbiologist diddled with the scanning electron microscope. He stopped in front of the glass cage at the back of the room and tapped on the glass.

"Don't do that," Friden said. "Speedy hates it when people do that."

The mouse stuck its whiskered nose out of its bedding and sniffed at the air before burying itself once more, apparently less perturbed than its owner. Richards didn't understand why Friden was so attached to the kind of rodent Richards had killed by the thousands on his farm as a kid, but it was important to him that his staff felt comfortable in their new surroundings.

He'd learned a lot about people as a venture capitalist. It required more than an almost prescient ability to
see the merits of an idea and the confidence to invest
an absurd amount of money. To be successful you had
to believe in the men and women behind the vision and
have faith in their ability to achieve it.

Sure, he'd swung for the fences and missed more
often than not, but all it took was connecting with the
right pitch one time, and he'd knocked at least a dozen
out of the park in the last twenty years alone, from
household names like Google and Amazon to pioneers
in the fields of biotherapeutics and organic agricultural
solutions. If there was one thing he'd learned from his
father, it was that you could never lose when you gam-
bled with someone else's money, and the way his old
man saw it, that was exactly what you had if you didn't
have the dirt under your nails to show for it, which was
why it had seemed like the greatest possible posthumous insult to sell the family homestead to a corporate
farm and roll the dice on a single bet. Richards was almost disappointed when he didn't lose everything on a
company called Quantum Link, a dedicated online
gaming service that subsequently diversified and
changed its name to America Online.

He'd honestly thought that by now his team of scientists would have laid bare all of the secrets frozen
beneath them. It had been almost too easy boring
straight down through the ice and immediately seeing
the inhuman skull covered with sediment. He'd almost
believed it was his destiny to be the first to prove the
existence of extraterrestrial life. Ever since that night
in the cornfield, it had felt as though every decision
he'd made throughout the course of his life had con-

spired to bring him to the bottom of the world, where all signs pointed to the proof he sought.

And here he was now, with that evidence within his reach, and yet, for the life of him, he couldn't seem to grasp it.

"There," Friden said, and slid his chair back from his workstation. He gestured toward the monitor with a flourish.

Richards stared at the image for several seconds before he finally spoke.

"What is it?"

"Exactly. I can tell you what it was, and I have a pretty good idea of what happened to it, but I haven't got the slightest idea why."

Richards dragged over a stool from the station beneath the Class II biological safety hood, which allowed for the sterile preparation of slides and solutions, and perched on top of it. The image on the screen reminded Richards of a plasma globe in the sense that what almost looked like bolts of lightning radiated from a spherical mass. It was misshapen on one side, where it appeared as though its insides had leaked out.

"What you're looking at is a species of archaea, a microscopic single-celled organism capable of surviving in environmental and temperature extremes that kill all other forms of life. We collected this one from the lake below us. It's the same species we found fossilized on the Vigarano meteorite from Italy. Until this morning, none of these buggers had produced any of these filamentous appendages. Then, all of a sudden . . ." He zoomed out and the screen filled with a dozen similar bacteria. ". . . *boom!* All of them shoot out these feelers and attach themselves to everything within reach."

"They look like cocoons."

"Kind of. I would have said they look more like nerve cells connected by a web of dendrites. Regardless, no sooner was this reaction triggered than their cellular membranes collapsed and their cytoplasm leaked out."

"Triggered?"

"There's no other explanation. Some external stimulus had to have caused the transformation. So I started thinking about every little variable that could have provoked it. Did I do anything differently when I prepared the samples for the slides? Did I spill anything on them or otherwise add an element of unpredictability? And then it hit me. It wasn't anything I did."

"So what caused it?"

"Let me show you."

Friden swiveled around to face the table under the hood, where he'd prepared several slides.

"The SEM gets incredible detail, but it's not able to image living organisms. A light microscope can, at the expense of magnification and resolution, which means we have to stain the archaea to better see them."

He switched the monitor from the SEM to the light microscope and clipped the slide to the mount. A few twists of the dials and the image came into focus. Tons of fluorescent green dots stood apart from what looked like a nebula.

"Each of those green dots represents an individual organism. If you look closely, you can see them move in little spurts."

"What's the significance?"

"Right, right. I'm getting to that." Friden hopped up and looked around the room as though searching for something. "I do my best thinking while I'm moving. Gets the juices flowing, you know? So I was pacing the corridor when Mariah comes barreling down the hall and nearly runs me over."

Dr. Mariah Peters was a geologist Richards had hired to map the terrain beneath the water and ice. Her previous work at Gunung Padang, the largest megalithic site in Indonesia, was crucial in determining that a hill thought to be the neck of an extinct volcano was actually a manmade building. It was her familiarity with volcanic rock and her wizardry with ground penetrating radar that allowed her to visualize the pyramidal structure beneath the layers of ash and soot that had accumulated on it from the eruptions of a nearby volcano. And considering the unstable geological nature of Antarctica, there was no one better suited for the job. In fact, she was the first one to document the nearly undetectable irregular infrasonic pulsations coming from somewhere beneath the ice.

"You know how she has that sonar drone down in the lake? The one she's using to map the bottom? Anyway, it's programmed to alarm if it malfunctions, so this alarm is going off and Mariah is all panicked, right? So I ask her what's going on and she says there's something wrong with the hydrophonic array that picks up the sounds that bounce back to the unit from the ground. There's this huge spike in the signal, right? Only it's not a malfunction at all. The sound waves are actually being amplified by some sort of hollow chamber, which causes them to reverberate or resonate or whatever. The point being that this happened at the same time I was preparing my slides."

"What did she find?"

"She's still working on it. Can we get back to me?"

Richards gestured for him to proceed.

Friden finally found what he was looking for and pulled an MP3 player from underneath a mess of notes and candy wrappers. He put both earbuds against the slide, one to either side of the microscope lens.

"The sound waves they use to map the lake floor are approximately one kilohertz. That's essentially the sound range between the eighteenth and twentieth frets on the high E string of an electric guitar, so I played this solo from Metallica's "The Unforgiven." It's got this nice long bend on the twentieth fret. I've got it primed at the right spot. Just watch what happens."

He unpaused the song and a high-pitched note erupted from the earbuds, sending sonic vibrations through the liquid medium on the slide.

On the screen, the green dots became fuzzy as filaments branched outward, seemingly connecting all of the dots together into a giant irregular matrix, before suddenly becoming hazy and losing definition.

"That right there," Friden said. "That's where their membranes rupture and the cytoplasm leaks out."

"Why?"

"The resonance at that particular sound frequency caused these microorganisms to essentially fulfill some sort of biological imperative in a matter of seconds. Something preprogrammed into their DNA." He looked at Richards as though waiting for the lightbulb to go on over his head. "You still don't get it. How about this? Inside of every cell is a fluid called cytoplasm. Sound waves like sonar pass through this fluid, but not without interacting, in this case with the chromosomal DNA floating freely inside that fluid. This interaction somehow stimulated the genes to accelerate the growth rate of its fimbriae—those finger-looking thingies—but in the process altered the chromosomes to such an extent that the plasma membrane and the cell wall ruptured."

"But first it activated some portion of the DNA that it wasn't currently utilizing."

"Bingo."

"So what are the implications?"

"That's what I intend to find out."

"What do you have in mind?"

"Varying the frequency maybe?" He removed his earbuds from the slide, unclipped it, and was about to set it back with the others when someone banged frantically on his door. He dropped the slide and it shattered on the floor.

The door opened before either of them could answer. Mariah stuck her head in. Her dark hair was mussed and her brown eyes were wide with excitement.

"You have to see this," she said and ducked back out into the hall.

"The hell, Mariah? Can't you knock like a regular person?" Friden said. He picked up the broken glass and set it back under the hood. It wasn't until he saw the droplets of blood pattering the stainless-steel countertop that he realized he'd been cut. "You've got to be kidding me."

"Get a bandage," Richards said.

"'Get a bandage.' Are you serious? That's how you show concern for an injured employee?"

"I have a hunch you'll survive."

Richards hurried to catch up with Dr. Peters. By the time he reached the corridor, she was already back in her lab, where he found her studying a row of monitors mounted above her immaculate workstation.

"This." She tapped a computer monitor with a pixilated square shape composed of varying shades and concentrations of gray and black. Several parallel lines radiated from one side, as though it were photographed in motion. "This right here. Do you have any idea what this is?"

"It's the bottom of the lake," Richards said.

"This is a map of the data points corresponding to the amplitude of the reflected sonar waves plotted on a grid. The black objects are solid surfaces that reflect the sonic impulses at ninety degrees, meaning they're horizontal. Everything else is at an angle somewhere between horizontal and vertical—the X and Y planes— and represented by these varying shades of gray. In a nutshell, three-dimensional objects displayed in two dimensions. Now look at this image over here."

She directed him to the adjacent monitor. Bands of different width crossed the screen, the uppermost of which was thinner and lighter in color. At the top was an indistinct triangular shape that appeared to cast a shadow.

"This is a visual representation of the raw data, just like you'd see during an ultrasound in a doctor's office. It's essentially a cross-section of the ground from top to bottom. Now watch what happens when I combine the two sets of data to produce a three-dimensional re-creation."

She typed commands on her keyboard and an image appeared on the third screen, this time clearly representing the bottom of the lake and the structures buried beneath the thick layer of sediment.

"Now do you see?"

Richards leaned closer to the screen, where, despite the limited resolution, he could clearly discern several manmade structures. Most of them were rectangular and in different stages of collapse, but it was the largest one in the center that captured his attention.

"My God," he whispered. "It's a pyramid."

"And that low-pitched hum we've been monitoring? It appears to be coming from inside of it."

8

EVANS

El-'Amarna, September 20—today

Until a representative from the Egyptian Ministry of State for Antiquities arrived to supervise the formal excavation, there was nothing more Evans could do. They'd photographed and digitally recorded the cave from every conceivable angle, plus they'd used a FARO laser scanner to create a 3-D model so lifelike it was hard to distinguish the virtual walkthrough from the real thing. It had already been twenty-four hours since Evans had personally spoken to Tihrak Mamoun, the Minister of State, whose job it was to micromanage every aspect of archeology in Egypt and preserve what remained of one of the world's most majestic heritages, which was why it was so surprising that there hadn't been a representative on-site first thing this morning as promised. While Evans had no intention of violating any of the terms of his agreement with the government and risk forfeiting all future rights to dig in Egypt, he'd never known the ministry to leave anything to chance.

He'd already sent photographs of the gnawed bones

to a forensic odontologist for her analysis, but without the indentations from which to mold a cast, she could only speculate. Digital images of the designs carved into the ceiling found their way to one of Andrea's colleagues in the astronomy department at Yale, who excitedly confirmed the precise positioning of the stars corresponding to a date more than three thousand years ago using a computer-generated overlay. Samples of coprolite were ready to be bagged and shipped back to Cairo for dietary analysis. There were even bones belonging to an extinct species of oryx that half a dozen zoologists and geneticists were nearly tripping over themselves to secure. There were so many mysteries that needed to be explored, chief among them the unclassified hominin species with the conical head, but there wasn't a blasted thing anyone could do until an official representative of the Egyptian government finally showed up.

Evans paced a figure eight around the lighting arrays erected in the center of the cavern. They dispelled everything resembling shadows and created an almost clinical workspace—were it not for the mounds of bones and the mummified corpse, of course, which seemed somehow smaller and less impressive. They measured the subject to be just shy of five-foot-nine, which marked him as taller than the average male of his time period by roughly the height of his elongated cranium. His fingertips had been filed down past the inguinal tufts and nearly to the first knuckle as a result of clawing at the earthen barricade and the stone walls in a futile attempt to escape. His most remarkable feature, however, was his teeth.

His incisors were spatulate and his canines longer

than normal, although it was impossible to tell how much longer since the tips had broken off, presumably while trying to bite into the hard bones. There was no way to evaluate the chewing surfaces without a panoramic X-ray or by physically opening his mouth, but the edges showed advanced wear for his estimated age and several of the premolars and molars were cracked all the way down to the roots.

It was hard not to rush to judgment and call this an entirely new species, at least not until he was able to send tissue and bone samples to the lab for genomic sequencing. He could feel it, though. This was something special, something truly unique.

Evans's entire career was built upon the idea of spontaneous genetic mutation, whether in response to environmental factors or through a fluke of nature. There was simply no other way to explain why so many protohuman species could arise from a common ancestor and have such different physical traits, let alone exist at the same time. *Home erectus*, *ergaster*, and *habilis* all walked the earth at the same time as their upright simian progenitors, *Paranthropus robustus* and *boisei*. *Homo erectus*, *floresiensis*, *heidelbergensis*, and *neanderthalensis* had coexisted with early *Homo sapiens* during the same 2,000-year span. Each represented a distinct evolutionary leap not just from its predecessors, but from its contemporaries as well. It wasn't just survival of the fittest, it was a full-on melee.

With the exception of the occasional overlap of habitat and interbreeding, the numerous hominin species evolved into what essentially could be considered regional variants, in much the same way as modern races. Outside of skin color, there are relatively few anatomic and physiologic differences between races, all of which have followed a similar evolutionary blueprint, despite extended periods of geologic isolation from one another. Not so with early hominins, who, following the last ice age and within the span of modern man's recorded history, registered phenomenal physical mutations that could neither be explained nor ignored, most noticeably the changes in the skull itself.

Seemingly overnight, modern man's simian shelf vanished and his sloping forehead gave way to an upright frontal bone. His cranial vault doubled in size to accommodate a brain twice the size of those of any of the other hominin species, and yet somehow it has miraculously remained the same size for more than 20,000 years.

And here before Evans lay a man like him, and yet one whose deformed head possibly held a brain at least 50 percent larger than his, one who potentially represented the next and most logical step in human evolution, and whose DNA just might prove his theory of spontaneous genetic mutation and hold the key to unlocking mankind's fullest potential.

For better or worse, he thought as he surveyed the piles of ravaged bones throughout the cave.

"Cade!"

Evans turned at the sound of his name, which had come from somewhere outside the tunnel. He had barely started squeezing through the hole when he heard the source of Andrea's excitement.

"It's about time," he said, and scurried toward the grumble of tires on gravel.

He emerged to find a blue Toyota pickup truck with an oversized camper shell and the insignia of the Egyptian National Police idling at the bottom of the ravine. A man wearing sunglasses and black fatigues climbed from the driver's side door. The silver star on his epaulets marked him as a lieutenant.

Evans cast a discreet glance at Andrea, who appeared every bit as uncomfortable with this development as he was. The entire country was well on its way to becoming a police state in response to the advance of Daesh, but even so this felt like overkill. He expected a plain-clothed representative from the ministry to step out from the opposite side, yet the silhouette in the passenger seat didn't move. It wasn't until Evans was halfway down the rocky slope that he was able to shield his eyes from the sun well enough to see the second officer fiddling with the glove compartment.

Andrea made a move to join him, but he waved her back. She retreated to join her graduate students in the scant shade cast by the neighboring escarpment. They'd covered every major contingency, from shakedowns by crooked cops and thieves to a caravan of trucks flying the black flags of ISIS funneling into the valley. There were enough provisions inside the royal tomb to withstand a monthlong siege and a satellite phone programmed with the numbers of the six closest American embassies.

"Dr. Evans," the lieutenant said in a thick Arabic accent. It was a statement, not a question. He knew exactly who Cade was. With the sun behind him, it was impossible to clearly see his features or what looked like a thin package in his left hand.

"That's right." Evans pulled off his work gloves and shoved them into the back pocket of his jeans. "What can I do for you?"

"We were dispatched at the request of Minister Mamoun, who sends his regards and apologizes for being unable to be here in person."

Evans smiled and nodded to the officer in the truck, who inclined his chin ever so slightly in response. Neither man appeared to be an immediate threat. They merely appeared aggrieved, as though doing their best to remain professional while performing a task they felt was beneath them.

"Surely the minister recognizes the importance of this discovery and is eager to take a look for himself."

"I know nothing about that, sir. Our orders are to deliver this package to you and escort you back to Cairo."

He held out the package and waited patiently for Evans to take it. The moment his hand was free, the officer leaned against the hood and lit a cigarette.

Evans glanced back at Andrea before turning the package over and over in his hands. It was roughly the size of a notebook, wrapped in plain brown paper, and sealed with a red sticker with Arabic writing that he had to tear to open the parcel. The manila envelope inside was taped closed. He peeled the tape, lifted the flap, and shook the contents to the edge where he could reach them. There was an iPad, a plane ticket from Cairo to Johannesburg, South Africa, and a photograph of remains nearly identical to those in the cave behind him, only a whole lot less ancient.

He looked up in surprise at the officer, who merely

blew smoke from his nostrils and asked in a distracted tone, "Shall we be on our way then?"

Evans couldn't find the voice to respond. He just turned without a word and headed back to the camp to gather his belongings.

9
JADE

O. R. Tambo International Airport
Johannesburg, South Africa

Jade still didn't know what in the world she was doing there, let alone how she'd talked herself into dropping everything and boarding a commercial plane in Maiduguri bound for, of all places, Johannesburg. She figured it was only a matter of time before her work took her to South Africa, which the U.N. was monitoring closely for crimes of genocide as more than 70,000 Caucasians had been murdered since the African National Congress rose to power, but she hadn't figured it would be this soon. Then again, this wasn't really work, at least not as it pertained to her contract with the International Criminal Court. The U.N. had been surprisingly happy to release her from her obligations in Nigeria and had even been kind enough to provide transportation to the airport at whatever ungodly hour she'd been awakened.

She'd been soundly asleep in her hotel room in Gubio, twenty miles southeast of the burned village of Musari, when she was roused by a sharp knock on the door. At that point, she couldn't have been asleep for more than a couple of hours, just long enough to find herself disoriented and uncertain of where she was. Her notes had been spread across the comforter covering her legs, and her computer was open on her lap. She'd left on the lamp, which revealed a gecko staring down at her from the wall.

A second knock had startled her so badly she'd knocked her laptop to the floor. She'd been halfway to the door when she realized she was only wearing a nightshirt and panties and scoured the floor for whatever pants she'd been wearing the night before. She'd had the presence of mind to don her hijab before answering the door.

The Canadian peacekeeper Billings had retreated a step and apologized for disturbing her in such a manner. By then she'd recovered just enough of her wits to feign a reasonable measure of outrage. She hadn't seen him since that first day in Musari, where she'd spent forty-eight hours straight documenting the atrocities of Boko Haram. There had been 204 people in that mass grave, each of them with wounds that needed to be photographed and causes of death that needed to be meticulously logged. Women and men alike had to be examined for rape and samples collected from their violated genitalia, scraped from beneath their fingernails, and swabbed from their teeth in the hope of building a database of DNA that could be used during the prosecution.

Without the aid of dental records, they'd only identified a third of the victims when she returned to her hotel, emotionally drained and physically exhausted. She was beginning to suspect they would never be able to identify all of them, including the girl with the cranial defect who'd been buried beneath the mother and her infant. Her mouth had been disproportionately small, her chin too narrow, and her eyes had seemed to bulge from their sockets. Beare-Stevenson Syndrome, a genetic condition that caused the bones of the skull to fuse prematurely, often presented in a similar manner.

Jade was ashamed of her initial reaction, which was undoubtedly the same one that poor girl had endured her entire short life, one of shock and revulsion at a face that had not only looked different, but alien. In the end, though, the girl's deformity had brought her a swift and merciful end compared to the other twenty-six abducted women, who were still out there being abused in ways Jade refused to even imagine.

Her first thought had been that Billings was making a romantic overture. He'd been holding something behind his back and wearing an expression she couldn't interpret. Every other time she'd seen him there had been no mistaking who was in charge. His uncertainty had caused the fine hairs to rise along the backs of her arms. He'd handed her a file folder clearly marked Top Secret and waited in the threshold until he'd politely suggested that she invite him inside, where he stood with his back against the door while she perused the contents.

The first couple of pages had caught her off guard as they pertained more to her work stateside in conjunction with the offices of various medical examiners. As a forensic anthropologist, she was often called upon to appear in court as an expert witness in relation to evidence collected from crime scenes, specifically that related to osteology and physical remains. While

DNA testing was becoming more widely accepted, misinterpretations and flat-out mishandling of samples had tainted its reputation and had led to the release of innocent men wrongly convicted and guilty men who went on to kill again. Thus it was imperative that someone like Dr. Jade Liang, with her impeccable credentials and respected position in the field, be willing to sign off on potentially fallible results in order to sway a jury.

There were several pages of PCR—polymerase chain reaction—tests that consisted of rows of black lines of varying width reminiscent of bar codes, if they were squashed and stretched like taffy. The labels had been redacted, although she could tell there were four different samples being compared. The PCR worked by using an enzyme to chop up segments of DNA, which were then placed in adjacent wells and exposed to an electrical current that caused them to flow through a gelatinous medium that separated them by size. This allowed for the visual comparison of similar samples that may have only differed by seemingly insignificant amounts of DNA, like with paternity testing.

All four of the rows were nearly identical, suggesting a large amount of shared genetic material. One section had been circled by hand in red and didn't correlate to the other three. The following page had shown the genomic makeup of that small section in detail, broken down into paired horizontal lines composed of four colors, almost like the bars on a soldier's dress uniform, and represented the actual pairing of nucleic acids that composed the DNA helix. Above and below each line had been the combinations of amino acids that formed individual genes.

"This can't be right," she'd said.

"Ma'am?"

"These lab results . . . they're—"

"Above my security clearance, ma'am."

She'd plopped down on her bed and wondered if she was still asleep and dreaming.

Now here she was, nine hours later, sitting on a private plane with honest-to-God propellers and pontoons instead of wheels, with three people she'd never seen in her life and a pilot who looked a whole lot more like a bear than a man, without the slightest clue as to where she was going.

Jade watched the tarmac streak past through the port-hole windows of the Basler BT-67. She wished she knew their destination. It seemed illogical to fly her down to the southern tip of the African continent just to head back north again, and a plane this size couldn't hold enough fuel to reach Argentina to the west or Australia to the east. Maybe Madagascar? The only thing to the south was ice and snow, neither of which appealed to her in the slightest.

There were six high-backed leather chairs in the cabin: four on one side, two on the other, facing each other across small tables to either side of the offset main aisle. The man across from her had sun-bleached hair and skin so tan it accentuated the age lines on his face. She thought he was probably a software designer or money-market manager, something that paid a lot and demanded little, allowing him to spend the majority of his time surfing, at least until she noticed the muscles in his forearms and the crescents of dirt under his fingernails and revised her guess to construction worker.

The girl beside him wore a heavy gray sweater with skintight black jeans and looked like she hadn't been outside in months. Her black-framed glasses were disproportionately large and her bangs were short. One side of her hair had a green streak, the other red. She barely looked old enough to drive, let alone to get a tattoo of doves in flight behind her ear. Her left hand moved restlessly, her fingertips tapping a frenetic rhythm on the pad of her thumb.

The man to her left had his eyes closed, but she could tell that he wasn't sleeping. He appeared to be soaking in everything around him without openly doing so. He had broad shoulders and a tapered waist, but carried himself in a manner that somehow seemed to diminish his size. Everything about him was so ordinary that she had to look at him several times before she was able to get a good idea of what he actually looked like. She wondered if he tried to make himself look just like everyone else, anonymous even in such close quarters.

The plane banked to the south, offering a panoramic view of the city sprawled below them, the spike of the Hillbrow Tower driven into its heart. The prospect of being at the mercy of forces beyond her control was simultaneously terrifying and exhilarating. She was grateful that Billings had agreed to track the GPS signal from her cell phone so at least someone would know where in the world she was.

"Everyone settle in," the pilot said. "Get some sleep if you can. We've got a long flight ahead of us."

The red sun bled through the windows as it descended toward the horizon. The plane gained altitude and the land fell away beneath her. The ocean shimmered as though countless rubies were submerged just below the surface.

She knew it was only a matter of time before the waves turned to ice.

10
ROCHE

Martin Roche had been instinctively skeptical of William Connor. Then again, he was instinctively skeptical of everyone. It was more than his nature; it was a consequence of his training and of reading literally tens of thousands of private emails in which people bared the darkness inside their very souls. He knew what people thought about crop circles and how little respect they had for those who studied them. Even the most generous among them considered his field a pseudoscience at best, while most were quick to make snide comments about little green men, which was why he never discussed his findings with anyone.

He posted his research on his website, which he'd gone to great lengths to ensure couldn't be found without searching the right combinations of words that only people like him would know, and even then it didn't appear on any of the major search engines. There was no mention of who he was, where he lived, or anything that could be considered even remotely personal.

It was there he organized his photographs, temperature and radiation graphs, germination data, and every other quantifiable trait. There was only a handful of others who'd been granted administrative permissions so they could add their data to his own, and he'd never once spoken to any of them directly, online or off, let alone in person. The way he saw it, he was treading a fine line when it came to his agreement with the NSA. He might not have been sharing agency secrets, but with the way the news of crop circle discoveries was suppressed, he was obviously poking around where someone might not want him to go, someone with power enough to manipulate the mainstream media and dictate the dissemination of information on the Internet, and there were only a few government agencies, and even fewer private individuals, with that kind of power.

Roche knew how paranoid that made him sound, but he'd eavesdropped on too many phone calls to think for a second that there were any secrets left in the world, which was why he hadn't been surprised in the slightest when the initial contact was made through his website. Granted, the email had been sent semi-anonymously from a Hotmail account, but he hadn't been out of the game so long that he'd forgotten how to track the sender's IP address, which corresponded to a business computer registered to a man named William Connor. Fortunately, Roche still had friends inside the NSA who owed him a few favors, and within a matter of hours he had everything he could ever want to know about William Stephen Connor. Distinguished career as a Navy SEAL. Highly decorated: Silver Star, Purple Heart, Combat Action Ribbon, Afghanistan Campaign Medal. Medically discharged after a bullet to the chest cost him a lobe of his lung. Lured into the private sector by an executive security firm in Los Angeles that catered to the entertainment industry. Went freelance and spent the last six years in the employ of a venture capitalist named Hollis Richards, who seemed to have a sixth sense when it came to betting on a long shot and who spent a sizable amount of his ungodly fortune in ways that piqued both Roche's personal and professional curiosity.

By the time he went to bed on the day he received the cryptic email with the attached photograph and the e-ticket to Johannesburg, he'd already determined exactly where he was going, if not why. He remained on high alert and kept his instincts attuned to his surroundings. He'd known SEALs in the service, men who were every bit as smart as they were lethal. More important, he'd learned much about men with enough money to influence current events, and not only did Richards qualify, he'd done an exceptional job of keeping out of the public eye, at least until a subsidiary of his private corporation reached a land-lease agreement with the Norwegian government and backed what on the surface appeared to be a geological survey of the Drygalski Mountain Range. A routine oil, gas, and mineral survey, however, didn't require the construction of an arctic research base stocked with state-of-the-art scientific equipment so specialized that Roche had to Google its uses.

If there was one thing he'd learned in life, it was that knowledge was the currency of power, and it was best not to let anyone know how much he had, so he sat quietly and discreetly studied the others, who appeared every bit as uncomfortable as he was and seemed to know even less. Roche would have recognized them if they were part of the small world of crop circles, in which he sometimes thought he was the only one not actively making a documentary.

The woman with the dark hair and emerald eyes looked at each of them in turn, nodded to herself as though reaching some sort of decision, and removed a folder from the satchel beneath her seat. When she spread its contents out on the table in front of her, Roche realized that despite everything he had learned, he knew absolutely nothing.

He recognized the PCR—polymerase chain reaction—tests. He'd commissioned several for various species of crops to determine if whatever made the circles had altered their DNA, but their genes were nothing like these. These had to have come from some higher order of animal, whose relation to his work couldn't have been less clear.

"Tell me if one of you can make some sense of this for me," she said.

"It's a PCR test," the tan guy across from her said.

"Thank you. I might never have figured that out on my own."

"You asked."

"No, I asked someone to explain the data to me, because from where I'm sitting, it looks an awful lot like the subject has twenty-four pairs of chromosomes."

"That can't be right," Tan Guy said. He turned the page so he could better see it and furrowed his brow. "Where did you get this?"

"You didn't get the same thing?" Green Eyes looked from him to the younger girl, then settled upon Roche. "That's not why you're all here?"

Tan Guy pulled a folded eight-by-ten photograph from the back pocket of his jeans, opened it, and flattened the creases before handing it to her.

"Where did you get this?"

"From the police officer who picked me up. Technically, from the Egyptian Minister of State for Antiquities, but—"

She spun it so that it was right side up for him and tapped the subject of the photograph.

"I took this picture."

Roche caught a glimpse of a dead girl's face, her eyes staring blankly at the camera from beneath another woman's arm.

"So you can verify its authenticity?"

"Verify its . . . ? I examined this girl's remains before personally covering them with a tarp."

"Hold up, hold up." He took his cell phone from the backpack stuffed under his seat and rifled through his pictures until he found the one he wanted. "I took this picture in a cave under the royal tombs in El-'Amarna less than a week ago."

Roche visibly flinched at the sight of it. Very rarely did anything take him by surprise, but the sight of the picture he'd received from the IP address corresponding to William Connor's computer did.

Tan Guy cocked his head and stared at him for a long moment before speaking.

"You've seen this, haven't you?"

Roche brought up the image he'd received. The composition was different, but there was no doubt the subject was the same. His showed a close-up of a mummified face with deformed features and an oblong head. He set it on the table beside the folded picture of a dead girl he could clearly see shared similar physical traits.

"What about you?" Green Eyes asked. She nodded to the younger girl, who wore an expression of complete and utter confusion. The tapping of her fingers momentarily ceased, but started right back up when she spoke.

"I don't think I'm in the right place." Her voice trembled, as though she were on the verge of tears. "This isn't right at all. I don't know anything about dead bodies. I'm a graduate student in seismology."

Her fingers became a blur of motion. She self-consciously tucked her hand under the table she shared with Roche.

"What brought you here, honey?" Tan Guy asked in a soft, reassuring voice and placed his hand on her forearm.

She closed her eyes, drew a deep breath, and composed herself.

"The president of the university called me into his office and showed me this picture. He said he also received a seven-figure donation in exchange for—how did he phrase it?—borrowing my expertise. I thought he was joking, but he made it clear just how serious he was by personally driving me back to my apartment to pack."

She set her iPad on the table, enlarged a thumbnail image to fill the screen, and turned it so they could all see.

Roche was better prepared this time and kept his expression studiously neutral.

"What is it?" Green Eyes asked.

"It's a crop circle."

"You mean like little green men?" Tan Guy said.

Roche barely resisted the urge to punch him in the throat.

"I don't know anything about that, but I do know what this symbol is."

Roche's heart raced when she tapped the picture he'd photographed himself. The one of a crop circle resembling a star with rings at its points, and a sixth point in its center.

"Sound waves aren't just an auditory phenomenon. They're physical waves in the electromagnetic spectrum, like light and X-rays, only with much longer wavelengths. While they don't have mass, per se, they do interact with matter. In fact, every sound has a different wavelength, so it affects matter in unique and characteristic ways. Think of the way a subwoofer makes your chest vibrate. The air in your lungs essentially creates a hollow chamber for the sound waves to resonate."

"Like a high-pitched tone shattering a glass," Tan Guy said.

"That's how human hearing works," Green Eyes said. "Tiny hairs on the basilar membrane in the cochlea detect auditory vibrations and the brain interprets them as sound."

"Exactly. We use a modality called cymatics to create visual representations of sounds at different wavelengths to demonstrate their interactions with matter by exposing a very shallow tray of water directly to a given tone. This creates little designs—for lack of a better term—that we call 'standing waves.'" She swiped her screen to the next image, which showed a sample of water illuminated by a blue light. It was pentagon-shaped and looked almost like a flower. There was a perfect star in the center, at the points of which were spherical blebs of water. It was identical to the crop circle. "This here? This CymaGlyph corresponds to a tone of 22.2 Hertz, which is the exact same sound my equipment picked up from the Cascadian Subduction Zone immediately prior to the tsunami off the coast of Oregon."

The day after the crop circle formed, Roche thought. He remembered hearing the breaking news on the radio while he was taking his daily measurements of germination rates. For the life of him, he couldn't see how her sound image was related to his crop circle, but there was no way he could chalk it up to mere coincidence.

"Well," Tan Guy said. "I guess now that we're more confused than we were when we boarded this infernal plane, anyone want to take a stab at where we're headed?"

"Troll Station," Roche said. They were the first words he'd spoken in hours and came out rougher than he'd expected. He cleared his throat. "It's a Norwegian research station on the Princess Martha Coast of Queen Maud Land."

"Antarctica?"

"How do you know?" Green Eyes asked.

A ringing sound arose from beneath the table with the PCR results spread out across it. Tan Guy looked at each of them before realizing with a start that the sound was coming from his backpack, which he pulled out from under his seat and balanced on his lap. He unzipped the main pouch and pulled out an iPad. In the center of the display was a FaceTime logo and a button to answer the incoming call.

He tentatively hit the button and the face of the man responsible for gathering all of them on this plane streaking toward one of the most inhospitable regions on the entire planet appeared on the screen.

11
KELLY

25,000 feet above the Southern Ocean

"Greetings everyone. I'm thrilled to see you all made it. My name is Hollis Richards, and I'm sure you have a lot of questions. Rest assured, they will be answered to your satisfaction in due time. I just wanted to reach out and thank each of you personally for dropping everything and getting on a plane without knowing exactly where you were going. I know it couldn't have been easy taking that leap of faith. Believe me. I apologize for the secrecy, but I have no doubt you'll understand completely when you reach your destination."

"Which is where, exactly?" the lady with the emerald eyes asked.

Richards smirked. His image briefly froze before jumping to a slightly different location.

"You'll find out soon enough, Dr. Liang."

"Troll Station," the guy next to Kelly said.

"Very good, Dr. Evans. I'm surprised, though. I would have wagered that it would be Mr. Roche who figured it out."

Evans glanced at Roche, who subtly shook his head.

"Just a lucky guess," Evans said.

"I don't believe that for a second, but that's neither here nor there. I suppose it's only fair that you get to keep your secrets, too." Richards smiled into the camera and seemed to look directly at Kelly. He reminded her of a cross between the guy from the Dos Equis commercials—the Most Interesting Man in the World—and Santa Claus. She could tell he was enjoying holding his knowledge over their heads. "How are you doing, Ms. Nolan? I'm sure you've had enough air travel for a while."

She forced her hand into a fist to halt the incessant tapping. Her fingernails bit into her palm.

"For a lifetime," she said.

"It will be worth it. Trust me. And just so you don't think I'm *all* bad, I'll leave you with a parting video I'm quite confident you'll enjoy. See you all in about . . ." He glanced at his watch. ". . . five hours. Try to get some sleep in the meantime. You're going to need it."

There was a clattering sound as he turned his laptop toward another monitor, which initially blurred with wide horizontal bands before the picture resolved. The time and date stamp in the corner indicated that it had been recorded at 16:18 on September 11th, nine days ago. The numbers in the opposite corner were paused at a point more than two hours into the recording.

At first, Kelly couldn't tell what was happening. It was too dark and the lone beam of light swung in a manner that made her stomach queasy. She recognized the splashing sound of someone slogging through water. When the beam finally settled, she let out a startled gasp.

The camera focused on the ground at the edge of a body of water of indeterminate size. The shallows were murky with disturbed sediment that sparkled in the light. The rocks at the bottom were furry with algae, while those above the surface bore the stratified markings of high tide. And in the transition zone rested a skull, turned slightly away from the camera with only a portion of its forehead, cheekbone, and upper jaw breaching the surface. It had a strangely conical cranium. Although with the way it was broken, she could only guess as to how large it had actually been.

"It has to be thousands of years old," Liang said.

"Forget how old it is," Evans said. "It shouldn't even be there."

The camera zoomed in on the face. The light reflected from the standing water in its hollow socket. Ripples abruptly formed at the edges, concentric rings that dissipated as quickly as they appeared.

The screen went dark before reverting to the Face-Time logo.

Kelly and the others sat in an uncomfortable silence marred by the buzz of the propellers, the drone of the engine, and the hiss of air blowing through the vents.

Kelly thought about the ripples. Had there been any around the skull itself? She couldn't remember seeing any, but the camera had been zoomed in so far that they would have been at the very edge, if they'd been there at all. She'd grown up in Astoria, so she knew all about rocky shorelines. There'd been no salt residue, which meant the body of water in the video had been freshwater and of considerable size for it to reflect the influence of tides, but there hadn't been anything resembling waves. The surface had stilled quickly after the cameraman stopped moving. There had to be another source for whatever force caused the ripples that had caught the cameraman's attention.

It suddenly hit her that she was probably there for just that reason.

If that were the case, then what kind of unstable environment was she potentially walking into? More important, why her? She'd gotten lucky predicting that earthquake, and everyone knew it. That she'd recognized a pattern was undoubtedly more a matter of coincidence than actual skill. Her methods needed further testing. Truth be told, she was still overwhelmed by the fact that had she not taken action, thousands of people would have died. Even with her intervention, five people had drowned that night, and their lives weighed heavily upon her conscience. She'd been over and over the data and concluded that there was absolutely nothing she could have done differently, a fact that was of precious little comfort.

Kelly realized that everyone was looking at her and glanced at her hand, which was doing its thing again.

"Sorry." She tightened it into a fist again and squeezed it between her thighs. "It has a mind of its own."

She'd had MRIs of her head, cervical spine, and brachial plexus in hopes of finding whatever anomaly of the nervous system caused what essentially amounted to an extraordinarily complex tic, but the scans hadn't revealed anything useful. No amount of trying could replicate the motions and she could make it stop anytime she wanted. It simply started when she found herself in a situation outside of her direct control. Her psychiatrist had called it a physiological manifestation of acute anxiety, at the core of which was surely some repressed psychological trauma fighting its way to the surface, despite Kelly's insistence that there had been nothing even remotely traumatic about her childhood.

Her mother had simply referred to it as "fretting"—a cute reference to the nervousness and the fact that it looked like she was playing an air guitar—while she'd come to think of it as a background program running on a computer, a screensaver of sorts that kicked on when she experienced stress. It was during the process of searching for a way to make it stop that she'd discovered the field of seismology. She'd learned early on that the tracts of nerves that carried both conscious and unconscious commands from the brain to the rest of the body could be peripherally stimulated by external magnetic fields, and that stimulation could produce an electrical current strong enough to trigger the neural pathways. The earth itself generated a large magnetic field that constantly exerted a tremendous amount of force and, in the process, produced an omnipresent infrasonic hum that interacted with the human body, despite the fact that no one could hear it.

Further research had shown her that sound vibrations traveling through any material from air to water and wood to metal produced mechanical energy. There were crystals—quartz, topaz, and even sugar—that utilized what was known as the piezoelectric effect to convert that mechanical energy into electricity, which served as the foundation for astonishing new technologies that could capture the power of the waves and the wind, and—she firmly believed—harness the inexhaustible energy produced by the earth's own magnetic field, much like she suspected her hand did. Especially at fault lines where the tectonic plates actively moved against one another, creating enormous fluctuations in the magnetic field like the one that had caused the tsunami. A single event of that magnitude could theoretically provide enough electricity to light the entire West Coast for several years.

Kelly glanced up to find the crop circle guy, Roche, openly studying her.

"You saw something on the video," he said.

"Maybe."

"What did you see?"

"A ripple."

"A ripple?" Evans said. "Did you not see that skull? Do you have any idea what it means?"

"We all saw the skull," Liang said. "It's the same mutation you and I both found in the field."

"It's more than that. You all saw its features and proportions. They were undeniably human. Not just of the *Homo* genus, but *Homo* freaking *sapiens*. If that video was taken in Antarctica—"

"As we're meant to believe," Liang interrupted.

"Right. If we assume that video was shot in Antarctica, then there's no way that skull should be there."

"Are you suggesting someone planted it there?"

"I'm not suggesting anything. Follow my logic. *Homo sapiens* didn't appear until two hundred thousand years ago and didn't migrate out of Africa until sixty thousand years ago. Don't you see? Scientists claim Antarctica has been covered with ice since the Neogene Period, fifteen million years ago. Even with advances in shipbuilding, modern man didn't even discover Antarctica until the nineteenth century. So either that skull is just a couple hundred years old—which any archeologist worth his salt can refute at a glance—

or at some point during those sixty thousand years man found a way to cross the Southern Ocean, navigating glaciers and surviving the extreme temperatures, which would cause us to question pretty much everything we know about the history of mankind."

"There's another alternative," Kelly said. "What if Antarctica hasn't been under ice for millions of years?"

Evans cocked his head and looked at her as though seeing her for the first time.

"There's no point in speculation," Liang said.

Roche leaned back in his chair and closed his eyes.

"You're right," Evans said. "We need to approach this without any preconceptions. Maybe Mr. Talkative over there has the right idea. I, for one, could use a little shuteye."

Kelly knew she should try to sleep, but there was no way she was going to be able to turn her brain off. She leaned against the window and stared down upon the cold black sea, where the first glaciers drifted beneath the wispy clouds.

12
ANYA

Troll Station, Queen Maud Land, Antarctica

Troll Station was little more than a collection of industrial buildings scattered across the barren, snow-spotted tundra. Everything was painted bright red for those occasions when the furious storms kicked up out of nowhere and reduced visibility to the tip of your nose. Anya hadn't been in Antarctica long enough to experience one, but she'd heard the stories. The old-timers had used the opportunity for outside training, tethering themselves together with climbing ropes and practicing limited search-and-rescue missions in the direct vicinity of the research station. The way they told it, it hadn't taken very long for them to realize that if they ever needed to utilize those skills, they were in big trouble.

Fortunately, right now it was smack-dab in the middle of what qualified as summer at the bottom of the world. The sun was out, and it was a balmy three degrees below zero, the perfect day to receive their newest arrivals. She'd barely left Chicago five days ago, and already it felt like that had been a different lifetime. Richards had thought it would be a good idea for her to be at Troll Station when they landed so she could share her experience acclimating. All of the other scientists had been with the team since its inception two years ago and had spent countless hours working under such cramped conditions, so none of them had been able to provide anything resembling helpful advice when she transitioned from living in the Windy City, which she'd always considered comparatively restrictive, to what essentially amounted to house arrest. Of course, their accommodations weren't the only things that required a little extra time to get used to.

Truth be told, she would have fought tooth and nail to get out of the station, if only for the morning. There were only so many hours in the day one could devote to research before starting to go a little stir crazy. She hadn't realized how much the ordinary nuisances in her life contributed to her overall sense of well-being. Driving to work. Going to the grocery store. Heck, even walking to the mailbox. They were luxuries she was no longer afforded. The Richards Group had spared no expense on their accommodations, but there was simply no substitute for the sensation of the sun on her face.

She heard the approaching plane long before she saw the first sparkle of reflection from its fuselage.

Anya still had a hard time believing that it was four in the morning and the sun was out. The Norwegians were still sound asleep, those who hadn't made the pilgrimage to their summer station in Tor, anyway. She was happy enough not to deal with them this morning. For as nice as they were, she needed some time alone in her head before the return trip to the Drygalski Mountains, which was more than a little unnerving, at least the way Richards intended to take them.

The red and white plane came in across the ice sheet covering the frozen sea. It buzzed the rooftop of the station and descended toward the ridgeline, where Richards and Connor waited near the packed-ice landing strip.

She hiked up the bare rock slope to where the *nunatak* abruptly gave way to the seamless white that stretched inland for as far as the eye could see. The Drygalski Mountains were little more than a serrated blade against the horizon.

The wind struck her squarely in the face when she stepped out into the open from the lee of the escarpment that swaddled Troll. The breeze might only have been blowing at a few miles an hour, but it felt as though it were coated with icy barbs that raked her bare flesh.

She pulled her balaclava up over her mouth and nose and crunched across the grated snow to where Richards approached the plane with his arm raised in greeting. The pilot hadn't even slowed the propeller blades, let alone opened the hatch. Their benefactor's enthusiasm was contagious. Despite his many eccentricities, she couldn't help but smile every time she saw him. He was the kind of person who just seemed to draw others to him and make them feel important, not because of him, but *to* him.

Connor stood at the edge of the runway. He was never more than ten feet from Richards at any given time. Theirs was a relationship that transcended a mere financial transaction, but to what degree she didn't care to speculate. All she knew was that anyone with designs on Hollis's life—although she couldn't imagine him capable of making a single enemy—would have better luck feeding themselves through a meat grinder than getting past Connor.

Anya reached Richards's side as the door opened and the stairs swung down onto the snow. Excitement radiated from him in palpable waves. His entire face was covered with a yellow balaclava designed to look like a smiley face; she could see the real thing in his eyes. He winked at her and clapped his hands in his customary manner.

"What do you say? Shall we do this then?"

"No time like the present," Anya said. Her breath gusted back over her shoulder. Ice had already formed around her nostrils and over her mouth despite her mask.

The people on the plane had absolutely no idea of the wonders that awaited them. She remembered being in their shoes, stepping tentatively from the plane into an arctic wasteland without the slightest idea what she was getting herself into. No amount of explanation would have prepared her for the journey ahead, and the mere idea of robbing them of the sense of awe and wonder they were about to experience was criminal. In fact, she almost envied them.

The first passenger appeared in the doorway, wearing a brand-new red parka he'd probably just put on for the first time. The others peered curiously from behind him.

"Welcome to Antarctica," Richards said. "Come, come. We're burning daylight."

He laughed at the joke he'd made a thousand times and rushed to greet his guests.

13
EVANS

42 miles south-southeast of Troll Station

Evans had been cold before, but this was something else entirely. It was as though the wind somehow passed through his body and froze the very marrow inside his bones. Even with the vents open wide and the heat directed into his face, he couldn't seem to stop shivering. If he somehow managed to survive this infernal journey, he'd never complain about the Egyptian heat again.

The Terra Bus was a cross between a Greyhound and a motorhome, if their offspring were bred to a monster truck. It had six sixty-six-inch wheels with tread so deep it could probably roll over his foot without making contact. The 250-horsepower Detroit Diesel Series 50 engine clocked in at twenty-five miles per hour, which felt a whole lot faster bounding over the imperfections in the thick ice, and burned through a kerosene-based fuel called JP-5 at a rate of roughly a gallon a mile.

All of their gear—what little they had, anyway—was stowed in the enormous cargo hold behind the rear wall, which left room for a dozen high-backed seats, aligned in three rows of two to either side of the center aisle. The driver, a man named Al Alberts from Alabama—whose sole job it was to drive this vehicle when infrequently called upon, droned on about the specs without seeming to take a breath, despite repeated attempts at conversation by those seated behind him. Richards smiled and encouraged him, while discreetly confiding that it wasn't only the scientists who were hired for their expertise. It was a small gesture, but one that went a long way toward setting Evans at ease. He figured the best measure of a man was how he treated those whose station in life didn't always command the utmost respect.

"This here's as far as we go," Al said.

The engine roared and the Terra Bus juddered to a halt. From his side of the vehicle, Evans could see only a vast expanse of white interrupted by the occasional rock formation. The granite escarpment on the other side was rimed with a crust of ice.

"There's nothing here," Liang said.

Since none of them had been able to sleep, they'd spent the remainder of the flight talking and trying to figure out what to expect when they reached Antarctica. Jade's background was similar to his own: they both studied the deceased, although from vastly different historical perspectives, in an attempt to discern not just their causes of death, but their lives in the days and weeks leading up to their ultimate denouement.

"This ole girl might be about the most powerful thing on wheels, but even she ain't getting up into those hills without tracks like a tank."

Al popped the seal on the door and the subzero air rushed into the cab.

Evans cringed.

The stairs lowered from the side door with a hydraulic hum. Al bounded down into the snow and tromped to the rear to unload their supplies.

Kelly blew out a long exhalation and rose from the seat opposite him. Her face was so pale that the streaks in her hair stood out like traffic lights. The front pocket of her parka bulged where her hand did its thing.

"Where are we?" she asked.

"We call this place Snow Fell," Richards said. He offered his hand and helped her down stairs that were already becoming slick with ice. Evans followed her into the brutal cold and around to the back of the bus. "It's a bastardization of the Icelandic word *Snæfell-sjökull*, which is the name of the volcano beneath which Otto Lidenbrock found the entrance to the center of the Earth in Jules Verne's classic novel. It really just means 'snow glacier mountain,' so I figure this qualifies." He inclined his head toward the frozen cliff. "I also like the play on words, if you get my *drift*."

Jade rolled her eyes, but Evans couldn't contain a chuckle. There was something endearing about Richards, an almost childlike quality, as though he completely lacked self-consciousness.

The mountain was really more of a jagged out-cropping reminiscent of a shard of broken glass embedded in the accumulation. A fin of snow blew from the pinnacle and stretched like a slipstream across the sky overhead. It was strange to think that this was just the peak of a mountain nearly concealed beneath two vertical miles of ice.

Richards took Kelly's bag from her, slung it over his shoulder, and led them away from the bus toward a structure erected against the face of the cliff. Connor had already cleared the drifted snow from in front of the pressure-sealed door and held it open for all of them to pass through. The interior was more than shielded from the elements; it was actually warm. The floor subtly vibrated with the thrum of the gas generator that fueled the heat blowing through the exposed ductwork overhead. The antechamber was empty, save for the arctic gear hanging from the walls and the grate set into the floor to drain the melting snow from their boots.

Anya—who introduced herself as a postdoctoral fellow in evolutionary anthropology, but barely looked old enough to drive—waited for everyone to enter the chamber and for Connor to seal the door behind them before opening the door at the other end. She smiled coyly at them and ducked through the doorway into a natural formation that smelled of earth and dampness, with the faintest hint of diesel smoke.

"What is this place?" Roche asked, echoing Evans's thoughts.

"Once upon a time it was a Nazi communications outpost, quite possibly the fabled Base 211," Richards said. "This is all of the original equipment over here. Most of it still works, if you can believe that. We decided to leave it as something of a memorial, but we removed all of the swastikas and other paraphernalia, for obvious reasons. We replaced the original concrete bunker and radar tower with that modular unit to help contain the heat and minimize the buildup of humidity in here, which nearly destroyed the maps on that wall ahead of you. We had them sealed in archival-quality polypropylene in an effort to preserve the original hand-written notes. If you look closely, you can still make them out. Assuming you can read German, of course."

His laughter echoed through the cavern.

Evans had never seen anything like this place. It was as though he had stepped from his era into another time, if one could ignore the overhead vents and conduits that connected the domed lights hanging from the cavern roof.

"Why would anyone in their right mind put a communications outpost all the way out here?" Jade asked.

"They wouldn't," Roche said. "There were no satellites back then. This is all short-range VHF equipment. They didn't design this station with the intention of intercepting Allied communications. They were looking for something."

He nodded toward the far corner of the room and what almost resembled the entrance to a mineshaft. The stone wall beside it was etched with designs that appeared surprisingly ancient.

"Very good, Mr. Roche." Richards smiled and clapped him on the shoulder. "But not entirely accurate."

"How so?"

Evans walked toward the earthen orifice and stopped dead in his tracks.

The petroglyphs.

They were the same symbols as he'd discovered in the cave under the Royal Tombs of Akhetaten.

"They weren't merely looking for something." Richards looked at each of them in turn. "They found it."

14
JADE

Jade wasn't used to not being in control. Her life was structured in such a way that nothing was left to chance. That was the whole reason she'd gone into forensic anthropology in the first place. Her mother had died when she was twelve, leaving her alone with her father, an organized and meticulous man of Japanese ancestry who believed that within his private domain the chaos of the outside world could be bent to his will. If something broke, you learned how to fix it. If you wanted to eat something, you learned how to cook it. And there was no point in learning if you weren't prepared to commit yourself to absorbing the totality of the available knowledge. So before she could even begin to come to grips with her mother's passing, she'd embarked upon a quest to discover everything she could about the nature of death itself, launching her obsession with imposing some sort of order upon the maddeningly random events that had culminated in her mother's death.

Walking through a tunnel braced with petrified wood beneath a mountain at the bottom of the world was far outside of her comfort zone, but the mystery intrigued her. Based on what she'd discovered in Nigeria and the picture she'd received with the plane ticket, she could only assume that somewhere ahead of her lay the secret to understanding how the two sets of remains were related.

The overhead lights cast strange shadows from the imperfections in the rock walls, where it was almost surprising not to find spiderwebs or any other sign of life that didn't exist in this frozen environment. Evans stayed by her side. Under normal circumstances she'd have told him to back off, but she drew a measure of comfort from his proximity. Roche, not so much. He made her uncomfortable, although she couldn't figure out why. Maybe it was the whole crop circle thing, which had immediately branded him as insane in her book. He was still in the cavern behind them, taking pictures of the symbols carved into the stone. She didn't much care for people who talked all the time, but she vastly preferred them to people like Roche, who seemed to take in everything around him without giving the slightest indication of what he was thinking.

The tunnel opened into another cavern. The back half was covered with a sheet of ice, above which a metal walkway extended. It wasn't until she saw what looked like the top of a submarine protruding from the ice that she realized there was water underneath it.

Richards's footsteps clanged from the pier as he walked out over the frozen water. He stopped at the end and, with a flourish, gestured toward the miniature conning tower.

"This astounding technological marvel is what they

call a personal submersible. It holds a pilot and six passengers and has a depth rating of a thousand feet."

He braced one foot beside the hatch and raised it open. The ice surrounding the conning tower crackled and water burbled across the frozen surface, through which the outline of the vehicle appeared vague at best. The vessel's name was stenciled on the side of the conning tower: *Nautilus*.

"Another reference to Jules Verne," Jade said. "I'm starting to sense a motif."

"I grew up in rural Kansas," Richards said. There was a hardness to his voice that hadn't been there before. "My father farmed wheat. And his father before him. You could walk a full day in any direction from our house and not see anything other than wheat, wheat, and more wheat. My earliest memory is finding a box of science fiction books in the loft of my grandfather's barn, and even at five years old I'd wanted nothing more than to be anywhere else. They were old and yellow and the spines barely held them together, but inside of them I found my means of escape to other places. Other worlds."

His expression momentarily clouded before his smile emerged once more and he clapped his hands.

"What do you say? Shall we get this show on the road?"

Connor stepped across the gap and lowered himself through the opening.

"The *Nautilus* can travel up to three knots," Richards said. "That's three and a half miles an hour for you landlubbers. She has the maneuverability to pass through some pretty tight places—not that we ever really put that to the test, mind you—and she's equipped with eight hours of air, which is way more than we'll ever need."

"For what?" Kelly asked.

Richards took her hand and helped her from the pier.

"To reach our destination, of course."

"Which is . . . ?"

"At the other end of this lava tube."

Unlike the others, Jade didn't find Richards's coyness endearing. She was cold and tired and in no mood for games.

The submersible's headlights lit up the ice, revealing just how thin it was. There had to be a source of geothermal heat somewhere down there.

Jade hopped out onto the sub and straddled the hole. A short ladder led downward into a cabin that reminded her of a stereotypical bachelor's pad from a seventies movie. The seats were plush and tan and seemingly only lacking an end table with a lava lamp between them. There were two chairs in the front, three in the middle, and a sofa-like bench running the length of the back. They were all narrow and set very closely together in order to cram them all into a space the size of a walk-in closet.

She ducked her head and descended into a giant glass sphere clamped between three stabilizers, like a marble in a bird's claw. The two to either side had spotlights directed straight ahead into the greenish water and down at the rocks below them. Walking across the transparent floor was disorienting, as though her feet were striking the ground well before her mind thought they should. She took the nearest seat on the bench, right behind the ladder, and stuffed her bag under her seat.

"From inside you'll be able to see everything," Richards said from above her. "And just wait until you see what that entails."

Evans climbed down and sat in front of her in the middle row, opposite Kelly, who pressed her hands and the tip of her nose to the glass bubble in an effort to look back up at the frozen surface.

Anya slid down and sat next to Jade.

"I know how overwhelmed you feel right now," Anya said. "Trust me. I was in your shoes not even a week ago. There's really no way to prepare yourself. You just have to see it to believe it."

"And when will that be?" Jade asked.

The younger girl smirked.

"Not much longer now."

Roche took the middle seat between Evans and Kelly, leaving Richards to seal the hatch behind them and climb over their legs to reach the front passenger seat. The control console formed a half ring in front of Connor and him. Two video monitors showed images from cameras mounted to the side stabilizers. The headlights diffused into the murky water, through which a curtain of bubbles rose.

The motor whirred and the cabin lights dimmed. The digital readouts imbued the sphere with a reddish glow as it inched away from the dock. A cloud of sediment churned from beneath them and rose like smoke toward the ice. The depth gauge and the GPS readouts started to move. The rocks fell away beneath them and the submersible canted forward.

Jade felt a twinge of panic as they dove straight toward the ground.

"It's okay," Anya said. "The first time I thought I was going to pee my pants, too."

The submersible leveled off and entered a tunnel barely larger than it was. The lights limned stone walls that were furry with sludge that reminded her of the East River. She realized with a start that it wasn't an aggregation of pollutants.

It was life.

15
KELLY

"**B**ecause of the ice, most people don't realize that this is one of the most volcanically volatile regions on the planet," Richards said. "This entire area is essentially alive with geothermal activity. Lava tubes like this one are formed when a volcano erupts and produces lava flows, which cool from the outside in. As the outer layers harden, the molten core continues to move, leaving a hollow passage in its wake. The residual heat causes water trapped beneath the ice cap to remain in a liquid state. We're only now beginning to discover all of the lakes and the networks of rivers and conduits like this one that connect them."

Kelly watched the slimy walls pass as she listened to Richards talk and imagined how specialized these organisms had to be in order to thrive in such a brutal and isolated environment. There were species of bacteria called *archaea* that had evolved to thrive in the absence of oxygen and at temperatures that cooked higher orders of life. She'd studied a species found in hydrothermal vents on the ocean floor that metabolized sulfur so it didn't poison the surrounding ocean.

Most scientists believed that similar organisms were responsible for processing methane and producing the earliest atmosphere as a by-product. She could only imagine what purpose these microbes served.

"Antarctica hasn't always been covered by ice. We've found fossils of leaves and bones that contradict the prevailing wisdom that it froze fifteen million years ago. In fact, I'm more inclined to believe that it was free of ice until a mere fifteen *thousand* years ago."

Kelly glanced at Evans, who'd proposed the same thing on the plane. He sounded exasperated when he spoke.

"That can't be right."

"Why not?" Richards asked. There was a note of amusement in his voice.

"Because that would change everything we think we know about the history of our species."

"It would, wouldn't it?"

"What evidence do you have to support your theory?" Roche asked.

"Oh, I didn't mean to imply that the theory was mine. The credit belongs to a professor named Charles Hapgood, who first put forth the idea of crustal displacement some sixty years ago. It was so well received at the time that Albert Einstein wrote the foreword when he published and then-President Dwight Eisenhower instructed the Strategic Air Command to provide him with any and all relevant scientific data to support his assertion that an abrupt shift in the Earth's crust caused the sudden movement of all of the continents on the planet at once."

Kelly rolled her eyes.

"Continents don't suddenly do anything," she said. "Even the Cascadia Subduction Zone—one of the most active fault lines in the entire world—only moves at a rate of a few centimeters a year."

"Ah, but take a step back and look at it from an overall macroscopic perspective. What are fault lines?"

"Areas where two tectonic plates physically interact."

"And what are tectonic plates?"

"Pieces of the hardened outermost layer of the lithosphere—a combination of the crust and the upper mantle—that fit together like a broken egg shell."

"What causes them to move?"

Kelly sighed.

"The intense heat produced by the Earth's core makes the molten rock in the mantle churn, taking the plates along with it."

"What is the mantle?"

"None of us are in the mood for a geology lesson," Roche said.

Kelly agreed. If Richards was trying to lead them to some kind of epiphany, he certainly wasn't taking the most direct route.

"Just hear me out," Richards said. He gestured for Kelly to proceed.

"The mantle makes up more than eighty percent of the Earth's interior. It's predominantly solid, but at such high temperatures behaves like a liquid."

"How so?"

"This molten material rotates around a solid iron core, which actually revolves at a different rate than the planet's surface."

"So we have a thin outer crust spinning around an

inner core a fraction of its size on a thick cushion of fluid," Richards said.

"Which is exactly what caused the continents to drift apart in the first place," Kelly said.

"Precisely."

"But that process took hundreds of millions of years."

"Because the Earth's rotation is constant?"

"Relatively so. As a whole, it seems to be slowing down. There are certain times in the year when its rotation changes slightly due to the physics of the conservation of angular momentum. The angle of the Earth's axis doesn't perfectly match its angular momentum because the planet is somewhat lopsided and subject to the gravitational forces of the sun and the moon."

"And those forces aren't always constant."

"Right. Since the orbits of both the Earth around the sun and the moon around the Earth are elliptical, the gravitational forces they exert are constantly changing, causing the Earth to precess on its axis, like a top wobbles as it spins."

"So—to use your top analogy—what happens when those external forces continue to increase that wobble to the point that it falls?"

"That can't happen. The core exerts a much stronger gravitational force than any external influence."

"So it would correct its own rotation."

"It's not really as simple as that. You have to take into consideration the strength of the magnetic field it produces and the velocity of the rotation at a given point in time."

"But it would, wouldn't it? Or else it would be thrown out of orbit and across the galaxy."

"Something like that."

"What would then happen to the crust, which is more heavily influenced by these external forces, during such a correction?"

Kelly paused to consider the implications. Such a correction was indeed possible—in theory—but there were so many contributing factors that she could only speculate. She weighed her words carefully, knowing that she'd fallen into Richards's verbal trap.

"The mantle's rotation around the core would accelerate at a rate exponentially proportional to what would essentially be a minor decrease in the rotational velocity of the iron core."

"Causing all of the tectonic plates to suddenly shift like a driver going through the windshield of his car in a head-on collision."

"That's a bit extreme. I would say more like the ball bearings surrounding the axles in the car's wheels as it brakes."

"It's a fine theory," Roche said, "but without anything resembling concrete evidence, that's all it is: a theory. It's no different than an ancient society believing this place was frozen by an ice god."

"Maybe it was aliens," Evans said.

"Funny."

"Here it comes," Anya whispered from behind her.

Kelly glanced out the window, then back at Richards, who swiveled in his seat to face them. He could hardly contain his excitement.

"If it's proof you want . . ." He toggled a switch and spotlights burst from the sides of the stabilizers, illuminating the walls of the lava tube as they fell away and the submersible drifted into a larger body of water. ". . . then it's proof you shall have."

Kelly's breath caught in her chest. She hit her forehead against the glass in an attempt to better see.

"Oh, my God."

16
ROCHE

The lava tube opened into an underwater canyon that branched in multiple directions. The gray rock was stratified and eroded into shapes reminiscent of the sandstone formations from the old Road Runner cartoons. Ripples formed where they broke the surface, maybe fifteen feet overhead. The sediment was the color of ash and billowed in the submersible's wake, revealing jagged rocks riddled with what at first appeared to be veins of some dark mineral. It took Roche a moment to realize that they were actually the fossils of some sort of plant. If he looked closely, he could clearly see the stems and the feathery wisps of foliage.

The implications were staggering. For there to be plants, there needed to be exposure to the sun, which meant that at some point this area was not only above the ice, it was warm enough to sustain vegetation.

He was held so enrapt by the fossils that he didn't immediately realize that they weren't the source of the others' excitement. The massive stone formations weren't merely the result of the random nature of geology; they were aligned in such a way as to create a veritable colonnade around the mouth of the lava tube. The rocks buried under the sediment were the remains of the megaliths that had once rested on top of the columns. In fact, now that he truly saw them for what they were, he could tell that the formations themselves were enormous slabs like those at Stonehenge, only reshaped by the erosive forces of eons of running water.

The submersible rose from the stone forest and breached the surface. Roche practically crawled into Kelly's lap and leaned against the glass in an effort to see the tops of the megaliths standing from the water. Even with as many as had fallen, he could still discern the outline of two concentric rings leaning toward one another. Some even touched, forming peaks like the surviving arches at the ancient ruins in Raufarhöfn, Iceland, known as Arctic Henge.

"Have you been able to date this structure?" Evans asked. His assessment on the plane had been spot-on. This changed absolutely everything they knew—or at least thought they knew—about the origin of mankind, but how did that pertain to Roche's work with crop circles and the picture he'd received in his email? "The oldest known megalithic structures in the world only date to the Ghar Dalam Phase of the Neolithic Period, maybe seven thousand years ago at the most. This henge would have to be easily twice that old."

"This environment makes carbon dating unreliable," Richards said. "We're not in any hurry to draw any attention to our findings yet, either. Hence the secrecy. The last thing we want is for the entire scientific community to descend upon our little discovery."

He winked at Anya, who smirked in response.

The surface of the water was a strange shade of light

blue caused by the reflection of the ice dome that had formed over the lake. There were no supports and yet the dome appeared infinite, stretching off into the far distance in every direction beyond their limited range of sight. It seemed physically impossible for such a fragile structure to support countless tons of ice, and yet here they were, cutting through the water toward Lord only knew what.

Connor killed the headlights and eased off the throttle.

Roche couldn't see a blasted thing until his eyes adjusted to the darkness and he was able to make out a faint glow in the distance, which resolved into several dim orbs as they neared.

"We have to be careful not to make it too bright," Richards said. "The organisms that live in the shallows are quite delicate."

"What kind of organisms?" Jade said.

"We've discovered more than twenty species of phytoplankton, zooplankton, and crustacean-like ostracods, the majority of which aren't found anywhere else on the planet. Dr. Friden is having a field day naming them."

A floating dock materialized from the wan light, bobbing gently on the waves.

Connor pulled right up to it, deftly swung around the rear end, and backed up until the pontoons grazed the top stabilizer.

"Are you ready for this?" Richards asked.

Roche glanced at the others, who wore mixed expressions of apprehension and impatience.

"Are we waiting for a drumroll or something?" Evans asked.

"My dear," Richards said. "Would you care to do the honors?"

"Absolutely," Anya said. She hopped up, scaled the ladder, and popped the seal to release the hatch. The air that rushed past her was frigid and smelled faintly like the aftermath of a hailstorm. "Are you guys coming or what?"

Roche grabbed his bag from underneath his seat and caught a glimpse of the sludge-covered rocks through the glass bottom. They looked just like those from the video they'd watched on the plane. Until that very moment, nothing about the alien-looking remains had felt real. Suddenly, his pulse raced at the prospect of at long last gaining some sort of insight into his life's work. Crop circles historically formed in close proximity to primitive megaliths. That was the whole reason he'd moved to England in the first place, but he'd always been quick to dismiss the involvement of an extraterrestrial race in favor of any even somewhat rational explanation, even in the absence of one. Physical remains would mean that perhaps it was time to at least entertain the notion that perhaps there were factors in play beyond his ability to comprehend.

He watched Kelly and Evans ascend the ladder behind Jade and Anya before starting up after them.

"Wait for me, Mr. Roche," Richards said. "I want to see your reaction."

Roche stopped and looked down at the older man. There was no hint of mocking or deception in his expression.

"This is going to blow your mind," Richards said.

Roche climbed onto the roof of the submersible and stepped off onto the pier, which sagged under his weight.

Waves sloshed against the pontoons as he followed the others toward dry land. The strange acoustics made their footsteps sound hollow. The weak lights were little better than complete darkness and made footing on the rocky shore treacherous.

Sheer cliffs rose up into the ice, which adhered to the stone in frosted curtains. A raised platform had been erected in a natural crevice and used as the foundation for a shaft leading up into the ice. An oddly thin and elongated elevator car rested on the concrete, its taut cables seemingly too thin to bear even its empty weight.

Connor opened the elevator door with a clang that reverberated throughout the cavern. Roche instinctively looked up, half-expecting to see cracks racing through the ice overhead.

"Don't worry," Connor said. "It would take an atomic bomb to bring this cavern down."

He said something else, but Roche didn't hear him. His pulse thundered in his ears as he veered away from the others and approached the icy surface of the cliff. He thought he saw . . . No, he couldn't have . . . could he?

The stone beneath the ice was smooth and gray. Granite, he guessed.

He pressed his palms against the ice. It had to be a good four inches thick. He recoiled when the freezing water ran over the backs of his hands and into the sleeves of his jacket.

"Perhaps this will help," Richards said.

Roche stared dumbly at the flashlight in Richards's hand for several seconds before taking it from him. He thumbed the switch and shined the light directly at the ice, revealing the shapes carved into the stone. He stepped back and raised the beam in an effort to gauge the full extent of the design.

There was a solid circle inside a larger, thinner circle, which served as the center for three smaller, solid circles positioned at the points of an equilateral triangle. Each of the smaller circles was contained within a thin halo, much like the enormous one in the middle. He'd seen this design before. In fact, he had a picture of it on the wall in his garage with all of the others. It was the same design as the crop circle that had appeared in Broadbury Banks, England, nearly twenty years ago.

He stepped back even farther and swept the light across the face of the cliff. There were similar designs as far as he could see in either direction.

17
RICHARDS

The portable construction elevator was roughly the size of a walk-in closet with Plexiglas windows that offered a disorienting view of the ice and steel rigging towers racing past in a blur. The car had been designed to hold up to four tons and accommodate sixteen people. He'd had the unit customized so that it utilized two cranes on the surface and opposing mast rigs for both redundancy and speed. Even with those modifications, it still took half an hour to ascend through the two vertical miles of ice that would have sealed the shaft in a single day were it not for the warm air rising from below and the recycled hot water that coursed through the hollow framework.

Richards had employed a team of engineers to install every possible security measure to prevent them from plummeting straight down into the earth, but that didn't necessarily mean he was comfortable inside this cage. The lights were barely bright enough to create an aura around the car, which was exactly the way he liked it. The original lights had been so bright that in combination with the reflection from the ice he'd been able to see nearly a quarter mile straight down.

Connor worked the controls from the operator's room, which was little more than a bulge in the side large enough to accommodate a single person. His bodyguard was so good at unobtrusively surveilling any given situation and anticipating his movements that Richards often forgot he was there.

Just enough heat blew into the car to keep the tips of their noses and their cheeks from turning red. He'd learned early on that you never wanted to get too warm or the shock of the cold became more than just physically debilitating; it imparted an emotional impact not dissimilar to despair.

He talked about the logistical nightmare of getting supplies and manpower to such a remote location and the speed with which they'd been forced to work without cutting a single corner that might compromise safety. Something as commonplace as a broken bone or laceration could prove fatal so far from the nearest medical facility, which was why the early arrivals had received training in first aid, but even a skilled surgeon wouldn't be able to repair a ruptured appendix in this environment. While his speech had been meant to set his new arrivals at ease, he could see in their eyes that it was having the exact opposite effect. He was grateful when the intonation of the motor changed, signaling that they were nearing the top.

The cranking and grinding of gears grew louder above them until it was all they could hear. Richards covered his ears out of habit as they ascended into the lighted section of the shaft, and the air filled with exhaust fumes and the scent of motor oil. The car rose through the floor and into a warehouse built directly into the side of the mountain. The walls were reinforced with six feet of sound-dampening material to prevent the noise from triggering an avalanche. In addition to the massive cranes and cogs that operated the elevator, there were industrial-size hot-water heaters and generators, forced-air heaters, humidifiers, and fans that pumped the noxious fumes through miles of ductwork and filters before venting them on the other side of the mountain, where the prevailing winds carried them out to sea.

The elevator juddered to a stop, and he opened the cage door. Richards gestured for the others to follow him and led them through a maze of heavy equipment and pipes to the pressure-sealed doorway. He pressed the button, and the overhead red light came on, producing a high-pitched alarm that he felt more than heard. The fail-safe prevented both the inner and outer doors from being open at the same time and releasing the clamor of machinery into the fragile environment.

The reinforced steel door slid back into the wall and he led them into a bare white corridor with countless monitors and clipboards hanging from the walls. Dale Rubley, his chief engineer, seemed only peripherally aware of their presence as he entered readings into his logs. Even Richards knew better than to interrupt him while he was working. There were men who took their responsibilities seriously, and then there was Dale, who seemed to spend every waking moment averting life-and-death catastrophes, if only in his mind.

Connor hit the button to close the door behind them, sealing off the racket. The abrupt silence always made him yawn and tug at his ears as though adjusting to a sudden change in pressure.

He triggered the door at the far end of the hallway, which produced a flashing red light, but mercifully no siren. The adjoining building was roughly the same size, but seemed considerably larger without the heavy equipment taking up every square inch of space. Not that the tracked arctic vehicles were small by anyone's definition of the word. A half-dozen bright red Sno-Cats with wheels and tread that looked like they'd been stolen from tanks were parked near the massive bay doors, beside which were cabinets brimming with tools of all shapes and sizes. There were rows of skis and snowshoes and a fleet of snowmobiles with deep tread, from which long metal spikes protruded.

"These mountains are so steep that any sort of construction requires an extreme amount of creativity," Richards said. "This point right here offers the only access to anything resembling a road, which means that as much as we wanted to put the research station here, it was really the only place to put the garage. Of course, I think you'll all agree that we solved that particular problem quite nicely."

Richards waited for them all to catch up before pressing the button to open the door. This moment never failed to give him chills.

The door slid into the recessed wall and opened upon a glass corridor that offered one of the most majestic views found anywhere on the planet. The enclosed walkway led straight out over the nothingness between the two granite peaks. From this vantage point, you could see all the way to the South Sea across the seemingly interminable fields of white.

"We call this the Skyway. It's similar in design to the Golden Gate Bridge and spans the more than two hundred feet between the auxiliary buildings and the research station." He started across the bridge, his footsteps echoing ahead of him. "It has wind vortex panels rated up to forty knots to keep it from swaying. The power and heat conduits are run across a second, more traditional suspension bridge. You can kind of see it if you look way down there to your left."

"Forty knots isn't really all that fast," Kelly said. "We get stronger winds on the Oregon coast."

"The wind rarely blows anywhere close to that hard this far inland. Near the coast, though? That's a different story. Those katabatic winds have been recorded at almost two hundred miles an hour."

"That's reassuring," Roche said.

"How far up are we?" Jade asked.

"From the snow or from the ground?" Richards asked.

"Never mind. I don't think I want to know the answer."

"Two hundred feet," Evans guessed.

"Not quite that far," Richards said. "And I assure you that this Skyway is one of, if not *the* most stable suspension bridges ever built. Our team of engineers considered every conceivable safety measure when they designed this place. Each building is compartmentalized from all of the others in case anything unforeseen happens. If, say, the power station causes an avalanche, that building is designed to break away from the garage, which in turn is designed to break away from the Skyway, and so on. The research station itself has a standby generator with enough fuel to provide basic life support through the entire winter. While this station may look somewhat precarious, I assure you, there is no safer building on the planet."

"Where is this station?" Evans asked.

"Right in front of you."

"All I see is the side of a mountain."

Richards smiled.

"Patience, my friend."

They crossed the chasm beneath the blazing sun, which almost made him forget just how cold it was. Directly beneath their feet was a sharp ridge, to either side of which was a steep, snow-covered slope that led into the shadows of the deep valleys. Snow Fell, and the origin of the zigzagging trail through the foothills, was on the far side of the mountain range to his right. Richards preferred the thought of parachuting down the elevator shaft to driving down that road ever again, though.

He pressed the button to open the door at the far end of the Skyway and guided them up an iron staircase that clanged with every footstep to a broad landing. The sign above the door read ANTARCTIC RESEARCH, EXPERIMENTATION & ANALYSIS STATION 51.

Richards placed his finger on the button and turned to face the others.

"Once you pass through this door," he said, "your lives will never be the same."

He knew how melodramatic that sounded, but he feared even those words were insufficient to convey the wonder of what lay on the other side.

Richards pushed the button and the door slid into the wall.

"Ladies and gentlemen," he said. "Welcome to AREA Fifty-one."

BOOK II

If you want to find the secrets of the universe, think in terms of energy, frequency, and vibration.

—Nikola Tesla

18
ANYA

**Antarctic Research, Experimentation &
Analysis Station 51
Queen Maud Land, Antarctica**

"The research station itself is actually four separate modular units." Richards led them through the columns of light admitted by the skylights in the atrium, which was framed by four enormous square structural pillars that served to divide the otherwise open space. The closest pillar to the right had been converted into a climbing wall with rubber handholds so that the researchers could burn off excess energy and climb from the lower level as opposed to merely scaling the spiral staircase. Open doorways to either side granted access to the library and the computer room. "As I'm sure you can imagine, building anything in a location like this is next to impossible, so we needed something that could be assembled elsewhere and installed using a maximum of two helicopters and a minimal amount of manpower."

"Why not just build it on the flatlands like Troll?" Roche asked.

"Ask the British," Connor said with a smirk.

"What my colleague means to say is that the entire Antarctic ice cap is in a constant state of motion, which makes it notoriously unpredictable. Believe it or not, our friends from across the pond have had five bases swallowed by fractures in the ice. This station is made of a lightweight, space-age polymer and seated on hydraulic legs bolted directly to the mountain. There's no more secure way to anchor the buildings on this continent, not to mention the fact that it offers convenient access to the environs beneath the ice without the added risk of destabilization caused by the rapid changes in the environment."

Anya cringed at the mention of the changing environment, which had started innumerable arguments about global warming between members of the staff as both sides could produce compelling evidence to support their positions. The problem was that the scientific models were predictive, which inherently introduced a measure of speculation. The only thing that either side could agree upon was that the governments of the world politicized the hot-button topic and utilized an element of fear to control the narrative while making billions of dollars from the regulation of carbon emissions.

"There you are, Hollis! I've been trying to get ahold—" Friden stopped halfway up the spiral staircase when he saw the new faces. "Who do we have here?"

He walked straight up to Kelly and took her by the hand.

"Max Friden. *Doctor* Max Friden, actually. And who is this divine creature?"

Anya sighed. Living with the microbiologist could

be exasperating. He had a brilliant mind and was reasonably attractive, but he was like a teenager with his father's Viagra prescription. While she welcomed anyone who could relieve her of his unrelenting full-court press, she was surprised by a twinge of jealousy.

"Kelly," she said, and snatched her hand from his. Her fingers became a blur of motion, as though she were attempting to communicate in sign language. "Kelly Nolan."

"For our newcomers," Richards said, "Dr. Friden is our resident expert in microbiology. Since you've already met Ms. Nolan, allow me to introduce the rest—"

"Yeah, yeah. Nice to meet you all. Can I talk to you for a second, Hollis? You know, privately?"

"Dr. Fleming, my dear, would you mind taking over the tour for me? I'm sure our guests are eager to see their quarters. After all, it's been *one really long day*."

He chuckled at his pun, but it lacked his usual joviality.

"My pleasure," Anya said.

Richards excused himself and descended the stairs with Friden, who spoke animatedly in a hushed tone the moment their backs were to the group. Connor nodded farewell and trailed his employer at his customary distance.

Anya looked at those remaining, who all stared at her expectantly.

"All right," she said and clapped her hands just like Richards would have. It was amazing how quickly his mannerisms rubbed off on you. "We'll start with the research library."

She guided them between the columns to the right. An enormous bubbled skylight was set into the ceiling and cast a glare upon a cluster of tables and chairs. One wall was stuffed with books from floor to ceiling; the other was lined with microfiche viewing stations.

"I know how old-school this must seem, but the world's been too busy uploading porn and cat pictures to the Internet to waste any time digitizing old scientific texts and articles that are only of interest to the few of us left who can actually read. In here, you'll find scholarly monographs, journals, and books on pretty much every germane subject, from the diaries of early Antarctic explorers to genetic assays on practically every species of life-form on the planet. There are also novels over here. Our Internet access is intermittent at best, so don't expect to be able to watch much Netflix. Assuming you have any free time, that is."

Anya led them back across the atrium and into the computer lab.

"This row of computers over here is for personal use. They're equipped with FaceTime, various browsers, and even a few games, but like I said—"

"Lousy Internet access at the South Pole?" Evans said. "The hell you say."

"We're limited to accessing polar-orbiting satellites, and even then the Earth's magnetic field causes all sorts of interference."

She directed their attention to the opposite side of the room.

"These computers over here monitor all of the manual and automatic functions inside the station. There are closed-circuit security cameras pretty much everywhere, except inside the residences and the restrooms."

"Why do you need security cameras?" Jade asked.

"Big Brother is always watching," Roche said.

Anya stared at him for a long moment.

"Ohh-kay. That doorway back there leads to the electrical room where they keep all of the servers and whatnot."

She guided them through the atrium and down the stairs, which opened upon a vast space even larger than the level above it. The square columns served as little more than visual barriers between the rooms. They started in the industrial kitchen, which featured a communal cooking area with a long range, oven, serving table, a walk-in cooler, and a tiled dining room with cafeteria-style tables with individual chairs.

"That's a lot of seating," Kelly said. "How many people are here?"

"Including yourselves? I believe that makes eighteen, although you probably won't see too much of the night crew."

"Night?" Evans said.

"I know how funny that sounds, but the interior lights are on timers to replicate a sixteen-hour cycle. It takes a little while to get used to, especially coming from the northern hemisphere, where it's currently the middle of winter." She passed between the tables and rounded the coffee station. "This isn't a hotel. There's no housekeeping or janitorial staff. You're responsible for your own messes. And if you drink the last of the coffee, please brew another pot. It's common courtesy and only takes like thirty seconds."

They passed a pool table and the back of the staircase. A pinkish aura spilled across the floor from the seams of a large glass enclosure. The windows were blacked out from the inside and dappled with condensation.

"This greenhouse is the only research lab in the communal unit, and it's only here because of its proximity to the kitchen. We grow all sorts of fruits and vegetables, but like anywhere else such things take time. The greenhouse also serves as Dr. Bell's lab, so he gets a little testy when people just barge in."

Anya knocked on the glass door before sliding it open and pushing through the heavy plastic flaps hanging over the entryway. The walls to either side were lined with racks upon racks of plants in shallow growing trays, from the floor all the way to the ceiling. The rows of lights above them alternated red and blue bulbs to produce a purplish glow that made the green leaves appear white. A fine mist of water blew onto the plants from tiny brass nozzles. There was lettuce and kale, beans and carrots. Tomatoes and strawberries hung from spherical planters overhead, forcing everyone to duck as they advanced down the main aisle, which was essentially one giant grate through which the condensation drained.

Another glass door divided the greenhouse roughly in half. It slid open, and a man in rubber boots and a rain slicker passed through the plastic curtains. His face was red and round, much like everything else about him.

"I've told you all a thousand times to stay the hell out of my . . ."

His words trailed off and his angry expression softened when he saw the new faces. He spoke with a brogue and, like every Scot Anya had ever known, had a hair-trigger temper. He smoothed his slicker and straightened the brim of his rain hat.

"Dr. Simon Bell," he said, and brusquely shook

each of their hands with both of his. "Lord, what you must think of me. You have to understand that if I don't keep everyone from helping themselves, there won't be enough for everyone. People around here think it's funny trying to take my strawberries without me noticing"—he raised his voice to be heard outside the greenhouse—"but I always notice. You hear me? I always notice!"

He took a deep breath and visibly collected himself.

"You'll have to forgive me. I'm right in the middle of something and I'm trying not to lose my train of thought, which is why it's so bloody hard to get anything done around here with everyone"—again, he raised his voice—"doing their damnedest to pinch my bloody berries!"

"I was just showing our new arrivals around," Anya said. "We'll get out of your hair now."

She turned and started back toward where they'd entered.

"So what do you grow in here?" Evans asked.

Anya sighed, closed her eyes, and hung her head.

"What do I grow? You think I'm some sort of gardener, is that it? What do I grow? I don't *grow* anything. I, sir, am one of the foremost paleobotanists in the world. I replicate the proper conditions to germinate complex arrangements of genetic material to give life to biological specimens that pre-date the earliest quote-unquote higher orders of life."

"Pre-date?" Roche said. "By how much?"

Bell pursed his lips and stared at Roche for several seconds as though sizing him up. He grunted, nodded to himself, and turned without another word. He slid open the door and parted the opaque curtains.

"That is the question, isn't it?"

Everyone in the station had a pretty good idea what Bell was working on back there, but outside of Richards and a precious few others, he never let anyone into his private lab. He even kept a second lock on the inner door should anyone be so desperate as to pick the outer lock he'd installed following what the old-timers at AREA 51 referred to as "Watermelongate," a series of events that started with a missing melon and somehow culminated in a McCarthy-esque witch hunt.

Anya looked at Bell. A part of her expected him to rescind his offer and retreat, cackling, into his lair.

Instead, he opened the door even wider and said, "Do come along, won't you?"

Anya nodded and followed him into a realm like an overgrown tea garden. Mist swirled near the ceiling and clung to plants unlike any she'd ever seen. With the way the purple light seemed to bleach the leaves, it was impossible to tell what kind of plants they were. What looked like ferns grew from a long rack, while broad-leaved succulents and bamboo filled the racks above it. Shrubs with leaves like inverted spearheads grew from buckets. Some were nearly as tall as the slanted roof and were developing pealike seeds from the undersides of the leaves. There were countless racks of test tubes filled with agar and seeds in various stages of germination scattered throughout the room, seemingly wherever there was enough space.

"This is what Antarctica looked like some fifteen thousand years ago," Bell said. "Imagine, if you will, a Valdivian temperate rainforest like you would find on the southern Andean steppe. Picture an understory of ferns and bamboo, above which towering conifers and flowering angiosperms grow so tightly together that they block out the midday sun. Once upon a time, this must have been one of the most stunning forests on the planet, one that was something of a transition zone between the Chilean matorral and the Mediterranean forests of Southwest Australia."

"I've never seen anything like these over here," Jade said. She gently traced the leaves of one of the tall trees.

"No one has. This species of Glossopteris has previously only been identified through fossils, and yet here it stands in all its majesty."

"You're saying this tree is extinct," Evans said.

"*Was* extinct."

"How did you clone it then?"

"I didn't. I removed the seed coat and cultured the embryo in a modified Murashige and Skoog medium."

"Where did you get the seeds?" Roche asked.

"We collected them down there. Under the ice. You'd be amazed what all is down there. Granted, the seeds weren't in the best shape, but I was able to extract enough viable genetic material to get a handful to germinate."

"No amount of genetic material, regardless of the species, can remain intact for millions of years," Evans said.

"No, it cannot," Bell said. He smiled for the first time.

"Which means . . ."

"Precisely. The implications are astounding, are they not?"

That was exactly why Anya was here. If they were able to gather enough DNA from the seeds frozen down there to bring this species of plant back to life, then there was hope that they could do the same thing with her work.

19
RICHARDS

"**W**e found something," Friden said.

"The entrance to the pyramid?" Richards asked.

"Better."

Richards found that hard to believe. Ever since the discovery of the pyramid, he'd been unable to think of anything else. It was the whole reason he and Connor had tracked down their new arrivals. It was a historical and cultural anomaly, and one that perfectly meshed with his own theories. Many ancient cultures believed that there were certain points on the surface of the Earth where they could tap into the planet's energy. It was in these places that they erected their most sacred structures. The pyramid of Giza in Egypt, the Nazca lines and Machu Picchu in Peru, Stonehenge in England, The Persepolis in Iran, Mohenjo-daro in Pakistan, the Moai statues of Easter Island. If one drew lines from all of these places to one another and extended them around the globe, even more significant sites fell upon these so-called "ley lines." The Newgrange Tomb in Ireland, Petra in Jordan, The Pyramid of the Sun at Teotihuacan, and the El Castillo Pyramid at Chichen Itza in Mexico, and countless others. Not only did these lines mirror the planet's magnetic grid, their points of convergence marked the sites of the greatest discharge of electromagnetic energy, where unrelated primitive cultures separated by insurmountable distances decided independently to build megalithic structures that still stood today.

Ninety percent of UFO sightings occurred along these lines, a fact that Richards believed was in no way coincidental. Even his own childhood sighting fell upon a minor line that any number of maps confirmed passed through his family's land. And all of those ley lines converged right beneath his feet at this very moment, under the ice at the very bottom of the world.

It was here where the Nazis believed they would find the entrance to the lost city of Agartha in the center of the Hollow Earth, and here where it was rumored they built a fortress for the remnants of the dying Reich and a base where they could conduct their rumored flying saucer experiments. There were even those who believed that somewhere beneath the seemingly impenetrable ice cap were the remains of the mythical city of Atlantis, a theory Richards would have found laughable were it not for the megalithic ruins that couldn't have been more than ten to fifteen thousand years old hiding under what scientists speculated to be the accumulation of millions of years' worth of ice.

The stairs connecting the station to the subterranean levels passed through the eastern residential module. The discovery of the network of caverns had been entirely accidental. The anchors used to bolt the station to the mountain were twenty feet long. They'd already mounted the central unit and were in the process of setting the anchors for the lab unit when the third anchor fractured the surrounding rock. Subsequent sounding had shown the surprisingly stable formations some twenty feet deeper into the mountain and an external egress on the opposite side of the mountain. Utilizing them as a part of the station was his architect's stroke of genius. Not only did it spare him the cost of a full structural module and its installation, it gave them a natural conduit through which to vent their mechanical byproducts. Even that small amount of heat passing through the ductwork helped maintain a constant temperature of 68 degrees Fahrenheit. In fact, based on the combined weight of the equipment for the various laboratories, using the natural formation was actually far safer in the long run. All they'd needed to do was build the framework inside of it, run the electricity and ductwork, and they'd effectively increased the overall dimensions of the station by a full fifty percent. There was even potentially room for expansion with all of the various side caverns and tunnels he hoped to explore when things finally settled down.

The only real alteration they'd been forced to make was in mounting the eastern residential wing lower on the mountain, which meant connecting the lower level of the main structure to the upper levels of the residential modules to either side, creating a staggered appearance and a whole lot more stair climbing than he'd intended.

Friden's lab was closer to the end of the corridor inside the mountain, but he guided Richards into the nearest lab, which belonged to Ron Dreger. Richards had lured the lead driller from Advanced Mining Solutions to help create and maintain the elevator shaft. It had been his stroke of genius to utilize a rectangular configuration that could be heated on two sides by hot water running through the hollow mast rigs and the electrical wiring that powered the elevator on the other two. The failure of any one element would cause worse than the advance of the ice; it could totally destabilize the entire shaft and cause the collapse of the machine room perched on the ice high above it.

Truth be told, Richards suspected the engineer had a little something going on with Dr. Peters, who whirled to face them when they entered the room as though she'd been caught with her hand in the metaphorical cookie jar.

"It's about time," she said. "The suspense is killing me."

She was sitting on the corner of Dreger's desk, which was easily six feet long and covered with oily mechanical components in various stages of assembly. His keyboard was covered with dark smudges from his greasy hands, as was the joystick beside it, which he used for a whole lot more than video games.

"Did you tell him?" she asked Friden.

"I was getting to it," Friden said.

"We think we found a way into one of the structures," she said.

"Not the pyramid," Richards said.

"It's possible they're all connected."

"You said they weren't."

"I said sonar is unreliable beneath that much solid stone."

"So what are we dealing with?"

"We plotted all of the locations where we found remains onto the topographical map of the lake bed," she said. "From every little toe bone and finger to the skull washed up in the shallows and the one you found during the initial coring. We then compared them with the direction of the current and estimates of time and various geological forces. That gave us several predictive models of dispersal, all of which followed fairly standard alluvial—"

"We think we found the tomb," Friden said.

"The source from which the remains originated, anyway."

"Where else would they keep bodies?"

"We don't know anything about this civilization or the nature of its abandonment," Mariah said. "If it was abandoned at all. For all we know, the people froze in their tracks during the continental shift like all of the mammoths in the northern hemisphere."

"In fact, there's really only one thing we do know—" Richards said.

"That they're not human," Friden said. "Not entirely, anyway."

"I was going to say that the only thing we know with any sort of authority is that we don't know anything at all. At least not yet."

"So do you want to do this or what?" Dreger said.

"Do what, exactly?" Richards asked.

"I rigged a submersible drone like Mariah's with several different video cameras, one of them in the thermal range. We detected a stream of slightly warmer water coming from the ground near the northernmost rectangular structure."

"One-B?" Richards asked.

"Right. Closer inspection revealed the origin to be a

crevice between two stones we believe were once structural components, so I hooked a fiber-optic borescope to the drone and have it all primed and ready to feed the camera into the hole to see what we find."

Richards looked up at the row of monitors. They were all dark, except for the one in the center, where he could discern a subtle circular outline framing the live feed.

"No time like the present," Richards said.

Dreger rolled back to his station and took the helm. A few keystrokes in his three-fingered way and a light blossomed in the center of the screen. It took several seconds for the aperture to rectify the focus, revealing murky greenish water swirling with microorganisms and air bubbles and the algae-covered edges of the fractured rocks. He used the joystick to control the camera, which slithered deeper into the hole with halting, disorienting movements.

"You have to remember that the camera's only an inch wide, so while it looks like a giant opening, at its widest point it's only eighteen inches."

"How deep can it go?" Richards asked.

"Don't worry. We have a full hundred and twenty feet to work with. We have a better chance of the battery dying first."

"Is that a legitimate concern?"

"Relax. I have everything totally under control."

Richards perched on the desk on the other side of Dreger and leaned closer so he could better see. The edges of the field of view were slightly distorted by the configuration of the camera, causing them to bow outward like the edges of a bubble. The ground underneath the camera was jagged with chunks of rock and what looked like broken bones, although it was hard to be entirely certain beneath the wavering sludge. The sides passed in a blur as Richards focused on the advancing light. The rocks fell away to either side, and the camera inched into a dark space of indeterminate size. Dreger halted the camera and used its articulated neck to turn the lens nearly 180 degrees.

Richards realized he was holding his breath and forced himself to breathe.

The structure appeared to have collapsed upon itself, completely sealing off the right half. Sections of the ceiling were braced on the rubble, leaving a space barely large enough for a man to squeeze through on his chest.

Dreger fed the camera deeper and through another narrow orifice into a chamber that appeared largely preserved. Portions of petroglyphs showed through the algae on the walls, although not well enough to get a true idea of what they depicted. Not that Richards cared at the moment. He was too focused on the sheer quantity of hominin remains protruding from the sludge.

20
EVANS

Evans tossed his bag onto the bed and collapsed beside it. He'd already lost all concept of time and couldn't remember when he last slept or how long ago it had been. All he knew was that he was starving, but at least there was a plan in place to take care of that. If he could find the willpower to climb out of bed, anyway.

His personal quarters fell somewhere in size between a prison cell and his freshman dorm room, but they were more than adequate for his purposes. He had a bed and a desk and a wardrobe for his clothes. A private bathroom would have been nice, but the communal restroom was only a dozen feet down the hall, and there were only six of them on this level to share it. The same held true for the floor upstairs, where Anya had dropped off Jade and Kelly before guiding Roche and him down to what she called "the dungeon." He wasn't entirely sure he wanted to know why and he was too tired to ask.

The scientists and engineering staff were housed on opposite wings, primarily because of the schedules they kept, and the ease of access to the labs on one side and the Skyway to the power station on the other.

Anya had told him he had half an hour to change and shower or do whatever he wanted to make himself at home before meeting them all back in the cafeteria for a meal and a presentation. He was debating whether to unpack or shower when he fell asleep.

He awakened fuzzy and disoriented after an inestimable length of time. He staggered down the hallway and stumbled up the stairs. The others were already seated at the long tables, positioned in such a way as to see the flat-screen TV on the wall opposite the island where steaming trays of what smelled like spaghetti and a vegetable medley beckoned him.

"I'm so glad you were able to join us," Richards said without a hint of sarcasm. He stood beside the television with a whiteboard behind him. "Please. Help yourself to some food and coffee and join us. We had only just started."

"Started what?"

"My dear boy, surely you're wondering why you're here."

"Why spoil a good mystery?"

"The mystery, as you generously called it, was regrettable, however necessary. As you'll soon understand."

Evans gestured for Richards to proceed and served his dinner onto a plain white plastic plate. Now that he had his food, he didn't feel particularly hungry.

"Where was I?" Richards said. "Oh, yes. Feel free to judge me however you will. It's been a long time since such things mattered to me. All I ask is that you hear me out, because I believe it's important to understand how we all came to be here in the first place."

Evans sat at the back table beside Jade and near the coffee. He poured himself a cup and took a slurp from the marvelously warm drink.

"I was nine years old when I saw a UFO above my family's wheat field. Just three red lights in a triangular configuration—what supposed experts have since named a 'black triangle'—hovering overhead for what felt like a full minute before streaking off across the sky without making the slightest sound. No rumble of helicopter blades. Not so much as the whisper of an engine. I spent the next ten years of my life examining that memory, pulling it apart from every conceivable angle in hopes of finding some rational explanation for what I saw, yet the more I scrutinized it, the more I became convinced that what I'd seen was the genuine article.

"Now I know what you're thinking. Trust me. I've heard it all before. But I ask you to consider the fact that two hundred years ago most people believed that man was created by God and woman from one of his ribs. The mere idea of evolution would have been blasphemous. Think about this, though . . . every single one of the major religions has a similar creation myth. Even lesser and dead religions theorized we were placed on this planet by some divine force, some omniscient intelligence. My question to you is this: What if they were right?"

Evans sighed louder than he'd intended and found himself pinned by Richards's gaze.

"Sorry," Evans said. "My bad. Go on."

Richards's expression softened once more and his eyes grew distant.

"It was with that working assumption that I set off for college without two nickels to rub together or the support of my father, who had always planned on me one day taking over the day-to-day operations of the farm, just like he did. The rest, as they say, is history. I majored in finance and went on to become one of the most successful venture capitalists during the economic boom of the eighties, but that wasn't the only thing I studied. I have always forced an extreme amount of pragmatism upon myself and deliberation upon my actions, so I essentially created two different lives: one of respect and financial means, the other private and supported by those means. I started by absorbing everything I could about religion, which led me to the historical sciences, where faith was forsaken in favor of fact. The reality, I learned, fell somewhere in between."

Richards removed a remote control from his pocket, pressed a button, and a series of pictures appeared on the screen. He clicked through them as he spoke, not lingering on any one image. They showed ancient petroglyphs, cave paintings, and geoglyphs from various cultures, although each and every one of them featured a similar subject with wide eyes, a broad cranium, and a tapered chin, features ascribed to what were often referred to as Grays.

"From this ancient parietal art in Utah and Australia to these Sumerian and Egyptian petroglyphs and these Celtic and Mayan statues . . . nearly every primitive culture from every location around the globe created images of these same creatures, for lack of a better term. These same faces are still prevalent in our popular culture more than seven thousand years later. Name a single religion—or any other prevailing belief—that has endured over a longer period of time. Christianity, Judaism, Islam. Even Hinduism is barely more than five thousand years old, and its earliest Vedas and Sanskrit texts describe beings descending from the sky and the relationship between the stars and planets."

"The first thing you learn in archeology," Evans said, "is that you can't ascribe thought processes to ancient populations because you can only view their lives through modern eyes, not those of the time period. It would be like a future civilization digging up our culture and thinking that *Star Wars* was a religious doctrine and we worship the Force."

"Like I said, I approach everything with a healthy measure of skepticism. I consider nothing to be fact without irrefutable proof, and even then I remain open to evidence to the contrary, much as those who discovered dinosaurs were convinced they were reptilian before further findings suggested that not only were they warm-blooded, they were the ancestors of modern birds. I hope you will evaluate everything I present to you as evidence with an open mind, because that's exactly what you will need if we are to unlock the secrets sealed beneath the ice."

"What secrets?" Kelly asked. "And what does any of this have to do with seismology?"

"You'll see soon enough," Anya said. She was perched on top of the pool table on the other side of the coffee stand, drinking from a plain white mug. "This is all part of the process. Trust me when I say I was sitting right where you are now not so long ago."

"Thank you, my dear," Richards said, and clicked to a familiar image of the English countryside.

Anya raised her mug to him.

"So, as I was saying, the study of ancient cultures invariably leads to questions that simply can't be answered. Consider Stonehenge, a fairly simplistic monument as far as such things go. The stones weigh anywhere between four and twenty-five tons and were transported from quarries more than a hundred miles away. Think about the logistics involved with hauling such massive slabs across the countryside and then standing them on end. Imagine how these primitive people were able to raise other megaliths a full six feet into the air to place them on top of the upright sections without the use of pulleys, which weren't invented until more than three thousand years later."

A picture of the three Pyramids of Giza appeared on the screen.

"Or how about the Great Pyramid here in the middle, which was built during a twenty-year period in the Fourth Dynasty, and involved the precise placement of more than two million stone blocks weighing an average of one-and-a-half tons each, with some surpassing eighty tons. That's an average of more than three hundred a day, or roughly one every five minutes if they worked around the clock. Not only that, it was built at the geographical center of the Earth's landmass and has eight sides instead of four—a common misconception—which can only be appreciated from the air at dawn and sunset on the spring and fall equinoxes, just like the way the shadow of the serpent creeps down the steps of the Temple of Kakulcan in Chichen Itza on those same days. On top of all of that, it was built to align precisely with the cardinal points of the compass and, with the adjacent pyramids of Menkaure and Khafre, replicate the exact arrangement of the stars in Orion's belt. The same holds true for the ceremonial buildings in Teotihuacan and the Thornborough Henges in northern England."

He clicked through the images as he described them. Several featured lines drawn between the structures and the angles between them in a side-by-side comparison with Orion's belt.

"Then there's Angkor Wat in Cambodia and the Serpent Mound in Ohio, both of which were designed to mimic the constellation Draco. We're talking about ancient civilizations with no formal training in either architecture or mathematics building structures of such exactness and complexity that we couldn't replicate them even with today's technology were we given twice as long to do so, people who formulated the concept of precession—the way a spinning top wobbles around its axis due to the forces of gravity—and had an intimate understanding of the solar system more than six thousand years before Columbus proved the Earth wasn't flat, a revelation that occurred a mere twenty years before an Ottoman admiral and cartographer named Piri Reis created the map that led me here."

Evans pushed his plate aside and poured another cup of coffee. There wasn't enough left for another cup, so he started another pot while Richards switched to an image of a hand-drawn map. It was yellowed and the edges were tattered, but he could still decipher the hooked tip of South America and the coastline of Antarctica.

"This map was drawn in 1513. It's a compilation of several others, including Columbus's maps of the Americas. The crucial fact that you need to remember is that Antarctica wasn't officially discovered until 1818, and by then it was completely covered with ice. The coastline on this map was compared to a seismic profile made through the ice sheet by the Swedish-British Antarctic Expedition of 1949 and found to match so perfectly that the cartographical department of the United States Air Force investigated and concluded that the Piri Reis map had to have been made before the continent was buried beneath the ice. It was a gentleman named Charles Hapgood who initially brought the map to their attention and subsequently formulated his theory as to how this could have happened."

"Crustal displacement," Evans said.

"Exactly. But you probably haven't heard about his discovery of the Oronteus Finaeus map, which was drawn in 1531 and features the entire shoreline of Antarctica without the ice. The Bauche map of 1737 actually shows terrestrial details. Mountains, rivers, and lakes, several of which match bodies of water we're only now finding down there."

"You lost me," Jade said.

"The science of navigation wasn't discovered until five thousand years ago and seafaring vessels weren't common until the first millennium BCE. So if you figure that even the most aggressive theorists speculate that this continent has been under ice for ten thousand years, who had the ability to create these maps back then?"

Evans was at a loss. He understood the implications, but, for the life of him, couldn't come up with a viable explanation.

"Now fast-forward to the 1930s and the sudden interest of the Nazis in Antarctica, which stemmed from the scientific ministry's quest to find the origins of the Aryan race. The Ahnenerbe, as it was known, believed that the Aryans were the survivors of the lost city of Atlantis, and that they escaped through the Hollow Earth to find sanctuary in the hidden city of Agartha, the entrance to which was supposedly somewhere beneath our feet."

"That's absurd," Kelly said.

"The whole foundation of their ideology was absurd, but you have to understand that these people believed with the kind of veracity that rallied an entire nation to fight a war that changed the course of modern history. Whether they found what they were looking for or not is irrelevant, because they found *something*. Now what that something was we can only guess. There are rumors that this is where they developed their Foo Fighter program and launched their first flying saucers. Other stories suggest that they found or built a fortress where they could lick their wounds until they were strong enough to again take on the world. Regardless, what we do know is that two submarines from the notorious 'Fuhrer's Convoy' surrendered to authorities in Mar Del Plata, Argentina in

1945. On board were heavily bandaged passengers and Nazi relics worth millions of dollars. Among them was this . . ."

Richards clicked to the next slide.

Evans's pulse thundered in his temples.

"What in the name of God is that?"

21
JADE

"That, my dear boy, is an anthropometric face cast," Richards said. "It was a common tool utilized by early anthropologists in the study of indigenous peoples, whereby a subject breathed through straws inserted into his nostrils for several hours while layer after layer of plaster were painstakingly applied to his face."

Jade was familiar with the practice. It was a part of the sordid history of her profession and represented roots they tried to hide, if not actively cut out. Forensic anthropology was born from the minds of scientists who traveled the world with calipers and charts, measuring and cataloguing the physical differences between populations and races. Early pioneers like Bruno Beger, whose findings on the 1938 Ernst Schäfer Expedition to Tibet were considered revolutionary at the time, returned to Germany and utilized his newfound knowledge to help the SS identify Jews by their physical characteristics and was later convicted of accessory to eighty-six murders for his role in selecting and preparing victims for the Jewish skeleton collection at Auschwitz.

"Whether or not this was cast from a living subject is a matter of some speculation," Richards continued. "All we have to go on is the holes for the nostrils, which could merely have been neglected in the obvious haste involved with the casting, but we have no reason to doubt its authenticity."

She scrutinized the picture, looking for overt signs of forgery. The subject was simply too fantastic for it to be anything other than a fake. The mold was essentially an inverted face, which, when filled with clay or plaster, could be used to create a lifelike bust. The edges were worn and cracked and showed visible smear marks from the original application of the medium. Sections had crumbled to powder, leaving holes that would eventually erode the entire mold. If it was a forgery, the craftsmanship was flawless, but she could think of no other explanation for the features of the individual formed inside, which could have been cast directly from the remains of the girl she'd exhumed from the mass grave in Nigeria.

"Why haven't I seen this before?" Jade asked. "Anyone in the field would give an arm and a leg to have the chance to authenticate it, let alone create a cast from it."

"It came from what one might call a *private* collection, and we'll leave it at that for now." Richards smirked. "It was from this mold that we produced this . . ."

He clicked the remote with a flourish and a face appeared on the screen. It had a narrow chin, pursed lips, and a tiny nose. The cheekbones were rounded and helped frame eyes that protruded from the sockets to such an extent as to nearly flatten the bridge of the nose. The brow line was high and the forehead elongated. The holes in the mold had left blemish-like imperfections. Everything about it was realistic, right down to the closed eyelids, which made the subject appear to be sleeping almost peacefully.

"I had a roommate as an undergrad who could have sculpted this in a matter of weeks," Kelly said.

"We cast this in latex, and by doing so were able to replicate details nearly impossible for any sculptor to recreate." He flipped through a series of magnified images. "The bases of eyelashes on the eyelids. Severely chapped lips here and . . . here. The impression of this vein in the forehead."

"Say it is real," Jade said. "This individual could have been born with any number of deformities, all of which could have been exaggerated by removing the plaster while it was still wet. Like you said, you can tell by the edges of the mold and the periphery of the cast that it was a rushed job. Even if this is a true-to-life representation of the individual from which the mold was created, what point are you trying to make?"

Richards smiled patiently.

"Let me show you something." He clicked through a series of images until he found what he was looking for. It was a mummified face like the one she'd been sent from Evans's dig in Egypt. The similarities between the mummy and the bust were staggering. The following picture featured a skull, browned by time and thickened with accreted minerals. The three faces were shown beside each other and then superimposed upon one another. "We scanned all three of these examples into the computer and analyzed them using a program that compares more than a hundred structural markers on each face. Every single point of comparison was in the ninety-ninth percentile, meaning they only differed by standard individual deviation, no different than any three of us in this room."

"That still doesn't answer my question," Jade said.

"We're talking about three different sets of remains, found on three different continents, at three different points in time. What I'm saying is really quite simple. Anya back there—Dr. Fleming, I should say—found the skull in Russia, Dr. Evans shot the photo of the mummified body in Egypt, and any number of intelligence agencies can confirm that the submarine carrying the mold was in Antarctica before surrendering in Argentina. I believe they cast that mold from a recently deceased—if not actually living—individual descended from the same lineage as the other two, a lineage that somehow either survived the crustal displacement and was still extant on this continent three-quarters of a century ago or one whose technological knowledge surpasses our own and has the ability to travel at will over great distances."

"What are you suggesting?" Evans asked.

"I'm not suggesting anything. I'm merely presenting the evidence that led me here and what I found when I arrived."

"Which is what, exactly?"

"The first thing we saw upon boring through the ice was a skull much like the ones Drs. Evans and Liang discovered independently on opposite sides of Africa. It was while investigating the best laboratory to sequence its genome when I discovered that Dr. Fleming had unearthed a similar specimen in Russia and was already a step ahead of me. A few telephone calls and a considerable donation later, not only did I gain access to the findings, but I also secured the services and discretion of the Brandt Institute. Within a week they confirmed my suspicion that the two were nearly identical."

"Nearly?" Jade said.

"Their genomes differed by about half a percent, which corresponds to roughly the difference between any two human beings. The most exciting finding, however, was that carbon dating revealed them to be separated by at least eight thousand years, an enormous amount of time in terms of human evolution for them to remain so similar. When compared to modern humans, they also shared distinct similarities in terms of base pairings with native peoples from the same geographic locations."

"What about the additional chromosome?" Jade asked.

Richards tapped the side of his nose.

"Very good, Dr. Liang. What about that twenty-fourth pair?"

He closed the file on the screen and opened a different directory, from which he selected a graph with tall bars grouped in pairs and numbered one through twenty-four, the last of which included an additional XY label to indicate the sex chromosome. Each numbered pair was a different length than the others, although identical to that of its partner, and pinched near the middle to show the position of the centromere. Color-coded horizontal bands filled them like stacks of poker chips. Jade immediately recognized that they were chromosomes for two distinct, yet biologically similar species, save for the fact that one had an extra column that the other didn't.

"On the left we have *Homo sapiens sapiens*, modern man," Richards said. "On the right, our magnificent cone-headed friend. As I'm sure you've already noticed, the latter species has an additional chromosome, one even smaller than the sex chromosome, labeled number twenty-four for the sake of illustration. All of the previous twenty-three pairs are of the same length and have the same base pair arrangement, with the exception of chromosomes five, eight, and eleven, shown in detail here."

He clicked the button, and a new image appeared.

"They're inverted," Roche said.

"Specifically these three sections here, here, and . . . here. The interesting thing about chromosomes, as I'm sure most of you know, is that they have what's considered a 'controller' gene positioned at the very top. By inverting these sections and changing the 'controller,' we end up with a completely different genetic expression, even though all of the genes themselves are exactly the same. An inversion event of this magnitude is essentially unheard of, which makes a case for spontaneous mutation as opposed to gradual evolution."

Evans stiffened beside Jade, who glanced curiously at him from the corner of her eye before speaking in a tone that betrayed her growing frustration.

"Again I'm forced to ask: what about the extra chromosome?"

"That's just it. We simply don't know. We can map the genes right down to nucleotide pairings, but we can't tell what function it serves any more than we can wager a guess as to where it came from. That's why I brought you all here. I need your skill and insight to figure it out."

Roche spoke for the first time. The sound of his voice surprised Jade, who had nearly forgotten he was in the darkened room with them.

"You keep going on about evolution, and then you hint at the involvement of aliens. So which is it? Are you proposing we're dealing with a discrete humanoid species or an extraterrestrial life-form?"

"I know this must sound like the wishful thinking of an old fool, but in my lifetime I've seen many things for which there's no logical explanation. Things that *defy* explanation. Two hundred years ago no one would have believed in the possibility that we descended from apes, let alone that we were only one of several lineages that did. Maybe that's all this species is, too. Then again, maybe it isn't. Protohuman remains are largely limited to geographic ranges, and yet we've found these elongated skulls on every continent, and near every major megalithic monument. Say what you will, but I firmly believe that all of this combined makes a case for the fact that some higher intelligence has been with our species from the start, a higher intelligence I believe to be alien in origin."

Evans laughed.

"You had me right up until that last bit." He deepened his voice. "'A higher intelligence I believe to be alien in origin.' Someone fit this guy for a tinfoil hat, would you?"

"Then perhaps you can explain the extra chromosome, Dr. Evans?"

"Sloppy handling of the samples? Contamination?"

"No chance in hell," Anya said.

"No offense, kiddo, but these kinds of things happen to the best of us."

"Maybe to you."

Richards clicked the remote and a new image appeared on the screen. Jade stood so fast she bumped the table and spilled her cold coffee.

"This screen grab was taken less than an hour ago," Richards said.

"Where?" Jade asked. Her heart was pounding so hard she could barely hear his voice over it.

"Why don't I show you?"

22
ROCHE

"We only just found our way into what we believe to be a burial chamber," Dr. Mariah Peters said. "At this point we can't even be sure exactly what we're looking at."

Roche hung back from the others. He needed space to think. There was obviously something Richards wasn't telling them. A critical piece of the puzzle simply wasn't there. In his former life, he'd learned that the best way to conceal a vital detail was to hide it within a flood of information, which felt like exactly what Richards had done. He'd inundated them with the visual equivalent of a shock-and-awe campaign and set the hook so deeply there was no hope of extricating it. It was all he could do not to allow himself to be swept along with all of the others, which was growing harder by the minute.

"It's not a tomb," Evans said. "I've explored countless burial chambers from any number of ancient civilizations, and while all cultures have different funereal practices, none of them show such callous disregard for the dead. This demonstrates complete and utter lack of reverence. It reminds me more of an animal's den."

"Like the tomb you discovered in El-'Amarna," Richards said.

"Exactly."

Roche leaned against the back wall. While the lab was reasonably large and well equipped, it hadn't been designed to hold this many people. He was tall enough to see over the others, who crowded around the drilling engineer's workstation, where Dreger operated the underwater drone with a joystick. There were three monitors mounted to the wall above the desk. The one on the left showed a digital elevation model of the bottom of the lake, although if he were interpreting it correctly, there were several buildings surrounding what looked like an oddly symmetrical submerged mountain. A thermal overlay had been applied to differentiate the temperature gradients, the majority of which fell along the blue and white scale. A red beacon indicated the location of the drone, the footage from which was displayed on the center monitor. The same grayish-green sludge he'd seen from the submersible covered fallen structural stones and more broken and disarticulated bones than he'd ever seen in his life. Despite the eyes of the dead that stared blankly into the camera as it advanced between them, it was the third monitor that intrigued him most.

It was divided into three rows. The top two featured low-amplitude sound waves, while the third displayed smears of red, blue, and yellow that he recognized as a spectrogram. It appeared to have caught Kelly's eye, as well. She nibbled on her lip as she studied it, her fingers fretting restlessly at her side.

"Can you zoom in right there?" Jade said. She tapped the image of the submerged chamber of bones. "A little more that way. There. That skull isn't like the others. It doesn't show any sign of cranial deformation."

"We've found more ordinary skulls than misshapen," Richards said. "I'm afraid we're just interested in the latter."

"They're human," Anya said. "Based on the breadth of the zygomas and the mandible, they appear to be of aboriginal South American origin. The Inca had similar facial architecture."

"That means there were two distinct hominin species living here at once," Evans said.

"We're still waiting on carbon dating for confirmation, but that's our working hypothesis."

"What about those?" Mariah asked, and pointed at a cluster of animalian skulls.

"Some sort of deer maybe?" Dreger said.

"Has anyone bothered to perform any pathological assays on the remains?" Jade asked. "If we're dealing with some sort of mass burial, we need to be incredibly cautious. An impromptu mass interment could signify the presence of a nasty pathogen none of us have the antigens to ward off."

"That's one of the reasons we wanted your expertise," Connor said from the doorway. He'd inserted himself into their midst so quietly that even Roche hadn't heard him. "Dr. Friden's working on isolating any potential viral involvement as we speak."

"And has been for the better part of a month," Mariah said.

"Surely no virus could have survived for millennia in water that cold," Evans said.

"A pithovirus was brought back to life after being frozen in the Siberian permafrost for thirty thousand years," Jade said. "That's one of our greatest concerns about global warming. There's no telling what kinds of horrific germs are preserved in the ice or what effect they'd have on our modern immune systems if they survived the thawing process."

"Do you think that's what happened here?" Connor asked.

"I don't want to speculate. If Cade's right and this wasn't designed to be a permanent tomb, we can't afford to dismiss any possibility out of hand."

"*If* Cade's right?" Evans said.

"Would you be able to determine if they were infected with anything?" Richards asked.

"If the pathological process affected the integrity of the bone," Jade said. "Sure. But I wouldn't be able to tell you what kind of microorganism was responsible without analyzing the DNA."

"We already have PCR results and a full genome," Anya said.

"That's a start. Are you at least taking standard precautions—?"

"What's that sound?" Kelly interrupted. Her fingertips blurred against her thumb.

"What sound?" Evans said. "I don't hear anything."

Kelly tapped the monitor with the sound waves.

"That sound."

Roche caught Mariah share a knowing glance with Richards, who watched Kelly carefully when he asked, "What does it look like to you?"

"It's obviously an infrasonic sound wave. At first I thought it was a whale's song, but it's too rhythmic, and considering the lake is freshwater, completely impossible. Maybe an unstable fracture in the bedrock? Have you been able to triangulate its origin?"

"We believe it's coming from inside this structure here," Mariah said. She pointed at what Roche had initially thought to be a mountain.

"That makes sense."

"How so?" Richards asked.

"Look at the spectrogram." Kelly tapped the colored row beneath the sound waves. "These dark red bands represent the sound. See how they appear hazy near the end, almost like they're dissipating?"

"Yes?"

Kelly turned to Mariah.

"Can you subtract the sound itself?"

"Subtract the sound from the recording of the sound?"

"Right."

"The only thing left will be background noise."

"Can you do it?"

Mariah stared at her for a moment before nodding to herself. She leaned over Dreger's shoulder and typed several commands into the computer. The red bands vanished with the next cycle, leaving behind little more than a reddish haze where the end of the line had been.

"See that?" Kelly said. "That's an echo."

"I should have recognized it," Mariah said.

"Don't beat yourself up. When you work in the Pacific Northwest, you learn quickly that not only do you have to account for an acoustic wave, you need to account for its echo, which is easier said than done on a rocky coastline like we have in Oregon."

"You're suggesting the sound is echoing from inside the structure," Connor said.

"No, I'm *telling* you the sound is echoing from inside the structure. Look at the residual waveform. It's hardly detectable, but I'd wager a vital organ that if you amplify the signal you'll find the waveform is nearly identical to that of the original sound."

"The structure's hollow." Richards was barely able to contain his excitement. "You're certain?"

Roche crossed his arms over his chest and cocked his head. It seemed they'd finally found the missing piece of the puzzle.

"What is it?" he asked, and studied Richards's reaction for any hint of deception.

Richards glanced at Mariah and was about to respond when Evans beat him to it.

"It's a pyramid."

"More than that," Richards said. "It's the largest pyramid on the planet. We estimate its total volume to be just under three million cubic meters."

"That's what, twenty percent larger than the Great Pyramid of Giza?"

"What's inside?" Roche asked.

"That's the problem," Dreger said. "We can't find a way in."

"What do you mean?" Evans asked.

"There's no entrance. At least as far as we can tell."

"What about through one of the other buildings?"

"That's what we were trying to do when we found the tomb."

"It's not a tomb," Evans said.

"It's a room full of dead people. What do you want me to call it?"

"Definitely not a tomb."

"We're overlooking the key component," Roche said. "These structures were built before the lake was here. You have to factor the water out of the equation. This village was built on dry ground in the bottom of a valley surrounded by tall cliffs, like the ones near the elevator. Whatever sound it's making would have fallen below the threshold of hearing. The only reason we're able to detect it now is because of the water, right?"

"What's your point?" Connor asked.

"Let him finish," Richards said.

"My point is why would anyone build something that would create a sound no one could hear?"

"The flooding is responsible for the production of the sound," Kelly said. "That would explain the lack of symmetry in the repetitions."

"So if the water is causing it—"

"Then it's finding a way into the pyramid that we're missing," Richards said. He took a breath and appeared to be about to speak before losing his train of thought. His expression changed before their very eyes from one of excitement to extreme concentration. "You'll all have to excuse me. I have preparations to make."

"Preparations?" Evans said.

"Mr. Dreger?" Richards said. "Will you please alert me the moment you find anything?"

"You got it."

Richards stepped out from in front of the monitors and made his way toward the exit. Roche watched the live feed from the camera as the borescope slithered over a jumbled mound of bones and focused on the back wall of the chamber, where characters had been carved into the stone. He recognized them immediately and masked his surprise before anyone noticed.

"And the rest of you?" Richards paused in the doorway and turned to face them. "Try to get some sleep. We have a big day ahead of us tomorrow. We're going to need those brains of yours firing on all cylinders if we're going to get into that pyramid."

He turned and hurried down the corridor with Connor at his heel, the echoes of their footsteps drowning out their whispered conversation.

23
KELLY

Kelly was so lost in thought that she wasn't aware she'd passed her room until she was halfway up the stairs leading back into the main complex. She shook her head and descended back into the hallway, where she found Roche waiting outside her room.

"Got a second?" he asked.

"Sure."

She stopped outside her door and waited for him to say whatever he had to say.

"Inside?"

He must have seen the discomfort on her face.

"No, no. Nothing like that. I just want to run an idea past you and I don't want to do so out here." He inclined his chin toward the security camera mounted near the ceiling. "We can go someplace else if you'd rather."

"I think we should probably just call it a day. I'd be happy to discuss anything you want after a good night's sleep."

There was something about him that made her uncomfortable, although she couldn't quite put her finger on it. He was awkward in the same oblivious way of a lot of academics she knew, but he was quite clearly not from the hallowed halls of any credible institution. He carried himself with a rigidity she associated with the military and had eyes that always seemed to be watching. While he seemed harmless enough, the whole crop circle thing hinted at the possibility that there just might be something wrong with his brain in a way she ascribed to conspiracy theorists and people who taped over the cameras on their computers and cell phones.

She opened her door and slipped inside, leaving it open just wide enough so as not to appear as though she were closing it in his face, while giving herself the ability to do just that.

"I need to talk to you about standing waves. Specifically the images. What did you call them? Cymagraphs?"

"Glyphs. Greek for symbols. CymaGlyphs."

"The picture of the crop circle you received? I took it in England the day before the tsunami in Oregon."

"You're making that up."

"All of this would make a whole lot more sense if I were. How familiar are you with the standing waves for other sound frequencies?"

"I have experience with some of the more common frequencies, but I wouldn't call myself an expert by any stretch of the imagination."

"Have you ever seen one like this?"

He held up a drawing scribbled on a piece of scratch paper. She recognized it immediately.

"Where did you see that?" she asked.

"Can we discuss this somewhere else?"

Kelly stared at him for a long moment before opening the door and stepping out of the way. Roche entered and waited uncomfortably to be invited into the small room. She gestured for him to take a seat at the small table that doubled as a desk.

"Thank you," he said.

Kelly slid her backpack from the corner of the bed so she could sit between him and the door. She clenched her hands into fists so as not to betray how nervous she was.

Roche dug his cell phone out of his pocket, set it on the table, and turned it so she could better see. He set the drawing beside it.

"I drew this image after seeing it on the wall inside the burial chamber or whatever it was."

"You don't want to call it a tomb, that's for sure."

Roche smirked. It was a small gesture, but a human one that helped her relax, if only a little.

He brought the screen on his phone to life and enlarged a thumbnail image of a crop circle taken from some height above a green field.

"This was taken in Woodborough Hill, England, around the turn of the century."

Both his drawing and the photograph featured a small circle at the center of a much larger circle, like a fat donut, through the bulk of which spiraling lines passed in both clockwise and counterclockwise directions so as to create oblong triangles of increasing size toward the perimeter. The picture reminded her of the bottom of a pinecone. She'd studied the design in graduate school, although in an entirely different context.

"Based on your expression," Roche said, "I'm pretty sure you've seen it before, too."

Kelly nodded and took a moment to formulate her thoughts, which diverted her concentration and allowed her fingers to do their thing. Roche watched them with open curiosity unplagued by the judgment she'd seen in the eyes of so many.

"Most people don't realize that the atmosphere and the ocean share a complex mathematical relationship. The winds, the tides, the currents. None of them are randomly oriented. While there is certainly an underlying element of chaos, nature itself maintains a very rigorous sense of order. That's the whole foundation of the oceanic and atmospheric sciences, the sole reason we're able to generate anything resembling predictive models and forecasts, without which we wouldn't be able to anticipate the formation of a hurricane with enough time to clear its path. Every natural system is at its heart an equation for which there is no perfect, rational answer, like pi or phi, which is known as the golden ratio and defines a logarithm that produces the most common spiral in nature."

"I'm familiar with the concept. Nearly all crop circles utilize the golden ratio in some way. It's considered sacred geometry, if you subscribe to the whole New Age school of thought. A lot of researchers in my field speculate that advanced extraterrestrial life would use something universal like the laws of mathematics as a means of first contact since there is likely no correlation between our languages."

"Do you believe crop circles are made by aliens attempting to communicate with us?"

"I'm not sure what I believe, let alone that this whole golden ratio thing is anything more than an attempt to impose order upon chaos."

"There really is more to it than that, though." Kelly rummaged in her backpack for a pen, flipped over his paper, and drew a spiral that started small in the center and grew wider with each turn. "Think of a nautilus shell, a chameleon's tail, the seeds of a sunflower, a spiderweb. All of these living beings naturally create spirals that adhere to this mathematical equation. We deal with it every day in the oceanic sciences in the form of whirlpools, hurricanes, and even the curl of a breaking wave. Every aspect of the universe—from the microscopic double helices of a strand of DNA to the vast Milky Way galaxy itself—conforms to the golden ratio. What you have here is not only the application of the golden ratio to nature, but the physical representation of a specific sound."

He nodded to himself.

"You already knew that, didn't you?"

"I was optimistic, but I didn't know for sure. You could say my training is in mathematics, too, at least as it pertains to the recognition of patterns and probabilities. I've been thinking a lot about what you said earlier. If one crop circle matched the design of a standing wave, who's to say that others didn't? It took maybe five minutes to find this crop circle from Avebury, England, in 2005."

He minimized the image on his phone and opened another photograph of a crop circle that looked like someone had rolled a giant die in the middle of a field and it had landed on the number five, only the outermost dots were contained within large circles. He swiped to the next image and the CymaGlyph of a standing wave labeled 396 Hz. The way the sound interacted with the volume of water caused it to bulge upward in five distinct sections.

The patterns were almost identical.

"This one's from the same area, only a decade earlier."

The next image resembled the stereotypical web of a spider flattened into a field of wheat. The corresponding CymaGlyph, labeled 741 Hz, looked just like it, although how any sound could produce such a complex pattern in water was simply miraculous.

"I think someone is attempting to communicate using sound," he said.

"I've seen those standing waves before," she said. "Same with the one you drew. They're the most commonly taught because they correspond to the Solfeggio frequencies. You know, the major scale? *Do-re-mi-fa-so-la-ti-do?* The one that looks like a spiderweb? That's *so*. The box with the circles is the first *do*. The one you drew is *mi* and matches the standing wave at 528 Hz, which, whether you believe in such things or not, corresponds to a frequency that a growing number of biochemists believe is capable of helping to restore damaged DNA."

"Do you believe that's possible?"

"Believe what? That sound can be used to alter DNA or that aliens are trying to communicate with us?"

"Take your pick."

"I find it hard to believe that sound can have any sort of physical impact on something as small as DNA, but I guess when it comes right down to it, that's exactly how radiation gives you cancer, and it's essentially sound with a much shorter electromagnetic wavelength.

As far as aliens trying to communicate with us? Surely there would be much easier and more direct ways of doing so."

"That's my opinion, too, but suddenly we're dealing with an awful lot of coincidences, aren't we? I mean, what are the odds we'd be looking at the physical representations of sounds we associate with speech?"

Kelly opened her mouth, but no words came out. He was right, but it was a huge leap from geometry and physics to first contact.

"Thanks for your time," he said and rose from the table.

"That's it? Thanks for your time?"

"I appreciate you hearing me out. I guess I needed to talk to someone else to make sure it made sense when I said it out loud."

"Why me?"

"I figured you'd be the only one who'd understand."

"Understand what?"

"Maybe I was wrong."

Roche turned and headed for the door.

A part of her wanted to tell him off for being so condescending, and then it hit her.

She remembered the symbols carved into the cliffs to either side of the elevator. They'd meant nothing to her at the time, but suddenly in the context of their conversation they made all the difference in the world.

"Sound is the key," she said.

Roche paused with his hand on the door but didn't look back.

The implications of what she was about to say were staggering. If she was prepared to admit the significance of the standing waves immortalized in both stone and fields of crops, she had to acknowledge that she was teetering on the precipice of reason. If he was right, she had to be willing to accept that not only had first contact been attempted, it had already been made.

"That's how we get into the pyramid," she said.

He turned around, smiled, and left without another word.

24
RICHARDS

Richards blew through the door to Friden's lab, startling the microbiologist.

"Jesus! Doesn't anyone around here know how to knock?"

"There's water in the pyramid."

"Duh. It's in a lake."

"The core is hollow, but somehow water's getting inside."

"I refer you to my previous answer."

"Show some respect," Connor said. He leaned against the doorway and crossed his arms over his chest.

"You're missing the point," Richards said. "The pyramid has been submerged for thousands of years. Either it just sprung a leak—which would be ridiculously coincidental after all this time—or the water has always been inside. Now we all know that water evaporates, so if we're dealing with a closed system, there has to be some mechanism that allows water to both enter and exit. Do you follow what I'm saying?"

"I couldn't follow you with a bloodhound and GPS tracker."

"It would be a shame if something happened to that mouse of yours," Connor said.

"Are you seriously threatening Speedy?"

"I've got this under control," Richards said. "Why don't you wait outside, Will?"

Connor stepped out of the lab and closed the door behind him, although Richards knew his bodyguard was prepared to come barreling through the door without a moment's hesitation. While his old friend's dislike of the microbiologist was painfully obvious, Richards was confident that Friden couldn't hurt his feelings, let alone his physical being.

"You see what happens when you feed a child nothing but raw meat?" Friden said.

"Are you through?"

Friden shrugged and slid back from beneath the hood. He removed his goggles and tossed them onto his desk. He'd been wearing them for so long that they left the impression of a raccoon's mask around his bloodshot eyes.

"When was the last time you slept?" Richards asked.

"What day is it?"

"You're useless to anyone in this condition. Get some sleep, for crying out loud."

"Aw, come on. I was just having a little fun with you. You need to stop taking everything so seriously. It's not good for your health."

"I appreciate your concern, although I could say the same."

Richards gestured to the mountain of Red Bull cans overflowing from the trashcan.

"Touché." Friden swiveled from side to side in his

chair. "Let's start over then, shall we? Welcome to my laboratory. What can I do for you?"

"The pyramid's a self-contained system that allows water to enter and exit while maintaining some amount of hollow space. It's not just producing the sound; it's creating an echo."

"The water's making that humming sound?"

"That's the general consensus."

"And you believe it?"

"Without reservation."

Friden stretched out his legs and spun in a complete circle.

"So the water's coming from a source other than the lake."

"It stands to reason. The influx of water from the lake would likely cause the structure to collapse like all of the others."

"So what's the significance?"

"One of the others said something that got me thinking," Richards said. "Why would anyone build a structure that made a sound no one could hear?"

"They wouldn't," Friden said.

"Exactly. So we can consider the sound produced by the water entering the structure to be coincidental, but that doesn't change the fact that the pyramid was deliberately built with sound in mind."

"You lost me."

"Think about it. The hollow chamber inside somehow took a sound below the range of hearing and utilized its echo to amplify it to audible levels."

"A primitive resonance chamber."

"Precisely. So the sound is amplified exponentially by its own resonant frequency, like the way the string of a guitar reverberates inside its sound box, creating acoustic energy."

"You think there's a relationship between the design of the pyramid and the reason the organism's cell membrane ruptured when exposed to the tone at a thousand hertz?"

"It makes a certain amount of sense, wouldn't you say?"

"In theory," Friden said. "If we factor amplification and resonance into the equation, then we would need to use a tone with considerably less acoustic energy to stabilize the reaction."

"And it would have to be a sound the people who lived here could produce consistently. Isn't there some kind of ancient music scale?"

"You mean like major and minor?"

"Something along those lines."

"And just try every note in the scale and see what happens?"

"Have you had any luck with the frequencies you've chosen?" Richards asked.

"Do you have any idea how many different frequencies that generator Dreger cobbled together for me can produce? My children would be grandparents before I tried them all."

"You have children?"

"God, no. At least none that I know of." He knocked on his desk. "But that's not the point. My point is that until now I've been flying blind. I'll research ancient musical scales and try some of the more common notes. Maybe now I can finally make something resembling progress."

"Then I'll get out of your hair. Keep me posted, would you?"

"Where are you going?"

"To bed. Like a normal human being. You should try it sometime."

"Are you trying to seduce me, Mr. Richards?"

Richards rolled his eyes and headed for the door. Friden spoke to his back in a voice lacking his customary sarcasm.

"Let's say you're right and the pyramid was designed to amplify this specific sound. Think of how many millions of tons of stone and countless hours of hard labor were required to build it. And all for what? To create a resonance chamber for a single tone? What could they possibly do with a sound?"

"That's what I intend to find out."

Richards opened the door and joined Connor in the hallway.

"You're not one of those nutjobs who thinks that ancient aliens built the pyramids, are you?" Friden said. "Never mind. Don't answer that. As long as your checks continue to clear, I don't really care."

Richards closed the door and led Connor back toward the main complex, where he maintained his own private suite in the engineering wing. It bothered him when people mocked him for his beliefs, especially people like Friden, who were so close-minded that they couldn't see the forest for the trees. The evidence was everywhere around them, staring them right in the face and yet so few actually allowed themselves to see it.

The cafeteria was empty and the greenhouse securely padlocked. Someone had finished off the pot of coffee, but otherwise there was no sign of life. He cherished moments like this, when he could be alone with his thoughts and not under siege by questions and demands from everyone around him.

There was no one in the hallway, although he could hear the third shift rustling around behind closed doors, preparing to start their day. Richards's suite was actually a combination of three, customized at the factory to provide maximum privacy, not to mention a private restroom. The outermost portion belonged to Connor and was separated from Richards's quarters by another door and a short hallway with a separate, alarmed entrance.

"I'll be fine from here," Richards said and clapped his old friend on the shoulder.

"You sure? You don't seem like yourself."

Richards smiled.

"There's a bit of melancholy involved with knowing your dreams are finally within your grasp."

Connor nodded and watched him pass though the bedroom. Richards closed the door behind him and stripped out of his shirt and pants as he walked past his bed and bureau to the third chamber, which was little more than a walk-in closet, but was more than large enough to serve his purposes.

He closed the door behind him and sat on the lone stool in the center. The walls were lined with shelves upon which his collection of relics was displayed under Lucite and black lights to prevent degradation by oxidation and UV rays. These objects represented an investment greater even than the arctic station in which they resided and the culmination of his life's

work. In this small chamber was the proof others refused to see, pieces of a puzzle that were all about to
fall into place.

Richards stared at the golden relic that would always hold the place of honor, largely because it was
his first. The tiny sculpture was Incan in origin and
dated to somewhere between 500 and 800 CE. That it
was gold-plated wasn't nearly as fantastic as the fact
that it resembled an airplane, complete with triangular
wings and an upright tail fin. While one could make a
case for it being a bird, no one who took the time to
compare its measurements and proportions to a fighter
jet could see it as anything else.

The case beside it housed a fragment of the Polon-
naruwa meteorite that struck Sri Lanka in 2012, the
microscopic examination of which revealed fossilized
bacteria and algae genetically distinct from any known
terrestrial species. He had several Mayan carvings purchased directly from the Mexican government, which
had been protecting them as state's secrets for nearly a
century. They'd been unearthed from beneath the pyramid at Calakmul and featured depictions of spacecraft
and aliens. As did the Ica Stones in the adjacent display, designs carved into andesite and discovered near
Nazca, Peru, where the framed photographs he'd personally shot from the open hatch of a helicopter had
been taken. They featured designs painstakingly created by people who would never have been able to see
them from the ground, geoglyphs that were hundreds
of feet wide and only appreciable from the air. There
was a hummingbird, a monkey, a spider, and a 1,500-
year-old alien sculpted into the side of a mountain,

with its wide eyes, misshapen cranium, and arm raised in greeting.

He had skulls ranging in size from an orange to a watermelon, all of them deformed to some degree and collected from all around the world. There was a 12,000-year-old Dropa stone from China that was nearly identical to the disc brake from a car's wheel. Lizard people figurines pre-dating the Sumerian culture from Al Ubaid, Iraq. Miniature sculptures of cone-headed people carved from mammoth tusks and discovered at a Stone Age excavation in Russia. Ancient bronze gears and threaded screws in petrified wood. Egyptian petroglyphs with flying saucers, aliens, and designs of technology that should have been well beyond their documented ability to comprehend.

And then there was his most prized possession, the Betz Sphere, resting on a custom-made plinth at the back of the room, almost like an altar. It looked like an ordinary silver bowling ball emblazoned with an elongated triangle and was recovered in 1974 from a fire that decimated the woods surrounding the Betz family home on Fort George Island, east of Jacksonville, Florida.

Richards caressed its seamless contours.

He should have known all along that the secret would be sound.

The problem with the world was that when it came to aliens, people demanded a level of proof greater even than that of their own religious beliefs. They wanted to see UFOs and little green men. They lacked his patience, his vision. They looked to the sky as though waiting for proof to fall into their laps while he dusted for fingerprints, which he discovered all over the remains of every ancient society from the dawn of man through modern times. There was no doubt in his mind that extraterrestrial life had influenced the development of the human species. And it was only a matter of time until he had irrefutable proof.

Richards brought his lips to within inches of the Betz Sphere and hummed. He felt the vibrations first in his lips, then in his teeth as the sphere resonated with the sound. It continued to emit the tone even after he ceased humming. The noise degenerated into throbbing pulsations that grew farther apart with each repetition until they sounded like the heartbeat of a living being.

25
ANYA

September 21

Anya swam down through the frigid water toward the submerged ruins. She was one of the few scientists with diving experience, but she'd never dived under conditions like these. She'd explored the Mayan cenotes of the Yucatán as an undergrad and the Great Barrier Reef while on vacation. Both had been reasonably challenging dives, but when it came right down to it, they were warm water and close to civilization in case of an emergency. The water temperature here was 28 degrees and only remained in liquid state through a miracle of physics beyond her understanding. All she knew was that it was so cold she had to wear multiple layers of clothing beneath her thermoprene dry suit, which not only did her precious little good, but made her movements considerably more cumbersome.

Kelly trailed behind her. Although the more experienced diver, she lacked Anya's ability to catalog the remains *in situ*, a skill that just might help them figure out what happened down here that led to the interment of so many bodies. Truth be told, she and Kelly were also the smallest and had the best chance of squeezing into the ruins without causing their collapse, a task that was looking more and more impossible the closer she got to the tiny orifice.

The submersible drone hovered above it, shining its lights down onto the gap between stones.

"How are you doing down there?" Evans asked. He and Jade were on the inflatable Zodiac floating above them, monitoring their progress via the live feed from the cameras mounted to their diving masks. The communications unit projected his voice directly into their left ears. Inasmuch as it was Anya's job to analyze the remains, it was Evans's to gather details of the structure and function of the building, along with interpreting the petroglyphs on the walls.

Anya's upper lip grazed the microphone when she spoke.

"I don't see any way either of us is getting through that hole, at least not with these tanks on our backs."

Bubbles burbled from her regulator toward the surface, where she could barely see the silhouette of the raft through murky water roiling with sediment and microbes.

"How hard is the ground?" Richards asked. He was back on the shore, coordinating her efforts with those of the others, who were in the process of assembling some sort of acoustic sound system.

Anya swam to the mouth of the hole and thrust her bright orange dry gloves into the silt, all the way past her wrists. She dragged several scoops of mud away from the entrance, creating clouds of sediment that made it momentarily impossible to see, even with the twin lights affixed to her temples.

"It's soft," she said.

"Can you widen it enough to squeeze through?"

She looked through the settling cloud at Kelly, who shrugged noncommittally.

"Maybe."

Together she and Kelly excavated the sludge from the orifice until they reached the underlying stone. They had to wait for the cloud to settle before they could evaluate their work.

"I don't know," Anya said.

"I'm not worried so much about getting in as I am about getting stuck in there," Kelly said.

"If you do," Jade said, "release your main tank and switch over to your backup."

"Which is a fraction of the size and only holds five minutes of air."

"That's more than enough to reach the surface."

"Easy for you to say from all the way up there."

Anya flattened herself to the ground and peered into the hole. The mounds of rubble cast strange shadows and created a veritable maze through which she could only barely discern the path of the borescope through the sediment.

"No point dragging this out," she said and pulled herself into the fallen structure.

The slightest movement stirred the silt, diminishing visibility nearly to her mask and creating an overwhelming sense of claustrophobia. She was acutely aware of the sound of her own breathing and the finite amount of air strapped to her back. There wasn't even enough room to flipper without banging her knees and elbows. She had to continually remind herself of what awaited her at the end of the maze as she navigated the narrow confines.

She nearly cried when the walls finally receded and the ceiling rose high enough to allow her to raise her head. The chamber appeared considerably smaller in person, but no less impressive. The broken remnants of columns littered the ground amid a scattering of bones. Many were hominin, but the majority belonged to animals. While determining the species was outside of her skill set, she recognized antlers, hooves, and the unique splayed digits of paws. They'd all absorbed the color of the sediment and taken on the consistency of stone, but she could still clearly see scratches in the cortex she equated with scavengers.

"Walk me through what you see," Jade said.

"The majority of the remains are disarticulated and scattered in no apparent pattern. Definitely abandonment context. There is a complete absence of grave goods. No readily identifiable midden or coprolite."

"Are there any articulated specimens?"

Anya flippered slowly over the bones, her face mask mere inches from them so that she could see anything resembling detail as she fanned away the sediment.

"Found one," she said. "Individual number one. Sprawled, on back. Upper torso flexed, but incomplete. Bones from the lower torso and appendages are missing. Abandonment context, like everything else."

She came face-to-face with the malformed skull they'd seen on Dreger's monitor, with its wide eyes and elongated cranium. Its lower jaw was gone, but several of its upper teeth remained.

"Can you get a little closer?" Jade asked. "Those

teeth . . . it looks almost like there's a gap between the lateral incisors and the canines."

"They do have certain simian qualities I didn't appreciate on the other skulls since they didn't have teeth, although the way individual teeth vary, the observation is of questionable significance."

"Without another specimen."

Anya knew exactly what Jade meant and was already a step ahead of her. She found another partially articulated conehead near the back and behind a mound of bones that appeared to have been broken to scrape out the marrow.

"Individual number two," she said. "Part flexed, part sprawled, on right side. Semi-articulated, but not formally interred. Concentration of disarticulated remains. Abandonment context."

"Same cranial deformation?" Jade said. "Can you focus on the teeth?"

"All that's left are the molars."

"And the alveolar sockets?"

"The spacing is similar, if not as dramatic."

"You sequenced this species' genome, right? Did you compare it to all known hominin populations?"

"No, we ran it through a database of plants. Of course, we compared it against every known protohuman and simian genome. You saw the PCR results. It's genetically distinct."

"Outside of the extra chromosome?"

"The closest match is *Homo sapiens sapiens*."

"That's not very helpful, is it?"

Anya contorted her body in an effort to turn around in the small space.

"Wait!" Evans said. "Go back."

"Go back where?" Anya asked.

"The wall behind you. Not that way. No. There. Can you expand the field of view?"

"You mean get farther away?"

"Yeah. Not too far, though. I want to see—right there. Perfect."

Kelly added her light to Anya's and focused on the faded design, the majority of which had either been smoothed by eons of running water or had crumbled to the ground, leaving behind portions of what looked like two stylized men with their arms raised in adoration to either side of a figure with an elongated head. The markings surrounding them appeared to be little more than the scratches and dots she associated with Sumerian cuneiform, although these were organized into columns. Above them was a design like a giant sun, only the rays radiated outward from a smaller circle in the center and crisscrossed in spiraling arches. The entire piece was framed by a giant pyramid.

"Jesus," Evans whispered. "The human depictions look almost Egyptian. The stylistic similarities are astounding."

"That's the design Roche was talking about," Kelly said. "The one that represents the standing wave of a sound frequency of five hundred twenty-eight hertz."

"There are more over here," Anya said.

She turned sideways and used her palms to pull herself along the wall. Entire sections of hieroglyphics had crumbled from the wall. The remainder required a little imagination to piece together. There were bulls with long, curved horns and stags with massive racks of antlers. Something that kind of resembled a lion. A line of men holding aloft what looked like one of those long alpine horns from the cough drop commercials. Chimeric men with human bodies, animalian features, and spread wings. A giant disc perched on the head of each and their cheeks bristled with beards that culminated in exaggerated points.

"There's an entire pantheon on this wall alone," Evans said. "Is there anything on the ceiling?"

Anya rolled over and faced the fallen roof balanced precariously above her. She'd been totally fine until she saw just how unstable the entire structure was.

"Try to hold the camera still," Evans said.

"You're kidding, right? It looks like a gentle current could bring this entire place down and you want me to hold still?"

"You're doing great, Anya," Jade said. "We're here for you."

Each breath came harder and faster until Anya feared she was on the verge of hyperventilating. The rectangular stones were braced against each other at odd angles that defied the laws of physics. The sides that had once formed the ceiling were covered with a seemingly random design of dots and the lines connecting some of them together. There was something familiar about the patterns they created, but she couldn't quite put her finger on it. Evans made the connection for her.

"It's a star chart."

"I've got to get out of here," Anya said.

It felt like the chamber was constricting, compressing the air from her lungs. Jade said something, but Anya couldn't make it out over her own heavy breathing, which echoed inside her mask. She couldn't seem to catch her breath any more than she could control her body.

"Try to remain calm," Jade said.

"Are you okay to keep going, Kelly?" Evans asked.

"Yeah, but Anya's freaking out. She needs to get out of here."

Anya kicked wildly and connected with the wall. Twisted. Propelled herself across the room through the billowing sediment toward the lone egress. Bones passed below her in a blur. She caught a glimpse of one final body with a deformed skull, leaning against the wall near the collapsed threshold and the rubble that must once have been a stone door. The edges were gouged and chipped where it appeared as though something had attempted to claw the door from the frame.

Kelly's voice was in her ear, trying to calm her down, but she couldn't focus on the words. She was only peripherally aware that the other woman wasn't following her.

Anya burst from the makeshift tomb and slithered through the maze of rubble as fast as she could. Propelled herself out of the narrow orifice and straight up toward the surface. She didn't pause to catch her breath until she was safely aboard the Zodiac.

26
ROCHE

Roche was missing something; he could feel it. He paced the rocky coastline, his breath trailing him over his shoulder. Much of the face of the cliff was concealed by ice so thick it would take months to chisel down to the bare rock, obscuring all but the most prominent of the massive petroglyphs, which must have stood out above the ancient village like the Hollywood sign over Los Angeles. Each of these giant symbols must have represented a part of a whole, like letters in a word, the summation of which remained a mystery.

He'd spent the better part of the night in the research library, learning everything he could about the electromagnetic properties of sound, its physical relationship to standing waves, and any overlapping references to primitive cultures.

Numerous societies throughout history believed that sound was an elemental force of nature, much like the wind or the rain. It circulated along the surface of the planet in currents that could be tapped to provide a continuous source of physical and spiritual power, one so sacred that many believed it could bring man closer to God, undermining the control of organized religion by essentially cutting out the middleman. It was for that very reason that the sheet music for hundreds of medieval Gregorian chants—hymns that utilized the Solfeggio frequencies in an effort to commune directly with the Almighty—was confiscated by the Church and locked away in the archives of the Vatican.

The Vedic tradition of India was built upon the idea that there were seven chakras—centers of spiritual power—in the body and that each corresponded to a specific frequency of sound—the same Solfeggio frequencies—responsible for the healing of the body and the mind. Tibetan monks used their "singing bowls" to produce those same seven frequencies for the exact same reason.

Many New Age practitioners theorized that for every part of the body there was a specific frequency of sound responsible for healing, frequencies based upon the principles of sacred geometry and vibrational harmonics. They even claimed that sounds of the proper frequency could be used to alter moods and cure diseases. And while most of what they put forth as scientific evidence struck Roche as largely a product of anecdotes and wishful thinking, he did find several interesting studies more firmly rooted in fact.

One study demonstrated that subjecting chrysanthemums to certain sounds accelerated the synthesis of RNA and soluble proteins, meaning that some genes could be activated by sound and their rates of transcription accelerated to alter the structure of DNA and its physical expression. A Russian biophysicist showed that modulating certain frequency patterns could essentially do the same thing in human beings.

Sonic vibrations were used to separate contaminants from water at the molecular level, and were so effective in doing so that they were employed following oil spills and were even used to recycle drinking water on the International Space Station. Revolutionary scientists like Nikola Tesla believed that sound frequencies could be harnessed to produce inexhaustible amounts of free energy. He designed a device—the Tesla coil— that utilized electromagnetic force and resonance to create a wireless source of energy transfer. In fact, there were many archeologists who believed the Great Pyramid of Giza had been built to serve as an ancient power plant.

Who knew why the pyramid out there under the lake had been built, but if there truly was a correlation between it and the crop circles, then maybe they were on the precipice of unlocking one of the greatest mysteries of all time, the key to which was chiseled into the stone and preserved behind several inches of solid ice.

As far as Roche could tell, there were four main designs. They were separated by smaller petroglyphs similar to those inside the collapsed temple, only three-dimensional, statuesque reliefs carved from the stone like the faces of Mount Rushmore. There were more human figures, some with elongated craniums, and chimerical beings with circles upon their heads, which appeared to be revered like gods. They were larger than the rest and featured in positions of prominence, while the others raised their arms in adoration or knelt in worship at their feet. The reliefs read like stories he could have perused all day, were it not for the scene in the background that gave him goose-bumps. It depicted four stone pillars on top of which stood four figures, each with an enormous horn that reached all the way to the ground.

He found what was left of the pillars among the rocks on the shoreline. He probably wouldn't have no-ticed them at all had he not been specifically looking for them as they were a mere shade of gray apart from the others and unadorned by any designs. The rubble was concentrated on the ground in front of each of the four symbols, which he believed corresponded to dif-ferent frequencies of sound.

In addition to the one that looked like the number five on a die, which represented the standing wave of 396 Hz, were three others of increasing complexity. There was a hexagon inside a circle with an odd checker-board pattern that almost looked as though someone had pinched the corners and stretched them outward until they formed peaks, which compressed the squares out-side of the hexagon while drawing those inside farther apart. He'd seen the same pattern in pictures from Ave-bury, England, in July, 2002, and speculated that it matched the standing wave produced at 639 Hz, or *fa*.

The third featured the spiderweb crop circle from Alton Priors, England, in July, 1998, the one he and Kelly speculated matched the standing wave produced at 741 Hz, or *sol*.

The fourth reminded him of a flower with six large petals on the outside, between which could be seen the tips of six leaves. Inside was a circle that housed an-other flower with six petals, only at its heart was a six-sided star, at the core of which was a third flower with six petals. The design matched that from Alton Barnes,

England, in June 2003 and the expression of 963 Hz, or *ti*.

The fact that all of the designs had appeared in such a short span of time and within mere miles of each other in Wiltshire County—near Stonehenge in southeast England—was not lost on him.

"Where do you want this thing?" Dreger called.

He and Connor carried the makeshift frequency generator between them as they traversed the rugged shore. The unwieldy contraption was composed of several speakers built into a homemade wooden box designed to serve as a resonance chamber. It utilized an amplifier mounted to an oscilloscope, both of which connected to Dreger's laptop. Richards followed them from the platform beside the elevator, where a series of laptops served as the communications center with both the station and the Zodiac.

"How about over there?" Roche said, and pointed toward the ground in front of the sun design.

"You're the boss," Dreger said.

"I'm certain this will work," Richards said, and clapped Roche on the shoulder. "I have complete faith in you."

Roche had expected his theory to encounter resistance, but instead it had been met with enthusiasm. He supposed that should have been gratifying; instead it set off all sorts of internal alarms. It was like they'd already guessed that there was some relationship between the designs and sound waves, which confirmed his suspicions that they knew a whole lot more about what was going on than they let on.

He watched the Zodiac floating on the still lake in the distance for several seconds before joining the others at the edge of the water. They'd leveled the contraption on the rubble of the collapsed column and angled the speakers toward the submerged pyramid.

"Were do we start?" Richards asked.

"Three ninety-six hertz," Roche said.

Dreger opened the laptop and a frequency generator program that allowed him to input specific frequencies in cycles per second. A sine wave appeared on the oscilloscope at the same time as the speakers emitted a low-pitched hum.

"Louder," Roche said.

Dreger dialed up the volume, tweaked the waveform, and looked at Roche, who signaled for him to increase the volume until he could feel the tone resonating in his chest. Three figures stood up on the Zodiac and turned in their direction.

Connor had to shout to be heard over the sound.

"Nothing's happening!"

Richards knelt at the edge of the water and held his hand in front of the speakers. It appeared to take tremendous effort to hold his hand still.

Thud. The distant sound reverberated through the darkness.

Roche instinctively glanced at the dome overhead, expecting to see cracks racing through the ice, only there was no sign of movement.

He stood on top of the largest rock he could find and stared out across the dark water toward where the Zodiac swept its lights across a localized section of choppy waves. Bubbles burst on the surface as though the lake were boiling.

"It's working!" Roche shouted.

"What should we do?" Dreger yelled.

"Move on to the next one!"

Dreger shut off the deafening noise, and he and Connor hefted the box from the ground.

"What's going on over there?" Jade's voice was so loud through the speaker in Richards's right ear that even Roche could hear it. "It felt like the entire lake dropped out from under us."

"What do you see?" Richards said into the microphone as he bounded over the rocks, trying to keep up.

"Now? Just a string of bubbles, but it sounded like something exploded below us. And Kelly's still down there."

"What in the name of God is she still doing in the water?"

"Documenting the hieroglyphics for Evans."

"I thought both divers were back in the raft."

"Anya had to return, but Kelly said she was fine to keep going."

"Tell her to get out of that structure and hold on tight!"

"Hurry!" Roche said. "If these sounds are supposed to be played at the same time, we might already be losing whatever progress we made."

"What now?" Dreger asked.

Static burst from the speakers.

"Six thirty-nine."

A similar tone with a slightly higher pitch boomed across the lake.

Thunk!

This time the reaction was instantaneous. The lake dimpled and sent waves racing outward, nearly capsizing the Zodiac.

"Keep going!" Roche shouted, but the others didn't

need to be told. They hefted the speaker box between them with the laptop still perched on top and crossed the uneven shoreline toward the next symbol, where they practically threw it to the ground.

"Seven forty-one!"

Waves broke against the rocks and filled the air with spray.

An even higher-pitched tone erupted from the speakers.

Thud!

The ground trembled beneath their feet. Roche covered his ears and turned toward the lake, where the raft roared away from the volatile surface behind it. Even taller waves raced outward behind them as though a boulder had been dropped from the sky.

"Nine sixty-three!" Roche shouted.

Dreger and Connor lifted the box so quickly that they nearly dropped it. Roche caught the laptop before it could fall off and typed in the frequency as he ran. A sound like the emergency broadcast signal exploded from the speaker before they even set it down.

A resounding *thud* echoed across the lake.

The frigid water raced outward so fast that it was up to their knees before they even knew it was coming. They barely lifted the speaker box from the water in time.

Roche leaned into the current and fought for balance on the slick stones. He caught a fleeting glimpse of the top of the pyramid before the Zodiac and its light sped out of range.

27
KELLY

"What's going on up there?" Kelly screamed.

She'd been searching the fallen structure for any sort of hidden passageway into the pyramid while she waited for the LiDar unit, which would produce a three-dimensional map of the interior, to finish scanning when the sonic vibrations from the first sound hit. It almost felt like a whale had nudged the building from the outside, followed by a distinct tremble in the ground. Pebbles and debris had rained from the roof before the first of the massive blocks fell, starting a chain reaction. She'd swum as fast as she could, banging her head and shoulders and knees, as the entire building came down around her. The second sound had collapsed the entrance on her legs, but she was able to drag them out and it only cost her a flipper. Not that a full set would have done her much good with the way the sediment had risen into a seemingly impenetrable cloud.

Her only option had been to grab onto the nearest stone block and brace herself against the violent currents as the underwater world tore itself apart around her.

The third sound had created swirling eddies in the silt, forming momentary gaps through which she glimpsed the base of the pyramid. A stone slab dropped straight down into the mud, causing the ground to shake and revealing what almost looked like a doorway that had been completely concealed behind megaliths and sediment.

The fourth sound had caused the water around her to vibrate. The final stone slab fell away, exposing the darkness contained within.

A heartbeat later she realized what was about to happen.

She barely managed to secure her grip on the stone before the current suddenly shifted, intensified, and sucked her legs all the way over her head and toward the pyramid. A vortex formed in the doorway, inhaling everything within its range. Silt and debris assailed her like buckshot. Bones and rubble bounded along the bottom of the lake. She started to slip and screamed with the strain. It felt like her arms were being wrenched from their sockets.

Kelly soared backward and cartwheeled through the water before she even realized she'd lost her grip. She tumbled blindly along the current until it abruptly waned and left her drifting toward the orifice on an eddy she easily escaped.

"Are you all right?" Evans shouted.

"What the hell just happened?"

"We were hoping you could tell us. The lake felt as though it just dropped out from underneath us."

"That's because it did."

"What do you mean?"

Kelly swam through the settling silt until she could clearly see the doorway, which continued to suck in debris, although at nowhere near the same rate.

"Jesus," she whispered. "It worked."

"It worked?" Richards said.

"I'm looking directly into the pyramid right now."

"It worked!" Richards shouted into her ear. "Did you hear that, Mr. Roche? She says it worked!"

"Not without nearly killing me in the process," Kelly said. "You could have at least given me a little warning."

"You have my most sincere apologies, my dear. I genuinely thought you had returned to the surface with Dr. Fleming. Tell me you're unharmed."

"I lost a flipper."

She realized how lame it sounded as soon as she said it.

"What about the remains?" Jade asked.

"There's no way anyone's getting to them now."

"Did the LiDar finish scanning first?"

"Looks like it," Evans said. "We won't know if we're missing any data until we perform the reconstruction, though."

Kelly floated closer to the orifice, which had inhaled the majority of the sediment around it, creating a fan-shaped trench leading downward to the bare ground. The pull of the current was no stronger than the standard undertow to which she was accustomed, so she inched down the slope until she could barely see the rubble of the fallen structure behind and above her.

The ground was composed of fitted stones of varying size, and yet the seams were perfectly straight and so tightly joined she doubted she could fit anything wider than a razor blade between them. She braced the insulated dry boot she wore beneath the lost diving fin on solid ground and with the other leg flippered against the current for balance. She could hear the others talking, but she couldn't concentrate on their words as she watched the tendrils of silt pass her and disappear through the trapezoidal opening. The threshold was easily eight feet deep and framed by an aedicule of polished stones that each had to weigh several tons. She couldn't clearly see the inscriptions on them beneath the rust-colored mud.

The lights mounted to either side of her mask revealed little more than the sparkling silt settling inside.

"I'm going in," she said. The words were out of her mouth before she even realized she'd reached a conscious decision.

"We should wait until we know everything's stable," Richards said. "Dr. Peters said she just received reports of flooding from Troll Station. They said it was like a geyser erupted from inside Snow Fell."

"The aquifers are connected," Kelly said. "The water had to have somewhere to go."

"Exactly my point. Lord only knows what might happen to you if you get sucked down into one of those passages. We don't have the slightest idea of how many are down there, let alone where they go."

Kelly slid closer until the pull of the current was almost irresistible. The slabs that had once concealed the doorway were each easily two feet thick and had fallen into the ground in such a way as to create stairs leading up into what looked like a narrow corridor. Strips of copper, green with oxidation, ran vertically down the walls to either side. She could feel the heat radiating from them even through her dry suit.

She glanced up toward the Zodiac, which was barely silhouetted by its own lights in the distance. Her fingers fretted at her side but couldn't quite touch through the thick gloves.

"Kelly?" Evans said. "Are you all right?"

"Yeah." The bubbles from her regulator fled her into the darkness. "Couldn't be better."

"Wait for me. I'm changing now. I'll be right down."

"You know where to find me," she said and lifted her feet.

The current pulled her into the confines. She kicked against it and braced her hands on the walls to slow her progress. Her lights did little more than limn the tunnel, which remained straight for maybe ten feet before starting a fairly steep decline. Twin copper pipes, so green she initially mistook them for algae, traced the ceiling above her before branching upward through a seam between stones. Another dozen feet and she encountered a second tunnel that led upward from the ceiling at roughly the same angle of her descent. The bubbles from her regulator rose toward it before being swept downward into the earth.

Kelly smiled to herself. She knew exactly what that meant.

She swam up into the passage and craned her neck in an effort to see where she was going. Her beams formed a diffuse golden aura that constricted into twin circles on the surface, which she breached for the first time in what felt like forever. She took a moment to gather her bearings before she crawled out of the water.

She knew that sunken ships often contained large pockets of air, but was surprised to find what amounted to a giant airlock inside the flooded pyramid. The slanted stone roof was barely high enough to allow her to walk in an awkward crouch, every other step punctuated by the *flap* of her flipper, until she reached a point where the ground leveled off and the walls receded.

The chamber was maybe ten feet wide, but so tall that her lights diffused before reaching the top. The walls to either side tapered inward like the undersides of twin staircases, only each of the smooth stone steps had to be at least five feet tall. The sound of her footfalls echoed around her in a way that made it sound as though she were in a stadium filled with people clapping in unison. Bits of broken clay and rusted iron covered the damp ground. The high-water mark on the walls came up to her waist, but only to the knees of the three-dimensional statues sculpted into the walls as though emerging from them.

"Are you seeing this?" she asked. The echo of her voice was disorienting.

Evans said something, but his voice cut in and out to such an extent that she couldn't understand him.

The statues were so lifelike it felt as though they were watching her as she advanced into the chamber. They held their arms out to support massive wings with such realistic feathers that she half expected them to take flight. Their bodies were taut and muscular and textured with what almost looked like fine scales. All of their chests were bare, although the men wore elaborate loincloths and the women contoured skirts. Each had an ornate headdress that reminded her of the masks samurai wore into battle, only these were carved into the faces of various animals, leaving just enough space through which to see their intricately carved eyes and the bridges of their noses. There was a man with the face and horns of a bull, another with the beak and flared feathers of a bird of prey. A woman with the snout and antlers of a deer. A man peering from the mouth of a fanged serpent. And each and every one of them had a giant disk balanced on his or her head, held in place by a broad V-shaped mount, like the horns of a gazelle.

She passed a tusked man, a lioness, and some creatures she didn't even recognize before reaching the end of the vaulted chamber and a tunnel so small she was forced again to crawl for roughly ten feet before her lights fanned out into a larger chamber.

Kelly stood and turned in a circle, letting her beam sweep across the recessed walls. The hairs rose along her neck and the backs of her arms.

"Oh, my God."

Her voice echoed around her like so many ghosts whispering from the shadows.

28
FRIDEN

Max Friden groaned and tried to open his eyes, but the screaming pain in his forehead forced him to close them again. He raised his head and pried his watch from his cheek. He'd apparently fallen asleep on it and hadn't moved since. He smacked his tongue from the roof of his mouth and, somewhat disoriented, looked around his lab. He just needed some caffeine to take the edge off of his splitting headache, which he knew was caused by ingesting copious amounts in the first place, but that was a problem for another day.

"Sweet nectar of the gods," he said and killed off the remainder of a warm can of Red Bull he found on the corner of his desk. He belched and launched the empty can toward the trashcan with the others.

A glance at his watch confirmed that not only had he slept through breakfast, he'd nearly missed lunch. Again. This kind of thing was becoming habit for him, but he did his best work in the middle of the night. Always had, always would. There was something about being on the brink of exhaustion that seemed to free his mind from the constraints he unconsciously placed on it during the day.

After Richards left, he'd gotten right down to business and researched ancient musical scales, which led him to the Solfeggio scale, first documented in cuneiform by the ancient Sumerians more than seven thousand years ago and utilized in Europe clear through the Renaissance. In the process, he'd stumbled upon all sorts of New Age mumbo jumbo about its so-called sacred tones, including the belief that the note *mi*—528 Hz—could repair damaged DNA. While he found the notion laughable, considering it was roughly half the acoustic energy of the tone that had caused the membranes of the organisms to rupture, it seemed like a reasonable starting point.

He'd extracted samples of each of the twenty-eight species isolated from the lake, everything from algae to protozoans, and prepared slides with as many living specimens of each as he could. One by one, he'd mounted them on the light microscope and watched through the lens as he exposed the organisms to that infernal sound. If there was a more annoying tone on the planet, he couldn't imagine it. After a while he'd started to wonder if stabbing knitting needles through his eardrums wouldn't have been an improvement.

None of the eukaryotes—single-celled organisms like amoebae and algae—showed any appreciable reaction whatsoever, nor did any of the previously identified multicelled prokaryotes found elsewhere in the world. So much of the scientific method involved ruling out reactions in control samples. Without them, it would be impossible to qualify the reactions of the test subjects, which he had saved for last.

The previously unclassified archaea they'd discovered in the lake, those that had matched the fossilized bacteria from the meteorite and had responded so violently to the Metallica song, had reacted not only immediately to the tone, but in the precise manner he'd predicted. Their fimbriae had lashed out and attached to each other and the glass, creating a complex network reminiscent of the chains of neurons and dendrites that formed the human nervous system.

He'd held his breath waiting for their membranes to split and the cytoplasm to leak out, only to find that the system remained stable. Unfortunately, all it did was a whole lot of nothing. Once it was established and its little web was formed, there was nothing he could do to stimulate it to do anything else. Even exposing it to the same frequency that caused the earlier samples to pop had done nothing. Repeating the procedure with a second slide had produced the same results, confirming what at that point he'd known with more surety than anything he'd ever known in his life . . .

He needed to get some sleep.

No doubt he'd intended to lay his head down for a minute or two, but here he was—Jesus, eight hours later?—and he needed to do something about this mother-loving headache so he could get back to work.

He got another can of Red Bull from the mini-fridge and used it to wash down a handful of ibuprofen.

The slides with the archaea species were under the hood. At least he'd had the presence of mind not to leave them sitting out on his desk. A quick peek under the microscope reassured him that their integrated structure remained intact. In fact, it almost looked as though the network had become more tightly woven, but he could have just been misremembering as the small part of his brain that didn't actively hurt was still foggy with the residue of sleep.

Friden yawned, set the slide back under the hood, and inspected the second sample. It showed the exact same thing, which was great and all, but he still had no idea of its significance, if there even was any.

He laced his fingers behind his head, swung in circles in his chair, and contemplated everything he knew about this strange species of archaea, which had yet to be formally classified, although he was leaning heavily toward something ending with either Fridensii or Fridensis. All archaea had unique qualities that basically set them apart from all other types of life on the planet. They were prokaryotic, which meant they had no nucleus or other organelles, and while they were similar in size and shape to bacteria, their genetic structure more closely resembled that of eukaryotic organisms, especially the enzymes responsible for transcription and translation, the process by which genetic expression was achieved. They were capable of metabolizing energy sources that killed every other organism, from ammonia to metal ions to hydrogen gas, and thrived in extreme environments from the bottom of the sea to the heart of a volcano, which was why the theory that they could survive in space wasn't so absurd. In fact, many scientists believed that microbes like this one were responsible for processing methane to produce the oxygen that formed the earth's earliest atmosphere, which allowed for the evolution of higher orders of life.

That was why he hadn't batted an eye when Richards first approached him about this project. Well, maybe he'd batted one, but when it came right down to it, he did believe in extraterrestrial life-forms, if not in any of their more Hollywood-esque incarnations. The theory that life had been seeded on this planet by a meteorite meant that somewhere out there was at least one other planet capable of sustaining life, although one at a different stage in its own evolution. He couldn't help but wonder what life on Earth would be like in another sixty million years. Would mankind still be the dominant form of life, or would it have destroyed everything and returned the planet to these very organisms so they could begin the process all over again?

Maybe therein lay the key. It had been sound that triggered their strange behavior, and what was sound if not a low-energy electromagnetic wave? Higher energy had initially triggered this reaction, but at an unmanageable rate that had caused its destruction, yet in its current state that same acoustic energy didn't affect it in the slightest. What if that were the whole point of this phase in the species' development? While nature itself was random, its individual components tended to react in predictable ways to given sets of stimuli. What if this web was essentially the next stage in this archaea's life cycle, like a caterpillar encasing itself within a cocoon? And if so, what would be the result? The individual specimens weren't even moving anymore. They were just stuck there in one place, connected in a filamentous mass like gray matter in the brain.

Friden stopped spinning and mentally retraced his

steps. He was onto something. He'd made a break-through, but he couldn't quite grasp it. It was a tip-of-the-tongue sensation that he undoubtedly would have already worked through were it not for this blasted headache.

"Think, think, think," he said, knocking himself on the forehead.

That was it. What was thought if not a series of electrical impulses carried through the brain on tracts of nerves, which in turn conducted those impulses to the rest of the body? That was the whole theory behind freezing someone's head in the hopes of one day attaching it to a robot or a cat or whatever these nutjobs wanted to do.

"Battery."

Friden yanked open one drawer after another until he found what he was looking for. He pried the back from his cell phone and pulled out the battery, cords and all. A quick snip and the plug was gone, allowing him to expose the wires. He had his eye to the microscope before he realized he'd effectively just ended his game of Lara Croft Go and cursed out loud as he aligned the leads with the edges of the slide. The cell phone battery didn't produce a ton of juice, but it had more than enough to demonstrate the passage of the current through the water on the slide, which caused the thinnest fimbriae to snap and the smaller archaea to rupture. The larger individuals almost looked like they were boiling, until he recognized that what he had mistaken for little bubbles were actually tiny buds.

"Interesting . . ."

The buds pinched off and floated among the fimbriae. He grabbed his iPad and played the 528 Hz tone. The buds rooted themselves where they were and tapped into the existing network.

Sound caused transformation and electricity triggered multiplication, implying either that the threat of electrocution had caused asexual reproduction as a means of self-preservation or in response to the increased demand for conductivity. Considering the nature of the response to the higher-pitched sound, he felt confident excluding the former explanation, but if the latter were true, what would be the biological or evolutionary advantage of being able to conduct a charge? Maybe the conductivity was like the sound in the sense that the organism only responded properly to the correct frequency and he simply hadn't applied the right electrical charge for the system of function at peak efficiency.

Two steps forward, one step back. That was science all right.

Friden slid back from his desk and rubbed his eyes. Hopefully things would make sense after getting something in his stomach and attempting to drown himself in multiple pots of coffee. He poured some food into Speedy's dish, grabbed his iPad on the way out the door, and opened the file containing the archaea's genome so he could peruse it while he ate. Maybe there was something hidden among the sequences of DNA that he'd missed.

29

EVANS

Evans had dived once on vacation as a kid, but this wasn't anywhere close to the same thing. The dry suit was heavy and unwieldy and he could still feel the coldness of the water through the multiple layers of clothing underneath. The darkness didn't help, either. The lights mounted to his mask illuminated the water directly in front of his face, yet did precious little to give him even a general impression of his surroundings. When it came right down to it, he wasn't the right man for this particular job, but there was no one more qualified to evaluate what he'd seen on the feed from Kelly's camera.

She was waiting for him outside the entrance, which was unlike any he'd seen before. The inner structure, however, was reminiscent of the Great Pyramid of Giza the way both ascending and descending corridors branched from the primary passage. He followed her upward through the narrow tunnel until she crawled out of the water into a massive vaulted chamber reminiscent of Giza's Great Gallery, at least in terms of its overall structure. The style, however, was a fascinating amalgam of ancient cultures and styles. The statues with their magnificent anatomical detail and artisanship were like something from the classical age of Greece or Rome, while the gods themselves were a cross between those worshipped by the Egyptians and Sumerians, and yet completely unlike either.

"Are you coming?" Kelly asked from the far side of the chamber, where her lights illuminated a hole in the wall near the floor.

"Yeah."

Evans took off his flippers and reluctantly followed her on his hands and knees through the tunnel into a large room analogous to the King's Chamber in the Great Pyramid in structure, although entirely unlike it in every other respect.

"Wow."

"My thoughts exactly," Kelly said. "You can see why I wanted to wait for you before going any farther."

Evans stepped cautiously into the room. The floor was smooth, the stones perfectly joined. A greenish-blue spiral pattern wound outward from the center, where a single column supported the weight of the high ceiling. It was covered with the same oxidation as the design beneath his feet, but it scraped off easily enough to reveal the copper underneath. He glanced down at the pattern carefully worked into the stone and imagined this room as it must have been long ago. With the fire-light reflecting from the polished metal, the effect would have been breathtaking.

"What is it supposed to be?" Kelly asked.

Evans could only shake his head. He simply didn't know. The ancient Egyptians used the pillars inside their temples to tell a story. Most utilized a papyrus

motif to illustrate their creation myth—man being birthed
from the primordial marsh—but this one seemed entirely
ornamental in a way he attributed more to the showcas-
ing of wealth than anything remotely spiritual. The ancient Egyptians and Sumerians were the first to mine
copper ore, although this structure pre-dated them by
thousands of years. They principally alloyed it with tin
to make bronze for the sake of adornment, as copper itself was considered ordinary and unattractive.

A lone egress marred the opposite wall. It was roughly
the same size as the one through which Evans had just
crawled, although nowhere near as deep. He crossed the
room and peered inside. The tunnel appeared incomplete. It terminated against a flat stone barrier maybe
eight feet in. He didn't see the vertical shaft branching
upward from it until he was all the way inside.

"Did you go up here?" he called. His voice echoed
from both above and behind him at the same time.

"Up where?"

"I'll take that as a no."

Evans twisted his torso and cautiously rose to his
full height. The blocks to his left were staggered in
such a way as to create a staircase running diagonally
behind the rear wall before doubling back upon themselves and continuing higher. He was nearly to the top
when he caught a reflection from something on the
ground. It was a tarnished silver stickpin roughly two
inches long with an ornate T-shape inside of a circle at the
end. Upon closer inspection, the design looked more like
the elaborate cross-guards and blade of a broadsword.

"This shouldn't be here," he said.

"What shouldn't?" Kelly asked as she rounded the
bend behind him.

He held up the pin for her to see, then closed it in his gloved hand.

"What is it?" she asked.

"Beats the heck out of me."

He continued upward until a gap between structural stones opened upon a chamber maybe half as wide as the one below it, but easily twice as tall. There was an elevated black ring set into the middle of the floor that almost looked as though it had been designed to hold the pedestal of an enormous statue that was conspicuously absent. Thick copper bands radiated outward from it like the rays of the sun. Where they met the walls, they continued upward in straight lines all the way to the roof, where they again traveled inward and converged directly overhead.

Evans stood in the center of the ring and turned in a circle. His lights made the oxidized copper in the walls appear to turn around him like the bars of a carousel. There was no other way out of the chamber, at least as far as he could see. He crouched and used the blunt end of the stickpin to chisel away the black crust covering the ring, revealing the silver metal underneath it.

He stood once more with a perplexed expression on his face and turned to Kelly.

"What's down the descending corridor?"

"I don't know."

"Then I suppose it's time we found out."

He brushed past her and started down the steep stairs. Something about the pin gnawed at him. It was more than the fact that silver wasn't even first mined until five thousand years ago or that it had been formed into what could have passed for a lapel pin. If they were right about this structure being somewhere between ten and fifteen thousand years old, then none of these metals should have been here. Whatever society flourished here would have been more advanced than any other on the face of the planet for another five to ten thousand years, and yet here it sat, frozen beneath two vertical miles of ice and at the bottom of a lake carpeted with the bones of its former inhabitants.

What in the name of God happened here?

Evans crossed the spiral and passed the column. Crawled through the tunnel and blew past the statues. He barely remembered to put on his flippers before crawling into the hole and propelling himself downward into the water. He had to contort his body to pass from the ascending corridor back into the descending, where the current guided him deeper into the darkness. He'd gone maybe fifty feet when a small passage opened above him. He paused only long enough to acknowledge its existence before continuing downward to where the tunnel leveled off.

Everything was beginning to take shape in his mind. None of the walls were covered with the sludge that had formed on everything else on the bottom of the lake, which meant that the pyramid had been sealed until they figured out how to open it, and yet somehow someone had to have gotten inside to lose the pin. The only other people to lay claim to this part of the continent were the Norwegians, who undoubtedly wouldn't have granted Richards's request to build his station here had they known about the ruins directly below it, and the Germans, who'd installed their communications center right in the mouth of the tunnel that led straight into the lake. They must have also found a passage that led them into this pyramid, and the only other way in had to be from underground, which would explain the reports of flooding at Snow Fell.

The passage opened into a larger flooded chamber much like the one beneath the Great Pyramid, in the center of which the supposed bottomless pit was clogged with debris. This one had a similar hole, although it remained open. The current flowing into it dragged everything that wasn't physically attached to the structure across the ground, over the elevated rim, and down into the shaft.

Evans leaned back and braced his hands on the ground, but only managed to slow his advance. He barely glanced at the walls around him, which, unlike the higher levels, were bare and utilitarian. They weren't composed of blocks like the rest of the pyramid, but rather from an existing cavern that had been reshaped to meet their needs.

He slid along the ground until his heels contacted the rim of the well and slowly flattened himself against it, wrapping his arms around and leaning as far as he dared over the hole. His lights illuminated twin blurs of motion that from above resembled spinning paddle wheels and the lava tube underneath them through which a subterranean river flowed.

30
JADE

Jade sat on the edge of the elevator platform, beneath one of the weak lights, and opened her laptop on her thighs. She hadn't even been down here for half a day and already the lack of natural light was beginning to affect her psyche. She couldn't imagine how horrible a place like this would be in the winter when the sun set for months at a time, especially in such close confines and with so many other people. She was a solitary creature by nature. Not that she minded being in the company of others, but she needed her own space to which to retreat when she wanted time alone in her own head, a space a whole lot bigger than her quote-unquote suite in the research station.

The truth was that she was somewhat socially awkward and the effort of maintaining an amiable façade was exhausting. The others' voices, their mannerisms, their mere presence was already grating on her nerves. If the elevator hadn't been recalled to the surface to bring down the engineering crew and their equipment, she would have happily commandeered it and reveled in the silence all the way to the top. Immersing herself in her work offered her last hope of escape.

Her computer had already analyzed the data from the LiDar scan and reconstructed it into a three-dimensional model of the inside of the now-collapsed building they were calling a temple, whether that was actually the case or not. The reconstruction was so accurate that it was even more lifelike than a photograph, which could only capture details in two dimensions. This program essentially created a hologram that allowed her to visualize even the most minute details, like the depth of the imperfections in the stone or the striations in the cortex of a bone, and turn it on any axis in order to examine those details from every conceivable perspective.

Her first thought was that several individuals, possibly a family unit, had gathered their livestock and taken shelter inside the structure before some unknown catastrophe struck. Now that she had the ability to study the scene as a whole, however, a new narrative was beginning to take shape. The program allowed her to filter out the overlying sediment, allowing for increased visualization of the remains. Anya had described them as abandonment context, which was accurate in the strictest sense, but their overall arrangement lacked the randomness Jade associated with historical excavations and more closely resembled what she would expect to find in the wake of a violent attack.

The animal bones were clustered together as one would expect to find in the den of a predatory species. For the sake of clarity, she divided the other remains into human and nonhuman hominins. The human remains were similarly gathered, while those of the nonhuman hominins reflected what one might traditionally consider abandoned, as though these individuals had simply died and no one had survived to bury them.

In many ways it reminded her of a case she'd worked in conjunction with the ATF maybe ten years ago in Brownsville, Texas. Several undercover agents had infiltrated the Gulf Cartel's arms-trafficking operation, which funneled drug money into the U.S. and weapons back into Tamaulipas through Metamoros. The ATF had received actionable intel from one of its men on the inside and had surrounded the warehouse where the weapons were stockpiled, but something had gone wrong. Agents had heard shots fired inside and attempted to penetrate the building when it suddenly caught fire. By the time they were able to enter the smoldering ruins, everyone inside had been dead for some time.

The blaze had been deliberately started by the smugglers in an attempt to cover their escape, but backfired when they found the tunnel they'd dug underneath the building had collapsed. Their remains had been found in the same room as the undercover agents they'd executed, where they'd tried to barricade themselves from the fire, which worked remarkably well and might have saved their lives had they been able to keep the smoke out. Their asphyxiated bodies had been found in similar positions to those of the nonhuman hominins, leaning against the walls where they'd been overcome by the smoke, while their victims had been heaped in the center of the room like refuse, their clothes stripped from them in a futile effort to block the vents and the gaps under the doors.

The walls had been similarly gouged and scored by the various implements the traffickers had employed in vain to hack and carve through the cinderblock walls, right down to their final, desperate attempt to claw their way to freedom with their own fingers, which Jade believed was exactly what had happened inside the temple. If she looked at the submerged scene in that light, she could see how the rubble in the doorway could have been from a barricade that collapsed with the rest of the building. That didn't explain the teeth marks in the bones, however, or the fact that they'd been broken to harvest the marrow, unless they hadn't barricaded themselves inside, but rather had been sealed inside, where they'd survived for as long as possible on the human and animal remains.

Crunching rocks announced Anya's approach. She climbed up onto the platform and plopped down beside Jade without asking her permission.

"Looks like the laser scanner worked perfectly," Anya said. "You can even see the reliefs carved into the stone."

"That's the whole point."

"You use this system for crime scenes?"

"Some."

"I would imagine that most are pretty easy for someone with your skills to read."

"Most killers aren't the brightest people. They tend to leave trails that anyone with a modicum of common sense can follow blindfolded."

Anya laughed.

"That's what we try to do in archeology, too, only the majority of the clues have been destroyed by the elements or buried by time."

"That's the difference. In my field, I can't afford to guess."

"Finding that conehead must be eating you alive then."

Jade glanced at Anya from the corner of her eye. In a way, the younger girl reminded her of herself, right down to the sarcastic quips.

"You could say that."

"The one I found in Russia was the same way. Totally out of place with her surroundings and not really buried as much as cast aside."

"Two different scenarios, I assure you."

"Maybe, maybe not." Anya drew her knees to her chest and turned around so as to better see the others where they'd gathered around the makeshift command center on the opposite side of the platform. "It was the deformed cranium that got me thinking . . . what if the conehead wasn't supposed to be there? I mean, the remains were totally unlike all of the others we recovered from the site, all of which had been formally interred."

"I found mine in a mass grave filled with hundreds of other people, none of whom should have been there."

"You're missing my point. What if the act of the burial was coincidental? What if the conehead wasn't part of the village's population, but rather separate from it?"

"Like she just wandered out of the jungle in time to get shot with all of the others? That would be some pretty lousy timing."

"Not if there was something that served to entice her."

"What could possibly entice her? The sound of gunfire? The screams of the dying?"

"Maybe the smell of all that death."

"That's one hell of a supposition."

"I found my conehead on the fringes of a village fortified against an unknown enemy and later abandoned and burned to the ground. Where did you find yours again?" Anya smirked and hopped to her feet. "It looks like there's something going on over there. Care to join me?"

Jade glanced back at the others, who encircled the laptop connected to the station. She recognized the chief engineer on the screen, the one who'd been so caught up in his work that he hadn't even acknowledged them when they walked past. Rubley, she thought. Something like that anyway.

"Give me a minute," Jade said and watched Anya cross the platform before returning to the 3-D model on her laptop. She pictured the three nonhuman hominins sitting inside the stone room with no way out and only the carcasses on the floor to sustain them as they desperately clawed at the walls. She tried to imagine what they could have done to warrant being entombed in such a ghastly manner. And she thought of a deformed girl with the scent of raw and burning meat in her nostrils sneaking from the forest in time to take a bullet. Suddenly she couldn't help but wonder if Anya was right and the presence of the humans in relation to the nonhuman hominins really was coincidental. They might as well have been animals, like the rest of the bones, if their sole purpose had been to serve as food.

Jade closed her laptop and rose to join the others. One screen played the video captured from the camera on Evans's diving helmet as he passed through a veritable statuary of monsters, which emerged from the shadows before vanishing back into them. The camera focused on Kelly as she crawled into a small orifice and Evans followed. The image shook so badly it made her stomach queasy.

"This is it," Evans said. "Right . . . here."

On the screen, he emerged from the tunnel into a larger room where details were lost to the shadows until he looked down at the ground and a green design that spiraled away from an oxidized metal column.

"What did you say was on top of the column again?" Rubley asked.

"A big silver ring. Aluminum, I think."

"Like a donut?"

"Kind of."

"Then isn't it obvious?"

"If it were, Mr. Rubley," Richards said, "we wouldn't be taking up your valuable time."

"It's a Tesla coil," Rubley said. "What you have there is one great big source of electrical energy."

"What purpose could it possibly serve?" Evans asked.

Rubley leaned closer to his webcam and smiled.

"What do you say we find out?"

31
ROCHE

"The symbol is called an Irminsul," Roche said, turning the stickpin over and over in his hands. "It's essentially a pillar with wings, not a broadsword, although I'd imagine that in this context it has a similar meaning."

"And what would that be?" Evans asked.

Roche tossed him the pin and hopped down from the platform. The rocks made clattering sounds underfoot as he walked toward the lake, from the edge of which he could see the flashes of light in the depths as the engineering crew installed a pressurized seal over the door of the pyramid that would allow them to open and close it like the diver lock-out chamber of a submarine. The flowing water of the subterranean river underneath the structure would then serve to drain the lower level and restore a state of equilibrium. From there they could figure out not only how to make the ancient machine work, but what it was designed to do.

"It was a sacred symbol to the earliest Germanic tribes. It means 'great strength.' The Nazis later appropriated it, among other esoteric symbols, as sort of a rallying cry to the larger population. The people of the time were angry, disenfranchised. Not only had they just lost the First World War and countless fathers and brothers, their country had been broken up and its people saddled with crippling financial reparations. It was as if the whole country was in a funk, one from which it was rescued by a renewed sense of national pride. People wholeheartedly bought into something called the Völkisch movement, which promoted the idea that the German people were the descendants of a superior race of Aryans—the survivors of the sunken city of Atlantis—and were never meant to be subject to anyone, let alone the vindictive French and British. Absurd as it might sound, it was this very notion, of the descent from Atlanteans, that created the conditions that gave rise to the Nazi party."

"That's the dumbest thing I ever heard."

"Dumber than a society ruled by inbreeders who worshipped cats?"

"Ouch."

"My point is that there is nothing more powerful than belief, especially in a climate where people were basically willing to subscribe to any theory that placed them above their circumstances, but faith could only be stretched so far before people demanded an element of proof, which was exactly why Hitler commissioned Heinrich Himmler to form the scientific arm of the Nazi Party, the Ahnenerbe, which was dedicated to researching the archeological and historical roots of the Aryan race."

"The blond-haired, blue-eyed survivors of Atlantis?"

"That's something of a bastardization perpetuated by Western propaganda, but it makes a whole lot more sense than the truth, which is that they truly believed the Atlanteans fled their sinking continent into the Himalayas, from which they made their way into the Nordic countries—hence the blond-haired, blue-eyed thing—before ultimately taking refuge in a place called Agartha in the center of the Hollow Earth."

"People actually bought into that nonsense?"

"You tell me. You're the one holding the lapel pin of an officer in the Ahnenerbe."

Evans stared down at the pin for several seconds before he spoke.

"You're so full of crap."

"The Nazis set out to find the lost city of Atlantis, and here you stand at the edge of a lake at the bottom of which lies the ruins of a civilization that by all rights shouldn't exist, holding the proof of their success in your hand."

"Suddenly you're an expert on the Nazis. Let me guess, they were big into the whole UFO thing, too."

"Actually, they were, but that's beside the point. My grandfather served in intelligence during World War II. He taught me that the secret to beating your enemy is destroying not his country, but his motivation. Cities can be rebuilt, societies will rise from their own ashes, as long as the defeated can stoke the fires of their hatred to fuel their ideologies. If you take away their beliefs, eliminate their cause, you rob them of their will to fight."

"Wasn't their motivation to kill all of the Jews?"

"No one even found out about the concentration camps until after Germany fell. The hatred of Jews was a symptom of a larger disease, not the cause. The Jews represented the bankers and lawyers who imposed the punitive reparations. They were of Middle Eastern origin, not Aryan. Had the Nazis been able to find incontestable proof of their Aryan heritage, even in the final days of the Reich with Russia closing from one side and the Americans from the other, they would have been able to cling to that belief and rebuild with that same sense of entitlement, comfortable in the knowledge that the world belonged to them as the descendants of the mystical Atlanteans."

"Instead, they sacrificed an entire generation for that bizarre ideology."

"Exactly, although it's rumored that in their dying days, the Nazis built a fortress in Antarctica where they could bide their time until the world was again ripe for the taking."

"Do you buy that?" Evans asked.

"Every lie has an element of truth, doesn't it?" Roche said. "They obviously found this place before we did."

"So if the Nazis were here, what happened to them?"

"That's a good question," Roche said, and walked away down the shoreline.

It was more than a good question; it was a question for which the answer was of critical importance. They'd been surrounded by all of the evidence they would have ever needed to inspire the German people to fight to the extinction of the very last man, and yet none of that proof ever made it back to the Fatherland. The only feasible explanation was that they never left the Antarctic. Or perhaps this was the origin of the Fuhrer's Convoy that mysteriously arrived in Argentina in 1945. Maybe whatever secret they discovered here was so frightening that even surrender was preferable to facing it, a secret so terrible they'd taken it to their graves with them.

Now here Roche and the others were, more than three-quarters of a century later, discovering this civilization with its otherworldly symbols and alien-looking remains as though for the first time.

The engineering crew breached the surface and loaded their welding gear back into the Zodiac, where even more equipment was stacked in watertight cases, which they commenced unloading with practiced speed.

"You ever see such a well-oiled machine?" Connor asked.

Roche had been so lost in thought that he hadn't heard the other man approach.

"Military?"

"CEC."

"Civil engineering corps. You guys really didn't spare any expense."

"You want something done right, you call an engineer. You want it done fast, you call the Navy."

"Makes sense, you being a former SEAL and all."

"You've done your homework."

"What can I say? I've always done well in school."

"So well, in fact, that the NSA plucked you right out of the DoD's pocket."

"They needed a second baseman for their softball team."

"Is that why they drafted you right after you deciphered the code the Taliban used to secretly coordinate the movement of troops?"

"Which led to the deaths of more than three hundred men, women, and children."

"And saved the lives of countless American troops."
Roche sighed.

"What do you want, Mr. Connor?"

"I just want to know what we can expect this machine to do."

"How should I know?"

"You were one of the best cryptanalysts in the business."

"And here I thought you brought me all this way because of my singing voice."

"You left the NSA to pursue the symbology of crop circles. Don't tell me that you've wasted so many years and accomplished nothing."

"Unfortunately, that's exactly what I'm telling you."

"So it's just coincidence that these crop circles happened to match the standing waves of the frequencies that unlocked the pyramid. That they just happened to stimulate the inner workings of a fifteen-thousand-year-old machine, inside of which we found a Nazi relic, all within a stone's throw of a temple where three alien-like creatures with extra chromosomes were barricaded with the bodies of their victims."

"I think you have a very vivid imagination."

"So I'm not right to be concerned?"

Roche looked away and watched the SCUBA-clad engineers unload the last of the cases from the Zodiac.

"I didn't say that," Roche finally said.

"You haven't said anything."

"What do you want from me?"

"I already told you."

"And I already told you that I don't have the slightest idea what this thing is supposed to do."

"Then maybe you're not the right person for the job, after all."

"I never claimed to be. I helped you figure out how to get inside. The way I see it, I've done my part."

"Inside that pyramid is a primitive Tesla coil designed to supply power to Lord only knows what. We need to know what to expect when we turn it on."

"What are you really asking me? If this is some sort of alien technology and we're about to trigger an invasion?"

"Is it?"

"You're out of your mind."

"Which is probably what those people down there thought before they were slaughtered and dragged into that temple to be consumed."

"That's quite a theory."

"If I'm wrong, perhaps you'd care to tell me what happened to the German forces that beat us here."

Roche glanced away. He was wondering the exact same thing.

"We're powering this thing up in a matter of hours," Connor said. "If there's anything we need to know first, you'd better figure it out."

He turned and crunched back down the shore toward where Richards had been watching their conversation from the pier.

Roche again looked out across the lake toward the tip of the pyramid and for the first time wondered if maybe, like the Germans, he was about to find the proof that he'd been seeking for so many years.

32
EVANS

The airlock had worked just as planned, and by the time they'd ridden the elevator back to the surface the water had been completely drained from the pyramid, laying bare tunnels that exposed the inner workings of the machine. Evans supervised the exploration via the camera mounted to the side of Dreger's tactical helmet. It was the drilling engineer's job to ensure the stability of the structure and make sure the inadvertent flooding hadn't compromised its integrity, which seemed highly unlikely considering its age and the fact that it was a veritable mountain of fitted granite, but they couldn't afford to take any chances.

The twin blurs Evans had seen through the hole in the sublevel were actually waterwheels built into the narrowing of a subterranean river. The flowing water caused them to turn and drive a series of cogs, which in turn rotated a ring of magnetite around a rusted iron column wound with copper wire, the same column that continued all the way up through the chambers directly overhead. According to Dreger, it was a fairly simplistic electrical generator, although one phenomenally advanced for its time. He suspected there had to be a series of capacitors elsewhere in the pyramid to store the residual charge and a means of dissipating the excess, which was undoubtedly the source of the hum they'd been monitoring since their arrival. Based on the electrical potential of the system, he speculated that whatever the primitive machine did must have been pretty spectacular.

The room with the well terminated in a blind cul-de-sac, forcing Dreger to turn around and head back toward the upper levels. He was able to walk in a crouch through the corridors, which had looked a whole lot smaller while Evans had been swimming through them. Dreger's voice echoed from the confines in such a way as to make it nearly unintelligible. He talked nonstop, presumably as a way of dissipating his own nervous energy.

"The whole concept is based upon Faraday's law of induction." His camera jerked from side to side as he spoke. "The magnetite is essentially a big, permanently charged magnet. When it spins, it creates a changing magnetic field and induces an electrical current in the copper wire, which is wound so tightly that it looks like solid metal. The voltage generated is proportional to the number of windings, meaning it not only amplifies what already has to be an impressive charge based on how fast the water's making the wheel turn, but continues to do so for three vertical stories. Now maybe it loses some of that charge to the surrounding rock. . . ."

Evans tuned out Dreger's voice and scrutinized the live feed. The way the lights reflected from the damp walls and remaining puddles caused the aperture of the camera to constantly adjust the focus, yet he could still tell that there were no hieroglyphics or writing on the walls, which suggested that while the corridor served a purpose, it wasn't meant to be seen, unlike the gallery with its elaborate statuary. That implied the upper passages were ceremonial in nature and designed to impress upon a large number of people the might of the gods. So what kind of might had this theoretical audience been gathered there to witness?

He hated the idea that he was separated from the exploration by two miles of ice, but he understood the need to proceed with caution. He'd still get his chance to study the interior in person once the engineering team confirmed the safety of both the structure and the ancient machine. Once they figured out what it did, anyway. The fact that he was looped into Dreger's feed at least made it bearable, especially considering the engineer's willingness to take direction.

". . . those specific sounds were used to create just enough energy to lower those stone slabs," Dreger said. "Or maybe I should say the precise amount of energy. I mean, really, you've got to give credit where credit is due. All of this is way ahead of its time. For all of our technological advancements, we didn't figure out how to generate hydroelectric power until the nineteenth century. It's things like this that make me think those people who believe in all of that ancient alien stuff aren't so crazy after all. Shoot, how else do you explain someplace like this?"

"You should be coming up on the vertical branch any second now," Evans said.

Dreger glanced up at the ceiling every few steps as

he watched for the mouth of the passage Evans had seen earlier.

"Don't you ever wonder how any number of people could build these pyramids to such exacting architectural standards using quarried rocks so large it would take dozens of men to lift, seat, and form to fit so perfectly?"

"All the time," Evans said.

"Do you buy into the theory that there were ancient astronauts who gave our ancestors the technology to make things like this?"

"You're joking, right?"

The shaft opened above Dreger, who craned his neck and used the light mounted to his helmet to trace the contours of the square walls. He stood to his full height and turned in a circle until he was facing directly into another corridor that angled upward and away from the descending corridor.

"There had better be a raise in my future," Dreger said. He grabbed the ledge and pulled himself up, but not before Evans caught a glimpse of the deep scratches and grooves in the stone between Dreger's hands.

"What do you see?" Evans asked.

"A whole lot of the same."

"No designs on the walls."

"They aren't as smooth as the others, like they've been deliberately left unfinished."

"Because they didn't expect anyone to see them."

"Someone must have. These grooves in the floor almost look like someone dragged or pushed something heavy through here."

"Like a sarcophagus?"

"You think this is a tomb? That would certainly explain the smell."

"What smell?"

"Like something crawled in here and died. Not recently, though. It's not like the stench you get when a mouse dies inside your wall. More like . . . I don't know. Have you ever come across an animal that's been dead for so long that all that's left is bones?"

Evans recalled crawling into the hidden, bone-filled tomb in Egypt.

"Yeah," he said. "I think I know what you mean."

Dreger's light focused on a stone barrier and constricted into a smaller and smaller circle as he neared.

"This is as far as I go," he said. "No. Wait . . . it's just a bend."

He turned to his left and entered another ascending passageway.

"What's your location?"

"I would guess this branch runs parallel to the main ascending corridor, only about twenty feet deeper. Whatever's ahead should fall in line with the iron column. Maybe where they store the capacitors."

Dreger looked down and Evans got a decent view of the nicks and scratches in the stone. The majority were linear in nature, like one would expect to see where a sarcophagus was dragged across the ground, only they were of uneven depth, which shot a big hole in the middle of his theory. The dust on the ground had an almost brownish tint.

"Is that dirt?" Evans asked.

Dreger ran his fingertips across the ground and held them in front of his face. He rubbed them together and scrutinized the discolorations.

"I don't think so. It's some kind of powder."

"Rust?"

"No. It practically disintegrates when you touch it."

Dreger continued higher until his beam limned the end of the tunnel and diffused into the darkness beyond the threshold.

"Ugh," he said. "It smells even worse up here."

Evans glanced up from the monitor and around the cafeteria, which had been converted into a command center large enough for dozens of computers and the workers monitoring every conceivable function and variable. The main screen Richards had used to deliver his introductory spiel featured the feed from a camera positioned in the uppermost chamber with the inset silver ring, where Dale Rubley, the chief engineer, directed the installation of lighting arrays and collected electromagnetic readings. Jade sat cross-legged on the pool table, swilling coffee as she continued to study the 3-D model of the temple on her laptop. Anya hovered over her, visibly making her uncomfortable.

Evans covered the microphone on his headset.

"Hey!" Jade looked impatiently in his direction. "I think you guys are going to want to see this."

Evans returned his attention to the screen as Dreger advanced into a square chamber roughly the size of a garage. His beam spotlighted the bluish-green column of oxidized copper wiring, casting its long shadow across the rear wall. He stopped and turned his head from left to right to visualize the reliefs carved into the stone. They were similar to those on the cliff, only partially concealed behind spatters of what almost looked like an ochre-based paint. The camera panned to the ceiling and the stars carved into the granite, just like the tomb in Akhetaten.

"Jesus," Evans whispered.

"What is it?" Jade asked from behind him, but the images on the screen obviated his answer.

The bodies strewn across the floor at the back of the chamber were skeletal and partially clothed in what looked like formerly white snowsuits darkened by the absorption of bodily dissolution and stuck to the ground by a crust of adipocere and amoeboid shapes of what he now recognized as dried blood.

"They can't be more than a hundred years old," Anya said. "If that."

Dreger swept the camera across the broken and disarticulated remains, tatters of clothing, and blood so old it had evaporated to powder. A torn jacket still had a patch on the shoulder: three upside-down Vs, one on top of the other.

"That's a Marine insignia," Dreger said.

"American?" Anya asked.

"They were alive when they entered that chamber," Jade said.

Evans looked back at her in time to see the color drain from her face.

"How do you know?" he asked.

"The spatter patterns on the walls are arterial, which means their hearts were still beating when they were attacked."

Dreger made a gagging sound and the camera abruptly turned toward the egress. His footsteps echoed from the speakers as he hurried back down the passage.

"What in the name of God happened down there?" Evans said.

33
FRIDEN

Friden struggled to open the door to his lab with his elbow while holding a cup of coffee in either hand and an open bag of Cheetos balanced on his iPad, the whole works perched precariously on his forearms. A ham sandwich hung from his mouth, dripping mayo down his chin. He'd barely entered the kitchen when he made the revelation that had been staring him right in the face this whole time and rushed back down to the sublevel, grabbing his lunch almost as an after-thought.

He turned around and used his shoulder to flip the light switch. Stopped dead in his tracks. The sandwich fell from his mouth and knocked over his iPad, sending cheese puffs skittering in every direction. He stared at his workstation for several seconds while his mind tried to rationalize what he was seeing.

"What in the name of all that's holy . . . ?"

Friden set his coffee on the nearest flat surface, flung the spillage from his hands, and wiped them on his lab coat. His desktop looked like someone had rummaged through it as though searching for state secrets. The light microscope was toppled on its side, the glass slide shattered. The computer monitor lay facedown on his stack of notes, the majority of which had fallen onto his chair and the floor, where they were soaked with the remainder of his overturned energy drink.

He walked to the far side of his workstation and found a mess of printouts and utensils that had been stacked on the corner now littering the floor. Several of the books had fallen from his shelf, along with the framed picture of him with Carrie Fisher and one of the actual prop wands used during the filming of the second Harry Potter movie. He caught movement from his peripheral vision and glanced up at Speedy's cage—

"Are you coming or what?"

He jumped at the sound of the voice behind him and turned to find Mariah standing in the doorway.

"Do you get some sort of sick pleasure out of doing that, Mariah?"

"The others are already in the cafeteria. They're about to start."

"I know. I was just there."

"Don't you want to watch?" She looked around his lab as though seeing it for the first time. "For Christ's sake, Max. Could you possibly be a bigger slob?"

"Funny," he said.

"Seriously. What the hell happened in here?"

"Check it out. You wouldn't believe me if I told you."

She picked her way through the mess and stood behind where he crouched in front of the cage.

"Ugh. What *is* that?"

What almost looked like a gooey spiderweb had been spun in the corner of the cage over the mouse's nest.

"I think that's my archaea."

"You're joking, right?"

"I couldn't make this kind of thing up."

"There's no way—"

"I need gloves."

Friden toppled over in his hurry to stand and plucked a pair of examination gloves from the box in his top desk drawer.

"What are you doing?"

"Lift the lid, would you?"

He snapped on his gloves and waited for her to do as he'd asked. The wire-mesh aquarium top came away with a crackling sound, tearing the fibrous strands.

"You remember how that sound triggered the growth of the fimbriae?" he asked.

"The one that ruptured the cellular membranes in the process?"

"Right, but the transformation remained stable at 528 Hertz."

He pried back some of the strands, which stuck to his fingertips. Just like spiderwebs, they had almost no substance to them whatsoever. Speedy stirred in his nest, rustling the tattered tissues.

"So what was the end result?"

"Nothing really," Friden said. "At least not until I exposed them to an electrical current."

"Why would you do that?"

"They formed a network that reminded me of the way axons connect to dendrites in the nervous system."

"So you electrocuted them?"

"It made sense at the time. I wanted to see if they functioned in the same way and were able to conduct a current. The charge must have been too high. I killed a bunch of them, but stimulated a self-preservation reflex in others that triggered asexual reproduction in the form of budding. I guess they must have just kept on multiplying."

Speedy squeaked and burrowed deeper into his nest as Friden tried to unbury him.

"I follow your logic, however flawed, but I still don't understand why you would put it in with your mouse."

"I didn't. I left it on a slide clipped to the light microscope. It got over here by itself."

"*By itself.*"

"I know how it sounds."

"I don't think you do."

"Whether or not you believe me doesn't change the fact that it did." He brushed cedar chips and nesting material from the mouse's trembling back, revealing a patch of fur matted with blood. "Jesus. Poor little guy. What happened to—?"

Speedy rose to his haunches so quickly that Friden felt the mouse's hooked teeth inside the flesh of his fingertip before he even sensed what was coming. Rich red blood dripped from the hole in his glove.

"Son of a . . . !"

He jerked his hand from the cage and ripped off his glove. His entire index finger was covered in blood. He felt himself starting to swoon.

"Just hold still," Mariah said. She plucked a Kleenex from the box on his desk, wrapped it around his finger, and secured it with a strip of clear tape. "It might be touch-and-go for a while, but I think you'll live."

"He's never bitten me before."

"There's a first time for everything."

Friden returned to the cage and used his opposite hand to expose Speedy, who'd buried himself beneath his nest once more.

"You remember how Einstein defined insanity, don't you?" she said.

"I'll be more careful this time."

Friden pulled back the layers of the nest until Speedy had nowhere else to go. The mouse curled into a ball on the glass bottom, which was thick with clotted cedar dust. There was so much blood on Speedy's fur that it was initially difficult to find its source. He gently brushed aside the damp clumps until he found the wound at the base of the mouse's skull, where tendril-like appendages almost appeared to have been sewn into its spine.

Speedy turned and snapped at him, but Friden yanked his fingers out of range in the nick of time.

"Oh my God," Mariah said.

Friden stared down at the mouse, which stood on its hind legs, its little hooked teeth and whiskers red with blood. They were about the only recognizable features left of his face. His black eyes bulged from his head to such an extent that it didn't appear possible for the lids to close over them. His ears folded outward as a consequence of the swelling in his head, which almost looked like a misshapen bubble had formed beneath the fur. He screeched and rolled his head awkwardly back on his neck and started to twitch.

"What's wrong with him?" Mariah asked.

"I don't know. What should I do?"

"You're asking me?"

"Who else would I be talking to?"

"I don't know anything about mice. It looks like it's having a seizure."

Speedy fell to his side and contorted backward until the crown of his bulbous head nearly touched his spine. The mouse's feet clawed uselessly at the glass. Its right eye bulged—

Friden turned away.

Crack.

When he looked back, Speedy lay still, a pool of blood forming below his mouth.

"He broke his own neck," Mariah said.

"Oh, Jesus."

"What did you do to him?"

"Oh, Jesus."

"Snap out of it, Max!" She took him squarely by the shoulders and turned him to face her. "What did you do to him?"

"Nothing! I told you. It was the archaea from the lake."

She released him and he staggered away from the cage. Tripped over his desk chair. Landed on the floor.

"That's not the worst of it, though," he said.

"Wonderful. Please tell me you have more good news."

"Its genome," he said. "I recognized a sequence of proteins I'd seen somewhere else."

"Where?"

"The conehead's extra chromosome."

"You're kidding right?"

"There are only so many nucleic acids. Sequences

are bound to repeat. That's the whole reason I came back to my lab instead of watching whatever's going on down in the lake."

Mariah paced back and forth, gesticulating as she spoke.

"The exposure to sound made them change form. Electricity caused them to multiply."

"What did you say they found in the pyramid?"

Mariah froze and slowly turned to look at him.

"The whole thing's one big electrical generator."

"We can't let them activate it," Friden said.

"That's what they're doing right now!"

"We have to stop them." Friden pushed himself up from the floor and stumbled toward the door. "Before it's too late."

34
RICHARDS

If sound waves were the key to unlocking the pyramid, then it stood to reason that they would also be able to turn on the generator at its core. Richards was positively dying to find out what the ancient machine did.

"Start at three hundred ninety-six hertz," Rubley said.

They'd rearranged the monitors so that everyone in the cafeteria could clearly see them from the tables, although most everyone stood or paced. The main screen showed an image of Rubley in his arc flash protective suit, which would shield him from both high voltage and heat. It seemed only fitting to Richards that Rubley looked like an astronaut in his full-body white suit and hood with the reflective face mask as he prepared to ramp up ancient technology potentially of alien origin. Richards had wanted to be inside the pyramid with the chief engineer, but Connor had reminded him of the reason he'd spent exorbitant amounts of money on experts and that he should let them do their jobs. It was his friend's polite way of letting him know that he'd only get in the way.

Each of the men wore a battery-powered headset inside the hood of his suit that allowed him to communicate directly with the other engineers inside the pyramid and Richards on the surface, where the audio channels had been routed to the monitors corresponding to their individual cameras.

A high-pitched hum burst from the speakers, followed quickly by a crackling sound.

The main screen filled with static, behind which there was a blue flash. The picture resolved just in time to show bolts of electricity shooting across the ground. Rubley hopped backward and stepped up onto a wooden stool with rubber-coated legs.

"Did you see that?" Rubley shouted. "Magnificent!"

The upper chamber looked completely different with the artificial light, which lent it the same clinical feel as the monitoring station they'd set up in the gallery with the statues, the view of which was on the leftmost screen. Two other engineers in matching arc flash suits recorded the surges in electromagnetic energy at several different points both inside and outside the pyramid. One of them spoke into the microphone inside his hood. Richards recognized the voice as belonging to Armand Scott, who supervised overnight operations. He was the taller of the two, the other being Paul Rayburn, an imposing physical specimen who had to be one of the nicest guys Richards had ever met.

"We're registering thirty-eight kilovolts at the toroid and thirty milliamps of current at the doorway."

"Toroid?" Richards asked.

"The ring in the floor."

"Anywhere else?" Rubley asked.

"Negligible readings at the other three layers of the door."

"They figured out how to use the sound waves to direct the electrical discharge from the toroid toward the desired wiring route, using it almost like a distributor. I don't even know if I could do that."

Richards's understanding of electrical systems was fairly rudimentary, but he had a good enough grasp to know that the donut-shaped top of the Tesla coil, the toroid, was releasing an absurd amount of energy in kilovolts that passed through the copper wiring in the floor and traveled some unknown distance through the stacked stones to deliver an electrical current to the mechanism that released the outermost of the four megaliths.

"Magnitude?" Rubley asked.

"Fifty hertz."

"This thing's putting out the energy of an X-ray generator. Radiation readings?"

"Four millisieverts."

"Magnetic flux density?"

"Zero point five milliGauss."

"That's the same as an overhead power line."

"The granite's doing a phenomenal job of insulating it," Rayburn said. "We're not picking up any EMFs on the surface of the structure."

Richards looked around the cafeteria. All of the others had stopped what they were doing to watch. They all wore the same expression of wonder he felt on his own face. It reminded him of the classic footage of mission control in Houston during the moon landing.

"Bump the frequency to six thirty-nine," Rubley said.

"On your mark."

Rubley glanced up at the camera, then down at the floor.

"Now."

Another humming sound caused the image to vibrate. It quickly degenerated into static through which purplish-blue lightning bolts struck.

"It's starting to heat up down here," Dreger said from the monitor on the right, which showed the cogs turning the magnet around the base of the copper-wrapped iron pillar. He thrust his face into the camera to demonstrate the beads on condensation on his mask.

"I don't like this," Kelly said.

"Negligible change in the subterranean water temperature," Scott said.

"I'm telling you, the temperature just jumped enough that I could feel it through my suit."

"We have to wait," Jade said. "We can't risk compromising the integrity of what could very well be a crime scene of some historical significance."

"It'll be fine," Richards said.

"Not if the temperature rises too much. You assured me—"

"If activating the machine were going to damage the remains," Connor said, "it would have done so the first time we turned it on."

"Who's to say it didn't?"

"Then there's nothing we can do about it now, is there?"

Richards sympathized with her position, but they'd come too far to stop now. Not when they were so close.

"Maybe we should give it a little time to cool off," Roche said.

"Talk to me, control," Rubley said.

"We have slight increases in both kilovoltage and milliamperes versus the previous frequency, both of which were channeled directly to the electromagnetic mechanism that held the second megalith."

"What's the radiation level in here?"

"Well shy of ionizing," Rayburn said.

"That's not very comforting."

"Thirty millisieverts."

"Holy crap," Roche said.

"Let's keep going," Rubley said.

"Doesn't anyone else want to know how American soldiers ended up being killed down here?" Jade asked.

"I really don't like this," Kelly said.

"I want to take a step back," Rubley said. "You said the symbol for five hundred twenty-eight Hertz was featured prominently inside the temple."

Richards glanced at Roche, who offered confirmation with a nod.

"Affirmative," he replied.

"The next tone in the sequence is seven forty-one," Scott said.

"We already know what that will do. Don't you want to take this baby out on the open road and see what she can do?" Rubley looked up into the camera as though addressing Scott through it. "You said it yourself. The readings have remained stable through two progressions. If we're right, this will probably just activate another circuit in the series, but surely such a fantastic machine wasn't simply designed to be a primitive garage door opener. Let's find out what it was designed to do."

"That's the problem, chief. We don't know what's going to happen."

"Isn't that the whole point?"

"You're standing on top of a live wire installed by cavemen, for Christ's sake."

"In full protective gear. Give me five twenty-eight."

"I want my objection on record," Scott said.

"Duly noted," Richards said into the microphone on his headset. "Does anyone else share Mr. Scott's concerns?"

"We should hold off on this frequency," Kelly said. "At least until we're able to determine what it does. Those hieroglyphics from the temple showed the standing wave at five hundred and twenty-eight hertz. You remember? The carving that looked like two men holding a donut over one of those coneheads. The whole thing was inside a big triangle. What if this pyramid was built specifically for this one tone? For all we know we could be triggering some kind of meltdown."

Richards stared at the young girl with the streaks in her hair for a long moment before speaking. He could see the fear in her eyes.

"Please proceed, Mr. Scott," he finally said.

"You're the boss," Scott said.

The sound erupted from the speakers. Static filled the screen. Bolts of lightning flashed from every direction behind it.

The screams were instantaneous.

"What's happening down there?" Richards shouted.

The center screen flickered with discharge.

On the left, sparks shot from the control equipment before bursting into flames. The men were quick to action and turned the entire gallery into a swirling white cloud with their fire extinguishers.

Dreger shouted incoherently from the monitor on the right, which was hazy with the sheer quantity of steam firing upward from the hole in the ground like a geyser.

Richards felt paralyzed as he turned from one monitor to the next to the next until the tone suddenly ceased.

All of the screens simultaneously went black.

A shattering sound emerged from the static, followed by the tinkle of broken glass and an electrical buzz.

"Mr. Rubley?" Richards said into the microphone on his headset. The only response was shouting from the other men. "Dale? Can anyone hear me?"

"We have to help them!" Roche said.

"The elevator's already down there," Connor said. "We can't recall it prematurely or they'll be stranded until it gets back down there."

"We can't just do nothing," Kelly said.

"Somebody answer me!" Richards shouted.

"This is Scott." Richards almost sobbed at the sound of the engineer's voice. "We've lost all instrumentation. Jesus. I've never seen anything like that. It was as if the entire pyramid turned into a conductor."

"Can you reach Mr. Rubley?"

"We're almost there now, but we have to be really careful. There's water everywhere. I don't think it's carrying a charge, though. Where did it come from?"

Friden and Mariah burst into the cafeteria.

"We're too late," the microbiologist said.

"Can anyone up there hear me?" Dreger said from the third monitor.

"Ron?" Mariah cried. "Oh, God. Ron!"

"Are you all right, Mr. Dreger?" Richards asked.

"Yeah. Just . . . shook up. What the hell happened?"

"We had an arc up here," Scott said. "It raced down that corridor like a freaking freight train. You should have seen—Oh, God. Dale. Somebody help me! Christ, he's not—Wait. I've got a pulse. Help me roll him over. That's it. You take his legs. I've got his torso. We need to get him out of here."

"We have to help them!" Jade shouted. She grabbed Richards by the arm and turned him around. "He's going to die if we don't—!"

In one swift move, Connor removed her hand from Richards's shoulder and pinned it behind her back, between her shoulder blades.

"Enough, enough," Richards said. "She's right. We have to do something."

Connor released Jade's wrist. She looked like she wanted to claw his eyes out, but Richards couldn't deal with that now.

"Mr. Scott," he said into the microphone. "Do you think you can get Mr. Rubley to the elevator?"

"Are you telling me we're on our own? You can't just abandon—"

"Listen carefully, Mr. Scott." Richards spoke slowly and deliberately in the calmest voice he could manage. "The elevator is already down there. If we recall it, we'll be wasting valuable time that Mr. Rubley might not have. Do you understand what I'm saying?"

"Yes."

"Then I ask you again, can you get Mr. Rubley to the elevator on your own?"

"We're going to have to, aren't we?"

"I've got an idea," Dreger said. "You guys up there? Get that medical kit ready because we're going to be coming in hot."

35
DREGER

Dreger dragged Rubley into the shallows. Collapsed. Struggled to his feet and pulled the unconscious man by the collar of his protective suit. Slipped on the rocks and fell again. Rolled over and brayed in frustration.

Scott burst from the water twenty feet out, the beam of light from his mask carving through the darkness.

Dreger unhooked his regulator and cast the heavy tank aside. He splashed back toward where Rubley lay and hauled him onto the rocky shore.

Rayburn emerged behind Scott and the two men sloshed up onto dry land.

Dreger caught his heels and went down hard on his rear end, tugging Rubley up onto his legs. His light reflected from the chief engineer's mask, which obscured his face. It was a blessing, Dreger knew, as he'd already gotten a good look at the man's burned cheeks and scorched scalp, an image he wouldn't soon forget. Even if by some miracle they managed to get him to the surface while he was still breathing, they wouldn't be able to keep him that way for very long, not without medical intervention beyond their limited means at the station. The man's skin had been burned to such a degree that it looked almost fibrous, like countless pallid strands of taffy stretched taut from his jaw to his prominent cheekbones and skeletal nose.

"Is he still alive?" Rayburn asked.

"I think . . . I think so."

Dreger slid out from underneath Rubley and doubled over to catch his breath.

"He's breathing," Scott said from where he crouched over Rubley, watching the faintest hint of breath cloud the inside of the mask before dissipating.

"Get him into the elevator," Dreger said, and took off up the shoreline as fast as he could.

The smooth stones rolled and clattered beneath him, throwing off his balance and nearly sending him sprawling. His light swung wildly in front of him and made the entire world appear to jerk from side to side. He caught a glimpse of the ice-rimed cliffs and the concrete platform at the farthest reaches of his beam and tapped into reserves he didn't know he possessed.

Everything that had happened since they activated the machine was a blur. Stumbling blindly through the darkness, falling so often he'd resorted to crawling from the sauna-like lower level up the descending corridor until he saw the wavering light from the equipment burning at the top of the ascending corridor. Waving away the smoke as he searched for the others, who he found in the gallery, carrying Rubley between them. Putting on their masks and gear and battling with the makeshift airlock he'd cobbled together using the pass-through box from the modular clean room and several feet of ductwork. Trying to swim with one arm while holding Rubley to his chest with the other. He was only now beginning to feel the blisters on his cheek where the mask had cracked and admitted the steam. The agony would be excruciating when his adrenaline waned.

He leaped up onto the platform. The lightbulbs had shattered, covering the concrete with glimmering shards of glass. The sockets spat sparks, which at least meant there was some amount of electricity flowing to them. He prayed the power surge hadn't reached the elevator's motor in the equipment room and the cranes outside the building on the surface or they wouldn't be going anywhere anytime soon. Ran into the elevator. The breaker box was built into a hinged panel in the ceiling. He grabbed the handle, pulled it down, and scanned the schematics until he found what he was looking for. Unplugged the breakers and tossed them aside.

The hydraulic brakes were mounted directly to the rails to either side of the top of the car. Cutting off the power to them was the easy part of the process. The teeth of the gears were fitted into the notches in the rails that prevented the elevator from falling, even if the flow of electricity to them ceased. He yanked open the access hatch and was halfway up onto the roof when the others clattered into the cage and slammed the grate closed behind them.

"Go!" Dreger shouted as he climbed out onto the roof.

"Are the brakes still functional?" Scott asked.

"Not for long. Just get this thing moving!"

The motor whirred and the car lurched.

Dreger grabbed onto the railing for balance as the elevator started upward into the shaft. Only one of the spotlights still worked, but it was a far cry better than nothing. He inched away from the railing until he was within reach of the safety panel. Both sides had three sets of brakes, each of which looked like a garbage disposal with a bullhorn connected to a chainsaw engine. Not only did he have to disengage them one at a time, he had to jump back and forth between the two sides in an effort to keep them even so the car didn't get wrenched from the tracks.

An alarm blared when he disengaged the first.

"I forgot to pull the breaker for the alarm!" he shouted.

"I got it!" Scott yelled from below him.

Within seconds the racket ceased and was again replaced by the roar of the wind rushing past Dreger's ears. He disengaged the first brake on the opposite side and the car noticeably accelerated. The buzzing sound of the gears grew exponentially louder.

Someone shouted something from inside the elevator, but he couldn't make out his words.

Dreger released the second brake with a thud and lunged back to the other side. The car bucked underneath him and knocked him from his feet. He fought to his hands and knees and released the matching brake on the opposite side.

The elevator accelerated and started to shake. The buzzing became deafening as the lone remaining gears tore through the slots in the rails.

More shouting from below.

"I can't hear you!" he yelled, but he could hardly hear his own voice over the tumult.

The frozen walls blew past in a blur behind the rigging, which made his light flicker like an old reel-to-reel projector. He reached for the final brake, but lost his balance when the whole car abruptly jerked sideways.

"What the hell are you doing down there? You're going to get us all killed!"

Dreger struggled to all fours, released the last brake, and felt the side of the car completely disengage from the rail. The lone remaining brake screamed and produced a cloud of sparks and smoke.

It was all he could do to hold on to the roof as he crawled toward the final brake, which radiated so much heat he wasn't sure he'd be able to get close to it, let alone touch it. He rolled onto his back. Kicked at the safety rail over and over until it snapped out of its fitting. Pried it from the opposite side. Jammed it into the hydraulic valve. Leveraged it upward with everything he had.

Steam and scalding fluid fired from the rupture and spattered the roof.

Dreger scurried away from it as the elevator completely disengaged from the rails, transferring the entirety of its weight to the cables. The car banged back and forth from the walls and the rigging as it rocketed upward.

He slithered on his belly toward the hatch as the car threatened to throw him over the side. Grabbed the edge of the opening. Pulled himself over. Fell into the elevator. A moment of weightlessness. Then impact.

He saw stars and tasted blood in the back of his throat. Tried to push himself up, but his hands slipped out from under him.

The car wobbled and clanged. Hammered the rails.

The metal floor was warm and wet with what he initially thought was oil from one of the ruptured valves, until he looked up and saw the smeared handprints all over the console and the spatters covering nearly every surface.

Dreger pushed himself up and turned to see one of the others crumpled in the corner, his cracked diving mask covered with so much blood he couldn't even tell who it was.

The bottom corner of the door beside him was bent outward and the metal links snapped as though someone had repeatedly kicked it.

He scrambled over to the man and ripped off his mask. Rayburn's eyes were wide open and his features speckled with the blood he'd coughed into his mask.

"Jesus!"

Dreger scooted away from the dead man and bumped into something solid.

Turned and found himself looking into Scott's lifeless eyes.

The elevator shuddered. Droplets of blood rained from the ceiling.

Dreger followed them upward toward the breaker box and screamed. There was something up there, clinging to the ceiling. A shadowed, inhuman form.

He dove into the corner. Slipped on the blood. By the time he knew what he was doing, he was already through the gap in the bent door and pulling himself into the slipstream.

Searing pain in his calf. He bellowed in pain and jerked his leg free. Lost his balance. Grabbed for one of the support bars on the underside. Felt the cold metal slip from his wet hands.

The earth opened beneath him as he plummeted, screaming, into the abyss.

36
KELLY

Kelly's hand was fretting like crazy and there was nothing she could do about it. Every last ounce of her concentration was devoted to slowing her breathing to keep from hyperventilating. She'd never been so terrified in her life. The thought that anyone's life could depend upon her meager training in first aid was almost more than she could bear. She'd been a lifeguard in high school, for crying out loud.

"You know what you're supposed to do," Jade said.

"I know, I know. Stop saying that. You're making me even more nervous than I already am."

"I was talking to myself," Jade said. "I haven't worked on a living patient since med school."

"Pray you get the chance," Evans said.

The banging and clanging of the machinery was so loud it was like someone taking a sledgehammer to the inside of Kelly's skull. They could barely hear each other over the racket, let alone the hum of the elevator rocketing up the shaft. Dreger had overridden the safety fail-safes that prevented the elevator car from going faster than four miles an hour and at that very moment it was speeding straight up toward them at nearly twice that speed.

The pressure-sealed door alarmed when it opened and Connor hurried into the room, trailing a breeze of mercifully cool air that felt divine against the back of Kelly's neck and the rivulets of sweat rolling down her back. It had to be a hundred degrees in there.

"We backed all of the vehicles out into the snow to clear the way like you asked," he said.

"And you raided the medical suite to set up an emergency kit in case we can't make it all the way to the library?"

Jade nervously squeezed the Ambu bag in her gloved hands, waited for it to inflate, and then squeezed it again.

"I keep telling you our 'medical suite' is a closet full of Band-Aids and gauze. I did the best I could."

Connor assumed his position opposite Evans, at the trailing end of the makeshift gurney, which was little more than a board on two serving carts from the kitchen, but they were just going to have to make it work. The plan was as simple as it was rushed. Jade would tend to Rubley while Evans and Connor pushed him as fast as they could through the garage and the Skyway and into the station, where Anya would be waiting in the library with as much water as she could microwave in so little time and every surgical implement, painkiller, and towel she could find. Dr. Bell was harvesting as much aloe as he could from his limited number of plants to treat the anticipated electrical burns. Kelly's job was to tend to the others, whose injuries were presumably minor by comparison, although Jade had prepared her for the fact that by the time these men reached the surface, they would have burned through their reserves of adrenaline and would likely already be going into shock. She had a stack of crates she could use to raise their feet above their heads and a mess of blankets to cover them, although with as hot and humid as it was in the boiler room, she figured she wouldn't need them.

Richards was in the computer lab, desperately trying to contact the outer world to arrange for emergency medical transport. Last she'd heard, though, his efforts were severely hampered by magnetic interference.

The door opened again for Roche and Mariah. Their faces were bright red and their eyebrows and bangs frosted with ice. Roche crossed the room and gave Kelly a reassuring squeeze on the shoulder.

"There's no way you could have known what would happen," he said.

She nodded for his benefit. While what he said was true in the strictest sense, the fact that she'd recognized that *something* would happen and had failed to prevent it made her culpable, if only in her own eyes.

"Ron!" Mariah shouted into a handheld transceiver.

A crackle of static blared in response. They'd lost contact with the four men who were inside the pyramid when they entered the elevator, undoubtedly as a consequence of the same electromagnetic interference that plagued Richards. All they knew with any certainty was that the men had started up the shaft in the elevator, which was streaking toward them so fast that Kelly was beginning to worry it wouldn't be able to stop in time.

The elevator console featured a monitor with two vertical lines and a red beacon that rose upward between them. The numbers beside it rapidly counted down feet beneath the surface. The floor vibrated ever so subtly. Kelly crept closer to the wire cage and stared down into the dark shaft. A faint light materialized from the depths.

"It's coming!" she shouted.

"Is everybody ready?" Jade asked. She took several deep breaths in a visible effort to calm her nerves. "How long will it take to get a helicopter up here?"

"You don't want to know," Connor said.

"They'll need to send one for you, too, if you don't answer my question."

"Assuming we're able to contact someone? Maybe eight hours. Minimum."

"Oh, God."

"We can get a plane to Troll in maybe half that time, if he's stable enough to transport, but it will take longer than that to get him there."

"You saw them," Evans said. "They nearly drowned trying to get Rubley to shore. And the way Scott described his condition when they dragged him into the elevator? I'd be surprised if he's still—"

"Don't say it," Jade said.

The ground shuddered.

Kelly made a move to look down the shaft, but Roche held her back.

"Something's wrong," he said.

"What do you mean?"

Kelly leaned around him and caught a fleeting glimpse of the light on top of the car hurtling toward her. The wires sang as the elevator bounced from side to side, hammering the support rigs. Sparks flew from the impact.

"Get back!" Roche shouted.

The friction of the wires on the pulleys produced a buzzing sound and a burning smell.

"There's no way it'll stop in time," Kelly said.

Roche pushed her away from the cage.

"Find cover!"

Kelly whirled and sprinted toward the back of the room. Scaled a massive water pipe that nearly scalded her hands. Heard the screaming sound of shearing metal.

The elevator launched from the shaft and hit the roof.

The impact tossed her against the wall. She ricocheted to the ground and cried out when her shoulder struck the concrete. Metallic debris pinged from the pipe and embedded itself in the walls.

A billowing cloud of smoke enveloped her.

Kelly coughed and tried to shield her stinging eyes. Rose from behind the pipe and looked around the room. The others moved like specters through the smoke, silhouetted by the flames rising from the shaft.

One of the cables had torn a hole through the roof, admitting a column of light and snowflakes. The influx of frigid air caused the smoke to churn and cleared a path to the elevator.

She climbed over the pipe and hopped to the ground, which was carpeted with shrapnel and all kinds of debris. Pulled her shirt up over her mouth and nose. Steam whistled from a punctured pipe.

"Ron!" Mariah screamed, over and over.

Kelly crept across the room. The outer cage lay in ruins, the posts jutting from the moorings at odd angles. Thick black smoke gushed from the motor, which spat scalding oil and lubricants like sparks from a firecracker. The cold air caught her off guard. It was like walking into a freezer that flung ice crystals at her. Through the overhead gap, she could see the arm of the crane leaning away from the building, out over the nothingness. The cable attached to it was taut. The pulleys and gears that once supported it had been shredded and the girders knocked through the siding.

The ground bucked, and Kelly stumbled toward the shaft.

Roche grabbed her arm to steady her and spoke calmly into her ear.

"I need you to do something very important for me. Do you think you can do that?"

Kelly could see the elevator maybe fifteen feet down the shaft in a snarl of bent rigging and cables. It had turned at such an angle that it looked almost like a lopsided diamond wedged between the rails. The light from the roof shined directly into her eyes, making it impossible to see how badly injured the men inside were.

A groan of metal and the car shifted. Fell another five feet.

The floor shuddered.

Kelly shrieked in surprise and stepped backward so quickly she nearly tripped over her own feet.

"Can you do that?" Roche repeated.

She nodded her head.

"Listen to me carefully. I need you to get as many people out of here as you can. Tell them to head straight back to the station. Don't stop in the garage. Just keep going and cross the Skyway."

"What about you?"

"I'll be right behind you."

She stared at him through the blowing snow and smoke.

"Don't do this," she said.

"Get going." He nudged her toward the door. "And don't look back."

"Everyone out!" Kelly shouted. She grabbed Jade by the arm and Mariah by the back of her jacket.

A rumbling sound stopped her in her tracks. The entire building shook. She staggered sideways and looked up at the hole in the roof in time to see a wall of white eclipse it as the avalanche buried the building.

"Go!"

37
ROCHE

Roche leaned out over the shaft and stared down at the elevator. One of the cables had snapped, leaving it dangling by the other, which wasn't going to be able to support its weight for very long. When it broke, there would be absolutely nothing to prevent the elevator from plummeting straight down to the bottom.

He took off his jacket, stretched it out in front of him, and jumped before he could talk himself out of it.

"What are you doing?" Evans shouted.

Roche caught the cable and nearly swung right off. The metal braids sizzled in his hands, even through the jacket, as he slid into the smoke. He was ten feet down before he finally managed to wrap his legs around it to slow his descent.

Hot water fired from a ruptured pipe, boring a hole through the ice and producing steam that mingled with the smoke. The flames took root on the roof of the car, spreading outward on the oil from the ruined motor. Lights fizzled and popped. Sparks rained down into the darkness.

"See if you can find a rope!" he shouted up at Evans.

Roche buried his face in his shoulder and attempted to get a few deep breaths without inhaling any more of the smoke, which felt like it smoldered in his lungs. He loosened his grip and slid down. Barely managed to stop with the fire licking at the soles of his boots.

"Careful," he whispered.

With as precariously as the elevator was balanced, the addition of his weight could send them all careening to their deaths. His heart was positively pounding when he eased a trembling foot onto the car and risked transferring a small portion of his weight.

The roof was slick with oil and condensation. He had to brace the outside edge of his foot against the gearbox fitted to the rails. The rack-and-pinion safety devices had been disconnected, effectively removing the teeth of the gears from the rails to allow for maximum acceleration. By doing so they'd eliminated the system of brakes and fail-safes that prevented precisely this scenario.

Roche blew out his breath and stepped all the way down onto the elevator.

Metal shrieked. The car lurched, but miraculously held.

A climbing rope whipped past his ear and struck the roof with a resounding thump. He glanced up to see Evans yanking on it, testing its connection to whatever he'd attached it to.

The railings framing the roof were slippery, but at least allowed him to grab something other than the cable. He found the hatch to the interior and swung it open. A gout of smoke billowed into his face. He turned away and coughed until he could finally steal a breath.

Thoom!

The elevator shook.

Roche nearly bellowed in frustration when he turned and saw Evans scooting toward him with the rope in his hand.

"You didn't think I was going to let you have all the fun without me, did you?"

"You're going to get us both killed!"

"How did you expect to get them up there by yourself, huh? Fly?"

Roche grimaced. Evans had a point.

"Stay right where you are," Roche said. "I'll go down there and help them up. You get them to the top."

"Sir. Yes, sir."

Roche sat down, lowered his legs through the hatch, and looked down between his feet. Sparks flickered from the control console, which he could barely see through the roiling smoke.

No one shouted for help or reached for him through the haze. They must have been overcome by the smoke, which meant that he needed to get them out of there in a hurry.

"Give me the rope," Roche said.

"What are you going to do?"

"Just give me the blasted rope!"

Evans kicked the coil toward him.

"Thank you."

Roche wrapped it around his waist and tucked it between his legs. He coiled the proximal end around one forearm, the distal end around the other, and belayed himself through the hole. He twirled as he descended into the car, using his hands as brakes.

His heels were mere feet from the slanted floor by the time he saw it. The metal was covered with what could only have been blood, which trickled down the slope toward a massive tear in the side. The metal was shredded and curled outward. The bodies of two men were wedged into the hole, their masks broken and their dry suits torn.

"Jesus," Roche said.

He fanned the smoke away from his face in an effort to get a better look, but could see little more than the shadowed forms of the men on the ground.

A crunching sound.

The elevator dropped several feet.

Roche barely hung on.

"Get out of here!" he shouted up to Evans.

"What do you see?"

"Damn it, Cade! This thing won't support our weight for very much longer!"

Evans hesitated before reluctantly starting back up the rope.

Roche slid down the other end and gingerly stepped onto the slick floor. He was unprepared for the sheer volume of blood. He had to stretch his leg to find a patch of bare metal large enough to accommodate his foot and curled his fingers into the metal mesh siding for balance. Drew them away wet and sticky with blood. From this vantage point he could clearly see it dripping from one rung to the next, all the way down to where the two men clogged the hole, the edges of which were bent outward as though something had broken through from the inside.

"What the hell happened in here?"

A spattering sound from above him.

He looked up just as water poured over the edge of the hatch and rained down upon him. It rushed past his feet and threatened to carry him away with it.

Roche scooted toward the men. The smoke was so thick he could barely see them. He worked his hand through a crack in the broken mask of the nearest man and under his jaw line. Felt for a pulse.

Nothing.

The second man was pinned underneath the first, his hand supinated on the slick floor. Roche pressed his fingers against the exposed wrist, but he didn't have a pulse, either.

Thupp!

A massive drift of snow struck the roof. Slush fell through the opening and slid down the floor toward him.

Roche crawled back to the rope, grabbed it as tightly as he could, and groaned with the effort of climbing. Braced his elbows to either side of the hatch and drew his body onto the roof. The entire building shook and nearly knocked him back into the car.

"Hurry up!" Evans shouted. He leaned over the edge of the shaft beside the rope and reached for him. "Remember what they said about these buildings breaking apart?"

The cable tore through the roof and the snow overhead, offering a glimpse of the crane falling away from the building.

The elevator abruptly rose underneath him, tearing through the rails and raising him toward Evans so fast that he barely had time to grab the rope. The cable tore straight down through the rear wall of the building and jerked the elevator sideways.

Roche pulled himself over the railing and jumped onto the side as the car tumbled upward. Wrapped the rope around his wrist. Ran straight up the car even as it grew steeper and steeper ahead of him.

Pipes ruptured below him and fired pressurized streams of scalding water in every direction. The entire world turned to steam.

Evans vanished below him as the elevator cleared the shaft and accelerated sideways toward the wall of the structure, through which Roche saw open air and recognized exactly what was about to happen.

He leaped from the elevator and careened through the air. Hit something hard. Inverted. Covered his head with his arms a split second before he hit the ground. Pushed himself up to all fours.

The elevator bounded across the concrete and struck the wall with a thunderous crash. The entire building leaned. The floor canted downward.

"Oh, no."

Roche propelled himself from the ground and into a sprint. Evans was five strides ahead of him and halfway to the door.

Metal screamed as the car tore through the wall.

The floor tilted even more.

Roche shouted and ran for everything he was worth, leaping massive pipes and dodging projectiles as everything that wasn't bolted to the structure tumbled down the rapidly steepening slope.

Evans blew through the doorway a heartbeat before Roche, who realized with a start that the pressurized door at the end of the corridor to the garage was closed.

A rush of air at his back. The ground swung outward so quickly that he hit the wall and collapsed to his knees. He scrambled for balance and lunged toward the far end of the passage.

The pressure lock disengaged, the alarm blared, and the door slid back into the wall.

Kelly stood in the doorway, screaming words Roche couldn't hear over the deafening sound of the building behind him breaking away from the mountain.

Evans dove across the threshold ahead of Roche, who watched the seal around the corridor pull away from the garage as he passed beneath it. He landed on top of Evans and hurriedly turned around.

The corridor whipped out over the nothingness and flipped away from the building, which cartwheeled down the slope and struck the ice cap with an impact that shook the entire mountain.

Roche stood and approached the open doorway, beyond which snowflakes whipped past on the gusting wind. The power station's anchors had torn through the granite on their way out, exposing jagged chunks of rock that nearly concealed the useless elevator shaft. Tangles of metal stood from the snow all the way down the hillside to where the prefabricated structure was flattened and impaled upon one of the cranes.

He pressed the button to close the hydraulic door and collapsed to his knees.

38
EVANS

The standby generator only produced enough energy to power critical functions and the emergency lighting that cast a dim red pall over the entire station. It was housed in the engineering residential wing, at the point farthest from the now-historical power station, and had suddenly become the only thing standing between them and slowly freezing to death, which meant that maintaining it was now the sole priority of the two remaining engineers, Rob Devlin and Lukas Proctor.

The other eleven of them gathered in the uppermost level of the central complex, where the skylights provided at least a hint of normalcy. Mariah had cried herself out and sat in the corner of the library, staring blankly into the room and holding a mug of tea she had yet to bring to her lips. Friden was still down in his lab, despite the situation, which left the botanist Bell to keep Mariah company, although, truth be told, he was really in no better shape than she was. Joachim Wolski, who was in charge of inventory, ordering, and laundry, was sprawled against the wall, an empty bottle of vodka cradled to his chest and nearly concealed by his long black beard. Anya was kind enough to push a cart of drinks and snacks across the foyer to them every so often, before returning to the computer lab, where she and the others did their best to remain calm while trying to figure out what to do next, which was easier said than done considering they'd just lost nearly a quarter of their number.

Evans sat on a table at the back of the room, near the door to the server room. He needed space to think. This entire scenario—from the activation of the pyramid to the loss of the power station—was overwhelming, but what troubled him most was how four men had boarded the elevator and only two of them had reached the surface, and they'd been dead on arrival. Even if what Roche said about the hole in the side of the elevator was true, that didn't explain how two full-grown men could fall out of it, whether accidentally or not, nor did it offer a hint as to how the other men had died.

He could tell Roche was thinking the exact same thing. He leaned against the doorway with his arms crossed over his chest, observing the others with almost clinical detachment. The man was an enigma. Evans's first impression had been that something wasn't quite right about him, or maybe he was just a prick, but the way he'd run toward danger instead of away from it betrayed a chink in his armor-like façade. Underneath was a man seemingly at odds with what one would expect from someone who chased flying saucers, a man with whom he now shared an unspoken bond formed by the mystery surrounding the disappearance and deaths of the engineers.

The kid with the colored streaks in her hair was never far from Roche's side, a fact for which Evans was more than a little grateful. Had Kelly not come back for them and opened that door when she did, he and Roche would have been launched out over the canyon.

Jade was up in everybody's business, as she always seemed to be arguing for no other reason than she could. She demanded to know what Richards was doing about their situation, shy of dialing through the bandwidths and pleading into the static, which placed her at odds with Connor, who didn't take kindly to any sort of assault on his employer. The truth was Richards was taking the catastrophe the hardest. He looked like it was all he could do to battle through the onset of physical shock.

"I got it!" Allen Graves said. He pumped his fist and swung in a circle in his chair.

The computer specialist couldn't have been more than twenty years old and looked like Shaggy, had Scooby-doo's best friend decided to dye his hair purple. He had a bar code tattooed on the back of his neck and reminded Evans of the kind of guy who hung out in the plush chairs at a hipster coffee shop talking about the screenplay he was going to write.

The monitors around him lit up and immediately divided into quadrants, each of which featured the view from a different security camera. While Evans had noticed cameras around the station, he never would have guessed there were so many.

"I diverted power from the emergency lighting in the garage—why you would need it when you can simply open the doors is beyond me—to the security system, which means I can access the stored data from the last twenty-four hours. Minus the last hour or whatever that the system was offline."

"Is there a camera in the elevator?" Roche asked.

"He wants to know if there's a camera in the elevator. Are you kidding? You can hardly take a dump around here without an audience."

Evans hopped down from the table and positioned himself so that he could see all of the monitors clearly.

"Bring it up," he said.

"You know a 'please' would go a long way—"

"Mr. Roche said there were two bodies in the elevator," Richards interrupted. "That means two men are still missing and could be in desperate need of our help."

Graves stared at him for a long moment, then turned and without another word brought up the elevator camera and isolated it on the center monitor. The screen filled with seamless blackness marred by the occasional ripple of static. Horizontal bands wriggled up and down as he rewound the feed, searching for the most recent image. The time stamp in the corner scrolled back past an hour, then ninety minutes. An image of the control console appeared, and beyond it, the bare metal floor and the open grate.

"There has to be more," Evans said. "Let it run."

Several seconds passed uneventfully until there was a flash of light and the feed abruptly terminated.

"Whatever happened down there knocked out the camera," Graves said. "What did you guys do, set off an EMP?"

"That's exactly what we did," Kelly said.

Graves glanced at her.

"I like your hair."

"I'd like you to do your job," Roche said.

Evans smirked.

"Are there any other cameras down there?" Jade asked.

"Yeah, but they're going to show the exact same thing. Well, not the *exact* same thing. What I mean is that none of them will show you anything beyond the ninety-three-minute mark."

"Anything with a view of the lake?" Evans asked.

"We've got a camera on the pier."

"Show me."

Graves flipped through the cameras until he found the one he wanted and blew it up on the monitor in front of him.

"I'll run it back another thirty seconds or so."

From the vantage point of the camera, Evans could see straight down the dock to where the submersible was moored. Everything appeared in shades of blue. The lake stretched out beyond it into the distance, where he could barely make out the tip of the pyramid breaking the surface.

"The cameras down there are infrared, so you won't get the color scale of the terrestrial cameras, but I talked the boss here into springing for the thermal models that increase the contrast based on temperature gradients. See how the water looks almost black? That's because it's so freaking cold. A person would show up in shades of orange and—"

A golden light erupted from the water a heartbeat before the camera went dark.

"Whoa," Graves said.

"Back it up," Jade said.

"Can you pause the footage right before it goes dark?" Evans asked.

Graves scrolled back through the recording and played it one frame at a time.

"This thing records at thirty frames per second," Graves said, "which means that each of these images represents roughly thirty-three milliseconds."

The outline of the pyramid took form beneath the water first, as though it were limned with an ethereal purple light. It brightened from orange to red to a golden hue that intensified as it neared the point until it shot straight up into the air, not as a solid beam, but as twin spirals that formed a helix. The image went black a frame later.

Evans's pulse rushed in his ears.

"What in the name of God was that?" he said.

"No wonder everything's fried," Graves said. "A discharge of that magnitude? We're lucky anything up here still works at all."

"The men were inside it when that happened," Jade said. "What did it do to them?"

"I can't tell you what it did to them," Friden said from the doorway. "But I think I figured out what it was supposed to do."

39
ANYA

"You're out of your mind," Connor said.

"Look," Friden said. "I'm only telling you what I can prove. Any inference is your own."

"You're telling me that the pyramid was designed to mutate people."

"I'm telling you that I witnessed the application of sound and electricity to cause physical changes in an unclassified species of archaea of potentially extraterrestrial origin."

"Which is a far cry from a human being."

"Let him speak," Richards said. He looked like he'd aged a decade in the last few hours, diminishing him before their very eyes.

"Thank you," Friden said.

"Tell us again about the mouse," Roche said.

"There's nothing more to say. The mutated archaea somehow got into Speedy's cage, penetrated his skin, and messed with his nervous system, which caused him to nearly fold in half."

Jade looked up from Friden's iPad.

"I've never seen anything like this."

"See? She gets it. I'm apparently not the only one here with half a brain."

"You're giving yourself too much credit," Kelly said.

"That hurt."

"May I?" Anya asked.

Jade handed her the iPad. Anya immediately recognized the genome that had been sequenced from the remains she'd unearthed in Arkaim, right down to the extra chromosome. Four of the chromosomes were highlighted, including the fifth, eighth, and eleventh, which, as she already knew, featured sections that had been inverted, if not how. For the sequences to have been flipped, there had to have been some form of direct damage to the DNA that could have been caused by anything from radiation to the lytic action of an enzyme, some process by which the helix was severed and reassembled backward, completely altering the physical expression of the gene.

It was the extra twenty-fourth chromosome—the one she had taken to calling the Delta Gene after the mathematical symbol for change—that most intrigued her, not just because of what it represented, but because of its similarity to the genome plotted beside it, labeled *Unclassified Archaea ssp*. They were nearly identical. The implications were mindboggling.

"It incorporated its DNA into that of the host," she said.

"And in the process altered three other chromosomes in ways we can't even speculate."

Anya thought about Headhunter's Hall back at the Brandt Institute in Chicago. Nearly all of the specimens had been found near ancient sites in the vicinity of pyramids, ziggurats, and other sites sacred to once-prospering civilizations. The notion that primitive people like the Egyptians, Inca, and Sumerians had such an intimate understanding of technology and physiology was as hard to swallow as the idea that they could have accidentally built a machine capable of triggering a form of spontaneous evolution. But if they hadn't built them, then who had?

Roche stepped forward and glanced at the iPad as he spoke.

"Let's take this at face value and assume that everything is as you claim."

"Which it is," Friden said.

"What would the exposure to the combination of sound and electricity have done to the men inside?"

"Theoretically? Nothing. Outside of electrocution, anyway."

"What he means to say," Jade said, "is that without this species of bacteria—"

"Archaea."

"Fine. Without this species of archaea to serve as a catalyst, nothing could have happened to them beyond the charge we witnessed pass through Rubley."

"What about the steam?" Anya asked.

"Of course," Friden said. "Archaea are able to survive temperature extremes that would kill other life-forms. If they could thrive in that lake, I have no doubt they could survive its sudden heating and vaporization."

"So these microbes were inside the pyramid—in the air with them—when these conditions aligned," Jade said.

"None of this changes the fact that our men are dead," Connor said.

"Missing," Richards said.

"You didn't see that hole," Roche said. "It almost looked like someone tore a hole through the cage. And there was so much blood . . ."

"Even if they did—for whatever asinine reason— punch a hole through the elevator," Connor said, "there's only one way to go from there, and that's down. No one can survive a fall like that."

"What about the rigging?"

"You ever try to grab a steel bar when you're flying past it at ten miles an hour? It would practically tear your arm off. Besides, what are we actually consider- ing here? That these microscopic bugs could cause some sort of physical transformation?"

"I saw it with my own eyes," Friden said.

"And it ended up killing that stupid mouse of yours. What makes you think the same thing wouldn't happen to our guys? There's the cause of all your blood, Mr. NSA."

Anya glanced at Roche in time to see a flicker of anger in his eyes.

"There's one way to know for sure," Graves said. From the tone of his voice, Anya knew exactly what he meant.

"Can you get video from the bottom of the shaft, Mr. Graves?" Richards asked.

"I can try. If you're positive that's what you want."

"The safety of these men is my responsibility. The burden of that failure is mine to bear."

Graves licked his lips, then turned to face the monitors. One of the cameras pointed directly down at the elevator platform from where it was mounted to the cage above and to the side of the opening. A crack ran diagonally across the image, distorting it almost like a poorly aligned fold in a magazine. Chunks of ice the size of boulders had fallen down the shaft and completely sealed it off, bending and tearing the metal frame in the process. The platform itself was cracked and littered with rocks and debris.

"I don't see anything," Connor said. "Can you zoom in?"

"I can't zoom, but I can magnify the image. That will ruin the resolution, though."

"Please try, Mr. Graves," Richards said.

Anya's heart broke for the old man, who reminded her of her grandfather in a way.

Graves magnified the central portion of the picture, giving it a pixilated appearance. The cracks in the concrete and the edges of the boulders became indistinct, but the blood that leaked out from beneath them was still just enough warmer than the platform to show up as a lighter shade of blue. As was the mangled hand jutting from a crevice between stones, its ring and pinkie fingers shorter than the others.

A moan from behind her.

Anya turned and saw the anguish on Mariah's face before she collapsed in the doorway, sobbing, and buried her face in her hands.

"Mariah . . ." Richards rose and made his way to her side. He knelt and placed his hand on her back. "I can't tell you how sorry I—"

She looked up at him through wild, tear-soaked eyes.

"Sorry? You're *sorry*? How long do you think it takes to fall two miles, especially when the whole way down you know you're going to die?"

"Mariah, please . . ."

He reached for her, but she slapped his hand away.

"He told you to wait. We all told you! But you didn't listen, did you? You went right ahead with it anyway. You were so hell-bent on proving aliens built this horrible machine that you never bothered to consider what they designed it to do. Didn't you spare a thought for what would happen to the men who were inside the pyramid when they turned it on? Well, I'll tell you what happened. Four men are dead. My Ron is dead. And it's all your fault. So tell me, huh? Was it worth it?"

Mariah propelled herself to her feet and was out the door before Richards could even try to stop her.

Anya looked away. She couldn't bear to see the pain on his face. Granted, she'd never understood his obsession and considered his correlation of aliens and coneheads to be a product of his imagination, but there was a part of her that had been rooting for him to be right. His belief was innocent, almost childlike in a way. He was an old man who only wanted to prove that we weren't alone in the universe, and yet four men with whom he'd lived in close quarters and shared every aspect of his life for nearly a year had paid the ultimate price.

A voice materialized from beneath the static coming from the radio.

Richards dove for it and pressed the button on the microphone.

"This is Antarctic Research Station Fifty-one. Do you copy?"

"Antarctic Research . . . Fifty-one . . . This . . . Barnett . . . state . . . nature . . . your emergency."

The voice was barely audible and cut in and out.

"We've had an accident, McMurdo. Four men are missing and presumed dead. Do you copy?"

". . . repeat . . . Station Fifty-one . . ."

"We've had an accident, McMurdo!" Richards shouted into the microphone. "Can you hear me? McMurdo?"

Anya caught movement from the corner of her eye.

She looked at the top left quadrant of the monitor on the right, but there was no sign of what she might have seen. She recognized the laundry room, the back wall of which was dominated by the standby generator.

". . . breaking up . . . I repeat . . . nature . . . emergency . . ."

"I pray you can hear me, McMurdo. This is Antarctic Research Station Fifty-one. We've had an accident!"

There it was again. This time she saw it. The picture was small and the source of the movement indistinct, but it almost looked like a shadow passed across the floor. There was a design on the generator. A long black arc, like an inverted Nike swoosh. She was certain it hadn't been there a few seconds ago.

"Hey." She pointed at the monitor as a silhouette streaked across the screen in a blur. "Did you guys see—?"

The power died with a resounding thud.

The monitors went black and the emergency lights died.

"McMurdo?" Richards shouted. "McMurdo? Do you copy?"

His voice echoed throughout the dark station.

BOOK III

Extinction is the rule. Survival is the exception.

—Carl Sagan

40
MARIAH

September 22

It had to be easily twenty below, but Mariah didn't feel it. She couldn't feel anything. She'd passed into a strange realm of numbness, where her thoughts were sluggish and her body seemed incapable of responding to even the simplest of commands.

Mariah had only known Ron Dreger for a few months, but they'd clicked immediately. Never in her life would she have thought she would fall for the kind of guy who had oil permanently trapped in his fingerprints and always smelled of grease, and yet here she was, wishing she'd made more of what little time they'd been given. They'd never even gotten around to talking about the future. Honestly, they'd been so comfortable with each other that they'd never even felt the need to discuss the present.

She pulled up her hood and wrapped her arms around her chest. The snow blew straight into her face, forcing her to duck her head into the wind as she walked away from the garage.

She'd said some horrible things to Richards, who she knew would have cut off his own arm to save Dreger, but there was no taking them back now. Not that it mattered. Nothing mattered anymore.

Visibility couldn't have been more than fifteen feet, which was more than enough to see what remained of the elevator shaft. The wreckage of the building in the valley below was lost to the storm. It barely seemed possible that this ragged cliff had ever been stable enough to support a building that large. The glacier had calved away from the edge, leaving behind bent and broken rails that bent away from the exposed shaft, which they'd sunk straight down the sheer face of the mountain in hopes that it would provide an added element of stability, for all the good it had done.

She stood as close as she dared to the edge and looked down.

The part of her that had clung to the hope that she would find Dreger climbing triumphantly up the rigging died when she realized that no one could have survived such devastation.

Mariah collapsed to her knees and started to cry, the mere act of which caused her to sob even harder. She'd always been strong, not a pathetic, blubbering mess like she was now.

She laughed out loud at her own stupidity when she had to scrape the ice from her lashes to open them.

Dreger would have had a good chuckle at her expense.

The thought of him nearly started the tears flowing again. There was nothing more for her to do out here. He was gone, and if she stayed out here much longer she would be, too.

She pushed herself up from the ground and turned around.

The windswept snow crunched underfoot as she headed back toward the open door to the garage, which materialized from the storm in a different place than she'd expected, reminding her just how easy it would be to lose her bearings. Her head wasn't right. When the helicopter arrived, she needed to be on it.

She was nearly to the door when she saw the gouges around the seams. It looked like someone had tried to use a crowbar to force it open. She would have dismissed them as a consequence of the corridor breaking away from the building had those marks not been so clearly evident surrounding the remainder of the circular seal.

Mariah ran her fingers over the deep scratches, then looked back toward the shaft. The wind had already scoured her footprints clean, leaving behind little more than elongated dimples. There was another nearly identical set of impressions leading diagonally toward her from the edge of the cliff.

"Ron?"

The wind stole the whispered word from her chapped lips.

She whirled back toward the garage. The button to activate the door was covered with pinkish smudges of what could only have been frozen blood. There were smears on the door itself, as though someone had attempted to manually shove it into the recessed wall. Was it possible . . . ?

The hand she'd seen . . . the blood . . . maybe someone else had lost their fingertips in the fall. Or maybe they were just pinned underneath the hand and she couldn't see them from the angle of the camera. If anyone could have survived, it was Ron Dreger.

Mariah entered the garage and closed the door behind her. She switched on the flashlight app on her cell phone and pointed the beam at the ground. She'd been so overcome with grief that she hadn't noticed the water on the floor, which could have melted from the bottom of someone's boot or—

She stopped and stared down at a spattered drop of blood. She knelt and dabbed it with her fingertip. The edges were dry, but the center was still damp.

"Please, God," she whispered and crossed the garage as fast as she could without losing sight of the tracks.

There were more smears of blood on the inside trim around the door to the Skyway. Now that she really thought about it, the door had already been open when she passed through the first time. From here, there was only one way to go. She ran through the glass tunnel toward the complex. Blew through the opposite door and stopped halfway up the iron stairs.

She must have missed something. If he'd come this way, he would have walked straight past her, unless he'd done so before she even left the library, in which case he would have entered through the main foyer where everyone would have seen him.

The stairwell was silent and dark.

She shined her light over the bare walls and up the stairs. The beam highlighted smears of blood on the railing. She climbed up the stairs until she reached it. There was a smudged palm print on the wall high above it.

Something tapped her shoulder.

She reached for it and felt the cool dampness.

Looked up.

The grate over the heating duct hung open, revealing a square of darkness.

Mariah glanced again at the rail. If she climbed up on it and braced her hand against the wall, she could probably—

Another droplet struck the top of her head.

She raised her eyes again to the open duct.

The darkness descended upon her before she could scream.

41
ROCHE

"What do you mean you can't just call them?" Jade said.

"We have an intercom system, but without the power . . ." Connor said, and tapped the button on the wall a dozen times to illustrate his point.

"Don't they have walkie-talkies?"

"They're just down the hall, for Christ's sake. Why would we need to send them with walkie-talkies?"

"In case something like this happened."

"We're going in circles. There's no point—"

"I'll go," Roche said. "Tell me you at least have a flashlight."

"Yeah," Graves said. "Give me a sec."

He ducked into the server room and retrieved a rechargeable flashlight from its charger. It was thin and black and so small Roche could have closed it completely inside his fist. Graves must have read his expression.

"What?" Graves asked. "If I have to use it, nine times out of ten I'm holding it in my mouth so I can use both hands."

"You know what they say about the size of a man's flashlight," Evans said from where he leaned against the wall beside Jade.

"Very funny."

"I haven't been into the engineering wing," Roche said. "Walk me through it."

"Take Mr. Wolski."

"Joachim's not getting up anytime soon," Anya said. "Will?"

"Uh-uh. I don't leave your side, and you're not going anywhere."

"Just tell me where to go," Roche said.

He was running out of patience. Something about this situation didn't feel right. Maybe he could consciously write it off as the shock of losing four men in such a horrible fashion and barely escaping with his own life, but he simply couldn't shake the feeling. It was primal, an instinct honed by millions of years of evolution and sharpened to a razor's edge by his tenure in the service.

"It's a mirror image of the wing where you're staying," Richards said. "Go downstairs and through the cafeteria. You'll enter on the upper level. Take the stairs down to the lower level. The utility room is all the way at the end of the hall."

"Someone should check on Mariah, too," Friden said.

"Are you volunteering?" Connor asked.

"I'll do it," Jade said.

Evans scoffed.

"I take it you have a problem with that?"

"Problem? Nope. I just didn't see you as the touchy-feely type."

"You don't think I can be compassionate?"

"I've only known you for a few days, but I was kind of under the impression that you'd been sent back from the future to save us from the rise of the machines."

"A robot joke. How original."

"Technically, the Terminator was an android," Graves said. "It has living tissue over a mechanical endo . . . skeleton . . ."

Jade speared him with her stare.

"I'm going to need a flashlight, too," she said.

Graves was only too happy to vanish back into the server room.

"I'll bring Mariah back with me if I see her," Roche said.

He left the bickering behind him and headed for the stairs.

"Wait up," Kelly said, and hurried to catch up with him.

"You should go back with the others."

"They fight like my parents used to. I've had enough of that for one lifetime."

"Then stay behind me."

"We're just going into the next building."

She was right and he knew it, but he couldn't suppress the irrational sensation that something was very, very wrong.

"Are you guys going downstairs?" Bell called from the library. He shed the blanket he'd wrapped around himself like a cocoon, set aside his book, and met them at the top of the spiral staircase.

Roche clicked on the tiny light and a surprisingly strong beam shot down the steps ahead of him. He hadn't noticed the ubiquitous thrum of machinery until it was gone. The stairs thumped hollowly under his weight. He could already feel the cold air beginning to radiate through the shell of the prefabricated structure and wondered how long it would be able to contain its finite supply of heat.

"I need to water my plants," Bell said. "Without electricity to the hydroponic system, I'm going to have to manually replicate the proper conditions."

"We're going to the utility room to see if we can find out what's going on with the power. We don't have time—"

"I didn't mean to imply that I needed your assistance. I have a torch in my greenhouse. I just didn't want to blunder down the stairs in the dark."

"Isn't the smoke bad for the plants?" Kelly asked. Bell stopped and stared at her curiously as she descended the final few stairs. "What?"

Bell caught up as they rounded the staircase and approached the greenhouse.

"The British call flashlights torches," Roche said.

"Why?"

"It was invented by an Englishman," Bell said.

"And what did he call it?"

"That's not the point."

Roche shined the beam onto the door of the greenhouse. Bell unlocked it with a key he wore on a chain around his neck and slipped inside. A light appeared through the glass before the door was all the way closed.

The cafeteria was eerily quiet. The equipment sat dark and lifeless on the tables. It seemed like forever since they were all gathered down here to watch Rubley turn on the machine. So much had happened in the hours since.

Their footsteps echoed ahead of them, through the short corridor, down the stairwell, and into the silent wing. A part of him had thought for sure the lights would have been on by now, but the little voice in the back of his head insisted that they wouldn't be coming back on anytime soon.

Roche and Kelly descended the stairs into the narrow, pitch-black corridor separating the rooms from the outer wall, which was already cold to the touch. There was no banging of tools or frustrated cursing from the open door at the end of the hallway.

Roche stopped and listened.

"Wha—?" Kelly started.

"Shh."

There was no sound whatsoever.

The fine hairs stood up on the back of his neck. Something was definitely not right. He could positively feel it. His instincts took over and his military training kicked in.

"Stay close to me," he whispered.

Kelly must have sensed it, too. She took hold of the back of his jacket and followed him as he inched cautiously toward a room that smelled of detergent and chemicals, beneath which he detected the faintest hint of fried wiring. He resisted the urge to call out to Devlin and Proctor, the engineers who'd been tasked with maintaining the generator, and instead moved all the way up against the wall.

The bulk of the utility room was to the left of the entryway and remained out of sight. The partially closed door concealed whatever might have been behind it.

When they reached the threshold, Roche crouched and listened for several seconds before going in low.

He took a mental snapshot. Ducked back. Scrutinized what he'd seen even as the image began to fade. There was an industrial washbasin beside a wire rack stacked with bottled cleaners. A laundry cart with canvas sides in front of a washer and dryer. An open closet door past them, in the back corner of the room. A large rectangular cabinet that had to be the standby generator dominated the rear wall.

No sign of the engineers.

Roche turned and shined the light down the corridor behind them. All of the doors were closed and the hall was empty. There was no movement whatsoever.

"You stay here," he whispered.

Before Kelly could protest, he went through the doorway, low and fast. The door ricocheted from the wall behind him as Roche swung his light from one side of the room to the other.

Nothing moved.

He rose to his full height and crept slowly into the darkness. Pushed the laundry cart out of the way. Its wheels made a sound like peeling masking tape and left behind thin red trails that led to a much larger pool on the tiled floor, above which a spatter of blood dribbled down the generator. One of the panels had been removed from the front and the inner workings exposed. Wires were torn, components unplugged, and pipes disconnected. Blood shimmered from just about every surface.

A broad smear led away from the puddle and to the open closet door, where droplets swelled from the wet handle.

"Oh, God," Kelly whispered.

"Don't come in here."

Roche couldn't afford to take his eyes off the closet. The trail led straight inside. There was no way anyone could have exited the room by way of the lone egress without leaving tracks all the way across the floor and down the hall.

A broom stood in the corner. Roche grabbed it by the handle, snapped it with a solid kick, and flipped the remainder over so he wielded it above his shoulder like a stake. Held the flashlight backhanded in his left hand. Kicked the door open. Lunged forward, prepared to strike.

There was no one in the closet. Only floor-to-ceiling shelves, their contents strewn across the ground, their edges sticky with blood. The unit at the back had fallen forward and rested against the side of the one next to it.

Plat.

Roche froze and listened. Where could the men have—?

Something warm and wet struck his cheek. He slowly raised his eyes toward the ceiling, and the open vent directly overhead.

Another drop streaked from the edge of the duct and struck the ground in front of him.

Plat.

42
JADE

Jade shined the flashlight down the upper-level corridor of the scientific residential wing. The bulb was remarkably bright, especially for its size, but did precious little to illuminate anything outside of the beam itself. She and Anya called for Mariah and opened the doors one at a time, pausing only long enough to sweep the light through each small room before moving on to the next. They checked the stalls and the showers before descending to the lower level. They were about to head down the hallway when Anya abruptly stopped.

"Did you hear that?" she asked.

"Hear what?" Jade said.

"I don't know. I can't describe it."

Jade held her breath and listened.

"I don't hear any—"

Thump.

The sound was barely audible and reminded her almost of the sound a car door made when someone leaned against it.

She turned to her right and found herself staring

down into the stairwell that led to the subterranean labs. The beam illuminated the stairs and the bare wall of the landing.

"She must have gone to her lab," Jade said.

"I should have guessed," Anya said.

The temperature dropped with every step they took. The cavern wasn't nearly as well insulated as the rest of the station, which hadn't been a problem when there was heated air circulating through the exposed ductwork, but without power the coldness of the rocks permeated through the floor and a cold breeze trickled from somewhere ahead of them, presumably where the pipes shunted the exhaust to the opposite side of the mountain.

"Mariah?" Anya called.

The geologist's door was open and there was no light inside. Jade stood in the threshold and shined her beam across the impeccable workspace. The chairs were aligned with the computer station and even from a distance she could tell that Mariah hadn't crawled underneath the desk.

"This doesn't feel right," Anya whispered.

Jade could sense it, too, but she wasn't about to lend credence to something as irrational as a feeling. The human body was conditioned to respond to any number of external stimuli in nearly identical ways. Goosebumps rippling up the back of one's arms or the hackles prickling from one's neck could just as easily be in response to the decreasing temperatures as the instinctive reaction to impending danger.

"Dreger has—had—a lab down here, too, right?" Jade asked.

"Next one on the left."

Jade led the way to another dark doorway and shined her beam onto a mess of mechanical parts. Again, there was no one inside, nor any sign that anyone had been there recently.

"It's possible what we heard was just the heating ducts responding to the sudden shift from hot to cold," Anya said.

It was a viable theory. The heat would have caused the thin aluminum panels to expand, and the sudden transition to cold would have triggered contraction, making the flexible metal buckle. And why wasn't the power back on yet?

Thump.

Jade shined her light straight down the hallway and toward the source of the sound. It had come from the open doorway at the very end of the hall.

"Dr. Peters?" Jade called. "Mariah?"

There was no echo from inside the dark room, as though the sound had simply gone in there to die.

"What's down there?" Jade asked.

"That's my lab," Anya said.

Jade walked toward the end of the hallway. She shined her light into Friden's lab, which looked like a hurricane had torn through it. For all she knew, Mariah could have been buried under the mess and she never would have known. She was about to move on when she smelled it.

She turned and swung her light toward Anya's lab.

There was no doubt in her mind what that smell was. She'd encountered it many times in the course of her work, only it was totally unexpected in this context, which made her revelation all the more terrifying.

"Oh, God," she gasped. "Mariah . . ."

Jade ran down the corridor and into a large cavern, at the center of which was a self-contained modular clean room connected to the ceiling by a series of ducts that maintained the negative pressure. The door was closed, but there was a large square opening where the pass-through box had been. The smell was definitely coming from inside of it.

Maybe she wasn't too late. The scent of freshly spilled blood was drastically different than that of older blood that had been given time to congeal and commence with the onset of decomposition. It had an almost electrical scent that was more a sensation than a smell, like the lingering taste of touching a battery to the tip of your tongue.

Jade's footsteps echoed as she ran across the room. Grabbed the handle. Threw open the door. Hurried inside and shined her light onto the blood-covered floor.

She'd expected to find Mariah bleeding out from her slit wrists. What she saw instead was infinitely worse.

The clean room was roughly the size of a semi-trailer with bare white polypropylene walls. There was a laminar flow hood beside a fume hood to her left and twin Class II biological safety hoods to her right, their glass enclosures and stainless steel surfaces freckled with crimson. The floor was sticky with blood belonging to the body heaped against a surgical storage cabinet with drawers full of sterile utensils and shelves upon which rested skulls with cranial deformations and intact bones of all shapes and sizes.

"Oh, my God," Anya gasped, and clapped her hands over her mouth.

Jade immediately went into clinical mode, emotionally distancing herself from the horrific situation, and shined her light onto the remains.

"Is this her?" Jade asked.

"I don't . . . I can't be sure. There's so much blood."

Jade crouched beside the lifeless woman, who lay on her chest, her arms pinned beneath her, facing the cabinet. The source of the blood appeared to be a gaping wound on her neck, inflicted with the kind of savagery Jade associated with predatory animals. The edges of the wound were ragged and avulsed. The sterno-cleidomastoid, omohyoid, and thyrohyoid muscles were torn and retracted to reveal the severed ends of the decedent's common carotid artery and internal jugular vein, the cricoid cartilage, and the fascia covering the cervical spine.

"Jesus," Anya whispered. "What happened to her?"

Jade carefully stepped around the remains, leaned against the wall, and shined her light into a face that left little doubt as to the identity of the victim. The geologist's cheek had been lacerated from the corner of her mouth to her ear, revealing her back molars.

"It's Mariah, isn't it?" Anya whispered.

Jade nodded.

"We need to tell the others," Anya said.

Jade ignored her and swept her light across the floor. Theirs were the only footprints. There was no blood beneath the hole where the pass-through box had been, nor was there any on the lip or dibbling down the wall, which meant that either Mariah had been killed in here—which Jade considered extremely unlikely based on the nature of the wounds and the lack of arterial spatters on the walls—or else she'd been transported here after the fact, before her body had yet to fully bleed out. If that was the case, then there was only one way she could have been deposited inside the clean room without leaving a trail.

She shined her light up at the ceiling, at the point where all of the exhaust vents from the hoods joined to form a much larger duct. Someone had punched a hole through the aluminum from the inside. Congealed droplets of blood adhered to the sharp edges.

"Where does that duct lead?" Jade asked.

"Someone killed her!" Anya cried. "Someone who's in the station with us right now!"

"Calm down. Now's not the time to panic."

"Calm down? We need to get out of here!"

Jade took her by the shoulders and looked her directly in the eyes.

"Get ahold of yourself. I need you thinking clearly. Look at the nature of the wounds. They weren't inflicted by a man. There's some kind of animal in this station, which means that causing any kind of commotion will only serve to draw it to us."

"You're on your own." Anya jerked her arm from Jade's grasp. "I'm not sticking around to find out what did this to her."

"Right now this is the only place in this entire station where we know for sure that it isn't. What we need to figure out is where it might be. So I ask you again, where does that duct lead?"

"The hoods are equipped with HEPA filters that are nearly one hundred percent efficient down to three-tenths of a micron, so they're vented right back into the system air."

"You're telling me this ductwork runs throughout the entire complex."

"I assume so."

"Then right now it could be absolutely anywhere."

Anya started to cry.

Jade steeled her jaw and tipped up the younger woman's chin so that their eyes met.

"Listen to me carefully," Jade said. "We have to stay together. We can't allow ourselves to become separated or we'll be easier to—"

Thump.

Jade froze. Her heart rate accelerated and her pulse beat so hard in her temples that the corners of her vision trembled.

Anya had been right about the sound, if not the mechanism of its production.

"It's up there," Anya whimpered.

"Shh."

Jade estimated the noise had come from somewhere outside of the clean room, but definitely within the perimeter of the cavern.

Thump.

Jade flinched and released a startled gasp. The sound was closer this time. Maybe just outside of the modular structure. Her autonomic nervous system kicked in with a surge of norepinephrine. Her muscles tensed, and her respirations accelerated.

She shined her light toward the main duct overhead just in time to see the aluminum dimple.

Thump.

Jade whirled, took Anya by the hand, and sprinted back toward the station with her light slashing through the darkness ahead of her.

43
EVANS

"The power should have been back on by now," Evans said.

The computer room had grown significantly darker in just the last few minutes as the snow started to accumulate on the skylight. It wouldn't be long before the upper level of the station was as dark as everywhere else. Graves was searching for more flashlights in the server room, but the fact that he'd been in there for so long didn't bode well. Then again, he could have just been trying to escape the growing tension among all of them.

Mariah's accusation that he was responsible for the deaths of the men in the elevator had devastated Richards, who sat with his head in his hands and only occasionally raised it high enough to check his watch. If McMurdo Station had understood the gravity of their situation before their communication was cut off, they undoubtedly would have set the wheels in motion to prepare for emergency evacuation. Connor estimated they could have a chopper overhead in as little as eight hours. Assuming the intensifying storm didn't further

complicate matters. It was always possible that Mc-
Murdo would instead elect to coordinate a response
with the Norwegians in Troll Station, but despite their
proximity, it would probably take them longer to reach
AREA 51 by ground. Of course, Evans and the others
could always drive out of there themselves. The problem was there was no telling what kind of damage the
destruction of the power station and the resulting
avalanche had done to the road, even if they could see
well enough through the blowing snow to navigate the
treacherous trail.

They'd be able to see things more clearly when the
power came back on, both literally and metaphorically.
Until then, they just needed to remain calm and prepare for every conceivable contingency.

It was the situation in the elevator that troubled
Evans the most. Four men had boarded the car—three
of them presumably in decent physical shape—and the
only two who made it all the way to the top had died
during transit. Roche hadn't seen their bodies well
enough to identify them, and the only way the other
two could have fallen through a hole that size was if
they'd done so deliberately or if they'd been pushed.
Something had happened inside that elevator, but for
the life of him, he couldn't figure out what.

"Someone should have been back by now," Friden
said. "It shouldn't have taken very long to find Mariah.
I mean, where could she possibly go?"

"I'm going down there myself," Richards said and
stood with the force of purpose.

"No, you're not." Connor stepped into his path to
the door. "You're going to stay right there."

"What could possibly happen to me?"

"Nothing as long as you do what I say."

Connor crossed his arms over his chest.

Richards gently placed his hand on Connor's fore-arm and spoke in a soft voice.

"I have to fix this, my friend. You of all people should understand how heavily all of this weighs on me."

"And you'll run off and do something rash. That's why I'm not letting you out of my sight."

"I pay you for your protection, not for your counsel. And besides, there's no imminent threat that requires your services."

"Then it's my job to protect you from yourself."

"You know me too well." The hint of a smile crossed Richards's lips. "If I'd ever had a son, I imagine he would have been just like you."

"Isn't that the sweetest thing you've ever heard?" Friden said.

"I'm still not letting you out of this room," Connor said, although it was obvious the words had an impact on him. "So please . . . sit down and try to be patient. The power will come back on any second and then we can worry about—"

Thump.

Evans hopped from his seat and turned toward the source of the sound.

"What was that?"

"Are you all right, Mr. Wolski?" Richards called.

"You could run the bulls of Pamplona through there and still not wake him," Connor said.

Thu-thupp.

Evans stepped far enough out into the room that he

could see the open doorway to the library across the foyer. Little more than the vacant row of microfiche readers were visible in the wan light.

"Joachim?" Friden called.

Thupp-thupp.

Evans walked through the doorway and into the open foyer, which was considerably colder than where they were all crammed into the computer room. There was no one on the stairs and the main entryway from the Skyway was still closed.

"Are you all right in there?" Evans asked.

He entered the library and glanced to his right, where he'd last seen the bearded man curled up with his bottle of vodka, but Wolski was gone. Books had fallen from the back wall and into a heap on the floor. Blood dripped from the shelves where they'd been. He looked from one shelf to the next until he reached the ceiling and the open duct, the edges of which were red with Wolski's blood.

"Sweet Jesus," Friden said from behind him.

Evans whirled to face him and caught a glimpse of the crimson arcs draining down the wall.

"Everyone back in the computer room," Connor said.

Evans backed slowly away from the corner of the room, where it looked like an animal had been slaughtered and hauled up into the ceiling.

"Yeah," he said. "I think that's probably a good idea."

He was barely through the doorway when he heard the thunder of footsteps on the stairs and turned to see two shadows racing straight toward him. Roche and Kelly emerged from the stairwell, breathing hard, their faces drained of color.

"The engineers are dead," Roche said. "Whoever killed them pulled them up into the ceiling."

"The same thing happened to Wolski," Evans said.

"Weren't you right here the entire time?"

"We were across the hall."

"And you didn't hear *anything*?"

"Don't talk to me like I'm stupid."

"I'm not. I'm talking to you like you're deaf." Roche peered around the corner into the library. "How does something like that happen with you mere feet away?"

"How the hell should I—?"

More footsteps. Directly below them. Moving fast.

"Out of the way," Connor said. He shoved between them and drew a pistol from the holster under his jacket. Aimed it down the spiral staircase.

Jade came around the bend at a sprint with Anya right behind her. She saw the weapon. Threw herself to the ground. Covered her head with her arms.

"Don't shoot!"

"Jesus," Connor gasped, and pointed the pistol down between his feet.

"She's dead," Anya said.

"Who is?" Friden said from the doorway to the computer room.

"Mariah," Anya said. "Her body's in the clean room."

"There's some kind of animal loose in here," Jade said. "It went for her throat and nearly decapitated her in the process."

"Something attacked the engineers in the auxiliary room, too," Roche said. "By the time we got there, all that was left of them was a trail of blood leading up to a vent in the ceiling."

"What in the name of God is happening here?" Richards asked.

"I already told you," Jade said. "There's some sort of predatory animal—"

"There aren't any animals here," Connor said.

"I beg to differ. I've seen the evidence with my own eyes. It looked like she'd been attacked by a bear."

"There isn't a single bear on this entire continent," Friden said. "This is a marine ecosystem. The largest predators are whales. The only thing that hunts on land are the seals."

"Seals can be aggressive," Kelly said.

"But they can't drag people up into the ceiling, for Christ's sake!" Evans said.

"Then what is capable of doing something like this?" Roche asked.

No one answered.

"All that matters right now is ensuring our safety," Richards said. His voice was strangely calm, and the look in his eyes distant.

"Predators in the wild don't attack prey in groups," Friden said. "They pick off the stragglers when they become separated."

"Then everyone stays together," Richards said. "No exceptions."

"Is there anywhere in the station that isn't connected to the main ductwork?" Jade asked.

"Not that I'm aware of."

"Which room is the most secure?"

"The server room," Connor said. "It's compartmentalized with its own fire walls and EMF shielding."

"We can't hide in there forever," Kelly said. "How

long will it take for someone to get here from Mc-Murdo?"

"We don't even know for sure that anyone's coming," Friden said.

"They'll come," Richards said with complete certainty.

"There's no way anyone can get here in under eight hours," Connor said.

"Then all we have to do is ride it out," Evans said.

"But if whatever's in here with us finds us first—" Anya started.

"Then I'll put a crater in its skull." Connor held up his Beretta M9 semiautomatic. "If anything so much as sticks its ugly head into that room, it won't know what hit it."

Evans liked Connor's enthusiasm, but it didn't make him feel better in the slightest. Something was terribly wrong here and they all knew it. Mankind knew no natural predator, and if Friden was right, there wasn't even one large enough to be a viable threat on this entire godforsaken iceberg, which meant that either someone was lying and this animal had already been inside the station or they'd somehow brought it in here with them from the outside. And the only place they'd been where anything could have possibly survived was the biome under the ice.

"Then we need to barricade ourselves inside," Evans said.

He brushed past Friden and Richards on his way to the server room.

"All right, kid," he said as he opened the door. "Your secret hiding spot's no longer . . ."

His words trailed off.

"What is it?" Kelly said from behind him.

"Stay back," Evans said.

The banks of servers and equipment cabinets were spattered with blood.

44
KELLY

Kelly had never seen so much blood in her life. It seemed like everything was covered with it. Not only was it hard to imagine that a single body could hold so much, it was terrifying to think that mere minutes ago the guy to whom it belonged had told her how much he liked her hair.

Evans pushed her back out of the server room and closed the door, but it was too late. She would remember the way the blood dripped from the hole in the ceiling for as long as she lived.

"The garage," Connor said. "If we can get across the Skyway before it does, we can seal off all points of entry from this mountain."

"Where's Dr. Bell?" Anya asked.

"In the greenhouse," Kelly said.

"We need to establish a defensible position while we still can," Connor said.

"We can't just leave him behind," Roche said.

"And we can't split up the group."

"Then you do what you have to do. I'm not going without him."

"I'll go with you," Evans said.

"If we break into two even groups, the numbers are still in our favor."

"Unless there's more than one of whatever's out there," Jade said.

Kelly looked at her in the dim light. Until that very moment she hadn't considered the possibility.

"There's another option," Friden said. "What if we're not dealing with an animal at all?"

"We don't have time for this," Connor said.

Friden opened his mouth as if to say something but must have thought better of it.

"I'll go downstairs with them," Kelly said.

"Do what you have to do," Connor said.

"You secure the garage," Roche said. "We'll be right behind you."

"If you're not there by the time we're done barricading the ducts—"

"We will be," Jade said.

"You should stay with the others," Evans said.

"And you should really stop trying to tell me what to do."

"I'm giving you five minutes," Connor said.

"We'll only need three," Evans said.

"Be safe," Richards said.

Roche nodded to him and ducked out into the foyer. Kelly hurried to keep up with him and glanced back to make sure Evans and Jade were right behind her. The others took off in the opposite direction and headed for the Skyway.

Their tread was uncomfortably loud on the stairs as they wound down into the darkness.

Kelly stifled a shiver and rubbed her upper arms.

Despite the fact that it was getting colder by the minute, she felt a sensation of numbness spreading from her core and realized with a start that she was dealing with the onset of shock. She couldn't afford to let it take root or she was in big trouble.

The silence on the lower level was suffocating. Her heartbeat in her own ears was deafening and each cautious step echoed like the beat of a drum. If there was something in there with them, it would hear them long before they heard it.

Roche shined the flashlight from left to right ahead of him as he passed through the cafeteria, revealing tables covered with computers and monitors. Chairs were toppled, and the coffee cart was overturned in a mess of broken glass, grounds, and sugar.

The greenhouse emerged from behind the stairs, the seams around its blackened windows highlighted by an inner glow.

Roche stopped at the door and turned around. Shined his light past them and into the cafeteria to make sure there was nothing behind them.

Evans slid back the door and pushed through the vinyl curtains, which dripped condensation down the back of Kelly's neck as she followed. The light was inside the rear chamber and did precious little to illuminate the front half. The plants in the racks to either side passed in darkness. The grate in the floor clanged with every step. Evans hit his head on one of the hanging planters and cursed.

"Dr. Bell?" Jade said from behind Kelly.

Evans paused at the door to the paleobotanist's inner sanctum. He waited for Roche to duck into the greenhouse and close the door behind him.

"I don't like this," Roche whispered. "He should have heard us by now."

"He could be lost in his work," Jade whispered.

"Or wearing headphones," Kelly whispered.

"Only one way to find out," Evans said.

He slid the door open and passed through the curtains.

Kelly hesitated before following him into the inner sanctum. She had flashes of all of the blood in the standby generator and server rooms and wanted nothing to do with carnage like that, but she cared for the prospect of distancing herself from Evans even less.

The light came from the back corner, behind a rack brimming with saplings and a stand of primitive trees. The mist was so dense it nearly smothered the source of the glow. Impenetrable shadows clung to the bean trees and the bamboo. She wanted to call out for Dr. Bell, but something prevented her from doing so.

Evans crept deeper into the foliage, brushing branches and leaves out of his face. Kelly ducked and shielded her head with her forearm, which kept her from getting slapped in the face, but did nothing to shield her from the freezing droplets. Broken glass sparkled from the floor and crunched underfoot.

She watched the light as they neared. It was obscured by the bushy branches overflowing the five-gallon buckets Bell had used as pots. She was nearly on top of it before she saw the flashlight lying on the ground, its beam shining impotently onto the side of a dirty bucket and the blood shimmering on the floor.

"Oh, God."

Kelly turned away and caught movement from the

corner of her eye. Through the ferns. Motion. Low to the ground. A shadow moving among shadows, causing the fronds to sway.

Roche shined his light at the source of the movement.

What almost looked like a giant white egg bobbed up and down behind the ferns. Bell's pallid face stared up at her from the ground below it.

The egg abruptly tipped backward and revealed the face that had been buried in Bell's neck. Roche's flashlight reflected in crimson circles from its large eyes and the blood covering its misshapen face. It opened its mouth, arched its back, and issued a hissing sound.

Kelly screamed and ran for the door.

45
RICHARDS

Richards felt as though he were trapped inside his worst nightmare. Everything he'd worked his entire life to achieve was coming down around his ears. People had died because of him. Dreger, Mariah, Graves, and Wolski, for certain. And he could only assume that Rubley, Scott, and Rayburn hadn't survived whatever happened on the elevator, either. They were as much his friends as his employees. Lord only knew how many others might join them before those who remained escaped this accursed place, yet deep down he felt a remarkable sensation of calmness accompanied by perfect mental clarity. For all the horrors transpiring around him, he couldn't have been more excited. He knew with complete certainty that his lifelong dream of proving the existence of alien life was about to come true.

How many nights had he fallen asleep in his bed envisioning how this day would come to pass? How many times had he closed his eyes as tightly as he could and held his hands over his ears to shut out the sounds of his father's drunken rages while he prayed for the lights to again appear in the sky and take him away with them? How many times had he begged for the men in the black triangle to abduct his father and destroy that awful farmhouse and the horrors contained within its walls?

The passage of time had changed his expectations, but his belief had never wavered. The idea of little green men in flying saucers was antiquated. Any extraterrestrial beings possessing such advanced technology wouldn't content themselves with merely watching a lesser species bumble its way through an evolutionary process that could only culminate in self-destruction, not when it could easily supplant it as the dominant form of life or utilize humanity to its own ends, which is exactly what he believed had happened.

The seeds of life had been planted in the toxic methane swamps of the earliest incarnation of the Earth and eventually bore fruit in the form of primates that could be bent to the will of a superior intelligence and whose evolution could be carefully monitored and controlled. The earliest men had worshiped the gods from the sky, who had instructed them in building techniques beyond their limited comprehension and utilized them to construct machines of great power for their own mysterious needs. They were the gods at whose altars the ferocious Aztecs and brilliant Egyptians knelt, the celestial deities to whom Christians and Muslims alike prayed, the omniscient beings who had made man in their image.

Only it wasn't man as he was, but rather man as he would become.

Connor led the group down the stairs. The clanging of footsteps on the iron steps was deafening in the confines. The temperature plummeted as they descended. The cold air radiated from the Skyway and hit them like an invisible force as they passed through the open doorway and into the glass tunnel.

The wall to the left was white with snow, completely concealing the view of the frozen plains and distant Troll. A drift had formed overhead in such a way that it looked like a wave preparing to break over the right side, where snowflakes blew straight away from them and into the chasm between the vertical black peaks. The tube shuddered at the behest of the howling wind. Without the heat pumping through the vents, they might as well have been outside.

Connor was several strides ahead of them and nearly halfway across the bridge when a shadow passed over him and across the ground in front of him. Richards stopped and looked up at the rounded roof. The ice had been scraped away in spots and the snow sloughed off in others.

"Wait," he whispered.

Anya blew past him on one side, Friden on the other.

A dark shape was barely visible through the accumulation above them, moving at a frightening rate of speed toward the garage on the far side. Its shadow sped across the ground in front of Connor, who finally noticed and pulled up just past the halfway mark. He reached out to both sides to prevent anyone from passing him.

"Stay where you are," Connor said.

He looked up at the shape clinging to the outside of the structure and raised his pistol.

"Everyone slowly retreat to the station."

"We can't go back," Friden said.

"We sure as hell can't go forward."

A clump of snow tumbled down the clear side of the tube before being ripped away on a screaming gale.

Whatever was up there adjusted its stance with a scratching sound that carved lines through the ice.

Connor matched the movement with his weapon.

"Is the glass bulletproof?" he asked.

"Are you serious?" Richards said.

"I have the shot, damn it. Is this thing bulletproof or not?"

"I don't know. It wasn't in the specs."

The Skyway was made from the same polymethyl methacrylate as the tunnel under the shark tank at Sea-World and guaranteed to survive anything that Mother Nature could throw at it. Of course, Mother Nature had never been known to carry a Beretta M9 that could punch a hole through the side of a house.

Another clump of snow slid down the side of the tunnel.

Anya shrieked and ran back toward Richards.

A clattering sound overhead.

Clack-clack-clack-clack.

"Stop!" Connor shouted.

Anya froze where she was and closed her eyes. Tears streamed down her cheeks.

The sound ceased. The scratches in the ice were deep enough to score the Plexiglas, but weren't wide enough for them to see any details of whatever was up there.

"Don't . . . move," Connor whispered.

The faint shadow had halved the distance between Richards and Connor, who kept it in his sights as he moved stealthily toward it. He passed underneath it and swiveled as he walked, placing himself between it and the others.

"Now slowly—*slowly*—walk back toward the station." The shape advanced, but Connor retreated just far enough to keep pace. "When I start firing, I want you to run as fast as you can. Do you understand me?"

"Yes," Friden whispered.

"Answer me, Hollis. I need to know that you're going to do what I tell you."

"Don't do this, Will."

"Do you trust me?"

"With my life."

"Then do what I say. Do you hear me?"

"Yes."

"Then start walking."

Richards knew there was no point in arguing with Connor when he'd made up his mind, especially not when Richards's position was as tenuous as it was hard to explain. He wasn't so much concerned about his own life as much as that of what he believed to be an extraterrestrial life-form on the other side of the Plexi-glas.

He walked backward, one step at a time, never once taking his eyes from the shape he could barely see through the snow and ice.

Clack.

Clack.

Clack.

It inched forward and again Connor moved with it, just fast enough to keep it above his head.

Richards felt the subtle warmth of the station behind him. He was maybe thirty feet from Connor, and the others had nearly caught up with him.

Connor turned.

The shadow started to move.

The muzzle flashed and the Beretta kicked. The bullet pitted the Plexiglas.

The report was deafening.

Connor fired again and again. The bullets punched through the weakened Plexiglas and fractured the tube into a spiderweb of cracks.

Richards saw the expressions of sheer terror on the faces of Anya and Friden as they blew past him. The ringing in his ears made it impossible to hear anything other than the repeated discharge, which sounded like it came from miles away.

Anya pulled on his arm and shouted into his ear, but he shrugged out of her grasp.

Thoom!

Thoom!

Thoom!

The glass shattered and rained shards onto Connor, who ducked and scrambled backward. Clumps of crimson snow followed, a heartbeat before the shadow fell into the Skyway. Its legs crumpled beneath it when it hit the ground.

Its skin was smooth and black, like that of a killer whale, with the exception of its bare hands and feet, which were remarkably humanoid.

Richards stepped to the side in an effort to better see it past Connor, who stood over it and aimed his pistol down at where it lay.

"Don't," Richards said. "Please."

Connor turned toward him with an expression of surprise on his face.

That was all the distraction the creature needed.

It lashed out at Connor from the ground, striking him in a black blur and lifting him from his feet.

He shouted and fired. The bullet missed and punched a hole in the glass. Cracks raced down to meet it.

Richards couldn't seem to make himself move. He felt as though his feet were stuck to the floor and the world around him moved in slow motion.

Connor used his forearm to push the creature up from on top of him and fired repeatedly into its thorax.

Geysers of blood erupted from its back and spattered the Plexiglas, which shattered all the way down the side, dropping enormous chunks of thick glass onto the combatants.

Connor leaned back and looked at Richards.

A single word formed on his lips, one Richards read more than heard.

Run.

The creature buried its face in Connor's exposed neck. He and Richards locked eyes across the distance. Richards recognized the pain and the fear he'd never seen there before, along with the certainty of the situation. His friend was going to die.

Connor continued to fire until he emptied the clip, hitting the walls and the roof.

The creature jerked its head to the side and released a spray of blood.

The trigger clicked on an empty chamber several times before Connor's arm fell limply to his side.

"Will," Richards sobbed.

The creature's head snapped up from the ruin of Connor's neck and Richards truly saw it for the first time. Its cranium was elongated and the flesh of its scalp torn. Its eyes bulged from their sockets to such a degree that its lids had to remain mostly closed to contain them. The veins had ruptured, causing a skein of blood to form on the surface, so thick it was nearly black. Its cheekbones had broken from the inside in such a way as to make them appear broader and its chin disproportionately thin.

It crouched on his old friend's body and arched its back.

Richards realized that what he'd initially mistaken for skin was actually a dry suit. It was torn straight up the back, the flaps folded over the creature's bare, bony shoulders.

Its chest swelled and blood spewed from its mouth when it issued a torrent of clicking sounds.

Richards staggered backward. Tripped over his own feet. Hit the ground on his tailbone. Kicked at the floor to propel himself away from the monster.

Despite the deformities, he recognized the face of one of the engineers who'd been inside the pyramid when they activated it. A man who, until that very moment, he believed had died in the elevator.

It was Armand Scott.

46
ROCHE

Roche shined his flashlight directly into the creature's face. It swatted at the beam as though in an effort to get it out of its eyes, which reflected the light from behind a glistening layer of blood. It made a clicking sound and scuttled back into the foliage, through which Roche could barely see the seam of torn skin across its forehead and the bare, elongated skull above it. Even with the distorted facial architecture, that was more than enough. He'd looked down through the smoke at this same man's seemingly lifeless body in the elevator before it was wrenched up through the shaft and hurled through the wall of the power station.

"Jesus," he gasped, and backed toward the doorway dividing the greenhouse.

Paul Rayburn made a guttural clicking sound and retreated into the shadows.

Roche lost sight of him, but followed the shaking branches toward the rear wall and the broken panel that was the source of the glass scattered across the floor.

He turned and sprinted through the barrier and the racks of plants.

"Go!" he shouted as he burst from the vinyl curtains and knocked the sliding door from its track.

His light struck the backs of the others as they ran, casting their long shadows across the ground into the cafeteria. The moment they rounded the stairwell they'd be out of the range of his flashlight and cut off from what little light emanated from the greenhouse.

It was the perfect place for an ambush.

Roche leaped up onto the pool table, lunged over the wreckage of the coffee cart, and grabbed Evans by the back of his jacket.

"Stop!" he said as loud as he dared.

Jade and Kelly whirled to face him, their eyes wide with fear.

A clattering sound from the far side of the stairwell.

Everyone turned toward the source and followed the progression of the sound with their eyes.

It was hard to pinpoint precisely in the darkness and with the strange acoustics of the station, but Roche's best estimate placed Rayburn somewhere in the cafeteria, near the mouth of the stairs, which was their only means of reaching the upper level. Surely by now Richards and the others were already barricading themselves inside the garage. If Connor was serious about only giving them five minutes, they were already on borrowed time.

"What was that thing?" Jade whispered.

"You mean who—" Evans started.

"Shh!" Roche whispered.

He couldn't afford to lose track of Rayburn, not after what the man had done to Dr. Bell, assuming he was still a man. The way his eyes reflected the light, his movements and mannerisms, everything about him had a feral, almost animalian quality, as though something entirely unlike him somehow inhabited his form.

A sharp scraping sound, like someone bumping into a chair and causing it to scoot across the floor.

It was farther to the right than Roche had expected. Whatever now animated Rayburn's body, which he was certain had been lifeless when last he saw it, was circling around the far side of the cafeteria in an attempt to outflank them. All he could see in his mind was Rayburn's malformed face when he looked up from where he tore the flesh from Bell's throat with his teeth. They had nothing resembling a weapon and no alternate route of climbing to the upper—

Roche grabbed Evans by the jacket and pulled him so close that when his spoke, his lips nearly touched the archeologist's ear.

"The climbing wall on the other side of the stairs. Do you remember it?"

Evans hesitated before replying.

"I think so."

"Take the others around to it and get upstairs as fast as you can."

"What about you?"

"If you don't get to the garage before they barricade the doors, it won't matter what I do."

A clattering sound.

Roche swung his light across the cafeteria, casting shadows from the equipment-covered tables. He detected a hint of movement, low to the ground, but couldn't pin it down with the beam.

"Go," he whispered.

He didn't dare look away from the light as he searched for—

A chair scooted from beneath a table with a screech.

He hit it with the light, but by then Rayburn was already gone.

The shuffling tread of the others became muffled when they rounded the back side of the spiral staircase. He heard the tap of a boot on one of the ledges and a grunt as someone transferred their weight to the wall, but he wasn't the only one.

A shadow raced in their direction, sending chairs toppling to the floor and knocking a monitor from the table with a crash.

"Hey!" Roche shouted.

The sound of his own voice startled him more than Rayburn, who skidded to a halt on the tiled floor in a crouch and cocked his head like a bird of prey.

Roche blinded him with the light and hurried to his left in an effort to position himself between Rayburn and the others, who were maybe halfway up the wall and moving at a rapid pace.

Rayburn made a clicking sound and held his hand in front of his eyes.

Roche used the opportunity to go on the offensive. If he could somehow advance another ten feet and drive Rayburn back in the process, he might be able to reach the stairs, but he needed to buy the others more time first.

Rayburn scuttled toward the serving bar.

Roche ran to intercept. He couldn't afford to let him get behind the stainless-steel island or he wouldn't be able to see him. Worse, he wouldn't be able to blind him with the flashlight, although he couldn't imagine that ploy would work for very much longer. He needed to get into a position to make his move now, while he still held anything resembling an advantage.

"What happened to you?"

Roche spoke while he moved stealthily toward the stairs. He kept his beam in Rayburn's eyes and listened for the sound of footsteps striking the floor above him.

Rayburn propelled himself toward the kitchen, but Roche anticipated the move and cut him off.

The man crouched with his thighs drawn to his chest and his palms flat on the floor between his feet. He arched his back to an inhuman degree in an effort to lower his head far enough to shield his face behind his knee and made a clicking sound that echoed throughout the cafeteria.

Roche crossed one foot over the other as he moved sideways toward the staircase.

"Let me help you."

More clicking sounds.

Rayburn lunged in the opposite direction and sought refuge behind the nearest table, where he passed behind the legs of the chairs like a tiger behind the bars of its cage. His skin was a sickly shade of pale, almost gray. The vessels in his neck stood out in stark contrast and struck like lightning bolts across his cheeks, temples, and forehead before running out from beneath the raw skin and over his exposed cranium, where it almost looked like scar tissue was beginning to form.

A thudding sound overhead as the first of them hopped down from the climbing wall.

Rayburn made a high-pitched shrieking sound and feinted deeper into the cafeteria before scurrying back toward the stairs.

Roche struggled to keep his light on him and nearly tripped over the bottom step of the spiral staircase in the process.

Another set of footsteps joined the first.

Rayburn lunged at him and lashed out with his hand. Ducked back. Tried again to dodge the beam, which reflected from his eyes like headlights from those of a deer in the middle of the highway.

"Talk to me," Roche said.

Rayburn released a rapid-fire series of clicks and Roche realized with sudden clarity that Rayburn was attempting to do just that.

Roche started up the staircase backward, one step at a time, his flashlight never wavering from the creature's bloody face. It watched him from behind its raised hand, its teeth bared.

One final thump, and the thunder of running footsteps overhead.

Roche backed into the bend in the staircase and recognized what was about to happen. As soon as he rounded the turn, he wouldn't be able to hold the creature at bay with his light, nor would he have any kind of room to maneuver in the tight spiral.

The Rayburn-creature knew it, too. It shrieked and transferred all of its weight to its hands, its legs bunched beneath it like a sprinter at the starting blocks.

Roche had only one option.

A hideous smile formed on Rayburn's face.

Roche blew out a long, slow breath and steadied his nerves. In one fluid motion, he took his eyes off the creature, turned, and sprinted up the stairs.

47
ANYA

Anya screamed and ran to Richards. Grabbed him by the back of the jacket and pulled.

"You have to help me!"

The freezing air buffeted her in the face when she looked up and saw a man only vaguely resembling Armand Scott pounce to the ground from on top of Connor. Snowflakes blew sideways past him and stuck to the walkway between them. His cranial deformity was identical to that of the remains she'd unearthed in Russia, only the physical expression of the flesh was far more terrifying than she could ever have imagined. She'd envisioned its face as being similar to that of modern man, but there was nothing remotely human about Scott's appearance. Everything about him was alien, from the grayish cast of his skin to the way he twitched and moved in lurches, as though unfamiliar with the mechanics of motion.

Fissures crackled as they raced through the Plexiglas.

The creature scuttled forward and cocked its head, first one way and then the other. Blood dribbled from its mouth when it issued a hiss that sounded like steam firing from a ruptured pipe.

Anya screamed and threw herself to her knees.

"Come on!"

She grabbed Richards underneath his arms and shouted with the effort of lifting him. He found his feet, but couldn't seem to take his eyes off the creature.

"It's magnificent," he said.

"Hurry!" Friden shouted.

The stairwell echoed with the drumroll of footsteps hitting the iron steps.

Anya looked back and saw several silhouettes bounding down the staircase toward them. She jerked Richards so hard she nearly sent him sprawling once more, but he regained his balance and stumbled backward with her. She took advantage of his newfound momentum to drag him away from the creature, which lunged forward, cutting the distance between them in half.

A scream from behind her.

She whirled to find Kelly in the opening to the Skyway, her hands clapped over her mouth. When Anya looked back, the creature was within ten feet of them and tensed to make another advance.

More popping sounds from above her. The cracks spread through the walls in her peripheral vision. Chunks of Plexiglas fell to the ground between her and the creature, which released a series of clicking sounds and retreated into the blowing snow.

A loud snap and a cable sang past to her right. The entire bridge shuddered.

"Hurry, Anya!" Friden shouted.

"There's another one behind us!" Jade screamed.

"Start barricading the stairwell," Evans shouted.

"And then what?" Jade asked. "We'll be trapped in here without light or heat or any way to signal for help."

Anya pulled Richards toward them. If she could just cross the threshold at the end of the Skyway, they could seal the creature on the other side.

Another cable snapped and the floor dropped.

Anya hit the ground on her knees and barely scrambled out of the way before Richards landed on top of her.

The walkway sloped downward toward where the creature crouched. The domed Plexiglas shattered and dropped enormous shards between them. The storm raced through the gaps, creating a moving wall of snow between them that nearly concealed the creature as it approached, low to the ground and coming up fast.

A resounding thud.

The Skyway slanted downward, so steeply that Anya started to slide. She grabbed Richards by the back of the jacket with one hand and reached for anything at all with the other.

"Hang on!" Evans shouted and dove for her. He caught her by the wrist and halted her slide.

Another cable snapped and whipped the frozen glass beside them hard enough to shatter the glass and impale her cheek with tiny fragments.

Evans groaned and pulled her up toward the doorway, the seal around which was already buckled and peeling away from the building.

"Give me a hand!" he shouted.

Friden tentatively crawled to Evans's side, grabbed Richards, and pulled hard enough on the back of his coat to pry him from Anya's grasp, lightening her burden enough that Evans could drag her up the slope and over the fractured edge.

She scurried past Evans, turned around, and helped the others pull Richards into the stairwell.

Bolts snapped and structural rings disengaged. Bits of Plexiglas cascaded down the bridge toward where the creature crawled toward them.

A chasm opened behind it. Connor's body slid through, tumbled out over the nothingness, and vanished into the storm.

"Close the door!" Anya screamed.

The creature slapped at the floor with its bare hands as the bridge grew steeper, digging its fingernails into the tiles in an effort to gain traction.

Evans pried the door from the recess until the others were able to help him drag it across the entryway.

The creature shrieked and scrambled uphill, blood dribbling from the gunshot wounds on its chest.

Ten feet.

Five.

It was nearly upon them when the Skyway broke away from the building.

The creature's eyes widened. Its nails tore from the cuticles. It screeched and flailed.

The last thing Anya saw before they sealed the door was the expression of sheer terror on its face as it plummeted into the blowing snow.

"Someone help me!" Roche shouted from the landing at the top of the staircase, where he struggled to jerk the door from its slot in the wall. "It's right behind me!"

Anya rushed for the stairs and hit them behind Kelly and Jade, who were already halfway up. She barely had the strength to climb and had to use the railing to pull herself higher. She nearly lost her balance when her hand slipped in something wet, but she managed to stumble forward and made it to the landing, where the others already had the gap down to a mere foot. A dark shape streaked straight toward the opening from the foyer on the other side, the light reflecting from its inhuman eyes.

"It's coming!" Anya screamed.

She threw herself against the face of the door and used her shoulder to help the others drive it closed with a resounding thud.

The creature struck it from the other side, hard enough to knock her backward, but she braced herself and leaned into it again.

Kelly screamed beside her as the creature hurled itself against the steel door, over and over.

Until, finally, it stopped.

Anya desperately listened for any indication of what it was doing on the other side but couldn't hear anything over the combination of their heavy breathing and whimpering.

She pictured Arkaim, with its twin fortified rings, a veritable fortress that should have been able to withstand any siege, reduced to little more than scorched rubble in the middle of a field, and the strange remains she exhumed near its outskirts. She'd made a terrible mistake in assuming that the coneheaded species represented a terminal branch in the human evolutionary tree rather than an offshoot from modern man, one facilitated by something lacking in humanity, something subhuman, the outward physical manifestation of which looked an awful lot like the alien species referred to as Grays.

Only there was nothing fictional about this being.

The creature shrieked and threw itself against the door one final time. It released a torrent of guttural clicks, then retreated into the station. The sound of its footsteps diminished until she couldn't hear anything from the other side at all.

Anya stepped back and looked at the door. Her hand had left a smear of blood on the steel. She glanced down at her palm, expecting to find a laceration, but the skin was intact.

She took Roche's flashlight from him and traced the railing down to where she'd slipped. There was blood on the rail, and even more on the wall above it, leading up to a hole in the exposed ductwork. Her heart sank when she gave voice to what they were all thinking.

"We're going to die in here."

48
FRIDEN

"**W**e can't just do nothing," Jade said.

"I activated the McMurdo Protocol," Richards said. "They'll come."

"You said yourself there's no way of knowing if they understood the nature of our emergency, let alone if they're going to send anyone."

"Trust me. They'll come."

"We won't even know for what? Another eight hours? We can't just sit here waiting for whatever that thing is to come in here after us."

"It's an alien organism," Friden said.

He stared at the hole in the duct. They'd managed to cram everything that wasn't bolted to the floor or walls into the orifice, but it didn't make him feel any better.

"You don't know that for sure," Kelly said.

"The archaea from the lake is the same species that was collected from the Vigorano meteorite, which means that whatever you want to call it, it's extraterrestrial in origin."

"You're suggesting they were able to infest and subsume the bodies of these men," Anya said.

"Duh. Haven't you been listening? Once I triggered the metamorphic process in my lab, they immediately sought out a suitable host. You should have seen what they did to poor Speedy."

"Regardless of their origin," Jade said, "no species can stimulate such rapid and dramatic physical changes."

"You saw the PCR results. Tell me I'm wrong."

"It doesn't matter what it is or where it comes from," Roche said. "All that matters now is that we find a way to get out of here in one piece."

"It matters to me," Richards said. "And deep down I know it matters to you, too. You can't spend your life in search of something only to abandon your quest when you're so close to the end."

"I study symbols. That's all."

"Symbols created by extraterrestrial life-forms."

"I don't believe that."

"Then how else do you explain them?"

"You can't just say 'must have been aliens' every time you encounter something you don't understand."

"And yet here we are."

"Whatever that thing out there is, I promise you it's not running around the English countryside leaving messages in the barley."

"But those very messages led to its creation."

"And I suppose now it's going to whip up a spaceship and go abduct some drunken rednecks."

"Don't you think a species capable of building a machine as powerful as the one inside the pyramid would have the ability to achieve flight?"

"That's not some advanced life-form," Anya said. "You saw what it did to Connor. It killed him with its teeth, for God's sake. That's not a hallmark of superior intelligence; that's a predatory instinct."

"We've found the skeletal remains of coneheads near the ruins of pretty much every major ancient civilization on every continent," Evans said. "They've been buried or entombed near pyramids of similar structure at sites sacred to people who never possibly could have come into physical contact with one another."

"None of this changes the fact that what we need to do right now is establish a defensible position without anything resembling a weapon between us," Roche said. "Or else we need to figure out how the hell to get out of here."

"The only vehicles are on the other side of that canyon," Anya said.

"There's not even a foot trail down the mountain from here," Richards said.

"Bright lights blind them," Roche said.

"Then all we have to do is restore the power—"

"Don't you think I would have done that already if I'd been able to? It looked like someone tore the guts out of the generator. Are there any more battery-powered lights?"

"If so, I wouldn't know where to start looking."

"We could always start a fire," Roche said.

"With us inside? You're out of your mind."

"We can't just do nothing," Roche said.

He paced back and forth with the flashlight, shining it all around the barren room as though hoping to magically find something they'd all somehow overlooked. The beam settled upon the outer door and he turned to face them.

"Don't even think about it," Jade said. "If you open that door, we'll lose what little heat is trapped in here with us."

"How long before it dissipates on its own?"

"Like it hasn't already," Friden said. He wrapped his arms around his chest and tried to preserve his body heat. Once it was gone, there was no way of getting it back. As it was, they could already see their breath. Further decreasing the temperature would force them to prematurely abandon the stairwell, which he had absolutely no desire to do.

"There has to be another way out of here," Evans said.

"Not without the Skyway," Richards said.

"We could belay each other down the cliff," Roche said.

"With what rope?" Kelly asked.

"We could always jump," Evans said. "If there's enough snow drifted below us, we'll just sink into it until we lose momentum."

"The wind hardens the upper layers," Richards said. "It would be like landing on concrete from this height."

Friden tuned them out and concentrated.

He and the others couldn't just sit around waiting to either be rescued or freeze to death. They didn't have a prayer of surviving the elements, which meant that sooner or later they were going to have to take their chances with the creature inside in the station. If only he'd been given a better opportunity to study the organisms that had subsumed Scott's body, he might be able to predict the creature's behavior and calculate a way around it, but so far the only trait any of the transformed beings had displayed was unrestrained aggression. Even

Speedy, who'd never once bitten him prior to being infected, had immediately demonstrated overt hostility.

Friden sensed he'd just touched upon something important and retraced his thoughts.

For the alien organisms to elicit so much unbridled rage from their hosts, they needed some sort of catalyst. The production of hormones could trigger violent behavior, but such complex interactions with the endocrine system would likely be short-lived and fade altogether when the hormones diffused into the bloodstream.

He remembered how the metamorphosed archaea had resembled the axons and dendrites that innervated the human body, from the dense matter in the brain to the narrowest peripheral nerve tracts in the digits. What if the organisms' transformation wasn't simply structural, but functional as well? Was it possible that the network they formed—which he'd already demonstrated conducted an electrical charge—could actually be used as an interface to send neural impulses directly into the host's brain?

Spores of the *Orphiocordyceps unilateralis* fungus infected ants and released chemicals that hijacked their cognitive functions and caused them to climb to a suitable location for the dispersal of the fungus' spores before dying. The horsehair worm developed inside the gut of a cricket until it was ready to emerge, then caused the cricket to drown itself so it could slither out into the water. Was it so hard to believe that this species could do the same when all of the available evidence supported that theory?

If the pyramid had been designed to accelerate the next phase in evolution, then there needed to be some sort of intermediary, something capable of altering the

DNA at a cellular level and suppressing the pain response as the body was subjected to rapid and surely agonizing physical alterations.

He remembered the wound on the back of Speedy's neck and the tendril-like appendages knitted into the mouse's bloody flesh. From there, the archaea could have gained access directly to the central nervous system itself via the spinal cord.

And then it hit him.

Neither Scott nor Rayburn had been inside the chamber with Rubley at the heart of the pyramid, which implied that neither of them had been exposed directly to the organisms, the sound, or the electrical charge, which could mean only one thing.

Somehow they'd been infected while transporting Rubley's body from the pyramid to the surface, and if Roche was right about seeing their lifeless bodies in the elevator, then they were potentially dealing with a species that not only had the ability to animate the dead, but one whose numbers could be multiplying at that very moment.

49
JADE

Jade shivered and rubbed her arms. It was as though the walls were made of paper. She'd lost feeling in her toes and the tip of her nose, which seemed to run with a will of its own. She could positively feel her lips chapping. The lack of sleep was finally catching up with her. Her eyelids grew heavier with each passing second. She would have physically held them open if she could have made her hands stop shaking long enough.

It suddenly hit her that she was on the verge of hypothermia. She had never examined it in person, but she'd read more than her fair share of case studies. She'd often wondered why the dying didn't recognize their impending demise and attempt to do something about it. Now she knew just how easy it was to simply allow her body to shut itself down, like someone walking through a house and switching off the lights, one room at a time.

She forced herself to stand and stomped her feet. It felt like there were spikes embedded in her soles.

"We can't stay here," she said through chattering teeth.

"We're safer in here than anywhere else," Roche said. He coughed into his bright red hands. "It's been an hour and nothing's so much as attempted to get in here."

"How many degrees has the temperature dropped in that hour? Just imagine how cold it will be an hour from now."

"Better cold than dead," Evans said.

"If we wait much longer, that decision will be out of our hands."

She descended the stairs to where Kelly leaned against the railing, her hood drawn over her head and her chin tucked to her chest.

"Get up and move around, honey. You can't let yourself fall asleep."

"Just for a little while."

"Don't you all get it?" Jade said. "The human body is designed to minimize the pain of dying. The symptoms of hypothermia progress from shivering and fatigue to drowsiness, loss of coordination, and lack of concern for your own health. From there, it's only a matter of time before you stop shivering, your pulse slows, and you begin to lose consciousness. If we stay here any longer, this is where we'll die."

"You're being melodramatic," Evans said.

"Is anyone else here a doctor?" Jade asked.

Nearly all of them mumbled some version of yes.

"Medical doctors, you idiots." She stamped her feet and tried to wiggle her toes. "That's what I thought. So you need to listen to me when I—"

Thump.

Jade stopped talking and looked up at the ceiling. The noise almost sounded like it originated somewhere above her head, although with the acoustics of the stairwell she couldn't be sure. When she looked back down, Anya was staring at her with a panicked expression that confirmed her suspicion. It was the same sound they'd heard in the duct above the clean room.

The others rose one by one and moved closer to each other at the top of the stairs.

Roche shined his flashlight along the silver ductwork, from one side of the room to the other. They'd decided to save the second flashlight in case the first one's battery died, but she figured under the circumstances no one would object to a little more light. She pulled it out of her jacket pocket and directed it at the barricaded vent.

Thump.

The aluminum dimpled directly above her, a mere five feet from the lone outlet.

"It's up there," Kelly whispered.

"It's probably just the metal contracting as it gets colder," Richards said.

"No," Anya said. "We heard the same thing before. In my lab. Above the clean room, where we found Mariah's body."

Thump.

The metal bowed outward in such a way that Jade was certain she could make out the impression of two knees.

"We can't stay in here," she said.

"I'm beginning to think you might be right," Evans said.

Thump.

"We need a plan," Roche whispered. "We can't just run blindly into the station."

"There are blankets in the residential wings," Kelly said. "We could barricade ourselves in one of the rooms—"

"The cavern," Richards said. "It's deep enough inside the mountain that it doesn't freeze. That's the whole reason we used it for the labs in the first place."

"That's where all of the ducts converge," Jade said. "Where we first encountered it."

"But it's not there now, is it?" Evans said

Thump.

Jade conceded his point with a worried glance at the ceiling.

"There's an entire network of natural formations back there that we haven't even begun to explore," Richards said.

"Do you really think now's the time to do so?"

"The ducts don't run back there."

"That's good enough for me," Evans said.

A scraping sound overhead, followed by a clatter.

"There's no time for debate," Roche said. "Surely we can reach the cavern faster than it can, especially if it stays inside—"

More scraping. They'd covered the vent with the AREA 51 sign from above the door and used the same nails to punch through the aluminum. One of the corners bent downward, far enough to reveal a sliver of darkness.

Jade's legs were so stiff she wasn't sure she'd be able to run.

Roche leaned into the door leading back into the station and braced his feet. Evans blew out a long breath and did the same. Jade squeezed past them and curled her fingers into the slot where the door fit into the wall.

A popping sound, followed a moment later by the *ping* of a nail striking the bare floor.

Roche shoved first and the others followed suit. The door skidded into the recessed wall with a deafening screech. The moment the gap was wide enough, Jade slipped through, leaned her back against the door, and pushed it open.

"Go!" Roche said.

Jade shined her light into the dark station and sprinted toward the spiral staircase. Her footsteps echoed from the computer room and the library. She didn't risk a glance in either direction. Her sole focus was on getting through the maze of passageways by any means necessary. Surely by now any element of surprise they might have had was lost, and the creature was frantically crawling overhead in an effort to keep up. If it hadn't dropped down from the ceiling and was already nipping at their heels.

She stumbled down the stairs, slammed into the bend, and managed to get her feet under her before she tumbled down into the cafeteria. She blew past the kitchen and ran toward the scientific wing.

Shadows passed to either side, seemingly animated by the darkness itself. She couldn't breathe, couldn't think. Her primal instincts eliminated all extraneous functions not related to her immediate survival.

The flashlight beam knifed through the dark corridors far faster than her mind could make sense of the input from her eyes. She heard the footsteps of the others behind her, but was too scared to look back to make sure theirs were the only ones. Roche's light cast her wild shadow across the floor and up the wall ahead of her. She hit the staircase and descended into the lower level of the residential wing. Raced past closed doors as her beam constricted against the wall at the end of the corridor and the blind turn leading to the stairs to the sublevel. She shouldered the wall, shined her light down the stairs, and was halfway to the bottom when she heard a sound that stopped her dead in her tracks.

Thump.

She swept her light from one side of the corridor to the other. All of the doors stood wide open, but she couldn't see into any of them from this angle.

The others thundered around the bend and nearly collided with her.

"Shh!" she whispered.

She eased down the last few stairs and stepped silently to the ground.

There was no sign of movement. No sound whatsoever.

Jade was certain she'd heard it, though. Distant, which made it hard to pinpoint its precise origin, but far closer than she would have liked.

She shined her light into Mariah's lab as she passed the doorway. Everything appeared just as it had earlier.

Thump-thump.

She whirled and swung her light deeper into the corridor, toward the source of the sound. There was no doubt in her mind that it had come from the end of the hallway, somewhere above where the modular clean room sat at the crossroads of ducts.

They were out of time.

Jade ran straight toward it, through the open door, and toward the gap between the modular structure and the cavern wall. Their lead had evaporated, and they had no idea where they were going or even if there was anyplace ahead of them in the darkness to hide.

Thump-thump-thump.

She shined her light across smooth granite walls adorned with petroglyphs as she ran, searching for any branch that might lead deeper into the mountain, and prayed Richards was right about there being an entire network of natural formations in which to hide.

50
EVANS

Thump-thump-thump.

The creature was coming in fast. Evans could practically see it scurrying through the pitch-black duct as it raced to intercept them. If it made it out of the vent before they found a suitable place to barricade themselves, they were in big trouble. He couldn't afford to let that happen.

Kelly and Anya rounded the side of the clean room ahead of him and vanished into the darkness.

Evans broke away from the others and ran straight into the clean room. If he could somehow block off the duct, maybe he could prevent it from getting in. Worst-case scenario, at least he'd be able to buy the others a little more time.

"What are you doing?" Roche shouted.

"Keep going!"

"We don't have time for this!"

"Just go already!"

Roche's light cast Evans's shadow across the dried blood on the floor and up the cabinets at the back of the room, where the inhuman skulls stared down at him from behind the glass. He hurried between the rows of workstations to either side, watching the duct-work branching from the hoods as it converged—

There. A ragged hole fringed with razor-sharp metal slivers. He needed to fix that spot in his memory before Roche ran away with his light and stranded him in darkness. If he could drag one of the units underneath the hole and somehow wedge the stainless-steel examination table on top of it, he could block off—

Thump-thump-thump.

The sound echoed from the orifice above him. It grew louder and more insistent, until it was all he could hear.

He grabbed the fume hood by the sides and jerked it away from the wall, but it didn't budge. He bellowed in frustration, spun around, and tried the same thing with the closest Class II unit. It didn't even wiggle.

Thump-thump-thump.

The cabinets!

He rushed to the back of the room and tried to get a grip, but the cabinets were fitted so tightly together that he couldn't slide his fingers between them.

"Will these things still work without electricity?" Roche asked.

Evans turned to see Roche holding what looked like a slender candlestick connected to a rubber tube. It took him a second to realize it was a Bunsen burner. Roche cranked the knob on the side of the workstation and produced a hissing sound. The smell of butane filled the room.

Thumpthumpthump.

"You're out of your mind," Evans said.

"Do you have a better idea?"

Evans thought he just might. He turned back to the cabinets, threw open the glass doors, and rummaged around until he found what he was looking for. Several rechargeable stainless-steel drills stood beside a charger filled with batteries. They reminded him of his cordless drill back home, only sleek and streamlined, like pistols with long grips. Each had a different attachment. He'd worked with them in grad school. They were bone saws. He recognized the different bits. A Stryker saw. Cranial burs. Oscillating saws and various rasps. And the one he wanted: the bone drill.

He slapped a battery into the handle like a clip into a semiautomatic. Pulled the trigger. The drill bit spun with a high-pitched whir.

Thoomthoomthoom.

The noise grew louder and more distinct. The creature couldn't have been more than ten feet away and closing fast.

Click.

Click-click.

A bluish light washed over Evans from behind.

Roche cast aside the safety lighter and dialed up the burner until it issued a flagging golden flame.

"I'll draw it to me," Roche said. "The rest is up to you."

"I've got this."

"We're only going to get one shot."

"I said I've got this."

Thoomthoomthoom.

Evans had expected it to pause long enough to survey the room below it, but it didn't even slow down. It dove headfirst through the hole and crumpled to the floor. It was on its feet a split second later.

Evans pressed himself back against the cabinet. It lowered itself to a crouch in front of him, so close Evans could have reached out and touched its misshapen skull, over which the scalp appeared to be miraculously healing. If it so much as sensed him behind it, he was in deep trouble.

"Over here!" Roche shouted and waved the flame in front of him.

The creature hissed and struck at the fire.

Roche retreated several steps and allowed the creature to advance.

"That's right. Come and get me."

Evans needed to seize his opportunity the moment it presented itself. He watched the creature's neck. The skin was raw and ragged where the organisms had entered along the spine. The wound was held together by material that almost looked like a wasp's nest. The spinous processes of the vertebrae bulged from beneath the pale gray flesh, almost as though in an effort to break through.

It arched its back and released a guttural clicking sound.

Roche feinted with the flame.

It swiped at him and nearly knocked the burner from his grasp.

"We don't have all day!" Roche shouted.

Evans steadied his hands as best he could. Summoned every last ounce of courage he possessed.

Roche swung the flame at it again, only this time the creature was faster. It swatted the burner out of his hand. It hit the ground and immediately went out,

leaving Roche to lunge for his flashlight on the countertop beside him.

It was now or never.

The creature tensed to attack.

Evans pulled the trigger.

It suddenly turned around.

Evans caught a flash of reflected light from its eyes
as he grabbed the back of its head with one hand and
drove the drill bit into the side of its throat with the
other.

Retracted it.

Drove it in again.

The second stab hit the carotid and sprayed him
across his chest, up his shoulder, and spattered the cabinets behind him.

The creature hit him squarely in the gut, hard enough
to drop him to his knees. The drill tore sideways
through its neck. Evans found himself face-to-face with
the creature, their eyes mere inches apart. Within them
he saw unfathomable darkness and sentience of such
malevolence that it chilled him to his core.

The creature smiled at the recognition. Blood burbled past its lips and dribbled down its chin.

Roche dove onto it from behind and pinned it to the
ground.

Evans drew back his legs and watched the creature
thrash in an effort to scurry out from beneath Roche
while its blood continued to pulse from its neck.

Roche struggled to hold it down until its movements
slowed and its muscles went slack. It clawed at the floor
with its left hand. The expression on its face softened.
The fire left its eyes.

Roche rolled off of the creature and onto his rear end.

"Jesus," he whispered.

Evans nudged the body with his foot.

It didn't even try to move.

"It's over," he said and buried his head in his hands.

51
ANYA

Anya had never felt such overwhelming relief in her life. She'd thought for sure that this was where she would die. They hadn't even found a way out of the cavern when they smelled butane and heard the commotion inside the clean room. The shouting had abruptly ceased and she'd feared Evans and Roche were gone. She'd been so excited when they emerged from the clean room that she ran to them and hugged them both.

That was when she saw it, lying facedown on the floor in a pool of blood. The flashlight had been left shining across the floor in such a way that it spotlighted a face that only vaguely resembled that of Paul Rayburn. For all intents and purposes, he had become something alien, and whether or not that transformation was complete would forever remain a mystery.

She hadn't known him well, but he'd been nice to her when she first arrived and had helped her set up a camera to record her work in the clean room. He'd even been so curious that he'd assisted her with taking core samples from the bones and preparing slides for analysis. He hadn't deserved what happened to him any more than he deserved what they were about to do to him. She understood Jade's rationale, but it felt like a posthumous insult inflicted upon a man who'd already endured too much.

The others had lifted him onto the stainless-steel table and rolled him onto his chest so that Jade could examine his spinal cord. She'd retracted the skin from his neck and severed the nuchal ligament to expose the spinous processes. The organisms formed a brownish aggregate that looked almost like a muscle, only with fibrous appendages that entered through the foramen between vertebral bodies, where they fused with the spinal nerves. Amber-colored spinal fluid leaked from punctures in the thecal sac where the filamentous strands passed through and merged with the spinal cord.

"It went straight for the central nervous system," Jade said. "Look at the way it integrated with the nerve fibers."

"So it's using the host's nerve tracts to conduct its own electrical commands," Evans said.

"That's my working theory."

"Which seems reasonable, but we're missing the key component."

"Which is . . . ?"

"The source of those commands," Anya answered for him. "Where's its brain?"

Jade stepped back and held up her gloved hands. She looked from Anya to Evans before settling upon Roche, who sat across the room, perched on a tall stool, silently surveying the scene.

"Hand me that cranial saw, would you?" Jade said.

"We should wait," Anya said. "Our focus needs to be on getting out of here, not—"

"Don't you want to know?"

Anya had to look away. Of course she did, but after everything they'd just been through, all she wanted to do now was curl up in a nice warm bed and sleep until the world made sense again.

"And those retractors, too," Jade said. "I'm going to need someone to provide manual traction on the scalp."

"I can't watch this," Anya said, and left before she changed her mind.

She heard the buzz of a saw behind her and hurried into the hall, where she followed the sound of voices into Friden's lab. He had both of the Bunsen burners under his hood set on low, which provided a faint bluish glow. Kelly leaned over one, rubbing her hands together for warmth.

"I'm telling you," Friden said. "We're missing something."

He paced a trail through the cluttered room, chewing on the corner of his lip.

"Missing what?" Anya asked.

"Think about it. There were four men down there in the pyramid, but only one of them was actually inside the chamber when they activated it. Now we know Dreger's body is down there at the bottom of the elevator shaft, and we've seen what happened to Scott and Rayburn, but what about Rubley?"

"You heard them on the radio. It didn't sound like any of them thought he was going to make it."

"So what then? His body became some kind of infected vessel that spread the organism to the others?"

"Sounds viable to me."

"Then where's Rubley's body? I mean, if it was nothing more than a vector, then surely it would have still been in the elevator when it reached the surface. Roche would have seen it."

"He said he didn't get a good look at the bodies. Maybe Rubley's was one of them."

"He said he saw two bodies, and we had two men attack us. Are you saying that's just coincidence?"

"What are you suggesting? That his body was dumped out of the elevator before it got to the top?"

"Maybe he climbed out on his own," Kelly said.

The firelight cast the shadows of her tapping fingers onto the wall of the hood. They were the first words she'd spoken since Anya entered the room and sounded like they'd come from far away, as though Kelly were somehow vanishing inside herself.

Friden kicked an empty can of Red Bull. It hit the wall with a clang and skittered into the corner.

Anya put her hand on Kelly's shoulder.

"Are you going to be okay?"

Kelly cut sideways through the flame with her fingers.

"Not until I'm thousands of miles away from this horrible place."

"We just have to wait a little longer, until they're able to get a helicopter up here from McMurdo."

"That's what everyone keeps saying."

"You don't believe them?"

"After everything I've seen today, I don't know what to believe anymore."

Anya gave her a squeeze and walked around Friden's desk toward his chair, which looked plush enough to swallow her whole. She had no doubt that she could fall asleep in a matter of—

She stepped on something that made a metallic scraping sound and nearly rolled her ankle. It was the lid from the poor mouse's cage, which sat on the shelf to her right. There was a mess of cedar chips and bedding material, but she didn't see Speedy.

"What did you do with him?" she asked.

"With who?" Friden said.

"With Speedy. Who else?"

"Nothing. He's still in there."

"No, he's not."

"What are you talking about? Of course, he is. Where else would he be?"

Friden nudged her aside and looked down into the cage.

"This isn't funny." He ran his fingers through the substrate, the dust from which adhered to the sticky glass above the nest in the corner. "He was here. I'm telling you, he was right here."

"I suppose he must have climbed out on his own, too," Kelly said.

Anya stifled a chill.

"Jesus," she whispered, and ran back toward her lab and the clean room, where the others had made an oval-shaped incision in the creature's cranium and removed the center like a lid to expose the brain.

"Speedy's gone!" she said.

"What do you mean, gone?" Roche asked. He hopped down from his stool and looked her squarely in the eyes.

"Friden's mouse. The one he watched die. It's gone."

"Then it must not have been as dead as he thought," Jade said.

"Speaking of gone," Evans said. "Has anyone seen Richards?"

52
RICHARDS

Richards had lost all sense of direction and had no idea where he was. Nor did he really care, because if he was right about where he was going, he likely wouldn't be coming back anyway, and he was at peace with that decision. He felt the pull of destiny, as though every decision he had made in his entire life had brought him to this singular moment in time, a moment he'd known would come to pass since he was a child. Even now, he didn't question that all-pervasive vision as he shined the flashlight through the narrow crevice in an attempt to follow the mouse, which he believed to be his own spirit animal in a way, for it had come to him and him alone.

He'd been standing outside the door to the clean room, staring at the dead body of yet another man he'd failed to protect, when he heard a scratching sound from somewhere in the darkness to his right. Dr. Liang had been so lost in thought that he didn't think she even realized she'd handed him her light, which he'd directed toward the cavern wall, eliciting a squeak and a flurry of motion across the ground.

He had felt as though he were moving through a dream as he approached the spot where he'd seen the movement and the dark stain on the bare rock. It was smeared, as though painted by a brush that was barely damp, and yet there was no mistaking what it was.

The intermittent trail led straight back to the open door of the clean room, through which light and the subdued sound of voices spilled into the cavern. He'd detected more motion from the corner of his eye and followed it deeper into the cavern, where he'd seen it again, only this time more clearly. The mouse had been hunched on the ground, licking the blood from its little front paws. It caught him looking and rose to its hind legs. A flash of reflected light from its eyes and it was gone.

Richards was by no means an expert on mice, but he knew with complete certainty that Dr. Friden's was the only mouse on the entire continent. There'd been more paperwork involved with bringing the microbiologist's pet than there had been for Dr. Friden and all of his equipment. And he certainly didn't need to be a genius to know that whatever that mouse might have been, it most assuredly wasn't dead, despite Dr. Friden's opinions on the matter. Of course, Mr. Roche had said the same thing about the men he'd seen in the elevator, and there was no way that either Mr. Scott or Mr. Rayburn could have been described as such, which meant that either two of the most intelligent men in their respective fields lacked the necessary observational skills to qualify states as intrinsically disparate as life and death, or somehow the subjects had been both dead then and alive now, a revelation that opened all sorts of possibilities when considered alongside the theory that

Dr. Friden's archaea could conduct impulses through a network resembling brain matter.

There were several openings in the far back corner of the cavern, opposite where Jade and the others had run blindly into an earthen cul-de-sac. The trail of blood led to the wall, over the lip of a ledge, and into a dark tunnel, from the depths of which he heard the faint scratching of claws. He climbed inside and crawled maybe a dozen feet before the ceiling rose enough for him to stand. His light revealed walls etched with the same kind of petroglyphs as those inside the submerged temple. He recognized men and anthropomorphic creatures, animals and beings with conical skulls. What initially looked like stylized suns shined down upon them, although based on the shape and sheer quantity that filled the sky above the pyramids and figures, he realized they weren't suns at all, but rather flying vessels that proved he'd been right all along.

The tunnel narrowed to the point that he feared he might get stuck, before opening into another domed cavern. The temperature dropped a good twenty degrees as he advanced. He felt the movement of freezing air coming from the mouth of another tunnel to his left, inside of which his light shimmered from walls coated with ice.

The mouse stood on its hind legs in the center of the chamber, where several more trails of blood converged. One entered from Richards's right, where at the farthest reaches of his beam he could see a silver duct with a hole punched through its side, which must have served as a conduit between the station and the exhaust vents. His team had run the ducts through as many of the natural recesses as they could, and only drilled when absolutely necessary so as not to compromise the structural integrity of the mountain, which, he now understood, had allowed what lurked ahead of him unlimited access to the entire station.

Speedy dropped to all fours and darted into the orifice directly across from Richards, who focused on the passage so as not to have to contemplate the fact that the blood on the ground was damp enough to ice over.

The moment he entered the tunnel, he knew. He positively knew. The smell was so vile that he had to bury his mouth and nose into the crook of his elbow. The designs on the walls passed in his peripheral vision, but he didn't dare turn to examine them for fear of taking his eyes off the flashlight beam, at the far end of which the mouse alternately appeared from and then disappeared back into the darkness.

His footsteps echoed uncomfortably in the confines. The cold faded behind him. A distant sound, like an amalgam of a click and a cough, reverberated from ahead of him.

Uhr-uhr-uhr-uhr-uhr-uh.

Richards froze.

Millions of years of inherited instincts cried out for him to turn and run, but the only voice he heard in his head was his father's when he told his old man what he'd seen in the sky above their farm. The cruel laughter had metamorphosed into the verbal abuse that had always heralded the physical pain to come. It was that voice that had motivated him to succeed in everything he did, if only out of spite, and that voice that gave him the strength to press on.

He lightened his tread and advanced slowly, cautiously. He heard that same husky, almost growling sound, but this time he didn't let it faze him.

The stench intensified until it made his eyes water. You couldn't grow up in rural Kansas without going to a slaughterhouse, which was exactly what this cavern smelled like.

Speedy stood on his hind legs in the mouth of the tunnel, beyond which was a larger space of indeterminate size.

Richards's heavy breathing and footsteps echoed from inside of it, where the awful smell became less an olfactory phenomenon than a physical one.

The mouse waited until he was nearly right on top of it before turning tail and scampering into the depths.

Richards's heart beat so hard and fast he feared he might have a heart attack right then and there, so close to realizing his lifelong dream.

He forced himself onward. Damn the consequences. If after all these years his body chose the moment of his greatest triumph to betray him, so be it. He wasn't leaving without seeing what he'd traveled so far and invested so much to find.

Uhr-uhr-uhr-uhr-uh.

The sound echoed from everywhere at once, making its origin impossible to divine.

He advanced into the darkness, shining his light from one side of the cavern to the other. The walls and ground glistened with blood, which made the tread of his boots sticky. Flowstone columns divided the chamber. He weaved through them, only peripherally aware of the designs carved into them, most of which were obscured by the accumulation of centuries of accreted minerals.

Movement ahead.

Richards shined his light through the maze of pillars, but couldn't see anything beyond open space and darkness.

Uhr-uhr-uhr-uhr-uh.

The noise came from directly ahead of him.

Richards took a deep breath. Blew it out slowly. Focused his resolve.

He strode out into the open and shined the flashlight onto his destiny.

53
KELLY

Their voices echoed throughout the passages.

"Richards!"

"Hollis!"

Kelly had spent a considerable amount of time in her youth spelunking in caves a lot like this one along the Oregon coast. She'd grown up in the same town where the movie *Goonies* was set and filmed and often drew pirate maps that would lead her to caves where she searched for the treasure of One-Eyed Willie. It was a secret she never shared with anyone as she knew how pathetic it made her sound, but it was vastly preferable to sitting at home alone or being forced to play with other kids, all of whom thought she was weird. There was even one kid who convinced her entire fifth grade class that her hand twitched because she was possessed by the devil. It was because of people like him that she prayed she would find treasure enough to move her mother and her far away from that place.

It was on one such adventure that she spotted a sea lion down by the shore. It dragged itself by one flipper across the sand and rocks and vanished into a crevice at the base of the cliff upon which she stood. By the time she picked her way through the forest and down the escarpment, the tide had risen up the beach and nearly to a cave she never would have seen had she not watched the animal drag itself inside.

She knew better than to even attempt to enter a coastal cave when the tide was coming in. There was no way of knowing how high the water would rise until you were drowning in it. And yet that day she had thrown caution to the wind, splashed through the tide pools, and dropped to her hands and knees. To this day, she still remembered with perfect clarity cocking her head and trying to see up a slope of talus into the shadows at the top. It had been so dark in there, and yet she'd kept crawling, a part of her clinging to the hope that the animal had been sent by some greater power to lead her to the treasure that would solve all of her problems, unlike the electrotherapy the doctors claimed would do just that.

The sea lion had been there, just as she knew it would, only by the time she reached it, it was already cold and lifeless. The others in there had been dead for much longer, judging by the smell and the fact that their bodies felt like jelly under their fur coats. It wasn't until years later that she learned they'd crawled in there to die because they'd been infected by a bacterium called *leptospirosis*, which she'd been extraordinarily lucky not to contract. The decomposition hadn't scarred her as much as the smell, which she swore was the same scent that now reached her from deeper in the warrens, where she knew there were things worse than dead sea lions lurking in the darkness.

"Do you smell that?" she asked.

Roche acknowledged her with a glance, but didn't reply, which for him, she was learning, was as good as shouting the answer at the top of his lungs. There was something about him that wasn't quite right, like he was there and yet not there at the same time, but there was also something about him that made her feel safe.

"There are footprints over here," Evans said. "Richards must have gone this way."

"How can we be sure they belong to him?" Kelly asked.

"They're still fresh."

"We shouldn't be doing this," Friden said. "We should just stick to the original plan and find somewhere to lie low and wait for the helicopter."

"What if it were you?" Jade asked. "Wouldn't you want us to come after you?"

"You can tell he came back here of his own free will. His are the only footprints, for the love of God."

"In blood," Anya said. "He left footprints in blood."

"Then he'll be able to follow them back, right?" Friden said. "Just like Hansel and Gretel."

"It's Mariah's blood," Jade said. "The creature must have dragged her body back here."

"And now it's dead," Evans said.

"You don't get it, do you?" Friden said. "Think about it. Rayburn and Scott were both dead, but they came back. Who's to say Mariah won't do the same? Or Devlin or Proctor? We shouldn't do anything or go anywhere until we find out what happened to Rubley."

"So in the meantime we just leave Richards to fend for himself?" Kelly said.

"He made a choice when he came down here. You know as well as I do that he never made a single decision he didn't want to make. He'd say the exact same thing I'm saying now. We should just go back—"

"No one's stopping you," Jade said. "All you have to do is turn around and start walking."

"But you have the only light," Friden said.

She smirked.

"I do, don't I?"

Jade pressed deeper into the cavern, clouds of breath trailing her over her shoulder. It wasn't until that moment that Kelly realized how much colder it had gotten. A frigid breeze caught her off guard when she stepped from the tunnel into a larger cavern.

Jade shined her light into the tunnel to her left, revealing ice on the ground and the walls. Kelly knew that ice needed precipitation to form, which meant that somewhere through there was an opening to the surface. Roche recognized it, too.

"How far down do you think we are from the Skyway?" Roche asked.

"Maybe fifty, seventy-five feet," Evans said.

Roche mercly nodded and followed Jade out of the breeze and into another crevice. The smell intensified tenfold, and Kelly felt the tears freezing to her cheeks. She was so scared she was crying, but the thought of stumbling blindly through the darkness was even more frightening than pushing on, despite what she feared lay ahead of them.

She thought about Friden's theory, about the organisms being able to reanimate the dead, but that simply couldn't be the case, not the way Rayburn had bled when they killed him. His heart had to have still been beating, which implied a measure of symbiosis or parasitism between the two species instead. That meant

Paul Rayburn had still been alive when they killed him. She prayed whatever part of him remained in his physical form had felt no pain.

Jade abruptly stopped and waved for the rest of them to do the same. She kept the light directed straight ahead, but cocked her head to the side as though listening for something. It took Kelly a moment, but eventually she heard it, too.

Footsteps.

Faint, distant.

Jade led them onward, slower than before. The crevice narrowed to such an extent that they had to scoot sideways. A faint glow emanated from somewhere beyond the end of the passageway.

The intonation of the echo of Richards's footsteps changed. Kelly was about to call out to him, but something stopped her.

There was another sound, barely audible, deep and at the lower edge of hearing. She clapped her hands over her mouth to stifle a gasp when she realized what it was.

The others froze. They were wedged in the tight crevice with nowhere else to go. Roche glanced back at her and she saw the same comprehension dawn in his eyes. He heard it for what it was, too.

Uhr-uhr-uhr-uhr-uhr-uh.

They weren't alone.

54
RICHARDS

"I know you're in here," Richards said. His voice sounded old and feeble in a way he never imagined it would.

He thought he'd known what to expect, but he was still unprepared for what he found. The den Dr. Evans discovered in Egypt, the one at the bottom of the lake, and the other with the remains of the American soldiers inside the pyramid . . . they'd been nearly identical. This was different, though. These weren't bare bones or mummified corpses on the ground in front of him. These were the savaged bodies of people he considered friends, people whose deaths already weighed heavily upon his conscience.

The bodies were heaped in the center of the cavern, their clothes ripped and their lacerated skin exposed. He saw the pained expressions immortalized on their faces and had to look away. There was so much blood on the ground that it had yet to coagulate or freeze.

His raised his light to the flowstone formation behind the remains. There were dozens of stalagmites of different height and thickness, like some hellish pipe organ, a veritable forest of spikes, from the depths of which he heard a shuffling sound.

"Come out where I can see you."

More shuffling sounds. He thought he saw movement through a gap between stalagmites, but by the time he caught up with his light, nothing was there.

The roof of the cavern was carved with the stars of the night sky, although the design had yet to be completed. It appeared to have started with Orion and expanded outward from there.

"Please," he whispered. "I need to see you."

Uhr-uhr-uhr-uhr-uhr-uh.

The sound reverberated from deep within the mountain. There was no doubt it originated from somewhere inside the jagged formation. His beam reflected from a pair of eyes that vanished as quickly as they appeared.

"Are you afraid of me?"

The answer caused his blood to run cold.

"No."

The voice was deep, barely audible, an almost hollow baritone at the lower limits of hearing. A vibrational sensation as much as a sound.

"You can speak?"

No response.

A silhouette passed between stalagmites. His light revealed a flash of gray skin, and then it was gone.

"I've spent my entire life searching for you."

Nails clattered on stone as it shifted from behind one stalagmite to the next. He caught a glimpse of its elongated head, red eyeshine from oddly circular orbs.

"Where are you from?"

"Everywhere."

It spoke in a strange, halting manner, as though un-accustomed to the physical mechanics of forming speech.

"Are you an alien?"

"All . . . life . . . alien."

More clattering of nails. A shifting of shadows.

"What planet are you from?"

"Many . . . worlds."

"How did you get here?"

"Always . . . here."

It passed between gaps, granting fleeting glimpses of a lithe, almost serpentine form.

Clack.

Clack.

"How do you know our language?"

"Host . . . knows."

"You assimilated it from Mr. Rubley?"

The shadow moved farther to the left. The flashlight shimmered from scales like those of a trout.

Clack.

Clack.

"The pyramid. It was designed to use you as a catalyst to evolve us, wasn't it?"

"Puzzle."

A light materialized from the darkness behind Richards, casting his shadow across the bodies and the flowstone formation.

"What do you mean, puzzle?"

"When . . . species . . . evolved . . . enough . . . to . . . solve . . . fail-safe . . . activated."

Richards turned at the sound of approaching foot-steps. The creature seized the opportunity, and with the clatter of nails darted deeper into the maze of stalagmites. Richards could barely make out its silhouette, pacing from one gap to the next, its hands raised in front of its face in an effort to keep the light out of its eyes.

"I don't understand."

"Species . . . no . . . longer . . . useful."

"So the machine evolves us into something more useful?"

"No . . . evolves . . . us."

"Into what?"

"Death."

"Your purpose is to kill us?"

Clack.

Clack.

"Why would you want to do that?"

The light shined directly on Richards from behind as the others emerged from the stone colonnade. He waved them back without turning around and hoped for once they did as he asked.

"All . . . species . . . serve."

"Serve what?"

"God."

"You're saying God is real?"

"Many."

"So both of our species serve these gods."

"In . . . different . . . capacities."

"Yours is to destroy us when we evolve beyond the limits of our usefulness?"

Clack.

Clack.

"And what is ours?"

"Build."

"Build what?"

"What . . . is . . . required."

"Hollis," Jade whispered from behind him.

Clack-clack-clack-clack-clack-clack.

The creature streaked across the cavern and vanished into the shadows. He saw just the faintest hint of its hunched silhouette before it vanished into the earthen wall.

"Please," Richards said. "I beg of you all. Please leave me alone."

He hurried across the cavern and shined his light into the recess where he thought it had gone, but there was nothing inside.

"The others like you failed," Richards said. "They're both dead."

"Not . . . like . . . me." The voice sounded as though it came from all around him at once. *"Drones."*

"Then your drones failed."

"We . . . make . . . more."

"We?"

"One . . . all."

"A hive mind."

A scratching sound. Claws on stone.

Skritch.

Richards couldn't pinpoint the origin of the sound.

"There are so many questions I want to ask you."

"One . . . more . . . than . . . others."

"How do you know?"

"Know . . . all."

Skritch.

"Then tell me. That night. In the field behind my house. All those years ago. What I saw in the sky. Was it real?"

"Show . . . you."

The voice came from directly above his head.

Richards looked up as it plummeted from where it clung to the ceiling. It was upon him before he could even brace for impact. It drove him to the ground with so much force that his hip broke. His head struck stone and he tasted blood. Struggled to keep his eyes open. Stared straight into those of an alien being.

There was nothing left of Rubley inside them. No hint of humanity.

His flashlight rolled across the floor. He heard shouting as though from a great distance. He opened his mouth to scream. Something dripped from the creature's mouth into his and lanced through the back of his throat. He sputtered blood and experienced pain beyond anything he'd ever imagined possible.

An electrical sensation preceded the arrival of the voices inside his head, millions of them, all speaking at once and in the same voice.

The eyes of the creature filled with the stars in the night sky and Richards felt as though he were speeding through them.

The universe revealed itself to him and laid bare its secrets.

In that fleeting moment, not only were all of his questions answered, but he saw the true nature of the species rapidly subsuming his consciousness. The insatiable hunger. The sheer malevolence. He understood the nightmare he'd unwittingly released and the events he'd set in motion.

A sensation of numbness flooded his veins, bringing with it the memory of a scared little boy hiding in a wheat field and the triangle of lights that carried him across the sky into eternity.

55
ROCHE

"**H**ollis!" Anya screamed.

Roche turned and pushed her back into the maze of columns.

"Go!" he shouted.

The creature raised its head from Richards's blood-spattered face and looked straight at him. Roche had never seen anything so terrifying in his entire life. It pushed itself up to its feet with spindly arms. Its skeletal framework showed through its gray skin. Its broad shoulders and wide pelvic girdle tented its flesh. It walked on its toes, its heels elevated, its legs flexed as though incapable of straightening its knees. Each step produced the clacking sound of nails striking the bare stone. It held its arms bent and cradled tightly to its chest, its clawed hands hanging limply.

It hunched its back, straightened its neck, and issued that horrible clicking sound as it rose to its full height.

Uhr-uhr-uhr-uhr-uhr-uh.

Roche pushed Kelly and Friden ahead of him and hurried to catch up before he lost sight of Jade's light. He slalomed through the colonnade, passing the silhouettes of the others streaking through the darkness until he reached Jade at the mouth of the crevice.

"Head through that frozen tunnel," he said. "If I'm right, it will lead you outside."

"And if you're wrong?"

"Cross your fingers that I'm not. Now go!"

She turned and sidestepped through the fissure as fast as she could. Roche helped Anya pass, then Friden and Kelly, and finally Evans, before sliding inside himself. Already the light was nearly gone, at least what little he could see through the bodies clogging the crevice ahead of him.

Clack-clack-clack.

The light abruptly faded.

A flash of eyeshine from behind him, near the ground and moving fast.

"Hurry!" he shouted, he hurled himself through the fissure until it was wide enough to sprint out into the cavern, where the others were already ducking into the tunnel, Jade's light reflecting from the ice.

Clack-clack-clack.

He lowered his head and charged after the others. The ground was so slick his feet went right out from underneath him. He managed to brace himself against the pipes bracketed to the walls to either side of him and used them to propel himself even faster. The sounds of their heavy breathing and thunderous footsteps made it impossible to hear anything else, but he didn't dare turn to see if it was still following them for fear of losing his balance.

The temperature dropped by the second. The cold infiltrated his body and formed barbs in his chest. He'd somehow forgotten just how cold it was outside and wondered if he'd made the right decision. He'd set them all on this course of action and it was up to him to make it work.

Jade screamed and threw herself to the ground.

Roche was nearly upon her when he saw why. A curtain of icicles had formed over the mouth of the tunnel. There was barely enough space between them to admit the ferocious wind and a barrage of snowflakes.

She rolled onto her back and kicked at the ice with her heels.

Cracks shot through the icicles and chunks fell away, but not nearly fast enough.

Roche could positively feel the creature gaining on him and realized that if they didn't break through right then and there, they were all dead.

"Down!" he shouted.

Evans hit the ground in front of him and shielded Kelly with his body. Roche planted his foot in the middle of the archeologist's back and used the traction to launch himself toward the wall of ice.

Roche clipped Friden's shoulder and narrowly avoided Jade. Covered his head and shouted. Led with his shoulder.

The ice felt like a brick wall when he hit it. For a split second he feared it wouldn't break, until it shattered like glass and rained down upon him as he burst from the side of the mountain. He caught a glimpse of clouds through the blowing snow and felt a sensation of weightlessness—

He landed on something hard and slid straight out across the canyon. His legs swung out over the nothingness and he barely managed to grab onto a thick cable before he shot over the edge.

Fortunately for him, the two pipes running through the tunnel converged outside the frozen opening, where they were bracketed together and supported by a massive steel arch that spanned the canyon. A web of cables reminiscent of those of a suspension bridge stabilized the pipes from above.

"Come on!" he shouted.

Roche pulled his legs up and braced them underneath him. Somehow managed to stand. Swayed as he stretched his arms out to either side for balance. The wind hammered him so hard that he had to grab the cables for support. He reached back toward the opening and took Jade by the hand.

"I can't do this!" she shouted.

"You don't have a choice!"

He pulled her out onto the slick pipes and guided her past him to the next vertical cable before offering his hand to whoever was next, but Friden was already crawling past him on all fours with Anya right behind him.

Roche made the mistake of looking down and quickly closed his eyes, but the damage was done. Long icicles hung from the pipes and formed a crystalline lattice over the supports of the arch, beyond which the ground only intermittently appeared through the blowing snow, so far down that the jagged rocks jutting from the windswept accumulation looked like a broken beer bottle.

A brutal gust nearly wrenched him from his perch.

"Hurry!" he shouted, and grabbed Kelly's hand as she lunged for him. Her foot slipped, forcing him to grab her around the torso and pull her to him. He'd barely regained his balance when Evans dove past his feet and slid across the pipes.

Roche looked back in time to see the creature emerge from the icy tunnel.

"Go," he said, and eased Kelly across his body, toward the opposite side.

"Not without you."

"Please," he whispered, but the howling wind stole the word from his lips.

He turned his back to her and faced the creature as it stepped down from the ledge and onto the frozen pipes.

Clack.

Clack.

"Don't come any farther," Roche said, although he knew it was a hollow threat.

He planted one foot on each pipe and grabbed the cables to either side. It was going to have to go through him to get to the others. He hoped they were taking advantage of every second he was able to buy them.

It lowered itself to its haunches and advanced in a loping crouch.

Clack-clack.

Clack-clack.

Its nails bit into the ice and scratched the metal underneath.

Roche took several quick steps backward and caught the cables again.

The creature effortlessly matched his retreat.

The clanging of footsteps on the pipes behind him was swallowed by the screaming wind, which hit him hard enough to make his feet slide on the ice. He struggled to maintain his traction. The creature used the opportunity to halve the distance between them. It was now well within striking distance.

A hideous smile formed on its misshapen face. Within

its eyes, Roche saw a being of pure evil, one not only well aware of its nature, but one that fully embraced it.

Roche had to stop it. Right here. Right now.

Regardless of the cost.

He staggered backward and braced himself for what he had to do next. He wouldn't get a second chance.

Clack-clack.

Clack-clack.

Its muscular form tensed in anticipation, ready to strike.

"I have one question for you." Roche locked eyes with the creature and prayed his expression didn't betray his intent. "Can you fly?"

He dove straight at it. Wrapped his arms around its slick skin. Drove it to the pipes.

Roche held on for everything he was worth and rolled over the edge, taking the creature with him.

56
EVANS

Evans was maybe a quarter of the way across the chasm when he glanced back and recognized what was about to happen.

He whirled and sprinted toward where Roche tackled the creature and dove the second he had solid footing. He hit the pipes on his chest and slid across the ice. His legs swung outward and rebounded from the vertical supports, nearly throwing him off the other side. He grabbed a cable and wrapped his arm around it as tightly as he could as he careened out over the open air. With his other hand he reached for Roche and managed to grab the hood of his jacket as he plummeted into the storm.

The other man's momentum nearly pried the cable from his grasp.

Evans shouted in agony as the metal braids bit into his palm and biceps. He wedged his leg under one of the brackets binding the pipes together and wrapped the other around their combined girth.

"Hold still!" he yelled.

Roche thrashed as though in an effort to take Evans with him.

Evans looked down and saw that it wasn't Roche at all, but rather the creature, which had managed to bury its claws into Roche's thigh. It tried to pull itself up, but only succeeded in tearing Roche's pants to the knee and darkening the fabric with blood in the process. Crimson droplets dripped from Roche's foot and joined the blowing snow.

"Let me go!" Roche shouted.

Evans's reply came out as a pained bellow. There was no way he was letting go. He didn't know how much longer he'd be able to hold on, though.

Roche reached up and took him by the wrist. Craned his neck to see around his hood.

"You have to let me go."

"You go," Evans grunted. "I go."

The distant ground momentarily materialized from the storm, more than a hundred feet down.

Roche looked away and reached for the zipper on his jacket.

"No!" Evans shouted.

He pulled on the cable with everything he had, but didn't rise in the slightest. There was simply too much weight.

The creature thrashed and scrabbled. Released a high-pitched scream.

Jade threw herself to the ice in front of Evans and grabbed him by the back of his jacket. Pulled as hard as she could. Friden joined her and together they were actually able to raise him far enough that he could readjust his grip on the cable.

The creature jerked against them and nearly took them all over the edge.

Kelly picked her way around and over Jade and Friden. It looked like she was going to go back into the mountain when she stopped, carefully knelt, and picked up an icicle. It was easily two feet long, and although its tip was broken, looked sharp enough to do serious damage.

She crawled to the edge beside Evans, worked her feet into the gap between the pipes and the bracket, and leaned out over the edge. Her eyes widened in terror and she screamed with the pressure on her knees. Swung the icicle. Hit the creature squarely on the shoulder.

It looked up at her, scurried around to Roche's back, and started to climb again.

Roche shouted in pain as the claws punctured his flesh from his thighs up his buttocks and to his back—

The shift of weight caused Evans to lose his grip. The cable burned his frozen hand, and were it not for Jade and Friden, he would have been halfway to the bottom of the canyon.

Anya knelt beside the cable, wrapped her arm around it, and grabbed a fistful of his jacket with her free hand.

Roche tugged at his zipper, but could only jerk it downward in tiny increments thanks to the weight pulling against the teeth.

The wind gusted and assailed them with snowflakes the size of moths.

The strain was more than Evans could bear. He could practically feel his rotator cuff tearing as his shoulder separated.

Kelly swung the icicle like a bat, but the creature managed to ward off the blow with its forearm.

Evans cried out and dropped several inches. He looked up and saw the strain on Jade's face. She wasn't going to be able to hold on much longer.

He realized what he needed to do.

Jade saw it on his face.

"Don't you dare! Do you hear me? Don't even think about it!"

The metal braids sliced through his palm as he slid another couple of inches. Rivulets of warm blood trickled down into his sleeve.

Searing pain in his ankle.

The creature's claws cut through his boot and skin alike. He felt them inside of him, against the bone.

It was trying to crawl from Roche to him.

He had to do something now. Before it was too late for the others.

"*I . . . go,*" the creature said. "*You . . . go.*"

The sound of its voice was worse even than the pain. Evans stared down at it and into the eyes of the entity that was responsible for the abandonment of Akhetaten and so many other primitive societies, and finally understood why the alien remains had been entombed where they never should have been found. The petroglyphs in Egypt and Peru hadn't been left as a record, but rather as a warning.

It narrowed its eyes and seemed to look straight into him, its stare like needles prodding his flesh.

"*We . . . know . . . you . . . now.*"

The icicle streaked across Evans's peripheral vision and struck the creature in the head.

Thunk.

The icicle shattered.

The malevolent expression vanished.

Its mouth went slack.

The claws tore down through his boot and disengaged from his foot.

Evans fought through the pain and clung to the cable.

The creature toppled backward and vanished into the storm.

His burden lightened, Evans pulled with everything he had left. Roche grabbed onto his legs and transferred his weight to the supporting arch.

Evans got one leg up and used it to pull himself onto the pipes. He buried his face between them and hugged them for dear life while the others dragged Roche up beside him.

Jade knelt in front of him and lifted his chin, forcing his eyes to meet hers.

"That was the stupidest thing anyone's ever done. You know that, don't you?"

She kissed him on the forehead and set about helping the others cross the bridge.

Evans leaned over the side and looked down, but he couldn't see a blasted thing through the blowing snow.

57
JADE

The pipes led to an orifice on the far side. Like the one on the adjacent mountain, it took some work to break through the ice, but they managed to get out of the elements before any of them lost fingers or toes. The pipes divided and went straight up a shaft to either side of an iron ladder, the rungs of which were so cold they threatened to absolve Jade of her fingerprints. The garage was reasonably warm, all things considered. At least the structure was intact and shielded them from the storm, which was about as much as they could hope for under the circumstances.

Jade breathed a sigh of relief when she saw the makeshift medical kit was still where they'd left it. It was probably the only thing that had gone their way in the last forty-eight hours. The wounds on Roche's legs had been so deep they would have needed stitches under normal conditions, but the best Jade could do was clean, bandage, and cover them as tightly as possible with whatever scraps of fabric she could find.

Evans's ankle had required additional immobilization and threats of violence if he didn't sit down and take his weight off of it. The others exhibited varying degrees of shock. The focus required to treat them helped her to suppress her own.

The silence in the garage was interrupted only by the howling gusts of wind that shook the structure hard enough to rattle the tools hanging on the walls and in the cabinets leaning against them. Eventually, she and the others would have to talk about their ordeal, but for now it was enough to be warm, safe, and in the presence of other human beings.

Jade made sure everyone was comfortable before ducking through the door between the massive garage bays and out into the storm. It wasn't snowing nearly as hard as it had been, although it had somehow managed to get even colder. She had trouble manipulating her hands well enough to chisel the ice from the handle of one of the arctic vehicles while balancing on its tank-tracks, but the door opened easily enough once she managed to do so. After trying a dozen keys on as many key chains, she found the one she needed and cranked the ignition. The engine roared and blasted her with heat from the vent in the dashboard.

There was probably enough room for them all to squeeze inside, but she didn't relish the prospect of trying to drive down whatever nightmare of a road led to Troll Station any more than she liked the idea of attempting to belay down the elevator shaft in hopes of using the submersible to reach Snow Fell. She was just fine killing time in the garage until the helicopter from McMurdo was able to reach them, thank you.

The console looked more like the control panel of an airplane than any vehicle she'd ever driven. The inset digital monitor featured readouts for functions she didn't immediately recognize. She found the knobs that controlled the headlights, windshield wipers, and the heater, which she dialed up as far as it would go and turned every vent so that it blew into her face. She found what she had prayed would be there affixed to the side of the dashboard and attached by a coiled wire to what looked like a car stereo. She turned it on and the cab buzzed with static.

Jade pressed the button and spoke into the transceiver.

"Can anybody hear me?"

She released the button and held her breath. Whatever bandwidth was already dialed in was undoubtedly set to a channel designated for routine communications, although likely one only the station used. She prayed the transceiver was powerful enough to reach Troll Station.

Jade dialed through the channels, one at a time.

"Mayday, mayday, mayday. This is Antarctic Research, Experimentation, and Analysis Station Fifty-one. We have an emergency. Does anyone out there copy?"

Only static replied.

"Mayday, mayday, mayday. This is Antarctic Station Fifty-one. We have several dead. Others are wounded and in need of medical attention. Do you copy?"

Surely there was someone out there. Anyone. There had to be somebody monitoring their situation.

Again and again she tried. Channel 13, 14, 15.

She was in tears by the time she reached 16. The desperation in her voice was palpable.

"Please. Someone. This is Antarctic Station Fifty-one. This is an emergency. We need help."

"Copy, AREA Fifty-one. This is NGD. Acknowledge."

Jade sobbed in relief and talked so fast she could barely keep up with her own thoughts. The man on the other end listened dutifully and patiently and only interrupted for clarity. By the time she was done rambling, the adrenaline had fled her. She felt a level of exhaustion beyond anything she'd ever experienced, as though she could simply close her eyes and sleep right there, but something prevented her from doing so. She had a mental tip-of-the-tongue sensation, an elusive thought of seemingly great importance that she couldn't quite grasp.

And then it hit her.

Snow Fell.

She remembered the archaic German communications equipment and the question she had asked.

Why would anyone in their right mind put a communications outpost all the way out here?

It had been Roche who answered.

They wouldn't. There were no satellites back then. This is all short-range VHF equipment.

The lettering above the display read: VHF MARINE.

"Who is this?" she asked.

"NGD, ma'am. McMurdo Station."

"No, it's not." It felt like the ground fell out from beneath her. "This is a VHF transceiver and McMurdo is two thousand miles away."

"You just sit tight and stay warm, ma'am. We already have a bird in the air. It ought to reach your location in under thirty minutes."

"Who is this? How did you know—?"

A click preceded the eruption of static.

Jade dropped the handset, killed the engine, and headed back to the garage as though in a trance. She found the others huddled for warmth, but separately from one another, as though proximity were an unwelcome reminder of everything they'd survived.

Roche glanced up from where he was sprawled on the tabletop they'd cleared to serve as an examination table. He read something in her expression and raised his eyebrows to ask the question.

She nearly broke down again, but regained her composure before speaking.

"I found a radio in one of the cars and contacted someone who claimed to be at McMurdo."

"McMurdo's on the other side of the continent," Roche said. "You couldn't raise them from here on a remote transceiver."

"That's my point."

"What did he say?"

"They already have a helicopter in the air and it'll be here in under half an hour."

"Half an hour?"

"That's what he said."

"Did he identify himself?" Roche asked.

"No."

"Could it have been someone from Troll Station?"

"He didn't have an accent and he terminated the connection as soon as I started asking questions."

"I don't like this."

"You and me both."

Evans stood and tested his weight on his bandaged ankle.

"I don't care who sent the chopper as long as it takes me with it when it leaves."

"A helicopter can go maybe four hundred miles on a full tank of gas, at the most," Roche said. "And I can't imagine it being able to sustain speeds much greater than a hundred, hundred-ten miles an hour in this weather. So we're looking at a point of origin within a two-hundred-mile radius and a dispatch time potentially as long as an hour and a half ago."

"Connor said it would take a minimum of eight hours to get here from McMurdo. Maybe they got ahold of someone closer and arranged transport for us."

Friden wrapped himself like a pupa in his tarp and shuffled over to them.

"Why does everyone look so grim?"

"We're being evacuated within the half-hour," Jade said.

"No way. They must have some of those MKUltra psychics up there at McMurdo to get a chopper up here that fast."

"Or they were monitoring us the entire time," Roche said.

"Who?" Friden said. "McMurdo?"

"It's impossible to say for sure."

"You think someone tapped into the feed from the security cameras?" Evans said.

"Trust me." Roche hopped down from the workbench with a grimace of pain. "It's not that hard to do."

"So what does it matter?" Evans asked.

"Think about it. There's no way anyone could get a chopper off the ground and up here so quickly, least of all from the opposite side of the continent—"

"Unless they already had one ready and standing by for just this contingency," Jade said.

It all made sense, but if Roche was right, that meant that not only had someone known what they were attempting to do in the station, they'd been prepared for them to succeed.

A clanging sound echoed through the garage, followed by a high-pitched whistle of wind. A cold breeze diffused into the room. The temperature dropped so rapidly that the goosebumps prickled along the backs of her arms and up her neck.

"What was that?" Kelly asked.

"What's below us?" Roche asked.

"Just solid rock as far as I know," Anya said and looked at Friden.

"Beats the hell out of me."

"If the collapse of the power plant destabilized the entire mountain—" Evans started.

"Then this whole place could be about to come down," Roche said.

58
ROCHE

The ibuprofen barely took the edge off the pain. It felt like Roche had been stabbed repeatedly in the legs, which he supposed was exactly what had happened. The bandages were already saturated and he could feel the blood cooling as it trickled down his calves, but there was something wrong and he had to figure out what was going on before it was too late.

He hobbled to the far side of the garage and found a metal hatch set into the floor. A tool reminiscent of a hooked crowbar hung from the wall above it. He stuck the bent end in the hole at one end and used it to raise the hatch, revealing a ladder leading down into the pitch-black depths.

Cold air blew straight up into his face.

"What's down there?" he asked.

"Once again," Friden said. "No one consulted me on the blueprints, so I'm going to have to refer you to my previous answer of 'How the hell should I know?'"

"Very helpful."

"I live to serve."

Roche sat at the edge and dangled his legs above the ladder.

"I'm going to need the flashlight."

"What you need to do is sit back down," Jade said. "You're in no condition to be on your feet."

"If this building falls down the mountain, I won't be the only one who's in no condition to be on his feet."

He took the flashlight from her and shined it down the shaft, which was easily as deep as the one they'd climbed from the pipe bridge.

Every step brought with it a new level of pain. He could positively feel where the claws had passed through his tissue and muscles as though they were still there. His only option was to harness the pain and use it to sharpen his mental faculties. There were alarm bells going off in his head. The revelation that the chopper had been stationed within a two-hundred-mile radius was far too convenient and created more questions than it answered. Chief among them: Who was out there impersonating McMurdo Station?

Roche had thought the sheer number of security cameras throughout the station was overkill, but he, of all people, should have recognized how precisely they'd been placed for surveillance of nearly every inch of the station. If someone had been monitoring their live feeds, they would have known exactly what was going on inside the station at all times and would have recognized that something was wrong when the cameras went dark. They could have activated whatever emergency protocol was in place and had an extraction team in the air within minutes, but instead they'd elected to let whatever was about to happen play out. He knew how paranoid that sounded, but the time frame and logistics worked. The biggest problem wasn't that the pieces fit so much as the picture they formed when he put them together.

There was nothing he could do about that now, though. The only thing that mattered was getting them all out of there alive.

By the time he reached the bottom of the ladder, he was so cold his hands were shaking. He stepped down onto bare rock, knelt, and shined his light into a pair of narrow passageways, just like the ones on the opposite side of the garage. The cold air felt as though it were blowing at him from both directions at once. There was a grate over the tunnel to his left, which led back underneath the garage. He could see an industrial fan through the vent, its lopsided silver blades slowly turning at the behest of the frigid breeze. There was a faint hint of light at the end of the tunnel to his right. If he was correct, it led straight to the elevator shaft and served to help circulate—

The vent lay facedown at the end of the tunnel.

He shined his light at the ground. At the bloody palm prints smeared inside the aluminum ductwork.

That was how the creature got into the station after climbing out of the elevator, which meant it would have known about the exterior access on the other end.

Roche again spun and shined the light through the vent, toward the fan. It wasn't just lopsided. One of the blades was bent outward, creating just enough room for something to squeeze—

The beam reflected from a pair of eyes in the darkness behind the gap.

"Oh, God."

Roche leaped to his feet and climbed the ladder as fast as he could.

"It's down here!" he shouted.

He was halfway up when he saw the startled expressions on the faces of the others.

Clack-clack-clack.

"Close the hatch! Drag something heavy on top of it!"

Clang.

It hit the ladder behind him, the force from which sent vibrations through the metal.

"Hurry!" Kelly screamed. "It's right behind you!"

Roche climbed toward the surface. The strain on his shoulders was ferocious, but he battled through it and climbed out onto the garage floor. Evans grabbed him by the jacket and dragged him away from the hole.

Clang-clang-clang-clang.

Jade nearly slammed the hatch down on his legs in her hurry to close it.

"Come on!" she shouted at Friden and Anya, who dragged a tool cabinet across the garage. She threw herself onto the hatch. The creature struck the underside with enough force to lift it from the ground.

Jade screamed and tried to use her body weight to keep it closed.

Another blow from underneath and she rose several inches.

Evans hurled himself onto the metal beside her.

"Hurry up!" he shouted.

Roche crawled to where Friden and Anya slid the cabinet across the concrete and helped them push it over the lip and onto the hatch beside Evans.

Jarring impact from underneath rattled the tools in their drawers.

"Do you guys hear that?" Kelly shouted.

Another thud and the clamor of tools.

And then Roche felt it more than heard it, a subtle, metered thrum passing through the ground, which could only mean one thing.

Kelly ran to the door and threw it open.

The wind raced past her, spreading snowflakes across the concrete.

The thunder of chopper blades grew louder and louder until a Sikorsky UH-60 Black Hawk came in low over the bright red arctic vehicles. Its rotor wash returned the accumulation from the ground to the air and blew it through the door.

"Go!" Roche shouted.

Kelly ran out into the blowing snow and waved her arms over her head. Friden pulled Anya to her feet and the two of them sprinted to catch up with her.

The hatch rose again, toppling the cabinet onto its face and spilling wrenches all over the floor.

Roche dragged himself up on top of it and shouted at Evans.

"I don't know how long I can hold this!"

"Between the three of us—"

"There's nowhere for that chopper to land and it can't fight that wind forever. You have to go. Now!"

"You'd better be right behind us."

"Go!"

Evans took Jade by the hand and pulled her to her feet.

A collision from below lifted Roche from the ground.

The lid slammed back down so hard it knocked him from on top of the cabinet.

He pushed himself up from the ground and hobbled toward the open door, where Jade and Evans vanished into the swirling snow.

The creature struck the hatch again and the cabinet slid to the side, disgorging half of its contents with a cascade of steel. Another thump and the lid swung open with the squeal of hinges.

Roche limped out into the storm and shielded his face from the wind. The Black Hawk's front wheels bounced from the roof of one of the vehicles as Evans climbed onto the tank-like tracks and boosted Jade toward where a man in black fatigues pulled her up through the open sliding door and into the helicopter.

Evans glanced back at him. His eyes widened.

Roche knew exactly what that meant.

"Go!" he yelled and waved Evans onward, but even he couldn't hear his voice over the roar of the blades.

The soldier tugged Evans over the edge by the collar of his jacket.

A gust of wind knocked the Black Hawk sideways before it again set a wheel down on the vehicle.

The soldier turned away and for a moment Roche thought they were going to leave him. Another soldier attempted to hold Kelly back, but she fought through him and screamed at Roche.

"Run!"

When the first soldier turned around again, there was an assault rifle against his shoulder. He sighted down the long barrel through the scope.

Straight at Roche.

He dove for the tank-tracks and climbed up the side of the truck.

A flash of discharge and a deafening report.

Heat against his cheek.

The projectile passed so close to his ear that it singed the cartilage.

He dove through the open doorway and glanced back in time to see the creature slide through the snow on its back in a wash of blood.

"Lift off!" the soldier shouted.

The chopper bucked against the wind. Roche grabbed Evans's leg while Kelly pulled him across the floor and away from the open door. He saw the creature clearly, sprawled—unmoving—on the ground, before the Black Hawk banked out over the canyon and the creature vanished into the blowing snow.

59
EVANS

Wind-class icebreaker Aurora Borealis
120 miles off the coast of
Queen Maud Land, Antarctica

The *Aurora Borealis* was a Wind-class icebreaker capable of carving through the sheet ice like a chainsaw through timber. In its previous incarnation it had been known as the *USCGC Westwind* and had launched under the Stars and Stripes in 1943. According to the official story, it had been decommissioned and scrapped more than thirty years ago, which, as Evans could attest, was about the furthest thing from the truth.

He and the others had been whisked out across the sea to where the *Aurora Borealis* sat frozen in the ice, the Drygalski Mountains a memory behind them. The chopper had set down on a narrow landing pad, where a team of medics had been waiting to hustle them into a makeshift medical ward belowdecks.

Everything that had happened since was a blur, from the cleaning, suturing, and rebandaging of their wounds to the blood tests, mouth swabs, and the monitoring of every vital function. He'd felt like a pincushion by the time he was pushed out of the partitioned exam room in a wheelchair and down the corridor to where the others were seated at a long table topped with steaming trays of bacon, sausage, and eggs. A man he'd never seen before poured them coffee from a carafe. He wore the same black fatigues as everyone else on the ship.

Evans tried to read the situation by the expressions on the faces of the others, but they appeared every bit as confused as he was.

"That will be all," a deep voice said from behind him. "Thank you."

The medic who'd pushed Evans down the hallway and the man with the coffee exited without a word and closed the door behind them.

A man in a custom-tailored suit wheeled Roche to the table and parked him beside Evans, who started to ask what was going on, but Roche silenced him with a look and a quick shake of his head.

The man in the suit walked around to the head of the table and stood facing away from them, his hands clasped behind his back. Snowflakes tapped against the window in front of him, beyond which the seamless ice stretched from one horizon to the next. When he finally turned around, he offered them a halfhearted smile, took off his jacket, and draped it over the back of the chair.

"Please," he said, and gestured toward the untouched food on the table. "You must be starving."

"We just watched everyone in that station get killed in about the most horrific manner possible," Jade said. "You'll have to forgive us for not being the most gracious guests."

"We're lucky to be alive," Kelly said.

"And while we appreciate everything you've done for us," Evans said, "I think we're all more than a little curious about what the hell we're doing here."

"Where are my manners? Of course, of course." He had a politician's smile, blinding white and practiced. The kind that was meant to set people at ease, but tended to have the opposite effect. His dark hair was slicked back, and his eyes were so blue they seemed to stand apart from his face. His suit must have cost more than Evans made in a year. "Allow me to introduce myself. My name is—"

"Cameron Barnett," Roche said. "You're with the NSA."

"Your reputation precedes you, Mr. Roche, but I'm afraid your information is outdated. I *was* with the NSA. Now I represent our nation's more, shall we say . . . esoteric . . . interests in a somewhat less official capacity."

"Did Richards know you were monitoring his security camera feeds?" Roche asked.

Barnett smirked.

"Who do you think funds this organization?"

"And what organization is that?"

"You mean Mr. Richards didn't tell you?"

"I'm starting to think there are a lot of things good old Hollis didn't tell us," Evans said.

"The rest will come in time, but for now, all you really need know is that I represent an interagency task force established to investigate seemingly inexplicable phenomena with potential global ramifications."

"Try saying that five times fast."

"Which is why we use a code name." Barnett sat down at the head of the table, leaned forward onto his elbows, and tented his fingers under his chin. "Welcome to Unit Fifty-one."

EPILOGUE

Evolution has no long-term goal. There is no long-distance target, no final perfection to serve as a criterion for selection, although human vanity cherishes the absurd notion that our species is the final goal of evolution.

—RICHARD DAWKINS

Antarctic Research, Experimentation & Analysis Station 51
September 23—24 hours later

The men moved like ghosts through the deserted corridors, the lights mounted underneath the barrels of the M16 assault rifles seated against their shoulders slashing through the darkness. They wore full-body Level A Hazmat suits with opaque visors that concealed their faces. The yellow Tychem fabric was virtually impervious to every kind of chemical and biological contaminant, which seemed excessive to Barnett, but he didn't want to take any chances, especially when it came to what they'd found in the station.

The carnage had been even worse than the survivors had described. Fortunately, it wasn't his job to collect and examine the bodies—what was left of them, anyway—but he wasn't particularly enjoying his job at the moment, either. He'd just received word that his team had found the remains of his great-grandfather, Sergeant Jack Barnett, inside the pyramid. He'd been officially listed as Missing, Presumed Dead since he and his entire elite expeditionary squad vanished into the Antarctic hinterland so many years ago.

Barnett's grandfather, John, had been just a child at the time, but old enough to understand that as long as there wasn't a body, there was still hope. He'd spent his entire life in the service of his country, if for no other reason than to gain access to classified information and launch his own investigation into his father's disappearance. Barnett and his father, Robert, had followed in his footsteps, only their paths had taken them into intelligence, where they'd discovered secrets the world as a whole was unprepared to handle, secrets that led them to the doorstep of Hollis Richards and the eventual union that had brought Barnett to this precise moment in time.

Barnett dreaded the prospect of telling his grandfather that they'd found his missing father's body, even more so because he had no choice but to lie to him and tell him it had been discovered in the frozen wreckage of the squad's B-24D Liberator airplane. As he'd said a thousand times, there were truths that people simply didn't need to know, for their own protection.

Such was the case with everything that had happened inside this station. Richards's staff of engineers and scientists had been selected for more than their considerable expertise; they'd been chosen because they'd left few people behind who would notice if they didn't ever return. Their deaths would be officially reported, but there wouldn't be any grieving families calling for a formal inquiry into the circumstances of their demise. They'd understood as much when they signed on, even if they hadn't known exactly what awaited them in the remote Antarctic installation.

Barnett regretted delaying the extraction of the survivors as long as he had. The wait had cost several men their lives, including Richards and Connor, but when Richards had contacted him using the pre-established McMurdo Protocol, which started an eight-hour countdown to extraction, they'd only just lost video from the security feed. It had been Barnett's call to wait for the power to be restored, even if it meant the deaths of those who'd been inside the pyramid during its activation.

Of course, not even he could have predicted the events that followed.

His men advanced through the subterranean hallway and into Dr. Fleming's lab at the end. He was suddenly grateful for the heavy SCBA tanks on his back, which flooded his hood with oxygen so he wouldn't have to breathe what must have been an ungodly stench. The walls and floors were decorated with dried blood, especially inside the clean room, where Dr. Evans and Mr. Roche had reportedly killed Mr. Rayburn—who'd been officially reclassified as Subject B—with a drill, although his body was nowhere to be seen.

For not the first time, Barnett questioned the accuracy of the eyewitness accounts of the survivors. Dr. Bell's body hadn't been in the greenhouse as they claimed. Mr. Graves's remains hadn't been in the server room, nor had Mr. Wolski's been in the library.

Such misreporting was common in cases involving massive casualties and group hysteria, but he found it hard to believe that all of them shared the same delusion. At least not unless they were deliberately trying to hide something from him. He could only hope they were telling the truth about the den through the maze of tunnels at the back of the cavern, where they claimed to have found the creature Barnett's man had shot from the chopper at the point of extraction.

The trail of blood had been easy to follow through the forest of flowstone formations. The den had been precisely where they said it would be and exactly as they'd described, only there were no human remains. The ground where they'd been was thick with coagulated blood and the fluids of bodily dissolution, but there was no immediate indication as to where the bodies themselves had gone.

There was a riot of bloody footprints, the majority of which headed back in the direction from which he'd come. Only one set of footprints, so faded and indistinct he nearly overlooked them, led deeper into the darkness. The blood had worn completely off the tread after no more than half a dozen steps, but he extrapolated their course and followed it to a narrow crevice in the granite wall.

Barnett swept his light across the ground as he approached it. Smears and random droplets of blood converged at the orifice. The edges of the fissure and the walls inside were smudged with crimson handprints.

He raised his rifle and shined his light into the earth.

Something reflected his beam. Near the ground. Twin flashes of red. And then they were gone.

Barnett quickly lowered his weapon again and sighted down the barrel.

A mouse stood on its hind legs, licking blood from its front paws.

It stared at him for several moments before scampering away and vanishing into the impenetrable darkness.

Connect with Us

Visit us online at
KensingtonBooks.com
to read more from your favorite authors, see books
by series, view reading group guides, and more.

for sneak peeks, chances to win books and prize packs,
and to share your thoughts with other readers.

facebook.com/kensingtonpublishing
twitter.com/kensingtonbooks

Tell us what you think!

To share your thoughts, submit a review,
or sign up for our eNewsletters, please visit:
KensingtonBooks.com/TellUs.